G000113713

R E T R I B U T I O N

Something strange is in the garden!
Something strange is at the door!
Something strange is in the carpet
Now unwinding on the floor!

Retribution for an Ancient crime.
Retribution for the Romans!
Retribution for a seaside town
Retribution for the builder!
Retribution for the greedy man.
and for the Lottery winner!!
Retribution for the ghastly child,
Retribution for his parents!
Retribution for the ginger tom.
.... A cat that will eat fairies!

FIRST EDITION
published in 2000
by
WOODFIELD PUBLISHING
Woodfield House, Babsham Lane, Bognor Regis
West Sussex PO21 5EL, England.

ISBN 1-873203-64-0

THIS BOOK
BELONGS TO

. . . .

RETRIBUTION

A TALE OF SUPERNATURAL JUSTICE

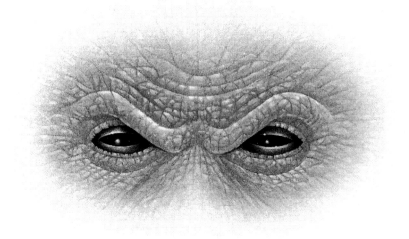

by

MIKE JUPP

Woodfield Publishing
WEST SUSSEX ~ ENGLAND

Enter PUCK.

Puck. Now the hungry lion roars,
And the wolf behowls the moon;
Whilst the heavy ploughman snores,
All with weary task fordone.
Now the wasted brands do glow,
Whilst the scritch-owl, scritching loud,
Put the wretch that lies in woe
In remembrance of a shroud.
Now it is the time of night
That the graves, all gaping wide,
Every one lets forth its sprite,
In the church-way paths to glide:
And we fairies, that do run
By the triple Hecate's team,
From the presence of the sun
Following darkness like a dream,
Now are frolic; not a mouse
Shall disturb this hallow'd house:
I am sent with broom before,
To sweep the dust behind the door.

William Shakespeare
(A Midsummer Nights Dream)
Act V Scene II

Contents

Acknowledgements

I WOULD LIKE TO TAKE THE OPPORTUNITY to thank the many friends and acquaintances without whom this tale could not have been told. You have only yourselves to blame!

Cliff Cropp, Graham Jacobs, John Nelson, Tony Jones (who allowed me to use his father's confidential report about strange goings on in deepest Sussex), the landlady of the 'Five Bells' in West Chiltington, Mr & Mrs Hodge, Carol Kalli, Wendy Hobson, Barry Belasco, Julia Young, Mark Coutts, Mark Adams, Chris Hackett, Les Eastaugh, Lester Hewitt, and June O'Sullivan.

To all the people of Bognor Regis, especially Kevin Smith, Steve Goodheart, Mel and Anne Young, Louise Adams, Maddy Johns, Barry Stokes, Steve Flanagan, Jamie Hunter, Kevin & Eileen at the Wheatsheaf, all the regulars at the 'Newtown Social Club', especially Stuart 'Fish' Laundon, Clive Osbourne, Alfie Law, Gary, Warren and Dave. And to everyone else who has helped me even though cider and senile decay has made me inadvertently omit them from this list!

Finally to my wife Nikki (who has stood by me through thick and thicker!) and my children, Eleanor and Merrin

This book is for them...

True Stories

In 1970, a property known as 'Firswood Cottage' in the West Sussex village of West Chiltington was purchased by a Mr King, who decided to have considerable alterations made before moving in. The contractors hired to undertake the building work were Messrs Griffin, Bray & Sons of Chertsey. They started work on 18th December 1970, but by the evening of the 5th January 1971 they had 'refused point blank to do any more work' because of 'disconcerting supernatural events'.

The rector of West Chiltington, the Reverend R.M. Jones, was contacted by Mr King on 5th January and asked for his help with this unusual problem. In a confidential report submitted to Church Authorities and the British Psychical Research Bureau, Rev Jones reported a number of inexplicable occurrences experienced by the builders. These included seeing a shadowy figure in the house and the garden; having items of equipment mysteriously vanish only to reappear in strange places; hearing disembodied voices and seeing an old man's face reflected in a mirror when no such person was actually present.

Later in 1971 the house in West Chiltington was allegedly exorcised by Dom Robert Petit-Pierre, the man on whom it is said William Peter Blatty based *The Exorcist*.

1971 was the year in which I moved to London from my home in Bognor Regis on the Sussex coast, to begin a career as a designer and illustrator in advertising and publishing. It was also the year I created two storylines that would eventually become the successful childrens' television series: *Bimble's Bucket* and *The Dreamstone*.

After ten years in the wonderful world of advertising and media agents I ended up with nothing.

In 1981 I began a career as a designer and writer for childrens' television programmes. After living in Holland, Germany and the USA, I returned to my family home in Sussex and purchased the house from my elderly mother. I converted a back bedroom into a studio, and landscaped the derelict garden, adding a large pond, a Rockery with a small waterfall and a little statue.

After ten years in the wonderful world of producers and their broken promises, I again ended up with nothing! (Except a beautiful wife and two wonderful children, worth more than all the riches in paradise).

The tale of '*Retribution*' was inspired by two stories, one from West Chiltington and the other from my own life. Both are true.

Mike Jupp, 2000

Introduction

IF GHOSTS COULD CAST SHADOWS, there would be precious little sunshine across the land of West Sussex.

Between the wooded heights of the South Downs and the tea-coloured swell of the English Channel, a million shades drift silently over the fields and towns of the ancient realm. Rippling over the trees and hedgerows, darting between wetland and meadow, the heavy memory of German bombers is eternally dispersed by the flashing shadows of Hurricanes and Spitfires. Beneath them move cloudy, older phantoms, wandering in a time of civil-war chaos. Royalist and Parliamentarian cavalry still thunder silently across the county. Under them stir the feudal shadows of serfs and knights, who in turn overlay the eroded apparitions of countless foreign invaders. Far below, lurk murky spectres of Normans, Danes, Vikings, Romano-British, Roman auxiliaries and Roman citizens who once lived and prospered across the area. Finally, and almost unseen, are the faintest shadows of all: those dimly remembered folk of Celtic and pre-Celtic times who fade into the merest wisps of prehistoric souls who walked the ancient ground long before there was an 'English Channel'.

Binding together all those who had lived or passed through the area that would one day be the kingdom of the South Saxons, was a curious feeling, a belief, an unproven certainty that the lawful occupants of the land were still living alongside them.

These secret folk of forests, fields, marshes and coastline were rarely, if ever, seen. Nevertheless, they were accepted as real, and their domain was respected and revered by everyone ... without exception.

Many an unrecorded chance encounter with these secret folk became hearsay or was woven into anecdotal stories which, in turn, became the stuff of myths and legends. Green men and Robyn Goodefellowes stayed as foreign gods came and went. Each generation acknowledged the secret folk as a fact of life, and it was generally accepted that not only did 'the hidden ones' observe human affairs, but on occasion they actually intervened. Woe betide anyone who disturbed their habitat, or broke their law!

Gradually, a middle Eastern religious cult that worshipped a human being replaced the old rustic deities. The deforestation of the new county coincided with the development of the feudal system as more and more land became cultivated. Agrarian reform was supported by the Industrial Revolution; villages became towns and cities spread into the surrounding country-side. Eventually humans became far too sophisticated to accept the old lore of the country and, steered on by a jealous Church, converted the flimsy knowledge of the old beliefs into nursery rhymes and childrens' stories.

Despite all this, however, the hidden ones survive, watching in dismay as their environment is gradually eaten away, almost powerless to intervene – almost!

For country lore exists, just as it did on that distant Saturday afternoon at the beginning of a fateful winter, long long ago ...

CHAPTER ONE

PANIC ATTACKS!

· 1 ·

PANIC ATTACKS!

AN EVIL WIND FROM SIBERIA was pushing the heavy clouds so close to the ground that their undersides were being ripped to shreds by the trees that covered the hilltop.

It was just after noon on the first Saturn's day of the ninth month of the year 406 AD. A rabbit pricked its ears towards the wind and darted away across the slippery grass slope as the noise of humans grew louder. Seven men were struggling to reach the top of the hill. A path of sorts existed, probably fashioned by animals as much as by human beings, but even with their iron shod boots and sandals, the men found it difficult to walk on the slimy chalk ground.

A man the others called 'The Fox' was first to reach the top. He crouched down and carefully surveyed the huge sweep of land that lay below them to the south. He beckoned to the others, who nervously crept up and sank to the ground beside him. The Fox took stock of his ramshackle companions one by one, and then, raising his eyes to the heavens, took in a deep breath and slowly shook his head.

"The Empire's doomed..." he muttered to himself.

The Fox, Gaius Commius Vulpinus, wasn't exactly sure, but he thought he was about thirty-three years old. Short, stocky and brown-skinned, with a receding hairline, he was the only one of the group who was of Roman ancestry. The others had all been born in and around the area to non-Roman families and were auxiliary soldiers to the Roman legions, if 'soldiers' was the right word to describe them. 'Rabble' was more like the right word as far as The Fox was concerned.

Less than twenty-four hours before finding themselves over-looking that cold, wind-blasted hilltop, The Fox's men had been living a comfortable life as part of the garrison to a substantial private estate. The mansion farmstead had been built on the banks of the River Trisantona and Gaius Commius Vulpinus had been appointed prefect of the cohort. Under normal circum-stances this would not only have been a great honour but would also have increased his wages. These, however, were not normal circumstances. The Fox's commanding officer, the tribune, Julius Severus Vectis, had hurriedly obeyed the Emperor Honorious' order that the legions of Britannia should withdraw to Rome and defend the motherland against the Goths – and several other breeds of unpleasant foreigners. Consequently the Fox found himself in charge of about fifty men instead of the usual four hundred and eighty, whilst his commanding officer had marched off with the 'real' soldiers. Saxon raiders had been the thorn in Britannia's side for many years, and now that the legions had all but gone, they became bolder and more frequent with their raids.

The attack on the mansion had been swift and savage. In the ensuing panic, the inhabitants were either slaughtered or had fled in all directions. The six who had escaped by following the Fox were the lucky ones – Vulpinus by name, fox by nature!

The seven men looked down towards the peninsula of Seal Island, some half a day's march away. The light was beginning to fade but it was still strong enough for them to see detail in the majestic panorama below them. The forest spread south to the coastline – whilst further to the south-west, large cultivated areas broke up the endless woodland. The Fox turned to the southeast and narrowed his eyes. He could see a column of smoke rising up and being spread by the north wind.

"I'm going off to take a dump!" said the youngest of the group, a spotty awkward youth whose real name was Leo Verica. He had been named Verica after the king of the local tribe, the Artrebates, who had invited the Emperor Claudius to invade Britain nearly four hundred years earlier. The others didn't call him Leo Verica. His friends, not that he had many, called him Leo, whilst everyone else called him Verruca, a painful, disgusting thing that stuck to the bottom of your foot!

"I'm going for a…"

"We heard you the first time," interrupted the Fox.

"Well you didn't answer," pouted the youth.

"That's because we're not interested!" scoffed Alba Dun, a chubby, redheaded man with a thick black beard.

"Hurry up Verruca … and do it quietly. I can still smell those murderous Saxons," said the Fox.

"I bet even the Saxons smell better than Verruca!" said Alba. The others sniggered as the lad sloped off towards the trees.

The men continued looking towards the distant sea, each thinking his own thoughts. The Saxons were not the only things they had to worry about. The very fact that they were travelling on Saturn's day was bad enough. Everyone knew that Saturn's day was a day of evil omen, when battles should not be fought, no adventures or important tasks undertaken, and most importantly, no journeys begun! It was bad enough that the enemies of Rome were attacking them without risking additional punishment by the gods of Rome!

It was for that reason that the Fox decided to stay on the hilltop for the night. None of them felt like challenging whatever lurked in the darkness below, be it human or superhuman. There was also a more pragmatic reason for staying on top of the hill: it was a good defensive position. It might just save their lives if they had been followed by unfriendly forces.

As the Fox began to organise a temporary camp, Leo was climbing down an exposed tree root to a small, chalky hollow. He was about to relieve himself beneath the tree when he lost his footing and fell. He crashed through some bushes and rolled into a basin-shaped clearing of grass. A large oak tree stood at the centre of the hollow, surrounded by strangely patterned rings of small, white rocks. Clearly the oldest tree in the area, the lower branches were festooned with man-made votive offerings, some so old and decayed it was impossible to identify them.

Leo scrambled to his feet and pulled his sword from its sheath. He did not like this place one little bit. He was cold, tired, hungry and just a bit afraid. What's more, he was angry at the way his comrades had treated him. He was fed up with being the butt of their taunts. He walked towards the great tree, and looked at the strange offerings that swayed in the breeze. He kicked at some of the stones in their peculiar patterns, then slashed at the hanging charms.

It felt good to relieve his pent-up feelings, so he began to vent his anger and frustration on the tree itself. At first he sliced branches at random, but then began to hack at the huge trunk. Pieces of bark split and flew in all directions as his attack become more and more frenzied until eventually the storm of his fury began to abate. Finally, he carved his name into the white, living wood that had been exposed beneath the mutilated bark.

With precision he cut the wood until the wounds, bleeding with sap proclaimed, 'Leo Verica Maxima Rex rules Britannia'. Exhausted, he stepped back to review his handiwork then, satisfied with the results, he piled some of the hacked bark into a little ring to make a seat. Then he piled some of the stones and broken offerings into the seat. The youth undid his clothes, sat down and made an unpleasant offering of his own.

"You took your time! What you been doing, eh?" asked Alba Dun when the youth returned.

"What have you got there?" snapped the Fox in a worried voice.

"Triumphs!" exclaimed Leo, and he held aloft some of the charms he had hacked from the oak tree.

The Fox pushed Alba Dun aside and grabbed at the boy's hand, snatching one of the peculiar objects to examine it carefully. Without looking up, he spat out a question.

"Where'd you get this?"

"Over there, when I went for a ..."

"Show me!!" hissed the prefect. He grabbed the young man roughly by the shoulder and thrust him back to where he was pointing. When they reached the hollow and stood before the ancient oak tree, Leo gleefully pointed to his name carved on the desecrated tree and to the makeshift latrine. The Fox had gone white with anger.

"You fool... you moron!" hissed the Fox. "Don't you know what this place is? Do you realise what you've done?." The smile faded from Leo's lips. He had no idea what his commander was talking about but he had no doubt he was in serious trouble. He stiffened and answered,

"No, Prefect Gaius Commius Vulpinus!"

"This is a sacred Druid site," answered the Fox with icy calm. "*The* sacred site by the look of it. Good grief! Not only have we upset Saturn by travelling on his day, but also you have just gone and severely pissed off every local deity between here and Italy! Well, my lad, you can keep guard tonight. And if you fall asleep... you're dead! Do you understand? Dead!" whispered the Fox into the lad's ear.

"Yes Prefect," gasped Leo, terrified by the Fox's words.

The two of them hurried back to the rest of the group and the Fox told them of Verruca's act of gross sacrilege. The men were seriously worried. The gods of Britannia were a surly lot, especially the sort of deities that the Druids worshipped! Now, through his irreverent vandalism, young Verruca had very likely opened up the gates of Hades ... and all manner of nastiness was probably already on its way to get them!

Under the command of their prefect, the men had dug an entrenchment of sorts in the middle of a thicket of gorse bushes. Now they huddled under their blankets, invisible from human gaze, but as it wasn't only humans they were afraid of, the Fox made sure they had some warning of attack, so Verruca was posted to guard them as they slept.

There was no fear of Leo Verica dozing off. After the Fox's dire warning he was in a state of abject terror. He stood without moving, nervously rolling his eyes towards the slightest sound. It was going to be a long, dark night for the spoiler of the shrine!

Some time well after midnight, the wind dropped and a gap began to open in the low clouds. A silver glow gradually washed over the landscape as the full moon began to make its presence felt. Menacing shadows began to appear besides indistinguishable objects that had now appeared in the moonlight.

Leo listened intently to the noises of the night, for, since the wind had dropped, there seemed to him to be more, not fewer, sounds floating in the darkness. Distant things howled, growled and rumbled, whilst things closer to the hilltop clicked, whistled scuttled and hissed. A small cloud cut the moon in half for a minute or less. When it had passed the moonlight now restored, all the myriad noises that Leo could hear abruptly ceased. The silence was deafening in the still cold air.

Suddenly, several small, dark shapes ran in all directions past the shivering young guard. They were moving so swiftly that it took Leo a few seconds to comprehend that he was watching the flight of panic-stricken rabbits. The silence was shattered by the frantic clattering of bird's wings as they fought to escape their roosts. The pandemonium increased as creatures sped across the hilltop in sheer terror.

"Oh Mars! Mercury and Minerva!" gulped Leo Verica. "Someone's coming up the hill!" The words escaped from his lips in a hoarse whisper.

The young man turned towards his sleeping comrades and began to move towards the protective gorse bushes when he felt all his joints begin to stiffen and his muscles to relax. He stopped and stood helplessly as a peculiar new sound grew louder. It was a splintering noise, the sound of cracking, splitting bark followed by the groaning and squeaking of heavy wood under intense pressure. Leo struggled to turn his head towards the sound before his body became completely paralysed. He tried to shout a warning but his open mouth had frozen.

A huge, dark shape was gradually rising into the moonlight from below the hill, coming from the direction of the Druid's oak hollow. Leo could now only move his eyes, straining them to make sense of the vast block of blackness that was creaking towards him. Beside his foot, a thin, black line rose up from the ground, spreading above the youth's head into the moonlight. Leo began to move. That is, Leo began to be moved! His whole body gradually floated silently backwards away from the bushes.

Inside his head he was deafened by the sound of his own unheard screams.

IT WAS THE STIFLING, UNNATURAL SILENCE that awoke the Fox. He immediately looked up from under his cloak and saw the grey dawn sky above the thorns of the gorse bush. Cautiously, with sword at the ready, he poked his head above the foliage. He watched for several minutes, moving his head around slowly. As there appeared to be nothing threatening in the vicinity, he carefully awoke the others. The men clambered stiffly to their feet trying to avoid the needle-sharp gorse thorns, as they warily made their way out of the bushes.

"Verruca!!" hissed the Fox. "Verruca ... where are you?" he whispered loudly.

"Prefect! Look! There he is – over there!" shouted one of the others. The Fox looked to where the man was pointing and saw the youth sitting on the ground facing towards them. The Fox moved slowly forwards, staring into the grey half-light of the dawn. Something was not quite right. He approached the sitting form of Leo Verica.

"Verruca!? Everything all right? Ver..."

The Fox stopped and instinctively gripped his sword in readiness. The young lad appeared to be grinning; a moronic fixed smile was spread from ear to ear as he stared with coal-black eyes towards the bushes. Alba Dun joined the Fox, looked at the seated youth and gasped. Leo Verica was dead. His cheeks were stuffed with acorns, which had caused his mouth to expand, giving the impression of a grin. Acorns were embedded in his nostrils and his coal-black eyes were actually two more glistening, dark acorns. The men looked closer and saw several waxy, white limb-like structures protruding from his thighs and calves. These growths twisted away from the body and sank into the ground. The closer the men looked the more tendrils they could see, protruding from his clothing and splitting through his exposed skin. The lad was literally rooted to the spot.

Alba Dun had seen enough. He backed away, turned and ran screaming down the slope of the hill to the south. As all his military training evaporated, the Fox turned in panic and chased after Alba Dun. The others didn't ask what had happened, they just turned and ran, following their companions down the hill, away from that accursed place.

Behind them, the hilltop faded as menacing, dark clouds lowered to embrace the ancient site. The seated body toppled over on its side as the wind sliced through the trees. A cascade of acorns burst from the splitting corpse and tumbled away down the grassy slopes. Above, the heavy clouds prepared to release their load. Soon the desecrated site would be sanitised under the cover of Druid-white, virgin snow. The clouds swept southwards across the Downs towards the distant, cold sea, inside them the messengers of winter prepared to be released.

THE ENDLESS, DARK GREY BLUR beneath a falling snowflake was becoming slowly but surely lighter in colour. In an instant, the cloud was gone and the world below appeared in dazzling, crystal-clear focus. The snowflake fell earthward, passing over a snake-like ribbon of foaming white surf that divided the iron-black winter sea from the darkness of a vast forest. To the east, the cloud stretched along the horizon, slowly turning from pink to violet as the pale winter sun approached.

Down and down the snowflake fell. Soon it was joined by a million more and together they spiralled and swirled over the cold countryside.

Eventually the forest began to thin, and as areas of brush and scrubland merged into cultivated land, a patchwork of little fields could be seen spreading inland from a distant bay. The snowflake tumbled towards the edge of that bay; the sea became lighter the nearer the snowflake fell.

About a mile inland from the sea, a great house stood alone in the middle of a large meadow. A strip of road as straight as an arrow led away from the house and gradually faded into the northern horizon.

A gust of wind snatched the snowflake and thrust it down towards the house. It was the first of a billion snowflakes that announced the beginning of that winter, and, as they began to settle, they slowly covered the end of an era.

A gravel path, wide and straight, bordered with neatly clipped low hedges, led to the great house. Four red-tiled roofs and one wooden tower looked down on a cobblestone courtyard and central fountain. The building resembled an enormous square doughnut and was easily the grandest house for many a mile. It had once been the scene of the hustle and bustle of everyday life. Even royalty had been amongst its many guests.

But suddenly it was empty. Hundreds of years of constant occupation had abruptly ceased. The last family had been the happiest occupants the house had ever known, and yet the man, his wife, the small boy and his older sister had all been forced to leave. The children didn't know why – but the adults knew. They knew that beyond the forest ... the monsters were coming!

They had been coming gradually closer over the last few months. Reports of Saxon pirates and their raiding parties were increasing daily. Now that they had been abandoned by their military guard, the man and his wife knew it would only be a matter of time before the grey reptile-headed ships clattered ashore close to their home.

That Saturn's day afternoon, when the Fox and his band were approaching the northern slopes of the South Downs, the man had seen smoke rising into the distant sky to the east. The smoke was coming from the direction of the neighbouring property at Buchanora Rex, less than five miles away. In an instant, his mind was made up. They would pack their remaining possessions – those which the departing troops had not already looted – and leave first thing in the morning.

Sunday arrived grey and cold, threatening their world with snow. Painfully slowly, the family drove their overloaded wagon towards the Selsey peninsular and its ancient seaport. They had been travelling for an hour or so when they were joined by a group of auxiliaries, a dirt-covered, frightened-looking rabble who were also heading for the port of Neptune at Novamare on the Selsey coast. The Fox, having finally negotiated the terrors of the forest, made it safely to an old military supply road and trudged the final few miles to the coast at an exhausting pace.

Late that afternoon the family, accompanied by their new 'guard', trundled into the once proud port at Novamare and embarked on one of the few remaining craft.

The family and the auxiliaries waited for the rest of the day on board the little ship. The captain wanted to make it worth his while before he set sail and there was still the chance of fare-paying stragglers appearing on the dock. Later that evening, the Fox told the assembled company, including the ship's captain and crew, about their own adventures. The captain listened nervously. On hearing of the ferocity of the Saxon attack he forgot all about additional passengers and prepared to make sail at first light.

On a cold, blustery moon day's morning, the little ship battered its way into a full gale that was sweeping along the Channel. Soon the land they had left was gone, smothered in the greyness of low, snow-filled clouds.

"The monsters will be in that cloud," the man told his young children.

Prefect Gaius Commius Vulpinus said nothing as he leant on the rail of the ship. He had overheard what the man said. He looked back towards the hidden shore. The Fox knew that the monsters the father was referring to came from the depths of the German forests. It was the monsters that came from the depths of hell that worried him!

The little ship pressed on through the mountainous seas, taking the family and the auxiliaries further south to a warmer, safer land.

DEAD LEAVES NOW FLUTTERED along the ground of the great square courtyard. The large, once-welcoming rooms at the end of the square were empty. Everything of value had been stripped from the house. Even the coloured glass that had once sent beams of rainbow light across the beautiful tiled dining room had gone.

When the first snows of winter arrived, they took the last remaining colour out of the bleak landscape. Across ploughed fields, the snowflakes tumbled. Urged on towards the abandoned buildings, the snow rode the razor-sharp wind. The wind hit the house, cutting through the tiles and bricks. Snowflakes streamed in through the black, empty windows of the stable and through the open doorways of the great house. Where once the warmth of the central heating had comforted the family and their many guests, there was now a sprinkling of frost. The only sound to be heard as the cold night closed in was the flapping of a forgotten curtain and the dry rustling of the wind-chased, frozen leaves that blew across the cobblestones.

Beyond the north side of the house lay a low-walled area of ground. A few scattered sticks and the remains of a scarecrow were the only evidence that once a lovingly tended garden had flourished on the site. Indeed so much delicious fruit and produce had been harvested from the little garden that the family had placed a small bronze statue beneath an old apple tree to thank the gods for their good fortune.

Mounted on a stone pedestal, the figure of the tiny bearded man with his goat-like legs played his pipes silently towards the deserted house. Snow had now covered over the statue's little horns and the tips of his peculiar pointed ears. He too had been forgotten.

The seasons passed, and as the little statue played his pipes to the passing years he watched sadly through empty eyes as the once-majestic house slowly fell. Tile by tile, brick by brick, the house crumbled. The monsters came and passed it by. It held no interest for them; they had no use at all for great houses with stables, gardens and fountains.

YEARS LATER some of them returned, not quite the monsters they had once been. They had changed. No longer fierce with swords, shields and armour, with boats that had the heads of dragons shaped on their bows, now they were more interested in building their own small stone farmsteads and in keeping pigs. The last of the useful bricks and timber had long since been taken from the site of the mansion. The grass and weeds invaded, roots dug into the cobbles, bushes and trees climbed out of the grassy mounds that hid the foundations and a green curtain of undergrowth gradually closed over the little bronze god. All memory of the house that had dominated the site for three hundred years was buried under the leaves of nearly sixteen hundred autumns.

CHAPTER TWO

A BARK RONDO

·2·

A BARK RONDO

One thousand, five hundred and ninety three years later
– a Saturday...

AN EVIL WIND FROM SIBERIA was pushing the heavy clouds so close to the ground that their undersides were being painted orange by the street lamps. The temperature was falling rapidly and the smoke of a thousand household fires swirled upward to be sliced by the same malicious north wind. An empty crisp packet twirled and tumbled along the damp, black tarmac of a deserted main road until a malevolent claw of cold air snatched it into the leaden sky.

A muddy, dog excreta-decorated lane led away from the main road and disappeared into a canopy of tangled branches. Concealed in the entrance to the tree-smothered lane a police patrol car waited to pounce on unsuspecting prey. Inside the car was forty-two year old Sergeant Len Chalcroft and his driver, Dave Norbren, a wiry blond-haired man some ten years his junior.

"You ready for the creatures of the night?" asked the younger man.

Sergeant Chalcroft took a drag from his cigarette and wound down his window.

"Eh!? Why, what's the time, Dave?" he asked.

"Coming up to ten forty-five," replied the driver.

Chalcroft blew a mouthful of smoke into the cold air and looked along the deserted length of the street.

"Yep... I'm ready. Bring 'em on!" he replied. "They'll be chucking up... chucking out... and chucking up again in that order," he added. He was referring to the battalions of Great British boozers who were about to be spewed from the local clubs and pubs into the cold November night.

Len Chalcroft pulled himself upright in his seat, adjusted his peaked cap and, after a final puff on his cigarette, propelled the burning stub from the car. The red glow of the cigarette arched from the window and spluttered into a clump of wet grass.

"Hurry up and shut that flippin' window, Sarge! It's freezing in 'ere," grumbled the driver, hunching his shoulders and drawing his elbows in towards the steering wheel.

"Don't you worry mate," replied the Sergeant as he wound the window up. "It'll soon warm up... oh yes!" he smiled and folded his arms.

In fact, nothing happened for over half an hour. The world in general – and the street in particular – remained eerily quiet. Then, as so often happens, it all began at the same time.

Chalcroft saw the twinkle of an oncoming vehicle's lights. The Policeman narrowed his eyes and stared hard at the approaching object. A moving traffic offence was heading towards them with only one of its headlights working properly.

"Oh dear, oh dear... and what do we have here then?" he said slowly and sarcastically, nudging his partner. "By the pricking of my thumbs, something wicked this way comes: open locks, whoever knocks! Start her up, Dave old mate... it's party time!" The police car rumbled into life as a bizarre vehicle meandered towards them.

Just a stone's throw away, Saturday night at the social club was drawing to a hot, noisy and smoky finale. The elderly rock band was being cheered for an encore (another rendition of 'Achy, Breaky, Heart'). The denizens of the snooker hall were leaving and the last tunes on the jukebox were being played out in the poolroom.

Donna and her friend Jade stood by the wall-mounted juke box and finished off their drinks. Their happy evening had comprised of chatting, exchanging friendly insults, bantering with their mates and eyeing up the 'talent'.

Shane, Darren and Lee had spent the evening trying to prove their pool prowess amongst the lads and swear like real men in front of the impressionable young women.

Last orders had been called at the bar. Lee swayed off to the toilet, while Shane and Darren's interest in pool evaporated as they contemplated going home with Jade and Donna. The three lads lived on the same estate as the two girls, and it didn't come as any surprise to Donna when Shane sidled up to her. He stood chewing his nails in front of them. After a quick glance of reassurance to Darren he spoke.

"Fancy a take-away?"

Donna and Jade and the other two girls giggled, then with a stern face Donna looked back towards Shane.

"We ain't got no money!" replied the dark-haired, large-breasted girl who wore a tight pink woollen sweater under a battered, black leather jacket.

"S'allright, we 'ave!" proclaimed Darren.

At that moment Lee arrived back from the toilets. He misjudged the doorway to the poolroom and smashed his shoulder into the wall, recoiled, then staggered forwards towards the jukebox.

"You goin' for ... hic! ... something ... hic! ... to eat, eh? I'll ... hic! ... I'll come wiv ya! ... hic!" slurred the almost-broken voice of Lee, who had drunk five pints of lager and three vodkas and could now see three of everything.

"Oh, flamin' 'ell! I'm not going if 'e's comin," pouted Jade as she frowned at the boss-eyed, acne-endowed youth.

"Me neither. Look at the wally! 'He can 'ardly stand up proper!" sneered Donna.

"I ... hic! ... I flip ... hic! ... flippin' can! ... hic!" insisted Lee.

"Don't worry, he won't be able to keep up, we'll lose him on the way," whispered Shane to Donna.

"I'll just ... hic! ... go to ... hic! ... the bog again. Won't be a ... hic! ... tic ... hic!" mumbled Lee as he wobbled off in the direction of the toilets.

"Quick, come on. Let's go!" ordered Donna.

The warmth of the club swirled into the night as the group tottered out into the cold. The fresh air blew away the viscous aroma of tobacco smoke, stale beer and various body odours and cut into their nostrils and stung their tired eyes as they walked briskly away from the club.

Lee swayed out of the toilet and discovered that his friends had vanished. He lurched over to a youth who was waiting for a taxi. Lee stared at the three identical youths and focused on the one in the middle.

"Here! ... hic! P-P-Pete. You seen mmmmm ... whassisname and ... hic! ... you know ... mmmm Dade and Jonna ... hic! Eh?"

"Yeah, they just left" said the lad.

Lee staggered into the youth, who gently pushed him away.

"F-f-fanks ... mmmm ... hic! Suvvleflitsnik ... mmmm ... hic!" babbled the awkward, incoherent Lee as he fell out of the club.

The others were several hundred metres ahead and were vanishing into the gloom of the blustery night.

"Come on, let's whip through 'ere," said Darren pointing towards the entrance of a cemetery.

"I ain't goin' in there!" protested Jade.

"What... you scared?" accused Donna in a mocking tone.

"No!" lied her friend indignantly.

"Right, well c'mon then!" hissed Shane and they fled through the entrance and into the municipal cemetery.

"Way-fer-me!" wailed a distant, plaintive voice from somewhere behind them.

"Oh no, it's Lee!" shouted Darren. "Quick lets 'ide over there!" he whispered loudly. The four youngsters ran off to be engulfed by the darkness.

They had been running for several minutes when Shane grabbed Donna's hand and pulled her towards an outcrop of headstones and carved figures that surrounded a huge and ancient yew tree. They tumbled giggling onto the soft grass behind a large stone angel that sheltered beneath the canopy of the great tree.

Shane and Donna watched as Darren pulled Jade behind some bushes on the opposite side of the path. The four teenagers listened intently for the approaching Lee. Noises filtered through the cemetery: a screech of faraway brakes melted into the muffled accelerating roar of a powerful motorbike. Distant shouts were hidden by the throb of a passing lorry and the swirl of the gusting wind.

It took a further three minutes for Lee to arrive at the entrance to the cemetery. He stopped and screwed up his eyes, staring painfully into the orange dampness of the empty street.

"Mmmmmm ... they've ... hic! Must've gone through 'ere ... hic! Ain't they?" scowled Lee as he looked up at the great iron gates. He began to totter backwards as he continued looking up. He corrected himself, leant forwards and pitched headlong into the darkness of the cemetery.

"Shh!" giggled Shane as he drew Donna close to him. "'ere comes the little plonker!"

"Oi ... get off! ... your 'ands are cold!" came a cry from the bushes that hid Jade and Darren. Lee trotted to a halt and dizzily looked around the path.

"I know your ... hic! ... in 'ere. Hic!" shouted Lee as he swayed from one side of the path to the other. There was the sharp sound of a hand slapping human flesh.

"Ow! Whatcha do that for?" cried Darren.

"Cos I don't like being groped!" hissed Jade.

Donna and Shane began to giggle, then Shane put his finger over his lips to tell the girl to be quiet.

Lee had spun round to try to pinpoint the location of the slap and voices. The cold wind confused his senses; the world was beginning to fade away. Now he stood rocking back and forth with a swaying, pointing arm raised to shoulder height.

Lee was just about to speak when his eyes closed and his arm began to droop down to his side. Then a hand grabbed his shoulder and a voice blasted into his skull.

"Boo!" screamed Shane, then he turned and ran towards the far exit, swiftly followed by Donna, Jade and Darren, engulfed in hysterical fits of laughter.

Lee screamed, tripped over the edge of the path, and plummeted into the grassy border. Pulling himself to his feet, he began to fall forwards again and the momentum of his uncontrollable body sent him sprawling over the low railings of an ancient memorial. He landed on a carpet of green stone chippings that covered an adjacent grave. As he lay there, fighting to keep his eyes open, he could hear the distant whoops and shrieks of the others as they fled to the opposite end of the cemetery.

Lee painfully dragged himself to his feet. He leant against a heavy marble pillar and unzipped his jeans. With one hand supporting his weight he relieved himself into a flowerpot and then across the headstone of someone called Hotham. The Siberian wind blew into his hair and a low branch from a nearby oak tree swished across his face.

"Way-fer-me!" he whispered weakly, and turned towards the path, but the coldness of the air drilled into him and once again he lost the struggle against gravity. He fell backwards against the oak tree and slid down its massive trunk into a sitting position.

"Way-fer-me!" he dribbled, as he stared into the gloom that stretched out before him.

He looked down at his left hand and saw that it was resting on a side root the size of a human thigh. Frustrated at his inability to stand and angered at the way his so-called friends had abandoned him, he decided to vent his anger on the tree. He fumbled in his pocket before pulling out a penknife. Lee opened it and began to stab at the tree's thigh-like root.

After a few seconds of angry stabbing, Lee's arm tired and he cut himself on his own blade. Had he fallen asleep? Or was he only imagining the thin black line that was rising out of some white marble chippings in front of him. Lee stared and screwed up his eyes, mesmerised at the sight of the strange rod-like structure slowly climbing vertically from the grave.

He decided it was either Darren or Shane fooling around. Gripping his knife, he thrust and slashed at the air in front of him to try and call their bluff. Lee staggered to his feet and flexed his shoulders in an attempt to look 'hard', then he waved the open knife at the peculiar object.

"Yeah? Come on then!" he slurred. "Come on, come on!"

Lee was aware of a noise that came from behind his left shoulder. He looked around and up into the blackness of the oak branches and then to either side of the gnarled tree. The distraction made him forget the enigmatic line that was still rising slowly above the grave.

Holding the knife in his outstretched arm, he walked towards the thick trunk of the tree and, after satisfying himself that he was alone, began to gouge out large chunks of bark. When he had eventually finished carving the semi-legible message it stated:

'Yo! Lee rules Bogham!'

The meaningless graffiti had been etched into the lifeblood of the venerable oak. Lee felt a weird tingling sensation stroke his spinal chord. He turned slowly around, and his jaw dropped open. The rising black line was now over four metres high and had begun to sprout side shoots. Lee slowly moved away until he felt the unyielding bulk of the mighty oak press into his back.

The black lines were evolving in front of him; networks of vein-like filaments were flickering laterally into the air. He realised that the black threads were forming into something he had seen before, but he could not remember what it was. Suddenly there was a loud crack from just above his head and an unpleasant splintering noise sounded to the left of his face. Lee's befuddled brain short-circuited and switched to primeval override and he was filled with the desperate desire to escape.

He tried to run but nothing happened! Only his right hand did anything; it opened and the knife slowly floated away from its grasp! Lee discovered he could move his eyes but every other part of him was held in an invisible vice-like grip. His mind screamed for someone to help him, but his mouth was frozen.

Then something moved beside him.

Lee's eyes hurt as he strained every muscle in their orbits to see what was happening next to him. Very slowly, in time with the staccato crackling sounds, a large flap of tree bark was peeling away from the huge trunk. In front of him the hovering knife was plucked from mid-air by a million tiny black threads that were emanating from the thicker black lines.

Lee felt the tree shudder as the bark continued to peel away from the trunk. A cascade of small, hard objects fell from the branches and the youth felt very real pain as he was struck time and time again. His eyes continued to strain to make sense of the tree bark, which was starting to ripple like cloth and was curling into a definite form: it was a hood, and under the hood a dark malevolent face-like structure was evolving.

To his horror, Lee felt himself being engulfed by a million threads. He was spun around and his face was thrust into his own graffiti. The pocket knife moved towards his back, and he felt his clothes being sliced away...

NOT FAR AWAY, Sergeant Chalcroft and his driver watched the eccentric vehicle weave a course along the central white line. It swept past the concealed entrance to the lane, trailing a cloud of blue and white smoke and a shower of sparks sprayed out from something that was dragging along the ground under the chassis. The smoke billowed from under the vehicle and also from the chicken-wire covered windows of a strange wooden hut that adorned the back of the van. The two officers leant forwards towards the windscreen.

"What the hell was that?" they asked in perfect unison.

"Whatever it is, let's have 'im!" commanded the Sergeant.

The driver slammed the vehicle into first gear and switched on the roof light array and as he did so a female voice crackled into the car.

"Foxtrot Lima Three. Control to Foxtrot Lima Three!"

"Foxtrot Lima Three. Go ahead!" answered Sergeant Chalcroft.

"Er, yes, Foxtrot Lima Three," said the radio operator. "Report of people dancing naked in the municipal cemetery."

Norbren raised his eyebrows and looked towards the wide eyes of Sergeant Chalcroft.

"Er, control, repeat message please," asked the Sergeant.

"Foxtrot Lima Three, I repeat, people screaming and dancing naked in the municipal cemetery at the Bichester Road entrance ... over."

"Yes, control, Foxtrot Lima Three, roger that! We're on our way!" replied the Policeman.

"Roger Foxtrot Lima Three, your message timed at twenty-three fifty eight ... Control out!"

Chalcroft slammed his hand on the dashboard.

"Scrub the van, Dave! I've been waiting years for this ... devil worshippers in Bogham! Let's go get 'em!"

The patrol car roared out of the lane, it's tyres spinning on the muddy surface, the lights on the roof illuminating the drifting clouds of smoke that had been created by the van. The car slewed round and sped off in the opposite direction from the strange half-timbered vehicle which had meanwhile pulled up to the kerb and stopped.

The cold wind blew the exhaust smoke past the stationary vehicle as the driver struggled to get out. The man stood swaying gently, peering into the thinning smoke. As the fumes cleared, he could not believe his confused eyes, for not only had the smoke dispersed it seemed to have taken the police car with it! He slumped back against the woodwork and glanced up towards heaven.

Foxtrot Lima Three swept into the cemetery approach road and was immediately confronted by a red and white creature running towards them. Dazzled by the lights, the flailing figure slipped and fell onto the cold tarmac in front of the patrol car.

"Careful Dave!" said Chalcroft as the two officers got out of the car and drew their batons.

The terrified, naked youth struggled to his knees, grimacing into the glare of the car's headlights. He stretched his blood-covered arms out towards the two men in a pleading gesture. The Sergeant ran to the pathetic shape of the injured Lee whilst the driver kept a close guard over his partner's back.

"Good grief!" cried Chalcroft as he saw the extent of the young man's injuries.

"Dave, get on the blower quick! Get medics! The kid's been carved up! All right son, you'll be all right," said the policeman to the freezing, terrified boy.

The ambulance rushed the mutilated youth to the Sussex County Hospital where his horrific wounds were soon being treated. The staff in the operating theatre were appalled by the extent and nature of his injuries.

The duty surgeon looked down at the latticework of cuts and scratches that had been scored into the back of the patient's torso, thighs and legs. After taking a deep breath, he leant closer to some of the deeper cuts that ran the length of Lee's back then, using a pair of small forceps, he began to probe the wound.

"Well I've seen some strange sights in my life," he exclaimed, "but just what on earth was he doing to get these things in his back?" He leant closer to the sedated youth's back and extracted numerous bloody lumps that had been buried in several deeply gouged furrows across Lee's shoulder blades. He rinsed one of the lumps in a pan of water, then lifted it up towards the theatre lights. The nurses and staff shook their heads in amazement at one of the many glistening acorns that the surgeon had removed from Lee's body.

EARLY THE NEXT EVENING, the occupants of Foxtrot Lima Three sat at a concealed ambush hideaway on the outskirts of the town. Conversation inside the patrol car revolved around the weird events of the previous night. Chalcroft looked out of the window and gazed as the approaching darkness. To the north, the cloud stretched along the horizon, slowly turning from pink to violet as the night closed in.

"I tell you there's a lot of it about: black magic, witchcraft and all that sort of thing" said the older man in an all-knowing way.

"Cobblers!" said Dave Norbren. "It's just kids. Any excuse to get their kit off. You mark my words, they'll have been some hanky-panky going on in that cemetery last night."

"Getting their kit off?" sneered the sergeant. "What, in the middle of November? It's cold enough for snow – in fact, I wouldn't be surprised if we got some tonight."

Dave didn't answer; instead he tapped his teeth with his fingernails and stared along the road. Chalcroft sucked in a mouthful of air, held out his hand and contemplated his knuckles.

"Mmm, you could be right! But I tell you, Dave that one was peculiar … and peculiar things have been going on around here for thousands of years!" Staring up out of the window at the endless dark grey blur above the patrol car, he automatically reached into his pocket and pulled out a pack of cigarettes. "There are more things in heaven and earth, Horatio..."

"Who's he?" asked Dave.

"Never mind," replied Sergeant Chalcroft with a sigh, "never mind. I'm sure it's going to snow."

CHAPTER THREE

BEYOND THE PAIL

· 3 ·

BEYOND THE PAIL

Ten months later ... a Friday ...

IT WAS ALMOST the autumn end of summer. The great cherry-red sun had finally, defiantly sunk into the mist-swamped fields beyond the little seaside town. High above in a wine-dark sky, thin strips of rose-lined clouds veiled the first twinkling stars of evening. The warm air held a scent of damp hay mixed with the sounds of clicking bats and the last swallows of summer.

Alongside one of the newly mown fields was a row of houses, and beside the last house was an area of derelict ground. Among the bushes and patches of clumpy grass was a mound of briers and ivy that had grown over an old, abandoned motor car. Various rusty objects and a fairly new supermarket trolley lay in and around a muddy puddle next to the car.

It was almost as though the untidiness of the waste ground was trying to invade the adjoining property. That property was Number One Romany Way, an old, thatched cottage with a glass conservatory that overlooked a huge garden. The straw of the thatched roof had once been a golden yellow and the glass of the conservatory had sparkled and shone, but now many panes were either cracked and broken or covered in grime, and the thatch was blackened with age and neglect.

The owner of the house was an old lady who lived there alone – alone, that is, except for Snaps, her ginger cat. The old lady's name was Miss Eleanor Forgetmenot and she had lived in the house for many years. She knew it needed repairs but she had very little money, and certainly not enough for a new roof or conservatory.

Although she wasn't rich, she was happy and content, and despite not being able to repair her home or redecorate the peeling paintwork, she had a lot to be thankful for. Above all her greatest joy was to walk in her beautiful garden.

Miss Forgetmenot loved to stroll along the flower-bordered path which curved and curled for what seemed like miles down to the trees and bushes that grew alongside the fields. She had spent many hours lovingly tending the flowerbeds and weeding the large rockery that rose up from the big pond, and on summer evenings she would sit in a little pink and yellow deck chair watching the golden-coloured fish swimming lazily in the clear, lily-topped water. The pond was surrounded by tall reeds at one end and at the other, where the Rockery was situated, a small waterfall had once cascaded into the deep, inky-dark water. The waterfall still flowed into the pond, but now it was no more than a trickle, owing to the twigs and branches that were slowly clogging the little stream.

The problem was that Miss Forgetmenot was now too old to carry out all the work needed to keep the garden in as beautiful a condition as it had once been. She couldn't afford to repair the rotting fenceposts, or prune the trees, or trim the hedges, or even to replace the chimney pot that had broken – and so, sadly, the further the garden spread from the house, the more of a tangled jungle it had become.

Although it saddened Miss Forgetmenot that the garden was becoming unkempt, it suited others very well indeed, for the old lady's garden had several secrets – and one of them was about to change her life forever.

The old lady knew about one of the secrets, but had absolutely no idea about the others. She did know that nearly 50 years ago, when the pond had been dug and the earth was being piled up at one end to make the foundations for the rockery, a workman had unearthed a lump of clay that was strangely heavy and resembled the figure of a man. Miss Forgetmenot had taken the figure and with a hosepipe and scrubbing brush had set about restoring the mysterious object. She was pleasantly surprised by what she discovered and put the little horned figure back on its newly-cleaned stone pedestal by the side of the pond. For 50 years the little man with the goat-like legs had played his pipes towards that waterfall.

What the old lady most certainly did not know was that if she thought that only she and her cat lived at Number One Romany Way, she was very much mistaken.

Many birds and animals had been attracted to the garden, for not only was the garden itself full of natural food but the old lady regularly left table scraps and titbits outside the kitchen door. Every hedgehog for miles around knew that there would be a delicious portion of cat food and a bowl of milk to be had at Number One.

Other, stranger creatures had also discovered that glorious garden. In fact, the ancestors of some of them had been on the land before Miss Forgetmenot had arrived and had transformed it into a garden. It was these creatures that were the real secret of Romany Way, a secret that the old lady could never have imagined in her wildest dreams!

And so it was that on that evening, when the air smelled of damp hay and was mixed with the sounds of clicking bats and the screams of the last swallows of summer, that a hungry hedgehog was snuffling through the long grass of the waste ground. He was heading towards the old lady's house, his mind full of thoughts of table scraps and titbits. Suddenly he stopped and sniffed the air. His coal-black eyes glittered as he glanced nervously towards the towering mound of briers and ivy beside which he had paused. It was the overgrown motor car. The hedgehog eyed it suspiciously and wondered whether it was empty or whether 'they' were having a meeting.

"Either way," he thought, "I've got to get to the house before them or there will be precious little left to eat!"

The hedgehog continued on his journey, quickening his pace, and head down he pushed his way through the dew-soaked grass. He was aware that it was almost dark and he did not want to be last in line!

Two small birds huddled together, trying to ward off the faint chill of the late evening. From their perch in an ancient apple tree, they watched the great orange disc of the moon as it struggled to free itself from the silhouettes of chimneys, trees and television aerials. Something swished the lush grass beneath the apple tree and the birds heard the sound of stifled giggling.

A light was switched on in a room at the back of Number One Romany Way, dispelling the inky darkness of the garden nearest to the house. The two birds ruffled their feathers and shuffled closer to the leafy shadows that shrouded the gnarled trunk of their old tree. There were more movements from below the safety of their roost and as they both looked down into the gloom they could see the occasional reflected glint of eyes as the light from the kitchen window flooded across the lawn.

Somewhere far away, a car alarm sounded briefly. The garbled shouts of late-night revellers mingled with the distant muffled 'clackety-clack' of the last train as it rumbled to a halt. A sharp 'clack' echoed through the garden as Miss Forgetmenot drew back the bolt on her kitchen door. Snaps the ginger cat rushed past her ankles, tail high, and vanished into the shadows. The old lady placed a plate of chunky cat food on a cardboard box. She

NO. 1 ROMANY WAY.

usually put the plate on an upturned bucket but it was missing tonight.

"Never mind," she thought. "I'm getting absent-minded. I must have put it somewhere else. It's bound to turn up sooner or later." After placing a saucer of milk next to the food, she stood and looked up to the heavens then, after taking a deep breath, she sighed and stepped back inside the kitchen, closing the door on the moist, still night.

The moon had freed itself from the roofs and telegraph poles and was gliding gracefully to the ceiling of stars. Now a yellowish-white, its light began to flood the land below. And in the garden of Number One Romany Way, the nightly ritual was about to commence!

Snaps the cat was creeping between the stalks of some tall border plants beside a pile of old fence panels. He stopped to sniff the ground.

"What is it tonight?" asked a voice. The cat relaxed his ears and carried on sniffing; he had recognised the voice.

"Chicken," he replied.

"Milk?" asked the voice from the shadows.

"Mmm, yeah. That's if the hogs haven't already drunk it." As Snaps slunk away into the darkness, the undergrowth rustled with the sound of another voice.

"Not tonight they won't have!" and there was the sound of cackling laughter from beside the woodpile.

The hedgehog had reached the tunnel in the thick hedge that separated the waste ground from the garden. He wondered how many more of his companions were in front of him as he entered the old drainpipe that acted as the tunnel. The pipe was about three metres long and he was almost half way when he heard grunting, snuffling and scratching noises, along with the sounds of gruff angry voices.

"Come on, come on! It'll all be gone by the time we get there! Put some muscle into it," said one deep voice.

"I'm trying the best I can," said another crossly

"Hurry up, I'm starving!" said a third.

The hedgehog came to what was usually the end of the drainpipe. Tonight, however, it seemed to continue further than usual, then stop at a dead end. Three other hedgehogs were huddled in the confined space. Two were impatiently watching a third who was pushing with all his might at the round metal wall that blocked the tunnel. Then he collapsed into the floor, panting.

"It's no good," he gasped. "I can't shift it!"

The animals looked at each other in the gloom, completely mystified. Thin tendrils of mist rose from the warm milk in the saucer. A small hedgehog, who had come from a different direction from his unfortunate cousins, had waited until the human had disappeared. Unable to contain his desire, he burst out from under a privet bush. His little legs pumped up and down for all they were worth. Strongly resembling a prickly guided missile, he made straight for the milky treasure that lay temptingly on top of the box. He was scarcely a couple of metres away from the saucer of milk when suddenly two huge shapes leapt out in front of him; two bearded, grimacing creatures making gargoyle faces. The little hedgehog instinctively curled himself into a ball and fell, bouncing and rolling along the ground. The two bearded creatures were Goblins!

The terrified hedgehog ball rolled uncontrollably past the goblins and into a thick flowerbed. There was a hiss, a scream and a wild thrashing of undergrowth! Snaps had been sniffing the ground at exactly the point where the spiky hedgehog cannonball had ploughed into the foliage. The cat leapt out of the flower border rubbing his nose. The goblins slapped their knees, doubled up with laughter.

The birds in the apple tree, having watched the antics below, settled down once more. This time they were happy to go to sleep knowing that Snaps the cat had retreated back inside the house. The still greenery of the mistletoe and ivy that almost covered the old tree began to rustle just above the snoozing birds. A dull yellow glow gradually lit the edges of the leaves and branches. The light was joined by another, and another.

The little hedgehog in the flower bed cautiously opened his eyes and began to unroll. He peered around the stems of the tall chrysanthemums to where the box and the food lay waiting, then with a snort he ran for cover, away from cats and annoying goblins.

The two goblins grinned at each other. One was named Wazzark and the other was Podfudger. Wazzark was the taller of the two and he was a little more than 30 centimetres in height. He bent his knee in a mock bow to his companion.

"After you, squire," said Wazzark.

"Fank you. I don't mind if I do," said Podfudger.

The pair tiptoed to the plate of food, cautiously looked around, then, when they were sure there was no danger, unfastened the little leather pouches that each had fastened to his belt.

"You'd better call 'em!" said Wazzark, pointing towards the distant apple tree.

"Do we have to?" pouted Podfudger.

"Of course we have to, it's in the rules" replied Wazzark. "B'sides, they don't eat much do they?"

Podfudger shrugged his shoulders. "S'pose not. Hey Wazzark, I know, I'll give 'em those rubbery bits in the cat food that you don't like!"

Wazzark was too busy wrapping pieces of the food into a large sheet of newspaper to answer.

Podfudger held up a ring of yellowish gristle and examined it at arm's length. "Whadaya fink this bit is?" he asked.

"I dunno. If it's cat food then it's probably a bit of a cat. C'mon, call 'em, I want to get back home!" said Wazzark.

"Why what's the 'urry?" asked Podfudger, looking into the shadows cast by the kitchen light. Wazzark had finished putting the food into his pouch. He looked up into the star-studded sky and took a deep breath.

"Storm coming!" he said.

At that moment, Miss Forgetmenot turned off the kitchen light and the garden was plunged into pure moonlight. Podfudger put the gristle ring back on the plate. Then, turning towards the apple tree, he made a soft whirring, clicking noise. It was the sound that the lights in the tree had been listening for. Three tiny, yellowish-green glows floated down from the tree, skimmed across the grass and headed towards the cardboard box.

"'ere quick!" said Wazzark "Take a swig of this." He slurped at the saucer of milk and then handed it to Podfudger. Podfudger took a mouthful of milk, then placed the saucer back on the box. As he did so, the three lights appeared over the edge and landed next to the plate, which had several small pieces of food left on the edge. Each of the lights was a tiny female form, lit by a thousand minute pinpricks of light that encrusted their spider-web robes. The fairies – for that is what they were – were extremely shy and secretive. Their leader's name was Ghisette and her silver hair was longer than that of her two companions. Unlike the other twenty or so fairies in the garden, she was not at all afraid of goblins and so she spoke for them all. Ghisette stepped on to the plate and looked down at the food. Wazzark scratched the back of his head and looked at the three tiny creatures.

"Enough?" he asked.

Ghisette studied the food, then clicked her fingers towards her two sisters.

"Enough," she replied in her tiny, musical, high-pitched voice. The two other fairies hovered gently near Ghisette. Each carried the cup of an acorn which, upside-down, made a perfect little food bowl. The fairies began to put the remaining food into one acorn cup. Wazzark lifted up the saucer of milk and, with the few drops remaining, filled the other cup to the brim.

Ghisette stood with her hands on her hips. Her dress was silver with tiny threads of gold that ran around the low collar and down to the threaded golden belt that hung just below her waist. At the back of her head, a high spider-web collar glittered in the moonlight. Attached to this was a cloak of the rarest golden spider silk, which trailed down to her ankles.

Wazzark looked down and whispered, "Hey Queenie, you'd better tuck yourself up well tonight!"

Ghisette looked up at the walnut-crinkled, leathery face of Wazzark. She frowned, folded her arms and tapped her foot.

"Oh, and why's that then Wazzark?" she asked suspiciously, expecting the usual smutty remark.

"Nothin' much," said the Goblin. "Just that I think you're in for a big one tonight!" With that, Wazzark nudged Podfudger in the ribs and they both chuckled and winked at each other.

"Do you?" replied the Fairy crossly. "And what makes you think that then?"

"Can't you tell?" said Wazzark. "Can't you smell it?" He pointed to the southwestern sky and took another deep breath. Ghisette frowned and continued tapping her foot.

"Good luck," whispered Wazzark, as he turned and headed across the moon-shadowed garden. "C'mon, Podfudger, they'll be hungry by now." Podfudger closed his leather pouch and stumbled after Wazzark.

"Bye Queenie!" he whispered.

Ghisette watched the Goblins until they had both dissolved into the shadows. Her sisters glanced nervously around. Ghisette raised her head to the southwestern sky, as the goblin had done, and sniffed the moist air. Immediately she caught the unmistakable scent and turned to the others.

"Storm!" she said urgently. "Quickly ... home!"

WAZZARK AND PODFUDGER were already scurrying back to their home. Home to the goblins was the Rockery above the pond. They shared their burrows with several other residents including two Elves (one Welsh and one Scottish), a Pixie and a visiting Leprechaun (who had come down from Kilburn in London for a holiday by the sea). Each had their own warm, little burrow, but for relaxation they would descend far beneath the Rockery to where Gnomes had dug out a spacious hall. The gnomes had left some years ago but they had agreed that everyone could use their home, including the hall, while they were away.

The goblins could see the dark outline of the Rockery as it began to tower above them. By now they had reached the reeds at the far end of the pond; in another few minutes they would be home. Wazzark stopped and grabbed Podfudger's arm.

"Hey, listen," said Wazzark.

"Oh, yeah," said Podfudger. "I forgot about them!" The goblins crept away from the pond. They found the little path that wound it's way through the tall grass growing up to the hedge. In the hedge was the drainpipe. Over the end of the drainpipe was the bucket. Inside the bucket were four confused and hungry hedgehogs.

The goblins crept silently up to the bucket. Wazzark picked up half a brick that was hidden in the grass next to the path. Then silently he sat down next to the bucket. Putting his ear to the cold, iron base he listened, then very gently he drummed his fingers on the bottom of the bucket.

"What was that?" said the hedgehog nearest to the obstructing metal wall.

"What was what?" asked another.

"That!" exclaimed the first, pointing at the wall.

Outside, Wazzark stopped tapping the bucket. He waved his hand at Podfudger and pointed at the bucket. He resumed the soft drumming. Inside the bucket, eight little ears pricked up.

"Yes ... I heard that!." The hedgehogs shuffled to the iron wall. Wazzark stopped tapping and held the brick at arm's length.

"It's stopped again," said the first hedgehog.

"What is it?" asked the second. Then all four of them pressed an ear to the cold, metal wall of the bucket – just as Wazzark struck the bucket with a mighty blow from the brick. There was a deafening clang! The bucket actually sprung into the air as the four rolled-up hedgehogs hit its roof.

Wazzark leaned close to the bucket and in a low voice he said, "You may as well find another garden tonight, 'cos there's no food left in this one. Still, at least the weather's going to be fine!"

Inside the bucket it was silent except for the chattering of tiny teeth. There was, however, a rather unpleasant smell.

Wazzark and Podfudger giggled as they rejoined the path under the apple tree which led to the Rockery. They walked silently by the side of the pond, their progress marked by the occasional plop of a frog seeking the safety of the water. They passed the last of the tall rushes – and there in front of them was the magnificent mountain with its pathetic trickle of water. Wazzark again grabbed Podfudger's arm and stopped him.

"Oi, Podfudger, 'ats off, bit of respect!" said Wazzark.

"Oh yeah, sorry mate!" said Podfudger.

And there in the moonlight next to the pond, a little ritual was performed by the goblins. Each goblin removed his hat, bent one knee and bowed his head to the ground. In front of them stood the statue of the little horned god with pointed ears. In unison, the goblins raised their eyes to the statue and both uttered the words "Thank you." Then they were up and off to the Rockery and the comfort of their burrows.

CHAPTER FOUR

THE STORM

THE STORM

GHISETTE AND HER SISTERS had gathered their share of the food and drink and were flitting across the lawn back to their roost in the apple tree. There was an urgency in their flight, for Ghisette could sense that the approaching storm was going to be dangerous. As Wazzark and Podfudger reached the base of the Rockery, they turned and looked back towards the old lady's cottage. The orange streetlight switched off, plunging the silhouette of the building into the surrounding darkness. The goblins watched as the three fairy glows flitted across the lawn towards the safety of their apple tree.

Wazzark and Podfudger began the climb up the slopes of the Rockery, delicately picking their footholds in the yellow Creeping Jenny and trailing Lobelia that smothered the weathered rocks.

The entrance to their burrow was halfway up the slope between two large boulders. Wazzark held a hand out to Podfudger and hoisted him up to where he was standing.

"Did you see that?" asked Wazzark.

"See what?" inquired Podfudger, turning to look at his friend.

Wazzark pointed to the sky beyond a line of trees. "Lightning," he said.

Podfudger took a step back from the entrance to the burrow and looked in the direction of Wazzark's pointing arm, then gasped.

"Look," said Podfudger. "The stars are going out!"

A great mountain of cloud was moving through the night sky towards the little seaside town. One by one the stars disappeared as the colossal wall of blackness engulfed them. A shiver of purple light silhouetted the line of trees as lightning flickered inside the cloud.

"C'mon," said Wazzark. "Let's get inside and tell the others. I reckon we'll just have time for supper before things get noisy."

"Whaddaya mean noisy?" said Podfudger as he climbed into the passageway that led down inside the Rockery. "I can't hear any thunder. You said it's a storm but I can't hear any thunder Wazzark!"

Wazzark took one more sniff of the night air, then he followed Podfudger down to the safety of the burrow. "You will, Podfudger old mate... you will!"

Snaps, the ginger cat, had not enjoyed his evening. For one thing his nose still throbbed with pain, which was a problem for it was the only nose he had. Normally he used his nose to push open the cat flap but tonight, in trying to avoid using his nose, he had caught his paw in the flap. Because he now couldn't use his nose or his injured paw, he had decided to strike the cat flap with his other paw and leap through the resulting gap.

Snaps struck the flap, which swung open with a resounding metal 'clack'. Unfortunately he must have struck it too hard, because as he leapt through the gap the substantial metal flap had rebounded off the top of the frame and like a guillotine, swung down on the tip of his tail. With a hiss like a derailed steam engine and a bloodcurdling yowl, Snaps fled to the safety of his number two bed behind the cooker. This was the bed he used when he was in trouble or when he did not want to be disturbed. His eyes half closed, he sat with his now-throbbing tail wrapped around his fluffed up body and stared at the cooker, which was no more than half an inch away, in an apparently comatose state.

Podfudger and Wazzark had reached the bottom of the stairs and now walked along a passageway that took them underneath the big pond. A door led to the 'Great Hall' as the gnomes had called it. Podfudger smiled as he saw the welcoming light glowing from the door's bulls-eye window.

Inside the Great Hall, the usual Friday night routine was being enacted. Two elves were playing pool in the centre of the room whilst around them, other fairy folk were either talking, half-heartedly watching the elves or playing darts next to the small bar that the gnomes had fitted into the hall. The atmosphere was warm, and smoky, for a visiting leprechaun was leaning against the bar smoking a blackwood pipe that gave off such a cloud of fumes that the others referred to it as 'Chernobyl'.

The leprechaun's name was Amoyka-ael Firbolg. This was somewhat of a mouthful for the likes of Wazzark and Podfudger, so they simply knew him as 'Cousin Moykle' – 'cousin' because all fairy folk are related in one way or another, much as humans and apes originated from the same family tree. 'Cousin' is also a term that many of the fairy folk use when referring to visitors or guests in the same way the English refer to their 'American cousins'. Thus Cousin Moykle's name was doubly appropriate he was both a relation *and* had originated from 'over the water'.

Fairy folk, just like their human counterparts, nowadays move around the country far more than they used to in the past. Transport is easily accessible to those of them who cannot fly, and it was not unusual for the occupants of Miss Forgetmenot's rockery to receive visitors from all over the place.

What the ancestral prototype of the fairy folk had looked like was a matter for conjecture. Wazzark had seen an illustrated chart depicting human evolution on a huge billboard that was advertising a car or something and had explained to the others that they too must have begun as a primitive-looking creature that dragged the backs of its hands on the ground as it walked.

"Och, well! It's still here then!" said a Scottish elf, pointing at Podfudger. This had instantly started a fight, which in turn led to a end of the discussion on evolution.

The fairy folk were an observant breedand had carefully observed human endeavour and learnt much from it. In fact, human endeavour had greatly affected the way they lived their lives and the most fundamental change of all was that they were now virtually unemployed.

Originally they had been used as a form of rustic police force, settling disputes between animals and generally acting as a catalyst between flora, fauna and the will of Mother Nature. That had been a time when their powers had been far stronger and more respected than was now the case. The spread of humanity and all its associated problems had removed so much of the natural habitat that they had become almost redundant.

The Scottish elf who was about to take his shot at pool was called Elfie. Elfie would swear a lot when playing. At least, the others thought he was swearing – it was hard to tell. Elfie came from Glasgow and when he made mistakes he began to speak a foreign language that the others found impossible to understand – which was just as well really!

Elfie's opponent was a Welsh Elf called Effans. Whereas Elfie was slightly built, wiry, and decisive with huge glasses that made him look intellectual, Effans was tubby, slow and cumbersome both in body and deeds. Effans looked like a rusty turnip. His large, round face, topped with a crest of red hair, was peppered with orange freckles. He also wore glasses, but whereas Elfie's were large and stylish, Effans wire-framed efforts looked like the bottom of two milk bottles. Effans annoyed Elfie. It wasn't just that Effans dithered and took time over his shots, or that he was half-blind and would knock whole pints of ale off the tables, it was the way he peered down the pool cue as though aiming with surgical precision, as though he had a thoroughly calculated plan of play – whereas in fact he had no such thing, he would just hit and hope! The coloured balls would fly in all directions, ricocheting off cushions and one another before finally coming to rest. That was what annoyed the Scottish elf because, without fail, Effans always managed to pot one of his own balls. Elfie almost believed that Effans was using some sort of magic – but he quickly dismissed the thought.

It was the thirteenth straight game and Effans had won every one of the previous twelve. Elfie surveyed the pattern of the pool balls – Effans was not going to win the thirteenth game! For in a rare piece of ill luck, Effans had left the final black ball teetering on the edge of the middle pocket. Even without his glasses Elfie couldn't miss that shot! The room went quiet as the others saw that Elfie was about to snatch a rare victory over the Welsh Elf.

"Me monies on de little fellah!" shouted a smoke-filled Irish voice from the bar.

"They're both little fellahs!" retorted another slurred voice.

"Would ye all kanedly shut yerr mooths!!" snarled Elfie down the pool cue. Elfie concentrated, his eyes focusing like lasers on the black ball. He could almost see a rail that the white ball would travel along, so easy was the shot. Inside his brain the trigger released, the message was travelling down his arm: "Now! But not too hard; don't follow through with the white ball; pot them both and that daft Effans will have won another game!"

"Grub up!" roared a voice as the door crashed open against the wall.

"*!!*!" shouted Elfie as a spasm in his arm made him lance the cue ball like a sword thrust. With a loud clack, both the black and white balls disappeared into the pocket.

"Ooh, bad luck boyo," smarmed Effans. "Still, never mind, Wazzark and Podfudger are here with the nosh, isn't it!"

Elfie sank his teeth into the pool cue as his glasses curled around his nose.

"There's a storm coming!" yelled Podfudger as the goblins shut the door behind them. All the occupants of the room followed the goblins to the bar where the food was laid out on a bar cloth.

"Tuck in," said Wazzark.

Over the years, the gathering of food had become an increasing problem for the indigenous fairy folk of West Sussex. Human beings simply didn't grow enough produce any more!

In the 'good old days' the fields were full of crops that anyone could recognise as food. There were urban allotments, orchards, beehives, and all manner of outlets for food gathering. Nowadays, the fields blossomed with lurid, multi-coloured plants like oil-seed rape, flax, tulips, heather, sunflowers, cactus and a load more inedible offerings.

These post-war, high finance farming methods had led to a migration of the fairy folk from the fields to the towns. The spread of farmland, the destruction of the hedgerows, the use of pesticides and new rural planning procedures had decimated the fairy population. The real reason humans thought fairies didn't exist any more was that they were not as plentiful as they once had been, and thus were hardly ever seen.

The rural changes had also led to the urbanisation of other creatures who competed with fairy folk for food. There were now urban foxes, urban badgers, urban deer, urban squirrels, and even urban birds of prey! This, combined with other, more common predators such as cats and dogs – made life difficult for the likes of Wazzark and his ilk.

Human beings still regarded fairies (who didn't exist anyway!) as a product of greeting-card companies and cartoon studios, or the creation of over-sentimental authors usually from somewhere in middle Europe. They were thought of as flitting around in rings, singing soppy songs, living under toadstools, drinking nectar from buttercups or sitting next to ponds with little fishing rods in their hands. Cutest of all were the ones who collected useless human teeth, usually from under pillows!

The truth was far less cute and cosy. In fact, fairies have become survivors, selective scavengers who, like the rest of us, have to work for a living! Food was around if you knew where to look for it. The problem was reaching it before every other creature in the district.

Dustbins were a firm favourite, as were greenhouses, garden cold frames and bird tables – especially in the winter – but favourite of all in the summer months was the ubiquitous barbecue! For humans, the peculiar fun of burning piles of food seemed far to outweigh the business of eating it – especially when alcohol was involved. The more drink that was consumed, the more uneaten burnt offerings there would be left for the fairies.

When food was plentiful in the warmer months, the fairies worked especially hard to collect stores. By the end of the autumn, the fairy folk of Number One Romany Way would always have just enough food put by to see them through the winter.

That most important commodity, beer, had recently become easier to obtain. Once upon a time it was only available, with difficulty, from behind pubs, off licences or clubs. The usual method of collection had been to painstakingly examine every 'empty' bottle and drain off the dregs, or to siphon off the ullage from old barrels. Now, however, thanks to many conscientious gardeners and their humane, eco-friendly slug-control methods, most of the gardens were awash with beer – hundreds of little yoghurt pots were sunk into flower beds filled to the brim with free, decent beer! What's more, the beer was getting stronger! Many gardeners had noticed that the slugs had been attracted to the beer. But although the beer was vanishing, the slug population was increasing! Stronger measures were taken in the form of beer with a higher alcohol content. Humane slug death was all the rage! This was a blessing for Wazzark, Podfudger and friends.

The occupants of the bar happily consumed the goblins' offerings.

"A storm you say?" Cousin Moykle, the leprechaun, tapped his pipe out into an ashtray. "Sure, we had one of those in Kilburn last month, a fellah drowned in his own basement – and dat is not blarney oi can tell ya!" A pretty female pixie called Pidwidgin turned to the leprechaun.

"You are silly," she said, and started giggling. Cousin Moykle looked at her. He opened his mouth to speak but then thought better of it and resumed tapping the embers of his pipe into the ashtray.

Outside in the cool of the garden the still night air was awakening. Leaves began to rustle as a breeze stirred the foliage. The bewildered, frightened and hungry hedgehogs had scuttled out of the drainpipe. Each had gone his or her separate way, but all were still confused about the strange metal wall.

Ghisette urged her sisters to hurry. The storm was fast approaching and with the breeze now becoming a substantial wind, they were finding it difficult to make headway as they flew low over the grass. Ghisette heard a cry from behind. The fairy turned to see one of the others fall to the ground, scattering food from the acorn bowl.

Just seconds later, the storm broke over the little town with a cataclysmic explosion of thunder. Almost instantly a cascade of hail blasted out of the sky. The hail drummed and rattled on Miss Forgetmenot's conservatory, smashing several panes of glass. The fairies were caught in the open. The hail fell on them like boulders. Ghisette beckoned frantically to the other two as she ran for cover under an old log. Elliel, the youngest, had received a glancing blow to her head; she was half-conscious as her sister Mirithin pulled her to safety.

The sisters watched as the white ice-balls bounced and danced around them. Then, as soon as it had started, the hail shower stopped and, as is the way with summer storms, the air was still again. What they did not know was that the clap of thunder and the hail shower were just the overture to a storm symphony that would last for nearly three hours.

Meanwhile, Snaps pricked up his ears and turned his head away from the cooker. He had heard a noise! So deep had been his trance that he had not registered the sounds of crashing glass. Eventually his instincts had conquered his brain and he awoke. There it was again; something was tapping on the kitchen window.

Snaps backed out of the cat flap without suffering any more injuries. As soon as his whole body was safely out, he spun around, the old panther instincts having returned. The cat stopped dead in his tracks and hunched low to the ground. Instead of mice or birds or any sort of prey causing the noise, there was nothing but the sounds of dripping water. Everything was splattered with tiny white marbles. Snaps picked up his paw and shook it violently. The ground was wet and cold – most unpleasant. He hesitated for a moment, and had just decided to risk the cat flap once more when a faint movement caught his eye.

Ghisette was wiping a streak of blood from the brow of Elliel when the rain began. Huge drops of water fell around the log, rustling the grass and slapping the leaves. Elliel was in pain, and, still slightly dazed, she was giving involuntary distress signals. The underside of the log and the surrounding grass were being lit by a gentle, pulsing blue light which was glowing from the Fairy. Ghisette held Elliel's shoulders.

"Elliel, Elliel! It's all right, you're safe. Elliel, can you hear me? Elliel, it's Ghisette!"

Mirithin had picked up a small piece of hail that was rapidly melting. She wrapped it in a handful of moss and dabbed Elliel's forehead with the ice-cold poultice. The emergency first aid proved successful. Elliel blinked and opened her eyes wide. She put a hand to her head and groaned:

"What happened?"

Ghisette stood up and ventured a few steps from the log, then turned back to answer her sister.

"You were hit by a hailstone. You're not badly hurt but you've been glowing ... someone may have seen you. Come on, we've got to get away from here!"

The rain began to increase. Small, watery explosions were detonating along the top of the log. Ghisette realised the extreme danger they were in: their home in the apple tree was still a considerable distance away; worse, in this heavy rain it was impossible to fly.

"Quick," whispered Ghisette, "follow me!." Elliel's wings trembled, and she began to rise into the air. "No, Elliel," cried Ghisette as she pulled the youngster back down. "We've got to walk – it's too dangerous to fly." Ghisette beckoned; the others followed.

Mirithin was confused. "Ghisette, you're going the wrong way – our apple tree's over there – look!." Ghisette turned, helping Elliel as she did so.

"We're not going home, Mirithin. We're going to the Rockery. We'll be safer there!"

Snaps, now tiger-like in attitude, was creeping through the undergrowth. He had often sat watching the wildlife documentaries on television, which the old lady so loved. "They have it easy," thought the cat. "Let's see how they would do in this place ... tuh! ... cheetahs? ... fastest cat in the world? ... I'd like to see one run sixty miles an hour around this garden ... it'd kill itself in minutes, all the rubbish that lies around this place."

A large raindrop hit the cat in the ear. Snaps shook his head rapidly and began furiously scratching his flooded ear with his back leg. Snaps overbalanced and fell into something soft, smelly and unpleasant. The cat screwed up its face in total horror when it realised just what it had fallen in.

The rain was falling heavily. Snaps hated rain. He hated whatever animal had left the marker he had fallen in. He was now in a deeply unpleasant, foul mood. Positive that something had made a noise on the lawn, the cat had begun to turn back to the house when he glimpsed a tiny blue light in the same place that he thought he had seen movement earlier. All thoughts of discomfort evaporated as another blue glow confirmed that something was indeed happening in the depths of the garden! The three fairies had left the safety of the log and were struggling through the tall, wet grass.

The cat slunk across the darkened lawn, tail low, ears pointing forward, eyes focused on the spot where the light had been. The rain grew steadily heavier and now the clouded sky was being illuminated by lightning. Snaps was totally concentrated on his prey – he knew that the blue light signified: fairies! And they were even more fun to catch than mice or birds – and far, far tastier.

There was a loud rumble of thunder and from nowhere a malevolent wind struck the garden. The cat was startled into action. He sprang across the wet grass and reached the log in a few rapid leaps. Snaps sniffed the ground. "Yess! Fairies!" he growled as he narrowed his eyes. Then, tail straight as an arrow, he hurtled towards the fleeing sisters. Snaps launched himself into the air. It was a mighty leap even for him and it achieved the desired result. A deafening crack of thunder split the air above the garden, lightning flashed all around. The cat landed with a soft thud directly in front of Ghisette. More lightning silhouetted the horrific, bedraggled shape of the cat. In a reflex move Snaps lunged with his paw and snagged Ghisette's cloak. The tiny screams were drowned by another clap of thunder.

It was soon apparent to the fairy folk in the Great Hall beneath the Rockery that this was not going to be an ordinary Friday night. Wazzark had been correct in his assumption that the storm would be a big one. It was – and it was directly overhead. The walls actually shook as the thunder blasted above them. Pieces of debris fell from the ceiling. A stone hit the bar next to Cousin Moykle's pint of ale.

"Well, would ye look at that!" exclaimed the Leprechaun. "A whisker closer and that would have done for me drink!"

"What's that boyo?" said Effans, turning to look at the leprechaun and in doing so he knocked over Elfie's half-full pint.

"Ah ferr heaven's sake, if yerr no the clumsiest git thart's everr lived and breathed!" screamed Elfie as his undrunk ale plopped into his lap. The goblins slapped their knees in mirth at Elfie, who was now standing and glaring at Effans, his crotch dripping with foam.

The lightning above the garden was now of the extremely dangerous variety. The white and blue streaks flickered between the clouds almost constantly. The great storm – for that is how it would be remembered both in truth and legend – had stalled over the seaside town. In the space of just one hour, more than two month's average rainfall cascaded out of the sky. The booming continued to be felt under the Rockery.

"Ah dat's great … c'mon ya dirty great beauty. Let's be havin' ye!" shouted Cousin Moykle as he stabbed the air above him with the stem of his pipe.

"Tee hee … you are silly!" giggled Pidwidgin the pixie.

The food on the bar had been consumed. Podfudger brushed his hands together to rid himself of troublesome crumbs. "Oi, Wazzark!" exclaimed the goblin, spitting food from his half-filled mouth. "Have you noticed something, well, peculiar like?"

"What, something other than Effans, Moykle, Elfie and Pidwidgin you mean?" answered Wazzark.

"Yeah," pondered Pudfudger.

"What?" asked Wazzark.

"It's getting lighter in here!" exclaimed the goblin. And indeed it was. Normally the rooms, corridors, tunnels and burrows under the Rockery were illuminated by small candles. The Great Room was slightly different, and unusual. The gnomes who had constructed the Great Hall had also built and installed a generator to produce electricity. The water from the stream had provided this natural power. The old lady had not been able to keep the little brook clear of debris and consequently the trickle of water that powered the Gnome's Mill only produced a dull background glow in the hall.

Wazzark looked around the room. "Blimey… you're right! It is getting lighter in here. You know what that means?"

"It means it's not as dark as it used t'be!" proclaimed Cousin Moykle.

"Tee hee hee," giggled Pidwidgin. "You are silly!"

Suddenly alert, Wazzark moved away from the bar. He surveyed the room and, stepping over to the wall, he peered closely at a gap in the rock. Wazzark turned back to the others; he held up a wet hand.

"The streams in flood! The lights are powered by the stream! If it's getting lighter it means the streams flowing faster!"

There was another resounding boom. The Rockery shuddered and in the rooms below, water began to drip from the ceiling. The lightning fizzed and flashed relentlessly. The rain poured, the wind blew and the thunder boomed and roared.

The little stream was now in full flood. A torrent of water had carried sticks, branches, dead leaves and all manner of garden detritus in a foaming mass along its course until it reached the waterfall. Some substantial broken branches had been lodged at the head of the waterfall. For years they had clogged the stream and it had never rained hard enough to dislodge the tangle.

Now the full force of the debris-filled flood surged over the top of the Rockery, sweeping away the dam of branches. Lightning flashed as a plume of spray billowed up from the surface of the pond. A metre-high wave welled up and spread rapidly across the entire length of the water. Great water-lily leaves disappeared beneath the flood only to reappear in disarray as the wave passed over them.

The little wheel embedded in the rock below the surface of the stream was now spinning furiously. A surge of electrical energy flashed through the gnomes' ancient wiring. The little electric lights that were dotted around the hall flared like miniature supernovae.

Several exploded, but enough light bulbs survived to turn the usually dim bar room into a photographer's studio. Reflections shone where no reflections had been seen before. Shadows were cast by the blinding lights, changing the whole aspect of the room.

Effans dropped his pint and stood blinking. He staggered forward, blinded by the light, and barged into Cousin Moykle who spat a mouthful of beer into the back of Elfie's head.

"Bloody 'ell!" exclaimed Effans.

"Ah! Joseph and Mary…" exclaimed Moykle.

"*!!***!?!!" exclaimed Elfie.

As Cousin Moykle wiped the ale off his chin and lapel, he turned to look at the brightly illuminated Welsh elf. The light was now so bright that Effans' red hair appeared to be a fire on top of his head.

"Oh God, 'tis awful ugly that y'are Effans," said Cousin Moykle as he began to refill his pipe.

"Look!" shouted Podfudger, and he jumped up and down pointing to the pool table. A steady stream of water was flowing from the ceiling. As they looked around, the fairy folk could see more and more streams of water coming from the ceilings and running down the walls.

"Bloody 'ell!" cried Effans. "We're sinking!"

"Don't panic!" shouted Wazzark. He stepped towards the dartboard and pointed down at the stone floor.

"Haven't you ever noticed these things! They're called drains!" Podfudger stepped over a little ribbon of water that was trickling into the grating below Wazzark's feet.

"Oh yeah" pondered Pudfudger. "Clever old sticks gnomes. They think of everything!"

Elfie, still wiping the back of his head with a bar towel, looked from the ceiling to the floor, then to the dripping pool table. He turned and frowned at Podfudger.

"Och well, they did'na thunk to poot the pool table somewhere dud they! Look – uts flooded!"

"Oh yes indeed," smiled Effans. "And I tell you what boyo – I'd still give you a thrashing on it even if it was completely under water!"

"Don't talk mince!" scowled Elfie.

Cousin Moykle lit his pipe and took a few puffs then, lowering the pipe to blow out the match, he spoke. "Ye know," said Moykle, and in an irritating way went through the pipe smoker's 'pregnant pause' ritual of taking another couple of puffs so as to add a sense of expectation and anticipation from an audience (if he still had one). "Dem gnome fellahs did get it roight! Dat tables in de perfect place. Look! Look at it! De waters drippin roight in t'middle of it!!"

"Now 'ow the heck can that be perfect if the whole thing's covered in water – you tell me that, boyo?" Effans folded his arms, lifted his chin and looked down his nose through two glittering lenses.

Cousin Moykle blew a smoke ring and then pointed his pipe stem at the Welsh elf. "Ah well, there it is y'see, me little Welsh carrot-top!"

"There what is?" asked Effans.

"Pool – that's whoiy it's called pool – pool cause it's full of water, so it is!"

"Oh ferr **!!*?!! sake!" said Elfie and strode damp-crotched to the bar and poured himself a whisky.

"Hee hee hee," giggled Pidwidgin. "You are silly!"

The fairies above ground were in quite a different mood. The rain slashed into Ghisette's face as she fought desperately for breath. Snaps had her tightly in his grip. He was oblivious to the storm that was raging overhead. His razor-sharp claws had torn into Ghisette's cloak and she was trapped fast. The cat just lay on the grass, his body extended, the white tip of his tail twitching on a half-buried tree root. Snaps growled and pondered whether to let the Fairy go and snatch her again or just to eat her straight away. As he considered, he heard a great crash and a splash from the direction of the pond. He did not like hearing odd sounds if he could not work out what caused them – it unnerved him. He decided to eat the fairy and go home to where it was dry, warm and quiet.

Elliel and Mirithin were struggling to contain a mounting hysteria. They taunted the cat from as close as they dared, hoping he would release his grip on Ghisette. Snaps simply ignored them. He fixed his gaze on the little struggling figure, mesmerised by the pulsating blue rays of light she was emitting.

The sky lit up with a blinding display of lightning. A network of white, veined light seared horizontally across the overhead clouds. It was followed by a titanic clap of thunder, so loud that the pressure from it shook the trees. The distant sound of shattering glass could be heard from all around as the thunder rumbled into the distance.

Snaps pulled his paws to his mouth. He examined the fairy closely then, with rasping tongue, he licked Ghisette along the length of her body. Mirithin flew across the face of the cat; she too desperately flashing her warning to the cat's eyes. But Snaps was oblivious to everything except his captured prey. He opened his mouth and closed his jaws over the fairy's head.

Elliel and Mirithin, both hovering only a metre from the cat's jaws, turned their heads away in horror. Then fortune intervened. Even as the last rumble of thunder was echoing into the distance, there was another gargantuan boom. A simultaneous flash of lightning exploded directly above the old lady's garden. The huge forked downstroke scored three direct hits.

Firstly, the chimneystack on Miss Forgetmenot's cottage roof disintegrated, showering a wide area with brick shrapnel.

Secondly, the supermarket trolley in the puddle on the waste ground exploded into millions of white-hot pieces of wire which fizzled and hissed through the air. Thirdly, the plum tree near which Snaps was holding Ghisette was split from top to bottom. For a second, the leaves became incandescent stars before they burst into flame. Then the lightning travelled down the trunk, following every root, searing and burning it's way deep into the earth.

At the instant of the lightning strike, the tip of Snap's tail was lying on a half-buried plum tree root. The flash passed through the root, through Snaps' tail and fizzled across the grass. The cat was very lucky, for although the lightning ignited his tail, his body only received a fraction of the charge. The energy passed along his tail to the point where his bottom and tail merged. Snap felt an excruciating burning sensation. He screeched and leapt into the air, hurling Ghisette into the wet grass as he shot off across the lawn to the cottage.

Elliel and Mirithin flew to their wounded sister. It had been a close call. Ghisette was covered in the cat's sticky saliva – she had been only one second from death. Ghisette struggled to her feet, grateful for the cool cleansing rain that was ridding her of the foul, mucous liquid. Seeing that she was safe, all three fairies turned to watch in amazement as a small fiery beacon trailed smoke across the lawn.

Snaps was still on fire as he screamed towards the cat flap. He took a flying leap at it, striking the centre of the metal plate at about thirty miles an hour. The flap smashed against the top of the frame and volleyed back on to Snaps, cutting two inches off the end of his tail. 'Every cloud has a silver lining' the saying goes. Well in Snaps' case the two inches of tail that he lost was the part that was on fire.

Snaps rolled and tumbled into the space behind the cooker, finally coming to rest in a terrified and exhausted heap. He listened to the hissing and popping of his burning tail before fading into a coma of pain. The storm rumbled on.

Wazzark, Podfudger, Elfie and Effans decided to go up to the surface to look at the storm. They followed in single file up the rocky passage that led away from the gnomes' Great Hall. Water was streaming along the floor and dripping from the walls and ceiling. A flash of lightning lit up the passage, its blue-white light illuminated the drops of water, turning them for an instant to falling sapphires.

"Cor, look at that!" said Podfudger as he ran ahead of Wazzark. The goblin reached the entrance which was blocked by a haphazard tangle of broken boughs, twigs and branches. Wazzark joined him and surveyed the obstruction.

"Right!" said Wazzark. "Let's get this lot shifted."

The two goblins and the two elves began heaving, pushing, pulling and shoving until the tangle of branches had been cleared out of the way. They emerged into the night and were amazed at the sight which greeted them. The four friends stood looking out from the shelter of the Rockery onto a scene of utter destruction.

Several orange glows lit up various parts of the horizon, the result of fires caused by lightning strikes. Strange lights flickered across the sky between the flashes of lightning. Leaves, twigs, branches and the contents of many dustbins were being hurled through the air by a wind that had now reached hurricane force. Over the roar of the storm could be heard the wailing of emergency service vehicles and the ringing din of hundreds of car and burglar alarms activated by the thunderclaps.

Below them, the once serene garden pond was a boiling, spume-filled expanse of splashing water. Foaming waves smashed along the banks of the stream and, as the water tipped over the rocks to the pool, the wind blew it skywards creating clouds of spray.

There was a loud crack and a bang near to the entrance of the cave. Instinctively the four friends ducked as a large piece of jagged wood buried itself into the ground in front of them. Another even larger object splashed into the pond, sending up a plume of water which was blasted sideways by the furious wind.

"Whoa, you can keep that!," said Podfudger. "It's bloomin' dangerous up here! I'm going back down!"

"Me too!" agreed Effans.

"Aye, me an all!" added Elfie.

The goblin and the two elves backed slowly away from the entrance, turned and scampered back down the wet passage.

"C'mon, Wazzark!" shouted the echoing voice of Podfudger. "It's not safe up there!"

Wazzark took one last look at the black pond below and began to move towards the passage when something made him stop and turn back.

The torrential rain had both cleansed Ghisette of the cat's saliva and stirred her into action. Elliel was weak from the earlier blow to the head and had to be helped along by both her sisters. The wind cut through the reeds and grass by the edge of the pond. Ghisette looked up and saw the black outline of the Rockery.

"Look – it's the mountain Elliel! Try and walk, we're nearly safe! Quickly Mithirin one last effort!"

Ghisette and Mirithin held their sister between them and struggled towards the Rockery. Although the wind was as strong as ever, the mass of reeds at the water's edge sheltered the path. The fairies even managed a short flight before the reeds thinned and the wind once again became too strong for the little creatures. Ghisette pulled Elliel on to her shoulders and began to crawl towards the rocks. Mithirin crawled behind her as spray from the waterfall swirled like smoke over the path. A huge gust of wind struck the open path between the reeds and the base of the Rockery. Mirithin watched in horror as Elliel was torn from Ghisette's back. The little fairy was flung into the air and was swept head over heels into the black, foaming water, where she instantly vanished.

Ghisette and Mirithin struggled to the edge of the pond. Water splashed over them as numerous objects fell into the swirling water. They screamed into the storm and began to flash their distress, but Elliel did not answer – she was gone. In disbelief, the remaining two sisters struggled to hold onto the grass, as twigs and leaves crashed around them.

"I thought so," muttered Wazzark under his breath. The goblin had seen the tiny blue flashes below the Rockery, and at first had thought they were reflections from the lightning that was still criss-crossing the sky. He carefully climbed down from the Rockery and, buffeted by the wind, reached Mirithin and Ghisette. Wazzark crouched down and picked up both the sisters. At first he thought their tiny screams were directed at him, but gradually he realised that something terrible had happened. Wazzark tried to understand what they were saying, but their hysteria and the roar of the storm made it impossible to make out anything.

The goblin turned back towards the Rockery, holding the sisters close to his chest. He clenched his teeth as needle-sharp hail stung his face.

Podfudger, Elfie and Effans had been back in the hall for some time. They were just beginning to worry about Wazzark when the door opened and the soaked, dishevelled goblin rushed in. The others gathered round as he gently placed Ghisette and Mirithin on the ground.

"There's been an accident," said Wazzark solemnly. "Quickly, get some blankets and warm clothes for these fairies."

"What accident? What happened?" asked Podfudger.

"It's Elliel, our sister," sobbed the tiny voice of Ghisette. "She's been killed."

"Killed! How?" asked Podfudger. Wazzark leant towards his friend and, looking at all the others gathered round, whispered: "Drowned! She was blown into the big pond and drowned."

Any excitement the storm had held for the fairy folk vanished. They stood, heads bowed, and remembered Elliel, their little friend, whilst above them the storm roared on through the battered night.

CHAPTER FIVE

COWBOY COUNTRY

·5·

COWBOY COUNTRY

MISS FORGETMENOT AWOKE to a beautiful, clear morning. The sun was climbing into the blue sky, she could hear the sound of birds singing and a lot of voices. The voices were coming from the street in front of her cottage. Pulling on her dressing gown, the old lady drew open her bedroom curtains and was shocked at what she saw.

Romany Way was covered in debris – indeed it was difficult to see the road at all. Fallen trees lay strewn between tangled telephone wires, smashed tiles, uprooted bushes, overturned dustbins and hundreds of broken, corrugated plastic roofing sheets. The residents were busy salvaging their possessions. An unusual feeling of camaraderie and helpfulness had descended on the town as the people came to terms with the extent of the damage.

The old lady dressed hurriedly. She was worried. Firstly she was baffled at what had happened for she, like many others, had slept soundly through the whole stormy night. Secondly, Snaps was nowhere to be seen, and thirdly, she worried if any damage had been caused to her property. She reached the kitchen and saw through the window that her conservatory was now just a frame; nearly every pane of glass had been broken.

Snaps heard the approach of the old lady as she came into the kitchen. The cat emerged from behind the cooker and, looking up at Miss Forgetmenot, uttered a pathetic yowl.

"Oh Snaps, good cat … there you are … I was worried about you. Oh! Are you frightened? Poor cat, never mind I'll get you some … oh!" The old lady stopped as she saw the grizzled, charred, furry object that had once been the end of Snap's tail. A frown came over her face as she took a dustpan and brush out of a cupboard. She stood over the unfortunate cat and waved the brush at him.

"You naughty boy!" the old lady scolded. "I give you plenty of lovely food and yet you will still eat birds!"

"Birds?" yowled Snaps. "Has she gone mad? That's not a bit of a bird! That's a bit of me!" He yowled again and turned, pointing his tail at the old lady.

"It's no use saying you're sorry," said Miss Forgetmenot. "You're a bad boy – there will be no dinner for you today!"

The cat stopped displaying its rear end as the old lady's dreadful words sunk in. "No dinner today" meant he would have to go and find something to eat and that meant – his shoulders drooped – the cat flap!

By mid-morning the whole town was going about the task of cleaning up and making good the night's damage. Charlie Wollock had been damaged that night, for Charlie Wollock, builder and decorator, had won the jackpot on the fruit machine in the Fresh Ferret public house and had proceeded to drink every penny of it. He couldn't even remember going home, let alone the worst storm in two hundred years!

Still wearing his clothes, the forty-something, bald, podgy man sat up in bed and scratched his stubbled chin. Through a clearing mist of recollection, the events of the previous evening were coming slowly into focus. Charlie smiled, lifted himself on to one buttock and plunged his hand into his trouser pocket.

"Blast!" he spat the word out in disgust. "I had four oranges. That's fifty flippin' quid! Where is it?" He shifted to his other buttock and searched his remaining pocket; that too was empty. The builder and decorator now became aware of the most awful headache, exaggerated by the realisation of how many spongers must have profited out of his winnings. "Blast!" he cursed through gritted teeth and fell back onto the bed.

The phone rang and the shrill sound cut into Charlie's brain. "Sod it!" he hissed, as he struggled to sit up again. He held a hand to his pounding forehead as the phone continued its attack.

"Leave me alone," he mumbled, but it soon became clear that the phone was not going to stop ringing. That meant it was someone who knew he was there, someone who he had been with the previous evening. Charlie hauled himself to his feet and staggered across his bedsit to the phone.

"Who is it?" he demanded in an irritated way.

"Wollock, is that you?" came a loud, brusque voice.

"Of course it's me. Who d'ya think it is, the Pope?" Charlie held the phone in front of his face at arm's length and glared at the earpiece.

"No, not Pope, more like dope," answered the tinny voice from the earpiece. The voice was that of Enoch Filch Esq., estate agent. Filch sat in his little agency office, situated above a bakery close to the seaside promenade. His business premises were about three quarters of a mile from Wollock's bedsit. The peeling, brown wallpaper of his office was appropriate to Filch's shabby business practice. Too many people had paid over the odds for his professional 'services' for him to have a good reputation in a very small seaside town where reputations, like unnatural deaths, were eagerly dissected.

Filch was in his mid fifties. His six feet two inch, chubby frame and affected accent gave him an obscure ex-military demeanour, an essential ingredient for a man in his line of business. He carried his lifestyle scars nobly: the grey swept-back hair, heavily greased, almost gleamed at his temples with nicotine yellow and his high forehead, pizza-like with red blotches, showed the intensity of his nocturnal drinking activities. In shiny grey suit and scuffed suede brogues, he was the master of his own empire, but fading though it might be, Enoch Filch was always an optimist. For him, clouds really did have silver linings – especially last night's clouds.

Filch leant back into his creaking, faded green leather director's swivel chair. He crossed his legs on to the desktop and gazed at his elderly shoes. With one hand he held the telephone whilst the other poked a ballpoint pen unpleasantly into a politically incorrect calendar. Filch sucked air in though his yellow teeth as he leered at the late Miss February. Slowly pulling out his pen he let the other voluptuous months drop down as he waited for Charlie Wollock's reply.

"What? Who's a dope?" came Wollock's voice from Filch's phone.

"My dear Charles, do you know what time it is?"

"Eh? Well, er … it's …" Wollock groped for answers.

"It's eleven thirty, Charles! Eleven thirty... and have you looked out of your window yet perchance?" enquired Filch.

"Er... hang on a minute, no why? Is it *that* late?"

"Go and look, Charles, out of the window. Go and look, there's a good gentleman."

Charlie stared at the receiver, put it down, turned and tottered across the untidy room and, reaching his front window, wrenched the grubby, grey curtains apart. Dazzling, excruciating daylight seared into his face and blinded him.

"Gordon Bennett!" he winced, as he swung his head away from the light. Slowly he turned back to look out at the world. His eyes adjusted quickly but it took his brain a little longer to comprehend what he was seeing. He was vaguely aware of the tinny voice from the phone at the other side of the room, but the chaos visible in the streets around his flat mesmerised him.

"Charles ... Charles! Come back to me! Wollock! ... Where are you?" continued the tinny telephone voice. Charlie stumbled away from the window and lunged at the phone. Grabbing the receiver, he shouted into the mouthpiece.

"Ere... have you seen what's 'appened in town?" Charlie held the receiver at arm's length towards the window as though it had eyes. "It's like a flippin' bomb's gone off. Oi! Enoch, there hasn't been a bomb again has there?" Charlie picked up the phone and carried it to the window, stretching the cable to breaking point to get another view of the street.

"No, Charles, not a bomb – much better! A violent, damaging, expensive storm causing lots of lovely damage to lots of lovely citizens' homes." Filch smiled and winked at Miss August.

"So... as you owe me money," Filch continued, "you had better get out there tooty-sweety and find some repairs that we can exploit – if you'll forgive that rather crude expression."

Charlie Wollock snapped out of his trance. "Eh? Whaddaya mean I owe you money?"

"Exactly that," answered Filch.

"How?" shouted Wollock.

"A little matter of a round of drinks and a taxi-cab home – something in the order of twenty quid, old boy. Anyway, we'll talk about that later. Now there's a good fellow, out you go and try to find what bounteous Mother Nature has presented us with before all the local cowboys beat us to it!"

Enoch Filch slammed down the receiver, leant back, crossed his arms behind his head and sighed a sigh of contentment.

Charlie Wollock pulled the cable in a fury and spat into the phone. "Twenty quid? Twenty quid? What round of drinks? I was flippin' paying last night, me – out of my winnings!" Charlie realised he was talking to himself. "Enoch! Sod it, 'es gone!" He wrenched at the phone in rage; the socket catapulted from the wall and struck him on the left ear. Charlie screamed in pain, tripped over his metal toolbox and crashed to the floor.

While this conversation was in progress, Miss Eleanor Forgetmenot was standing in her back garden looking up at her cottage. Her worst fears had been realised for the violent storm she had slept through had severely damaged her home. Number One, Romany Way, unlike the adjoining new 'link-detached' houses, was an old, thatched property. This morning, however, not much of the thatch remained, the chimney had vanished altogether, and the conservatory was a catastrophe!

The most serious consequences of the storm for the old lady were the numerous leaks in the roof. Water had been driven in through the gaps and saturated the wallpaper in some of her upstairs rooms. Miss Forgetmenot hurried inside to phone for help. "Oh dear, oh dear," she sobbed. "This is terrible! My roof's leaking and oh … if it rains again … the electricity … oh my!"

She disappeared into the house. Snaps had followed her outside. He sniffed the crisp, clean air and wandered off towards the wooded area at the end of the garden. Looking around, he became aware of the overnight additions to the old lady's lawn. A large area near the house was strewn with brick rubble, blasted from the roof when the chimney had been destroyed. Snaps prowled cautiously onward, threading his way through a maze of fallen branches.

Suddenly he froze. "Gaa! What's that?" he thought, as he fluffed up what remained of his tail in fright. A plastic heron from one of the neighbour's gardens had been blown through the air and was stuck upside down in the middle of the lawn. Snaps stared unblinking at the thing until he was quite sure that it posed no threat, then continued to thread his way through the debris-littered garden.

The old lady placed the opened Yellow Pages directory by her ancient telephone. Peering carefully down through her wire-rimmed spectacles, she placed a finger on the number of a 'Painter, Decorator, Handyman' and lifted the receiver. The phone was dead; no reassuring dialling tone, just silence. She replaced the receiver and tried several more times until she finally accepted that there was no hope – the line really was dead.

It was such a pity that old Henry Sprigg had died, she thought. Henry had been nearly as old as Miss Forgetmenot but he had been fit and active until the end. Henry had kept the old lady's lawn in reasonable condition for years, and for no reward other than her welcoming chitchat and endless cups of tea. Henry would have known who to contact and would have organised the repairs, but unfortunately Henry, like the phone, was dead. The old lady slumped into the chair by the useless telephone. She had no family to help her and no friends; the situation seemed hopeless. Quietly, Miss Forgetmenot began to weep.

Enoch Filch strolled around the 'display area' of his business empire (a haphazard selection of property photographs pinned to a large corkboard). Some were large, glossy pictures of extremely grand buildings that Filch had snipped out of *Home and Country* magazine, before adding his own 'sold' stickers. The properties that remained were genuinely his to transact. They ranged from the lower end of the market to the virtually uninhabitable. Filch, however, had a mastery of English adjectives and could make even the most miserable hovel sound attractive. He smiled, raised himself up and down on his heels then made a two-handed swinging motion with an imaginary golf club. Glancing at his watch he saw that it was mid-day – time for a Saturday lunchtime 'G&T' at the Regal Hotel.

As the day progressed, fate was weaving a spell that was gradually bringing Enoch Filch, Charlie Wollock and Miss Forgetmenot closer and closer.

Charlie Wollock entered one of the garages behind the row of flats in which he lived. Seconds later he emerged, enveloped in a cloud of blue-white smoke, driving what the vehicle registration book described as a van/utility vehicle. The hood and cab of the van were recognisable as the usual type of workman's transport, but the rear of the thing, which had rusted away years ago, was totally unlike any other normal van. Charlie could not be bothered to spend perfectly good beer money on an unnecessary expense such as a third-hand van. Instead he had built a peculiar wooden, hut-like structure which he had then bolted onto the back of the old wreck's chassis. He cut windows into it and covered them with chicken wire and finally painted the whole grotesque vehicle in a ghastly excreta-brown colour.

Charlie spent the afternoon driving around 'his manor'. The seaside town of Bogham was indeed a scene of devastation, but the repair and reconstruction work was already well under way. All the bona fide roofers, electricians, plumbers, glaziers and general repairers had been hard at work for hours. Following, and in some case preceding, them were the fraudsters, fakes and charlatans, more commonly known by the public as 'cowboys'. Unfortunately, many of these cowboy builders were not instantly recognisable from the genuine ones, and in any case, in an emergency such as this, the average homeowner's powers of observation were woefully low.

In Charlie Wollock's case, however, his reputation, like his van, was well known. That was why by five o'clock he still hadn't had one shred of luck. He decided to venture further afield. Some of the more exposed buildings between Bogham and Bichester must have suffered a severe battering, thought Charlie. He drove on through the winding lanes stopping occasionally to look at distant buildings. But the storm seemed to have pinpointed Bogham alone; even the trees were unscathed and he was only five miles away from the town centre. Charlie looked at his fuel gauge; it was getting low. He was hungry and, by now, extremely fed up. Pulling the van into a lay-by he swung round, and drove back towards the town.

No sooner had he driven past the sign that said 'Welcome to Bogham' ('twinned' with an unheard-of French village and an even more obscure hamlet in Bosnia or somewhere) when he spotted the flashing blue and orange lights of a police car and a council truck.

He wound down his window, which promptly fell with a clatter to the bottom of the door, and drew up beside a policeman who had motioned him to stop. Charlie kept his face well away from the officer, who leant over to speak to him. The policeman had not seen Charlie's van before and was so shocked with its appearance that instead of saying, as he had intended "You'll have to turn back sir, the road is blocked by a fallen tree," he actually said automatically, "Is this your vehicle sir? Have you been drinking?"

Charlie Wollock jerked his head further back inside the van, trying to hide any remaining fumes from the previous night. He panicked, and searching desperately for an answer, choked out the sound, "Wha?"

The policeman straightened up and, laughing aloud, looked the van up and down. "Sorry sir, you threw me for a minute. Is this one of those Korean jobs? They must have been drinking when they built it eh?! Ha, ha!"

Charlie, his face drained of blood, tittered nervously. "Er, yes officer … ha … ha …"

"Anyway the road's blocked, sir, you'll have to go back via the top road. There's a turning half a mile back on your right, next to a bus shelter". At that moment, the policeman was called away by one of the workmen. Very slowly and with all his driving skills mustered, Charlie Wollock manoeuvred his van around and cautiously drove away from the scene.

"Flippin' comedian!" Charlie muttered, but it had been a close call and he thanked his lucky stars that it hadn't been one of the local traffic Gestapo, in which case he would have been blowing into a breathalyser in less time than it takes to say "You're nicked!"

The drive back to Bogham via the detour took Charlie along some unfamiliar roads and by mistake, he turned into Romany

Way. He did not realise his error until he reached the crossroads at the end. Charlie had noticed the amount of debris that was piled up in bins and boxes and the occasional skip.

"Mm," he thought, "these houses are all reasonably new ... I wonder ..." He was just about to turn back and knock on a few doors when his hopes were dashed. In his rear-view mirror he saw several red and white vans parked along the road.

"Blast! Trust flippin' Hunter's lot to get all the good stuff ... typical!"

The vans belonged to one of Charlie's arch rivals, Jimmy Hunter, who owned a local building and roofing firm. Jimmy was a popular character around the drinking temples of Bogham, and Charlie was always the butt of his jokes and scorn. It would be no use him showing his face down that road.

Unsure of which way to go, Charlie turned his van to the right and it was then that he saw Number One Romany Way standing forlornly on the corner. He slammed on the brakes and brought his van to a halt, one wheel on the kerb.

From where he had stopped he could see nothing but trees, so Charlie decided to investigate the house. He reached into the glove compartment and pulled out his chequered flat cap. This was not just to cover his bald head but also to give him a 'builderish' look. None of Jimmy Hunter's men were anywhere to be seen, so Charlie Wollock, builder and decorator, strode professionally to the front door of Miss Forgetmenot's cottage and knocked confidently with the heavy brass doorknocker.

Miss Forgetmenot opened her front door and was confronted by the flat-capped figure.

"Oh, good evening. Are you from the electricity or the telephone?" she smiled.

Charlie was perplexed. "Um, er, why, should I be? Were you expecting them?" he enquired, rubbing his hand over his mouth.

"Well, I don't know," said the old lady. "It's my phone, it doesn't work – and the electricity, well, it can't be right, can it?"

Steering the conversation away from the old lady's initial questions, Wollock began his usual patter. "No, it can't be, not with that sort of damage. It'll be the storm that's done it," said Charlie loudly and decisively.

"Yes, yes. And then there's the roof and the chimney ... I'm not sure I'm covered with the insurance for that sort of thing – How will I get it repaired before it rains again?"

Aware of the old lady's anxiety and confusion, Charlie stepped up his attack.

"Ah, now that's why I'm here. We've got to repair it before it rains again ... winter's on it's way you know."

"Oh yes ... it won't last the winter!" said Miss Forgetmenot with a worried expression.

Charlie leant forward and peered into the hallway, making mental notes about the property. He put his finger to his mouth and, shaking his head, started 'tut, tutting'. "I'd better take a look, madam, especially with... you know ... the electricity." Wollock hadn't a clue what the old lady was talking about but there was obviously some sort of damage inside the house and he'd seen for himself the amount of straw thatch that was on the ground in the front garden instead of on the roof.

"Oh, come in, Mr ...?"

"Wollock, madam, but you can call me Charlie. Now if you'll show me the damage..."

The old lady led him through the house. Charlie was astonished at the sight of the huge, rambling back garden. His mind began to race. 'Enoch's going to love this one,' he thought. Through his daydreaming, he heard the old lady's voice.

"And you can see up there, my chimney's completely disappeared, I don't know where it's gone. And the roof is very bad I'm afraid – can you see Mr Wollock?"

Charlie snapped out of his cash-induced trance. "Ooh, tut tut, don't worry about that. Oh no, we'll soon have that back in working order, Mrs ... um ... Mrs, Mrs ... Madam."

"Forgetmenot, Miss Forgetmenot," she replied.

Charlie Wollock took a social club membership card out of his pocket and flourished it as though it was a professional document. Skimming a few pages, he suddenly pointed to something.

"Ah ha!" said Charlie. "Here it is … Miss Forgetmenot." The old lady was not sure what the meaning of the official-looking book was, but it certainly made her feel a lot happier that her name was in it.

"Right," said Charlie in his cheeriest voice. "Let's start mending, eh madam? I'll get some plastic sheeting inside the roof to stop it leaking."

The old lady was confused by the speed of events. She sat down for a moment to try to collect her thoughts. She had found her insurance documents before the appearance of Charlie Wollock, builder and decorator, but try as she might, the conditions were in such confusing small print that she was unable to read them.

"If only I had nice neighbours," Miss Forgetmenot had sighed. Her neighbours had only spoken to her twice in six years. The first time was to ask her to stop her cat defecating in their herb garden. Snaps loved the neighbour's herb garden. They had filled in an old ceramic sink with soft, moist peat in which they had planted some feverfew and chives. It was easy to dig a hole in the peat and just as easy to cover over the evidence, and Snaps loved flicking the yellow petals from the feverfew's flowers as he sat in the sink relieving himself. The only other occasion was to complain about the state of her overgrown garden. Nasty, common weeds were springing up in their flower borders, the seeds blown over, apparently, from the old lady's property. Miss Forgetmenot snapped back to the present.

Charlie was about to start phase two of his plan, physical labour, when Miss Forgetmenot asked in a worried voice:

"B ... B ... But, Mr Pollock... how much is this going to cost? I haven't much money, you know, and things are so expensive these days!"

Charlie beamed a broad, sympathetic smile, closed his eyes and gestured in the air with one hand (a technique he had borrowed from Enoch Filch).

"Wollock, madam, Wollock. And please don't worry about the money. It's in times like these that we must all stick together," smiled Charlie, as he opened one eye.

"But Mr Bollock ... I'm not sure that my insurance is in order. It's been a long time since I paid anything, you know," went on the old lady anxiously.

"Wollock, madam ... with a Wuh! But please ... it's Charlie. Of course you'll still be covered by the insurance. But that's not the important thing," he continued solemnly.

"It isn't?" replied Miss Forgetmenot.

"Oh no! What's important is... if we don't get some repairs done before it rains, I'm afraid it's going to cost an *awful* lot more!" He emphasised the word 'awful' as he strolled on to the grass and stood, hands on hips, looking up out at a cloudless, beautiful, late summer's evening. Not even a leaf (those that remained) was stirring.

"And it doesn't look too good over there, if you want my opinion!" he said, in an ominous, old country dweller's tone.

"Oh dear, oh dear," said Miss Forgetmenot as she looked nervously towards the horizon for signs and portents of doom that the knowledgeable Mr Colic had obviously observed. "In that case please do continue... please do!"

Charlie Wollock, protector of the poor, slapped his hands together and rubbing them vigorously, smiled at the old lady and turned to leave. "Righto madam, I'll get the plastic sheeting right away and we can start first thing in the morning! Good evening, madam ... see you at eleven o'clock! Bye for now!"

Snaps had missed this conversation as he had made his way across the garden and reached the corner of the pond. He stopped and looked cautiously around. He had reached 'their' territory! Strange things sometimes happened around that area of the garden. The cat stood on three legs, one of his front paws in the air. Next to him was the little bronze statue of the goatman. Snaps was puzzled. After all that storm and wind, with muck and grime flying everywhere, why was the little statue and its pedestal so very clean? He decided, as he'd done so many times before, that he didn't like the creature with the horns – something about it was creepy. Suddenly he heard a sound. 'Was that one of them,' he wondered, 'they don't usually come out until it's dark!'

Snaps turned away from the statue, giving it a last, quizzical glance. He lowered himself down into tiger position. Once again, there was a metallic scratching noise. Snaps moved silently through the long grass towards the hedge where the drainpipe tunnel ran through to the waste ground. Keeping the mutilated tip of his tail well clear of the ground, he slithered through the long stalks until he reached the drainpipe. There he saw two hedgehogs standing by the bucket that was still over one end. Snaps stood up and walked out of the long grass.

"Oh it's you lot!" he remarked with an air of disinterest. "I thought it was goblins or fairies or something."

"Did you put this thing here?" asked one of the hedgehogs in an accusing tone.

"What thing?" frowned the cat.

"This bloomin' bucket. Look, it's blocked our tunnel. We couldn't get through last night. We've had to walk all the way round today!"

Snaps didn't like hedgehogs; they were very 'lippy' creatures – well at least the bigger ones were. This was, he considered, because they knew he couldn't eat them and therefore they could afford to be cheeky.

"Now why would I want to put a bucket over the end of your tunnel?" he replied sarcastically.

The hedgehog looked at the cat, then at his colleague. "I dunno. Sort of stupid thing a cat would do maybe?"

"Or to stop us getting the dinner that the old dear leaves out for us!" added the other hedgehog. This remark struck home; Snaps never did see the reason for his mistress to hand out perfectly good food for that rabble. He decided that conversing with hedgehogs was beneath his dignity so, raising his nose and tail into the air, he turned away. The hedgehogs immediately noticed the burnt, stubby end of his once snowy-white tail. They sniggered and winked at each other.

"Oi, Fuzzy! Half your arse has fallen off!"

Snaps' face curled up in fury but he refused to be intimidated. The hedgehogs were rolling around in hysterics when the cat, without looking back, said firmly: "I wouldn't have thought you would have been so happy, what with that fox over there creeping up on you!"

The hedgehogs froze. "Fox?" they said in unison – then in terror they pulled frantically at the old bucket until it was far enough off the drainpipe for them to gain access and, like torpedoes, they shot off into the safety of the waste ground next door.

Back in the dubious comfort of his bedsit, Charlie Wollock had phoned Enoch Filch at his home. Filch's abode was a 1920s-style building on a private estate where a member of royalty had once stayed to convalesce after an illness. Filch had listened with growing eagerness to what Charlie had to say.

"… so I says to her, 'Right then, I'll be back in the morning to start work,' and she says, 'All right then!' Sounds good, doesn't it?" crowed Charlie.

"I should say so! Romany Way… Mmm, haven't been there for years, old boy. I thought they were all Legoland squats up that way with postage stamp gardens."

"They are, Enoch, they are, but not this one… Number One Romany Way is bloody huge – must be worth a million!" continued Charlie, enthusiastically.

There was a pause from Filch's end of the phone, then he coughed and replied, "I think we'd better meet, Charles. Today appears to be finishing better than it started. I'll be in the Fresh Ferret at eight thirty. Look forward to seeing you!" and with that Filch hung up.

Later that evening both men were to be found deep in conversation at a table in the darkest corner of the Fresh Ferret. Just before closing time Enoch Filch handed a large, thick, brown envelope to Charlie. Charlie smiled and frowned at the same time and after glancing furtively around to make sure he wasn't being watched, stuffed the envelope into his jacket pocket.

As luck would have it, the next morning, Sunday, was another beautiful day, a day in which not one vehicle belonging to Jimmy Hunter was to be seen anywhere near Romany Way as Charlie Wollock clambered out of his van. This time he was not alone; his young nephew Kevin was with him. To his friends and enemies alike he wasn't Kevin, he was 'Scud'. Only Charlie called him Kevin, but Scud didn't care, after all, he was only there to earn money, not exchange pleasantries with his daft uncle.

"Good!" explained Charlie as he slammed the van door, "None of blasted Hunter's crew about to cause aggro! Come on Kevin, get the gear out the back, and don't forget that dirty great plastic sheet."

Charlie, holding a clipboard for added effect, strode up to the front door of Number One Romany Way. He knocked confidently, looked about him, smiled and began whistling, without resorting to any form of tune. The door opened slowly and the old lady peeked through the gap. She observed the raised cap silhouette of the chubby Charlie.

"Oh, Mr Golly it's you. How kind, won't you come in. I'll put the kettle on, shall I, for a nice cup of tea?"

"Er, Wollock, madam, er, oh yes, yes very kind, very nice!"
Charlie followed Miss Forgetmenot into the house, looking back
as he did so.

"In 'ere Kevin, 'urry up!" shouted Charlie.

"I'm sorry, what did you say?" asked Miss Forgetmenot.

"Nothing madam, just talking to my lad, er ... my apprentice
Kevin," mumbled Charlie.

"Where d'ya wannit?" asked Scud as he reached the front door
with Charlie's toolbox.

"Round the back boy, round the back. You don't go through
people's houses with gear. Go on with you – get round the side!"

Seventeen-year-old Kevin was small for his age. He had all the
disadvantages of being genetically linked to the Wollocks such as
single-figure IQ rating, a foul mouth, laziness etc. But not only
that, he was exceptionally ugly, his face covered in so many spots
that it looked as though he'd been hit with a shotgun. His mates
called him Scud because he acted tough. He wouldn't have felt so
tough if he'd known that the local girls all knew him as 'Pizza Butt'.

Scud walked round the side of the house and met his official-
looking uncle as he came out of the back door, still clutching the
clipboard and waving a pencil. As soon as the old lady had
returned inside to make the promised tea, Wollock grabbed his
nephew.

"Kevin!" rasped Charlie, "I want you to get all the straw you
can find that's lying around the place."

"Wha'for?" asked Scud.

"Because I don't want the flippin' roof to leak for a while. I'm
no flamin' thatcher, and I'm sure as hell not going to pay for one!"
snarled Charlie under his breath.

"'Ow you gonna fix it then?" wondered Scud.

"You let me worry about that lad. Now, do as I say, get all that
straw picked up, we've got a lot to do!"

And indeed over the next two weeks Charlie and Scud were
kept very busy. In between jobs Charlie was constantly updating

information on his clipboard. On one occasion Scud wandered over and, peering over Charlie's shoulder, asked "How much does the old girl owe us then eh?"

"Old girl?" exclaimed Charlie, "I'm not flippin' worried about what the old girl owes us – it's blasted Filch I'm keeping me eye on."

"Eh, what's 'e got to do with it?" asked Scud, screwing up his pockmarked face.

"Never you mind, lad, never you mind!" answered Charlie mysteriously.

It was on a Friday afternoon nearly two weeks after Charlie Wollock had first banged on Miss Forgetmenot's door, that the repairs were finished. The telephone had been reconnected and the electricity was no longer a danger. Charlie and Scud had crammed the plastic sheeting up against the eaves under the thatch. Luckily for the pair of them, the majority of the damage to the thatch was on the south side, which faced away from the road. Nobody could see what they were up to, especially anyone like Jimmy Hunter. The pair had thrust armfuls of straw into the large gaps that were all over the thatched roof. These had been fastened down by strips of plywood, half a ton of nails and an ocean of rubber cement. Repairing the chimney stack and general decorating were far more in Charlie Wollock's line of work. He and Scud soon made fairly decent repairs (although even these would not have stood up to expert inspection).

The old lady, however, was very pleased, especially as on the day before the work was finished there had been a heavy rainstorm. Miraculously the bodged-up roof held and any water that did leak through was absorbed by the large amount of sawdust and newspaper that Scud had scattered over the attic floor.

Miss Forgetmenot saw the man and boy loading up their tools and carrying them out to their van (she supposed it was a van, although she never actually saw it because it was always parked around the corner 'so as not to cause an accident', Charlie had assured her). The old lady prepared scones and little cakes for her two saviours as well as tea for the man and lemonade for the boy.

"Oh, Mr Dolly!" called Miss Forgetmenot from her kitchen window, "I've made some tea for you and your boy!" Charlie and Scud were passing the kitchen with the last of their tools and equipment. Charlie put down the two tins of emulsion paint that he was carrying.

"'ere take these, and finish loading the van," said Charlie to Scud from the corner of his mouth.

"Oo's she callin' a boy?" mumbled Scud.

Charlie rubbed his hands together and loped towards Miss Forgetmenot.

"Mm, that's very kind of you madam," smarmed Charlie, "but unfortunately we've got to get back to our … suppliers … to um, collate our logistics. We have to do that after every job. Ho-hum, no rest for the wicked, as they say!" Charlie leant back with hunched shoulders, spreading his upturned palms in a Fagin-esque gesture.

"Oh but I've…," started Miss Forgetmenot.

"But look on the bright side! We've finished, and you're safe and sound. Snug as a bug, eh?" interrupted Charlie, slapping his hands on his hips. "Well, that's about it! As soon as we've given you our bill, you just pass it on to the insurance company and you can forget all about the whole thing" said Charlie.

"Oh, well I…" Miss Forgetmenot hesitated.

"So, I'll say goodbye, and if there's anything you need…" Charlie turned and strode away. He reached the front gate and, giving a final wave, disappeared round the corner. Confused with the haste of the workmen's departure, the old lady stood, teapot in hand, and gazed at the space vacated by the vanished Charlie Wollock.

Charlie reached the van. Scud was standing at the rear looking down at a flat tyre. A message had been chalked on the road surface. The message was in a speech bubble next to a crude cartoon of a man with a flat cap.

"Oi, Uncle Charlie… what's a 'toser'?" asked Scud, pointing at the road.

"Eh! What do you mean?" scowled Charlie.

"Well it sez 'ere you're a 'toser'!"

Charlie fumed at the misspelled graffiti and bared clenched teeth at the flat tyre.

"Flippin' Hunter's lot, I bet. Come on, get in, Kevin!" said Charlie.

"What about your spare?" asked Scud, pointing at the damaged tyre.

"I 'aven't got a flippin' spare!"

Charlie got into the van and viciously slammed the door. The windowpane dropped from its frame and plunged with a thud to the bottom of the door. Charlie started the van, and before Scud had finished fitting his seat belt, put his foot down hard on the accelerator. The rickety van lurched forward and sped away in a cloud of blue and white smoke, the offside tyre slapping the road noisily as the ramshackle vehicle clattered along. Scud looked at his uncle, his mind on the anticipated pleasures of payday.

"I wonder how much the insurance will give 'er, Uncle?" said Scud, trying to hint at payment.

"They won't give her doodley!" said Charlie, wrestling with the steering wheel as he tried to aim the van down the road. The flat rear tyre was making one side of the vehicle bounce like a pogo stick.

"Eh?" said Scud in alarm. "How do we get our money then?"

"Don't worry, you'll get your money, Kevin, oh yes! Don't you worry, you'll get your money!" an obscure smile curled up on Charlie Wollock's lips as the van smoked and bounced into the sunset.

Later that same evening, Enoch Filch and Charlie Wollock were again in the darkest corner of The Fresh Ferret. They were discussing an invoice that Charlie had presented to Filch for analysis. The two leant forward across the table, their foreheads almost touching.

"Now, you're absolutely sure about the insurance, aren't you old boy?" whispered Filch nervously.

"It's kosher, mate! I had another decko at it this afternoon. It ran out flamin' years ago. Blinkin' roof wasn't covered anyway."

Filch leant back in his chair and laughed. "And it still isn't if you've fixed it!" he guffawed. Charlie frowned, but the thought of their scam deflected the cutting remark and then he laughed as well. They lifted their glasses.

"Cheers!" they said in unison as a pint of bitter kissed a gin and tonic.

SNAPS HAD FOUND LIFE A LOT EASIER over the few weeks while Wollock and Scud were working on the house. In Snaps' case, he hadn't needed to use the hated cat flap once. The man, the boy and the old lady were opening and closing doors all the time.

The residents of the Rockery were not so happy. All the work being done to the cottage had interrupted Miss Forgetmenot's evening routine of distributing titbits. This had meant that Wazzark and Podfudger were forced to venture further afield than they were used to, and venturing further afield had its inherent dangers – dogs being highest on the list.

And so it was that on the very same evening that Enoch Filch and Charlie Wollock were deep in skulduggery at the Fresh Ferret, the old lady resumed putting out leftovers for the hedgehogs.

Friday night slipped mistily into Saturday morning. The cottage stood silhouetted against the orange, streetlamp-lit, sky. Miss Forgetmenot was sleeping soundly in her restored home. For the first time since the strangers had left, Snaps had to use the cat flap. The metal plate rose very slowly as a white paw probed outside. Gradually all the cat passed through the aperture until he was safely (and painlessly) outside.

"Oh, it's you," said Snaps.

"Oh, it's you," said Wazzark and Podfudger together. The goblins had not seen the cat for the two weeks whilst Charlie and Scud had been working at the cottage.

"'Ow's yer tail?" enquired Podfudger sarcastically.

The cat walked off without answering and without looking at the goblins. He was wishing that he was fifty times bigger. He imagined chasing the goblins across the lawn, cornering them, throwing them into the air, slapping them down with his paw, and biting off a leg or an arm. He drooled as he visualised jumping up and down on their dismembered, lifeless bodies, digging a hole in the neighbour's peat-filled herb garden enamel sink, dropping their decapitated heads one by one, face-up into the hole, defecating onto them, and then covering up the evidence.

"Yes!" thought Snaps, "I *hate* goblins!"

THE FOLLOWING MONDAY MORNING, a letter was dropped on to the front door mat of Number One Romany Way. It was addressed to 'Miss E. Forgetmenot'. The old lady put down her piece of buttered toast and walked from the kitchen to fetch the letter. Returning to her kitchen, she slit open the envelope with a little mother-of-pearl-handled letter knife. The letter was an invoice for work carried out at her property by one Charles A. Wollock, builder and decorator. An itemised list appeared below Wollock's letterhead that continued onto a second page. At the bottom of the almost endless catalogue of labours undertaken and parts supplied was the final total: the sum of thirty-seven thousand pounds! The old lady fell backwards into her chair, moving it so far back on two legs that she had to grab the table to prevent herself from tipping over backwards. The cat shot out from under her chair. Snaps had never seen movement that quick from his mistress. He stood looking back at Miss Forgetmenot, twitching his tail in annoyance.

"Oh my, oh dear, oh my ..." She sat motionless and the letter fell from her hand, but after a few seconds, the old lady closed her wide, staring eyes and her body slumped in relaxation.

"Oh, you silly girl!" she said to herself, "The insurance company will pay! Of course they will, Mr Folly said so! Oh dear, what a shock, Snaps! What a shock I've had."

The cat sat down, curling his tail around his front paws, and watched as the old lady slowly stood and walked off to the drawer where she kept her private papers. She found the appropriate papers, but, still not being able to read the fine print she searched her bureau until she came across a small, silver magnifying glass.

Within five minutes, the awful, desperate stomach-churning truth was revealed in all it's magnified certainty! The policy was ten years out of date. Ten years! It seemed only a few weeks ago that she had reminded herself to make sure she was insured. The old lady trembled and looked around her. She had never felt so alone and insecure.

"But no! It's a mistake. Mr Rowlock probably put the decimal point in the wrong place! That's what will have happened! Three hundred and seventy pounds," thought the old lady and she smiled in relief. "Three hundred and seventy. Oh dear, that's still an awful lot of money, but I think I've got that in the post office."

She found Aldwhyke Village Post Office in her phone book and dialled the number...

CHAPTER SIX

'PAY DIRT'

· 6 ·

'PAY DIRT'

THE TIME WAS JUST PAST TEN O'CLOCK in the morning when the phone rang at Charlie Wollock's flat. Charlie was making his second cup of coffee. Scratching his pyjama-clad backside, he shuffled to the phone.

"Yeah?"

"Mr Polly, is that you?" answered a frail voice.

"Eh? Who's that?" he coughed.

"It's Miss Forgetmenot. Mr Polly, I'm ringing about your letter, I've got your money here."

"Oh yeah? Good..." said Charlie, half-asleep. Then, realising what she had said, his eyes opened wide in astonishment. If she had enough money to pay his bill she was either a miser or was insured. 'Either way, Filch can't get his hands on the property – so the money's all mine!' Charlie grinned.

"Oh good!" continued Charlie, as respectfully as his voice could sound. "I know it's a lot of money, but what with inflation and all that..."

"It certainly is!" replied Miss Forgetmenot. "I can remember when three hundred and seventy pounds would buy you a house," she chirped.

"Oh yes, well I'm afraid it wouldn't today would it?" said Charlie. He made a quizzical face and scratched his head, thinking, 'What's the old bat talking about? Three hundred and seventy pounds?'

"No," continued the old lady, "I thought your bill said thirty seven-thousand pounds when I first read it! And dear me, you couldn't buy a house for that these days, could you?"

"What do you mean, you thought … when you first read it?" said Charlie.

"Why, the three hundred and seventy pounds, Mr Wally…"

"Now listen, lady. I don't know what game you're playing. The bill is for thirty seven thousand, not a penny more, not a penny less! And you've got a week to pay up!"

Charlie slammed down his phone in a furious temper. It was back to 'Plan A' after all – and that involved Filch. He paused for a second to think about having nearly forty thousand pounds in his pocket before coming back to reality and picking up the phone to give Filch the news that everything was going to plan…

TWO DAYS AFTER Miss Forgetmenot received the devastating ultimatum from Charles A. Wollock, builder and decorator, a certain Mr Henry Hobbs was sitting at home watching television. Home to Henry Hobbs was a high-rise flat half way up a tower block that overlooked the Bakerloo Line in North London.

For some time, Henry had been 'unable to work' owing to a catalogue of 'injuries' and 'inherited anomalies'. However, fortunately for the idle 48-year-old, the host of medical conditions ravaging his body only appeared to affect his capacity to work. Until recently Henry had been a driver for a local firm of minicabs called 'Cabs 'R' Us'. Most of the time, however, it had been more a case of 'Cabs 'R' U/S' (i.e. 'unserviceable') and the firm had become synonymous with late arrivals, breakdowns, getting lost and drivers with terminal body odour.

Henry, like Charlie Wollock, was podgy and balding, but whereas Charlie was crafty at working, Henry was crafty at *not* working. Life for the lethargic Hobbs was tolerable. He shared his home with his wife Harriet, who was forty, and his twelve-year-old son Harry. Harriet worked as an office cleaner for four days a week, whilst little Harry attended (or didn't, more often than not) the local comprehensive school.

Being married with a child had developed in Henry the natural gift of 'selective deafness'. For instance, he was able to hear such phrases as "Yer dinner's ready" or "Bert's on the phone, do you want to go for a pint?" whilst not being able to hear "Don't forget to put the rubbish out" or "Get Harry his lunch" or "The carpet could do with a hoovering".

It was on *that* Wednesday evening when Harry was playing 'earthquakes' in his room and Harriet was calling for help with the washing up from the kitchen while Henry sat in his favourite frayed and battered armchair, rolling a cigarette. A can of cheap Australian lager rested on the shiny arm of the chair, whilst Henry stared at the television waiting for the mid-week National Lottery draw to commence. Jackson, the family cat, strolled in and sat next to the electric bar heater. Henry frowned as he glanced at the cat and instinctively began scratching himself before smoothing the Lottery ticket which bore his chosen numbers.

The audience at the television studio, primed with American-style applause, clapped and whooped. A fading rock star flashed his embalmed smile and pressed a button to release the numbered ping-pong balls that would soon select the winning Lottery numbers. Henry lit his cigarette and poised his ballpoint pen. As the first ball rolled down the plastic tube, Henry could see that on it was the number six; he ringed a six on his ticket and looked back at the television as the second ball tumbled down the tube. The second ball was a seven. Henry realised that next to his ringed number six, he also had a seven. Events then started to become surreal. Another ball rattled out of the tube revealing the number eight, which was displayed at the bottom of the television screen. Henry had also correctly predicted this number and he ringed it on his ticket. At this point he began to have what could only be described as an 'out-of-body experience'. His senses dulled as the balls continued to roll out of the machine. He saw himself stub out his freshly lit cigarette, pick up the can and swig a mouthful of lager. Everything in Henry's world fell silent except for the rattling sound of the next ball in the plastic tube. So far, every ball that had been selected had corresponded to Henry's choices. The last ball was revealed. Without displaying any emotion and with half-closed eyes, Henry circled the last number on his ticket. He looked down and saw six ink circles surrounding his six chosen numbers.

"Henry!" screamed a voice. "Didn't you 'ear me? I asked you if there was any more washing up in there? Look at you sitting there gawping at the TV, I don't know why I ..."

Harriet Hobbs never finished her sentence for her husband erupted out of the armchair, scattering the contents of the ashtray and his can of lager across the room and simultaneously squirting a mouthful of lager at the television set.

"Gaa-arkk!" came a noise from his throat as he repeatedly thrust a pointing finger at the dripping screen. Harriet's bottom jaw dropped in amazement as she stared at her husband.

"Oh my gawd, he's 'avin' a 'art attack!" she thought, cramming her knuckles into her mouth, and trying to surpress instinctive fears about payments on his life insurance. The cat, confronted with the towering, jigging figure of Henry Hobbs, made a dash for the back of the sofa and safety.

Henry grabbed Harriet's arm and jumped up and down, waving the ticket above his head. He stopped, thrust the ticket under his wife's nose and then collapsed, sweating profusely, into the armchair, which puffed out a cloud of dust.

Harriet grabbed the Lottery ticket from her husband as he fell backwards and saw the ringed numbers. The scream emitted from the Hobbs's living room was so ear-splitting that young Harry Hobbs heard it in his bedroom, despite the excruciating noise of track three of his latest CD (a recording by the Tormented Turds, a heavy rock band). Harry wandered out of his bedroom, looked towards the television set and saw the lager froth still sliding down the glass. From there his gaze fell upon the crumpled form of his mother who had fainted and fallen to the ground. Looking over to the armchair he saw the zombie-like figure of his father staring into space.

"Dad, what's 'appened to Mum?" enquired the boy. "Dad... DAD!"

Henry sat motionless, both arms hanging limply over the side of the armchair. His legs stretched out in front of him and his lips were moving slightly. He became aware that Harry was shouting at him and slowly lifted his right wrist into the air and pointed at the television set. Without looking at the boy he mumbled, "We've won! ... I got all the numbers right ... We've won the National Lottery ... a rollover ... It's US!"

THURSDAY MORNING DAWNED crisp and bright over a mist-veiled Bogham. Cousin Moykle had decided to go and sit by the pond to enjoy his pipe. The leprechaun left the entrance to the Rockery tunnel and was puzzled by the brightness of the newly risen sun. He looked around before walking down the rocky path and realised what was missing.

"Well now, dere's a funny thing!"

Cousin Moykle produced a box of matches from his well-worn corduroy breeches. He pressed down the bowlful of tobacco with his thumb, then lit the pipe. After a few puffs, he pointed the stem of his pipe towards the trees on the far side of the pond.

"All de leaves have gone, so dey have!" said Cousin Moykle.

"Who are you talking to?" came a little voice from behind. Cousin Moykle turned around to see Pidwidgin coming out of the tunnel.

"Oi haven't been out in dayloight since dat dirty great storm, so oi haven't, an oi was thinking dat somethin' was de matter, and so it is. Look!" The leprechaun pointed with his pipe towards the strips of sun-gilded cloud. "D'ye see, Pidwidgin? All dem leaves, look, dere dey are … gone!"

The pixie gazed in the direction of the pointing pipe stem. The leprechaun was right, for autumn had come early this year. Most of the trees and many of the bushes had been stripped of their leaves during the night of the storm.

"Tee hee!" giggled Pidwidgin. "How can you see them if they're gone? You are silly!"

Cousin Moykle was about to enter into conversation with Pidwidgin, about to tell her of his observations and of their conclusions. Instead, he took another puff of his pipe, looked up at the sky and sighed as he thought 'It would be easier to explain the mysteries of the universe to mouse droppings.'

"Well oi'll be seein' ya later, boi fer now."

Cousin Moykle waved his pipe in the air and slowly descended the Rockery path. He reached the edge of the tranquil, dark-watered pond as the first rays of the new sun began to strike the garden. The leprechaun strolled past the tall reeds until he reached the little bronze statue of the goat-man. Cousin Moykle removed his cap and bowed his head before the horned figure.

"Top of the mornin' t'ya, sor! It's moighty glad oi am ta see ya lookin' so foin an' in one piece. An' now oi'll say good day t'ya. Good boi."

Cousin Moykle replaced his cap and walked away from the statue. Minutes later he reached a gap in the reeds where some large stones lay half-submerged in the water beside the grass bank. One stone was higher than the others and had become a favourite vantage point for the visiting leprechaun. Cousin Moykle stepped across the stones and sat down on the largest one.

Pidwidgin had watched Cousin Moykle walk away towards the pond. She watched as he disappeared behind the water reeds, his progress marked by a series of smoke trails. The pixie followed him until she reached the grass at the base of the Rockery. Looking nervously around and sniffing the air, she set off in the opposite direction from the leprechaun.

Pidwidgin's early morning task was to collect mushrooms for the others. While the pixie was looking for mushrooms, the others, apart from the leprechaun, were carrying out their daily duties. They had a rota for various jobs, such as waste disposal, gathering food and other provisions, laundry and all the usual necessary domestic chores.

The leprechaun had already completed his chore, even though he was a guest. Cousin Moykle was an expert candle-maker. He had been given a sack full of candle ends which the others had collected over the months and had set to work making a selection of beautifully crafted sticks. Now he had finished, he was looking forward to watching the world go by and puffing on his pipe.

Pidwidgin skipped along the edge of the pond to where she knew she could find some mushrooms. Everyone from the Rockery loved Pidwidgin. She was the youngest of the inhabitants, being still in her late teens. Pixies, as with most fairy folk, lived to roughly the same age as humans; it was only gnomes who lived considerably longer. Pidwidgin was also nothing like any of her kind, for whereas pixies were supposed to spend their time causing mischief and mayhem to man and beast alike, Pidwidgin preferred a quiet, uncomplicated existence. This little pixie enjoyed the company of the Rockery inhabitants. They were less rumbustious than the pixies she was used to, and they were all older than her. She felt safe in the company of Wazzark, Podfudger and the others.

The fresh, young, sparkling sun continued its slow rise into the crisp morning sky. Branches, reeds and grass were encrusted with tiny droplets of dew. Miniature rainbows were created in the treetops as the strengthening sunshine lit the watery diamonds. Pidwidgin had reached a clump of evergreen foliage that grew beside the reeds and was now on the far side of the pond from Cousin Moykle. Glancing across the water, the pixie felt reassured that the little man was nearby but she still continued to sniff the air once in a while for safety's sake.

Beneath the green, leathery leaves of the bush, Pidwidgin saw a crop of fresh, bulging white mushrooms. Taking a little knife out of the haversack she was carrying, she began cutting through the swollen stems of the fungi. Three minutes later she had filled the bag with more than enough mushrooms for all the Rockery inhabitants. She stepped out from under the leafy shadows and began to walk back towards her home. She made her way along the path beside the pond, close enough that her reflection was mirrored in the water's glass surface. Pidwidgin stopped to watch a shoal of goldfish swimming slowly alongside the bank, fascin-ated by the shimmering colours of the fish, which shone out at her from the dark waters. Sluggish in the night-cold water, the fish glided past the stems of some water lilies. Pidwidgin continued along the path, but she had only taken a few steps when the tranquillity of the pond was shattered.

There was a loud splash, which made the pixie spin round to look back to where the fish had been. Large ripples were spreading across the mirrored surface of the water. Pidwidgin watched as a big goldfish leapt high out of the water in panic. Then another flew, tail flapping, out of the same place. More and more fish of all shapes and sizes were leaping and splashing out of the pond. Puzzled by the sudden activity, Pidwidgin turned back to look into the water. The fish were darting around something strange that was lying at the base of the water lily stems. She leant over the bank to get a better look at whatever it was that was frightening the fish, and strained her eyes as she peered into the crystal clear water.

At first she could only make out a shiny object close to the lily stems, but as her eyes became accustomed to the refracted images she could clearly see that part of the shiny object was moving. Pidwidgin moved her face within a whisker of the water's surface, then slowly she realised just what she was looking at.

Cousin Moykle had closed his eyes and was enjoying the luxurious warmth of the sun on his wrinkled face. He puffed intermittently on his pipe, savouring the honey aroma of the smoke and enjoying the tranquillity of the morning.

A high-pitched scream splintered the moment. The leprechaun opened his eyes in shock, his jaw dropped and the smoking pipe fell from his mouth, landing in the water with a plop and a hiss.

"Holy Mudder of God!" he exclaimed as he scrambled to his feet, looking desperately around for the source of the noise. He slipped from the rock and only just managed to stop himself from falling head first into the water. Shaking like a leaf, he hauled himself back on to the large stone. Another, longer scream echoed around the pond. The leprechaun steadied himself and glanced back over his shoulder in time to see Pidwidgin screaming in terror, her arms flailing above her head, as she ran back towards the Rockery.

Elfie had been looking forward to his breakfast even before he had gone to bed. The elf had managed to acquire a magnificent pork sausage in a deal he had struck with a neighbouring elf. No one under the Rockery knew of the sausage's existence except Elfie.

One end of the gnomes' Great Hall served as a dining area for the fairy folk. On that particular morning, Wazzark, Podfudger and Effans were sitting at a wooden table eating their meagre breakfasts of assorted odds and ends from the communal larder. The two goblins were eagerly consuming their rations whilst Effans sat looking at the offerings on his plate.

"Wassup, Effans, not hungry?" enquired Podfudger.

"I'll have it if you don't want it!" chirped Wazzark. Effans said nothing as he tilted his head, examining the plate.

"Well boyo, that's the problem see … It!"

"What is it?" asked Effans as he pushed his nose close to the slop-filled plate.

"It's the same as we've got … look," said Wazzark, lifting a particularly viscous glob of bluish-green foodstuff with his fork. Whatever it was had the consistency of molasses and slowly trickled down on to his plate.

"Well, I dunno. Doesn't look right to me somehow. You may be eating it all right, but I'm bloody glad I didn't tread in it!"

"Look," said Podfudger, annoyed, "do you want to eat it or not?"

"Well, I dunno, there's nothing else is there? So I suppose I'll have to," moaned Effans.

"Well shut up and eat it then," snapped Wazzark.

The goblins finished off their breakfasts, lifting the metal plates and licking them clean. Effans put both elbows onto the table and began prodding the food on his plate. Wazzark and Podfudger leant back from the table and burped in unison.

"Lovely grub!" said Wazzark.

"I'm still starving!" said Podfudger.

"I believe you'd eat your own bloody mother if she had enough salt on her! Oh, it's no use, this is horrible. I can't bloody eat it!" Effans pushed the plate away in disgust. Podfudger made a grab for it and in an instant had scraped the contents on to his and Wazzark's plate. The goblins lifted their plates and poured the frog-spawn-like food down their open throats.

The three friends sat at the table for a few minutes in silence. Wazzark was thinking about where their next meal would come from. Podfudger was wondering what roasted cat tasted like. Effans was wishing he'd eaten his breakfast because his stomach was rumbling.

A door into the hall opened and the goblins and Effans looked up to see Elfie enter. He was carrying a large, brown paper bag. With a self-satisfied smile on his face he walked to the table and sat down with the other three. Effans looked at Elfie and, in an 'I-told-you-so' tone informed the Scottish elf that there was no breakfast left. Elfie said nothing as he put the paper bag on to the table.

"You did'na save me any then?" quizzed Elfie.

"Nope!" said the others together.

"Och well, neverr maind, I've gawt ma ain!" and with that Elfie plunged both hands into the bag and slowly extracted the magnificent sausage. Three jaws dropped open, three pairs of eyes bulged, and three pairs of lips began to dribble.

"Blimey!" said Wazzark.

Effans gulped and behind his thick spectacle lenses his eyes opened so wide that he looked like an owl.

"Bloody 'ell!" he cried.

"Cor! Where'd you get that?" asked Podfudger.

"Aye well … Neverr you bloody maind where ay gawt it! Just you remember tha' ye neverr saved me any o' y'o'n breakfast, ya bastards!" Elfie closed his eyes and smiled at his companions. Then, to add insult to injury, he produced a jar of sandwich pickle and half a crusty loaf. The Scottish elf began a mystic, almost religious pre-consumption ceremony. He removed the top of the relish jar and carefully scooped out a spoonful, which he tenderly spread along the length of the mighty sausage. He turned the plate round in a slow circle so as to examine its length and girth. Elfie leant over the sausage and slowly moved his nose along its entirety, sniffing and licking his lips.

"Aye … that's ready. Och, am I gonna enjoy eating you, you big beauty that ye are!"

Wazzark and Podfudger were dribbling copiously whilst watching Elfie's every move. Effans had gone into a trance as he gazed at the sausage.

"Can we have a bit?" whispered Podfudger.

"Aim so sorry … did ya say somethin'?" enquired Elfie.

"He said, can we have some … please?" said Wazzark.

"I see, I see, can you have some o' mai sausage?"

"Yes!" said Wazzark and Podfudger.

"No," said Elfie "get stuffed!"

By this time, Pidwidgin had reached the Rockery and, still screaming in terror, she began to run up the slope towards the tunnel entrance. The leprechaun had scrambled back on to the grassy bank and was running clumsily along the path in pursuit of the hysterical pixie. By the time Cousin Moykle had reached the Rockery, Pidwidgin had vanished inside the tunnel. Uncomfortably out of breath, the leprechaun stumbled over some loose shale and trod directly into some particularly runny cat excreta.

"Oh, Holy God! What's that?" cried Cousin Moykle in horrified disgust as he looked down at his diarrhoea-covered shoes.

Pidwidgin fled down the tunnel, her screams echoing around her as she rapidly approached the door that led to the Great Hall. Wazzark and Podfudger sat with drooping shoulders and piteous expressions as they watched Elfie prepare to devour his sausage. The Welsh elf had almost slipped into a coma of desire at the sight of Elfie's Epicurean preparation. Elfie raised his knife and fork above his plate.

The main door to the Great Hall flew open, crashing against the wall. Pidwidgin stood on the threshold and delivered a scream of such intensity that one of the lenses in Effans' spectacles cracked. The goblins were so startled they fell off their stools. Effans shot up in the air, catching both knees under the table. Plates, knives, forks, cups, saucers, pickle jars and a large sausage rose with perfect synchronisation above the table and over the cowering figure of Elfie.

"Shite!" screamed Effans.

"*!!**!!" screamed Elfie as he made a desperate attempt to seize the flyaway sausage, missing by a hair's breath and crashing to the floor in painful failure.

Pidwidgin ran screaming across the room and amid the crash and shattering of breaking glass and furniture she disappeared behind the bar.

The sausage hit the ground in a spray of relish and proceeded to roll furiously across the room. Elfie scrambled to his feet and, half-running and half-falling, tripped over Effans who was blocking his way.

"Ma sausage! Ma sausage!" screamed Elfie. "COOM BACK!" Elfie scrambled on all fours towards the slowing sausage. It was almost within his reach; a disaster would be averted!

Meanwhile, the portly leprechaun was running headlong down the tunnel. He could hear the commotion getting louder as he rapidly approached the door to the Great Hall.

Cousin Moykle ran puffing and panting into the hall and was amazed at the sight that greeted him. Crockery and utensils were strewn amongst the upturned tables and chairs. Various bodies were rolling around in a scrum, whilst the screaming shape of Elfie was scrambling towards him.

"No ... no ... no ...!" yelled the Scottish elf.

The leprechaun trod on something that gave way with a pop under his weight. Silence descended on the room. Cousin Moykle looked cautiously down and saw the excreta-covered, squashed sausage. He stepped back and, leaning down, examined the foul-smelling object that was fully 30 centimetres long.

"Holy Joseph and Mary," blasphemed Cousin Moykle, "Now how in God's name did that cat get in here?"

In the world above, the postman was leaning his bicycle against the privet hedge at the entrance to Number One Romany Way. He walked towards the old lady's front door and stood for a few seconds whistling quietly to himself as he sorted through a handful of letters. The letter he eventually pushed through the letterbox was another demand from Charlie Wollock.

An hour later on that Thursday morning, Miss Forgetmenot opened the letter. Inside the envelope was a photocopy of Charlie Wollock's invoice. The final amount had been underlined in red ink, and a scribbled note beside it added: 'In case there's still any misunderstanding'.

Miss Forgetmenot walked slowly into her front room. The light fought to penetrate the closed curtains as the old lady shuffled to her favourite armchair. She had not drawn the curtains and she did not switch on the standard lamp that stood next to her. She bent down and slowly sank back into the soft security of her old armchair. With tear-filled eyes she sat staring at the dull orange glow of the curtains. This was her home. She had loved and cared for it and now through her own negligence and an accident of nature she was going to lose it.

She thought of her strong handsome son, who would soon be arriving to clear up this awful mess. She imagined the dramatic scene as her son, dressed in his fine business suit, strode into Mr Wollock's office and confronted him with that awful invoice. No one would get the better of her son; he would make things right.

The old lady slipped further into her dream as she sat in the chair clutching the letter. Gradually she realised that there was a banging noise in her dream; or was it a dream? The banging became louder – was she dreaming? Miss Forgetmenot opened her eyes and, for a fraction of a second that lasted for years in her waking dream, she remembered she had never had a strong handsome son...

The banging started again. The old lady stood up, now fully awake and aware of her surroundings.

"Goodness me!" she said. "There's someone at my front door!"

Enoch Filch stood, raising himself up and down on his heels with his back to Miss Forgetmenot's front door. The old lady opened the door and Filch pirouetted around to face her, removed his brown trilby hat, bowed and presented his business card in one smooth, sweeping, theatrical gesture.

"Dear lady," he said, handing her the card. "My name is Enoch Filch and I represent an austere and worthy body of professional men and women of this town who are ever alert to shady practices and charlatanism."

"Oh!" said Miss Forgetmenot, taken aback by the eloquence of Filch's introduction.

"Oh indeed, dear lady, oh indeed," continued Filch as he fiddled with the brim of his hat. "It has come to our attention," he paused, looking behind him to the right and left as though searching for enemies. "It has come to our attention that you have suffered a particularly cruel blow of fate, vis a vis, storm damage, and ... humph! A certain ... humph! A certain regrettable oversight regarding property insurance?"

Miss Forgetmenot was completely amazed by Mr Filch's grasp of her predicament. "Why yes, I've had a lot of repairs done to my house, you know. I thought I was insured; he told me I was insured! Oh dear, and now I owe so much money ... whatever shall I do?" sobbed the old lady.

"Dear lady, dear lady. Please, please! I beg you there is no need for such miserable disconsolation! I can assure you that you are not alone. Our ... er ... group has been inundated with requests for assistance. Now, please! I beg you, keep my card safe and if events become too terribly beastly, please do not hesitate to telephone my number. Now, I will bid you good day." Enoch Filch bowed once more and, with his hat held out before him, retreated backwards as though in the presence of royalty.

"How extremely kind of you Mr ..." the old lady held up the card and looked closely at his name. "Mr Filch, how kind. Won't you stay and take some tea or coffee?"

Enoch Filch reached the gate, stood up straight and put his hat on. "Thank you, no, I'm afraid there are too many others like yourself that we have to visit. Too many others who are suffering from life's cruel vicissitudes; too many others who need comforting." And with those parting words, the saintly Mr Filch disappeared around the corner.

Miss Forgetmenot stood bemused on her doorstep, holding the man's card close to her face. Suddenly the world didn't feel quite so empty. She had a friend; an ally. 'What a pleasant man,' she thought, as she returned indoors to make herself a nice cup of tea.

Enoch Filch reached his old, abused, olive green Range Rover and climbed inside. He smiled and put on his leather driving gloves.

At the same time that the estate agent was driving out of Romany Way, Pidwidgin, who had taken refuge under a slops tray, was looking up at three astonished faces. Wazzark, Podfudger and Cousin Moykle were leaning over the bar to get a better look at the frightened pixie.

"What on earth's the matter with you?" frowned Wazzark.

"Did that rotten cat have a go at you?" asked Podfudger.

Pidwidgin shook her head. Cousin Moykle looked down over his shoulder at his cat-soiled shoes then, looking back, he said,

"Dere had been a cat dere alroight! But dat's not what was botherin' the little darlin'. Am I roight, Pidwidgin?" Pidwidgin nodded in agreement.

"Ghost!" said the pixie in a high, trembling voice.

"Ghost?" gasped the others.

"Where?" asked Wazzark.

"In the pond," answered Pidwidgin, beginning to tremble more than ever.

"A ghost in de pond! Well oil be!" exclaimed the Leprechaun and he scratched the back of his head.

"What's she talking about?" asked Podfudger turning to Wazzark.

"What was this ghost doing in the pond, Pidwidgin?" asked Wazzark. The pixie emerged from under the slops tray, stood up and began to get excited again.

"It was lying on its back waving at me from the bottom of the pond. But that's not all! The ghost … the ghost was Elliel and she was crying!" Pidwidgin started waving her arms in panic.

"All right, all right, calm down!" said Wazzark in a soft calming voice. "Listen, Pidwidgin, there's nothing lying on the bottom of the pond waving except possibly a fish!"

"And moi poipe" interrupted Cousin Moykle.

Wazzark frowned at the leprechaun, then continuing he said, "And it wasn't Elliel. She's gone, Pidwidgin; she drowned."

"When de ghost was wavin' at ye, did it have smoke comin' out of it?" asked Cousin Moykle.

"No!" sobbed Pidwidgin.

"Ah! Well dat's alroight then! It wasn't me poipe!" smiled the leprechaun contentedly.

"It was Elliel. She's a ghost! If you don't believe me, go and have a look for yourselves!" spluttered the pixie.

Wazzark, Podfudger and Cousin Moykle lowered themselves from the bar.

"Well?" asked Wazzark looking at the others.

"She's gone mad! Pixies do, you know," said Podfudger in a matter-of-fact tone. "They're so small and close to the ground that they get affected by weed killer and chemicals and stuff – it rots their brains."

The goblins and the leprechaun were joined by the dishevelled figure of Effans.

"Mad you say? Who's gone mad, Podfudger boyo? That pixie is it?"

"She hasn't gone mad. She thought she saw Elliel in the pond, that's all," frowned Wazzark.

"She probably did – and well dead and wrinkly she'll be by now, yes indeed," said Effans. Wazzark let out an exasperated sigh, he was trying to think of a rational explanation for Pidwidgin's plight.

"Look," said Wazzark "we don't want Ghisette or Mirithin finding out about this, they're upset enough as it is. We'll just have to go and find Squidget – she can have a look in the pond."

"Who's Squidget?" asked Cousin Moykle.

"She's a water nymph and she's Ghisette's cousin," replied Podfudger.

"Is dat a fact!" said the leprechaun in a surprised voice. "Maybe she can foind me poipe!"

Suddenly there was a furious cry from behind them. "Ye fat Irish bastard! Look what ye've doon ta ma sorsage!" Cousin Moykle lurched around to see Elfie holding up the ruined sausage on a fork, it's remains covered in dust, hair, and cat excreta.

"Oh! Dat's yours den?" answered Cousin Moykle.

"It *!!*#* was!" ranted Elfie, as he waved the stinking, desecrated object to and fro. The leprechaun looked genuinely surprised and said:

"Oi thoight a cat had don it. Begorra, what in God's name have ye been eatin'? Oh ye poor wee man. Ye need ta see a doctor so you do!"

"C'mon Podfudger," said Wazzark "Let's go to the river to look for Squidget."

"What! In broad daylight?" exclaimed the goblin.

"Anything's better than this madhouse," said Wazzark. "Besides, we can't leave Pidwidgin in that state. We've got to sort out this ghost of hers."

With that Wazzark pulled on his jacket and headed for the door, followed hurriedly by Podfudger.

At the same time as the goblins were leaving the Great Hall, Harriet Hobbs was answering the telephone. The voice at the end of the phone confirmed that they had indeed correctly picked the six winning numbers and that they were the only winners.

"What's he say, Mum, what's he say?" asked Harry Hobbs excitedly.

"Quiet!" said Henry Hobbs, "let yer mum talk to the man."

"What?" said Harriet to the man from the National Lottery. "How much?" Harriet put the back of her hand against her forehead then, with her eyes closed, she tottered unsteadily on her feet. "Chair! Quick, get the chair!" she beckoned. Henry picked up the nearby chair and placed it behind his wife. Harriet sat down heavily, "Don't tell anyone? ... Yes ... Yes ... Twelve o'clock ... Yes ... Yes ... My 'usband knows where that is ... Yes ... No, I won't ... Yes ... Bye ... Yes ... Thank you." Harriet Hobbs replaced the receiver and looked up from the chair at Henry and Harry.

"Mum ... Mum ... how much we won, eh? ... Tell us, Mum, tell us!" squawked the boy.

"The man said there was only one winner – us! And that we've won ninety-six million, eight hundred and fifty-five thousand, five hundred and twenty-two pounds ... and fifty-five pence," intoned Harriet slowly.

"Phwoar!" said Harry "is that a lot then?" Harry had only mastered talking with difficulty – maths was far beyond his comprehension.

"A lot?" shrieked Harriet leaping to her feet, "it's nearly all the money in the world!"

"What are we gonna do with it then, Mum, eh?"

"Well I know what I'm going to do ... I'm opening a slate down at the Witches Tit," smiled Henry. Harriet grabbed her husband by his string vest.

"Oh no you're bloody not 'Enry 'Obbs! We're going to the Dorchester 'otel tomorrah! I want you fresh as a bloody daisy, not smelling like a brewery! Now get down the corner and get me magazines!" commanded Harriet.

"The Dorchester Hotel? What in Park Lane?" asked Henry. "What are we going there for? We don't know anyone there – and what magazines?"

Harriet put her hands on her hips and began to tap one foot. "We're going to be presented with our cheque from the Lottery people at the Dorchester, an' we're 'avin our pictures took, that's what – an' I want me posh 'omes magazine before we go!" said Harriet.

"Why?" asked Henry.

"Because we're moving!" exclaimed Harriet.

"Movin'?" gasped Harry.

"That's right, my precious!" said Harriet, squeezing Harry's chubby, red cheek. "But first of all Mummy's going to take her darlin' little boy on a 'oliday!"

"A 'oliday?" croaked Henry and Harry together.

"I don't want a 'oliday!" griped Henry.

"Where are we goin', Mum?" cried Harry.

Harriet pointed her finger at Henry and, closing one eye, she glowered at her husband. "You may not want a holiday, 'Enry 'Obbs, cos you're whole life's a bloody holiday – but we do! An we're gonna 'ave one with or without you!"

Henry tutted, looked upwards and sighed. "All right, all right, where'd you wanna go then?"

"Bogham!" announced Harriet decidedly.

"Bogham?" coughed Henry. "What the hell do you want to go to that dump for – there's nothing there except rust and Zimmer frames?"

"Look you miserable old git, we're going to Bogham 'cos me Mum and Dad used to take me there when I was a little girl. An' anyway, we're not staying in Bogham, we're staying at Maislins," said Harriet Hobbs.

"What – the 'oliday camp?" exclaimed Henry.

"Ah wickeed!" shouted Harry.

The Hobbs family found it difficult to get to sleep that Thursday night. The expectation of the next day's events was like Christmas Eve, and the night before a birthday all rolled into one. The most difficult part of their fortunate circumstances would soon be over: that of keeping the colossal win a closely guarded secret.

Far away from the orange-lit sky of the noisy London night, in mist-shrouded fields beyond the houses of Bogham, Wazzark and Podfudger were searching the banks of a small river, the Alderbourne Rife, for Squidget, the elusive water sprite.

They had walked for miles that night without finding any sign of her – a long way for two small goblins – and they were exhausted. The only eventful incident was when Wazzark had a row with a particularly bolshy badger, which in turn bit Podfudger on the backside. By eleven o'clock on Friday morning, Wazzark and Podfudger were fast asleep in a cosy hayloft beside a farmhouse just outside Bogham.

Nearly seventy miles away in north London, the Hobbs family were dressed in their smartest clothes, eagerly awaiting a chauffeur-driven limousine which had been dispatched from the hotel to collect them. This transportation had been arranged by a leading national newspaper who had 'scooped' the story of the historic Lottery winners.

Harry Hobbs pressed his greasy nose against the balcony window and scanned the surrounding vicinity for any sign of a limousine (not that he actually knew what a limousine was). In the event, the boy was surprised when not one but several huge cars drew up outside. The multi-coloured fleet of vehicles swept into the tower block's car park complete with the flashing blue lights of a police motorcycle escort.

Harriet was getting more and more excited. The arrival of the fleet of cars had made her realise that it was all true! They now really did have more money than they knew what to do with.

Harriet, Henry and Harry were escorted from the building by several business-suited company representatives. In the car park they were invited to pick the car of their choice, five having been sent, each one a different colour.

"I wanna go on me own, Mum," pouted Harry.

"You can't, you're comin' with us!" growled Henry, who was irritated at having had to get up so early to put a suit on.

"Let 'im go on 'is own if 'e wants to," sighed Harriet, jumping to Harry's defence, as she usually did.

"Yeahh!" shouted Harry as he rushed off towards a huge, yellow stretch limousine with a satellite dish on its roof. A burly, uniformed chauffeur wearing dark glasses opened one of the car's many doors and Harry disappeared inside.

Harriet and Henry chose a gleaming white car. Together, they entered its cavernous interior and sat down on the back seat. They were joined by the chief representative from Tintagel, the company that ran the National Lottery. She was a black-haired, sharp-nosed woman in her thirties, wore a pair of bifocal spectacles and was dressed in a dark business suit. She gushed and fussed over Harriet and Henry, doing her best to explain the day's itinerary, after all, this was the most important task she had been asked to undertake in her job so far – the Hobbs's were the largest jackpot winners in the Lottery's history!

The entourage arrived at the Park Lane hotel and were greeted by a frantic media scrum. There were hundreds of photographers, journalists and television crews all battling to get nearest to the feted family. Eventually the Hobbs's were ushered inside the luxurious building and the glitzy, bow-tied, champagne-smiling jamboree was under way.

Henry and Harriet, with Harry in front of them, were asked to help hold up a monstrous, elongated bank cheque on which was written the staggering amount of their winnings. They smiled and a battery of cameras clicked and flashed in a fusillade of photo-fire.

It was the longest day of the Hobbs's life, but at the same time it seemed to pass very quickly. Before they knew it, the celebrations had danced and sung into the early hours of Saturday morning.

The Hobbs stayed at the hotel that night as guests of the *Daily Post* in exchange for the exclusive scoop of their story. Henry and Harriet eventually sank into bed at two-thirty in the morning. Harry had gone to bed many hours earlier after being violently sick in a flower tub – the result of eating six 'knickerbocker glories' in quick succession! Harriet snuggled up to her husband.

"Ere, 'Enry, I was thinking, you know, this morning when we were in the back of that big posh car." Henry lay on his back watching a large, brass fan blade lazily turning above him. He grunted in reply.

"Well, I was thinking. It reminded me of your old Ford Cortina. Do you remember when we used to get in that back seat, eh?" Harriet gave a girly giggle and snuggled closer to Henry.

"Heh, heh, yeah!" chuckled Henry.

"Yeah… up at Elstree, in them woods! Cor blimey, that was thirteen years ago." Harriet's advances had just begun to have an effect on Henry, when the thought suddenly occurred to him that Harry was now twelve years old and that he had probably been conceived in that old Cortina, parked in the concealed entrance to a field full of Brussels sprouts. All desire in Henry instantly evaporated at the thought of sex, conception – and especially at the thought of another Harry!

"Leave off, Hat," he muttered, "I'm knackered … See you in the morning."

And with that the romantic Henry Hobbs turned over onto his side and broke wind.

CHAPTER SEVEN

BEETLEMANIA

BEETLEMANIA

IT WAS JUST AFTER THREE O'CLOCK on that same Saturday morning when Wazzark and Podfudger finally found Squidget the water nymph. They had asked a water vole if he had seen her and the rodent had led the goblins straight to her within minutes.

Water nymphs were very closely related to fairies. They were slightly more robust in appearance, a little taller – and waterproof. Apart from that they were very similar. Squidget preferred to live in running water, and at the point where the goblins found her, the Rife flowed over a small weir. Squidget was extremely pretty. The Nymph had dark blue-black hair streaked with green strands, very large, deep green eyes and tiny pointed ears. Her silver-blue, lacy wings shimmered like quicksilver as they hung down her back and thighs. Her body was covered in exquisite, tiny scales and her little pelvic fins were of a pale gold.

"Oi, Squidget!" shouted Wazzark from the bank of the river. Squidget was sitting on an iron bar that rose from the centre of the weir.

"Squidget, come here," shouted Wazzark again. The nymph took to the air in her characteristic dragonfly style. She swished away from the goblins to the opposite bank and promptly vanished.

"She's disappeared!" exclaimed Podfudger.

"I can see that," frowned Wazzark. He shouted several more times across the bubbling water before giving up. "Flamin' fairies!" he muttered under his breath, "they're always mucking about!"

"No, we're not," said an indignant voice right in his ear.

"Aaarghh!" screamed Wazzark in fright. "Do you have to creep up on people like that?" he grumbled as he retrieved his fallen cap. "You frightened the life out of me!"

"Yeah ... and he hasn't got much of that left!" sniggered Podfudger.

"Shuddup you," snapped Wazzark.

"What do you want, Wazzark?" enquired Squidget as she hovered around the goblins. Ghisette had told the nymph all about Wazzark and Podfudger.

"We've got a ghost in our pond," said Podfudger in a proud voice.

"A ghost?" said Squidget.

"Shut up, Podfudger," snapped Wazzark again. "He means there's something in the pond that's frightening the fish. Pidwidgin said she saw something lying on the bottom," explained Wazzark.

"Yeah ... there's something fishy in our fish pond ... it's Elliel lying on her back waving up at folk," added Podfudger.

"That's not funny, Podfudger!" said Squidget in a voice so sad and serious that it made the goblin very embarrassed. The news had reached the nymph that Elliel had been killed during the storm although she did not know all the details.

"What's he talking about, Wazzark?" asked the water nymph, rightly assuming that she would get more sense out of the other goblin.

The three of them sat down and Wazzark explained to Squidget what had happened to Pidwidgin. The nymph agreed to go with them to investigate the pond so they set off towards Bogham as the moon appeared above the mist.

On the following Monday morning, Miss Eleanor Forget-menot received an ominous, threatening letter from Charles A Wollock. This time the letter threatened immediate court action and the confiscation of her property if she did not pay the money she owed. The old lady fell into a deep depression and then a rapid panic. She telephoned Charlie Wollock to try to come to some arrangement. The old lady wanted to discuss something called a 'second mortgage' with him (she had heard an item about it on the radio), but all she got was an answer phone voice telling her to leave a message. Then Miss Forgetmenot remembered the kindly Mr Filch and dialled his number.

Charlie Wollock was lounging back in a chair in Enoch Filch's office. He had just lit one of his roll-up cigarettes. Enoch Filch lifted his coffee cup to his lips and sat looking out of the window. He was about to take a sip when the phone rang. With unhurried composure he replaced the cup on its saucer and lifted the receiver.

"Good morning, Filch speaking."

"Oh, Mr Filch, it's Miss Forgetmenot here." Enoch Filch sat up straight, pushing his shoulders back into what he thought was a financially alert posture. Charlie raised one eye and looked over to the estate agent.

"It's the old dear!" exclaimed Filch in a loud whisper as he cupped one hand over the phone's mouthpiece and pointed at it with the other.

"My dear lady, how can we help you?" Filch continued, talking to the old lady whilst looking at Charlie. "Oh dear! Yes, of course that's serious. Yes, I'm very afraid to say that he is actually quite correct ... What? ... Oh yes, yes ... of course! Well, let me see, shall we say half an hour? Yes, good ... Goodbye Miss Forgetmenot."

Filch slammed the phone down in triumph, stood up and turned to the window, his hands held together behind his back. He watched the everyday scene being enacted in the street below.

"You're a wicked man, Charlie Wollock. You've upset a charming, defenceless old lady." A pigeon landed on the balustrade of Filch's balcony and swivelled its head towards the estate agent. It didn't like what it saw and flew quickly away. Filch turned and addressed Charlie.

"The poor lady has asked me to assist her in dealing with the demands of an incorrigible rogue who is hounding her for money! Any idea who that might be, Charles?"

"Haven't a clue Enoch ... not a clue," chuckled Charlie as he re-lit his homemade cigarette.

Enoch walked to a large, Edwardian hat and coat stand in the corner of the room and began putting on his overcoat and trilby.

"You realise," said Filch, "that naturally, I am uniquely qualified to help, and I shall, of course – as they say in the films – 'make her an offer she can't refuse'." Enoch Filch walked back to his desk and opened a drawer. He extracted a large cigar which he presented to Charlie. "Here, Charles, throw that ghastly thing away and have one of these." The estate agent handed the cigar to Charlie who put it into the top pocket of his red and blue chequered lumberjack shirt.

"Cheers, Enoch. If you don't mind I'll stick it in me pocket and sell ... smoke it later!" Charlie got up from the chair and followed Enoch Filch out of the room.

The two men said goodbye in the street. Charlie headed for a private drinking club whilst Enoch Filch climbed into his venerable Range Rover.

The drive from his office to the Ingletimber Residential Hotel for Gentlefolk took Filch just under eight minutes. The Range Rover turned into the private road where his destination's gravel drive was guarded by two imposing stone lions. Filch drew up outside the large mock-Tudor house. Built during the 1930's the house, like so many of the big houses in the area, had been converted into a care and nursing home for the elderly.

A small, stocky man of Asian appearance greeted the estate agent with an outstretched, gold-encrusted hand. Sonny Patel was the latest owner of the property. Patel had acquired the hotel two years previously and in that time he and Filch had successfully concluded several business transactions.

"Ah, Enoch my good friend. It is always a pleasure to see you. You are well, I trust?"

"All the better for seeing you, my dear chap."

Enoch shook Sonny's hand and the two men entered the building. They walked into the hotel's office, Sonny shut the door behind them and helped Enoch remove his coat, then went over to a large globe drinks dispenser and poured a gin and tonic for his guest.

"I take it that the 'business' of which you spoke earlier has been going well, mmm?" smiled Patel.

"Quite… quite. It's the usual thing, Sonny old man, the usual thing. Sad case really, but I'm glad to say that I think I can help!"

"Any next of kin?" asked Patel inquisitively. Enoch Filch made himself comfortable in a large, buttoned leather armchair and he accepted the drink from Sonny Patel.

"I'm not absolutely sure, but it doesn't look like it, old boy. Very sad," said Filch.

"Mmm, this 'sad case' Enoch, is the person particularly old?" enquired Sonny Patel.

"'Fraid so, 'fraid so, got to be eighty odd if she's a day," replied Filch, creaking about in the armchair.

"And this person…" started Patel.

"Lady … lady … very nice old lady," interrupted Filch.

"This lady," continued Patel, "this lady is, I presume, a lady of some wealth?"

"Ah, not yet Sonny. But don't worry, she soon will be, as will you, old boy, as will you!" Enoch raised his glass to the smiling Sonny Patel.

"It'll be about a week, I should think, Sonny. The usual arrangements ... strictly cash, of course!" said Filch.

"Oh, of course, my dear chap, of course!" replied Patel.

Enoch Filch finished his drink after finalising the opening gambit of their mutual skulduggery. He left the hotel and drove away from the waving, smiling Patel. He headed northwest and was outside Number One Romany Way in a matter of minutes.

Miss Forgetmenot welcomed the philanthropic Enoch Filch into her home. She had made a fresh pot of tea and arranged some dainty teacakes and shortbread on her best china. Filch declined the tea on health grounds and began his subterfuge. He explained that he had often dealt with situations like the one in which she found herself and told her of the many satisfied ladies and gentlemen who were comfortably settled in their new surroundings thanks to his efforts.

With all the gilded phrases he could command, he app-roached the dread subject of her debts. He explained that she would have to pay the horrendous amount one way or the other, and that because she had no insurance to fall back on or reserves of cash, she would have to use her capital assets to pay the debt.

"And I'm afraid that means the property... unless you have any relatives or friends who could assist you?" Enoch Filch leant forward, fighting hard to hold back the welling crocodile tears.

"No ... no there's no one I'm afraid," said the old lady, sadly.

"Well look," continued Filch in an upbeat, positive way, "as I said to you on our previous meeting, my team and I are at your disposal. Think the matter over and, if and when you come to a decision, please ring me and I will be with you immediately."

He leant forward towards Miss Forgetmenot and gently touched her hand in a gesture of reassurance. "In the meantime I will give your dilemma my most serious consideration."

The thought that such a perfect gentleman could be anything other than scrupulously honest never occurred to poor Miss Forgetmenot. She had no one to advise her on matters of finance or any other deeply personal issues. The crisis the storm had brought about was so completely incomprehensible to the old lady that Enoch Filch's patter had won her over entirely.

"I don't know how to thank you, Mr Filch," said Miss Forget-menot as the estate agent prepared to leave.

"Tut, tut, think nothing of it, dear lady. That's what we are here for, to help!" And once again Enoch Filch drove away from Romany Way, leaving the old lady in a happier and more confident frame of mind. He really was a gentleman!

THE LIGHT OF THAT LATE SUMMER DAY began to fade. Street lights were beginning to glow as tired and hungry children were being called in for their tea. Squidget had returned to Romany Way with the goblins. She had spent the day above the Rockery asleep in the stream and awoke to the sound of Ghisette's voice calling her. The water nymph unwrapped herself from her bed of pond weed and swam to the surface. The cousins embraced and greeted each other, then they sat close together while Ghisette told Squidget what had really happened to Elliel on the night of the storm.

"She couldn't swim then?" asked Squidget.

"No," said Ghisette, looking down.

"And no one's found anything?" asked the nymph quietly.

"No, nothing," replied Ghisette looking to the sky and wiping away a tear. Squidget was asking Ghisette some more questions about the pond and what Pidwidgin had said when Wazzark, Podfudger and Cousin Moykle appeared.

"You ready?" asked Wazzark.

"I'm ready, but where's Pidwidgin?" asked Squidget.

"Hiding!" said Podfudger.

"Ah, you'll not see dat little pixie until you've got to de bottom of dis pond business," said Cousin Moykle.

"Well that's what Squidget's here for, to get to the bottom of the pond. Come on, before it gets too dark! Cousin Moykle, show us where Pidwidgin was standing," said Wazzark.

The leprechaun led the group away from the Rockery towards the pond. It was a quiet evening, the sun was dipping down towards the rising mist and the garden's nightly routine was beginning. A column of gnats rose and fell by the waters edge, scattering as a bat scythed hungrily through it. Somewhere in the garden a hedgehog was snorting through a flower bed searching for slugs.

"It was about here," said Cousin Moykle, looking over to the far side of the pond to get his bearings. "T'be sure, oi can see me favourite stone over dere."

Squidget flickered into the warm air and slowly hovered out over the water.

"Ghisette," called Squidget, "any Dytiscus?"

"Yes" said the fairy, "quite big ones, be careful!"

"Thanks," said the water nymph, and with a soft plop she disappeared below the surface of the water.

"What's a Dy... Dytic... Dytickle us?" Podfudger asked, turning to look at Wazzark.

"I dunno!" said Wazzark.

"It's a great big water beetle and it's dangerous. It would be to a fairy anyway," whispered Ghisette with a shudder.

"What about a Squidget?" asked Cousin Moykle.

"She'll be all right if she's careful," replied Ghisette.

Squidget took a look back towards the surface. The ripples had spread away and the pond was calm once again. The nymph saw the faces of her friends as they peered into the pond. She darted away towards the thick, rubbery stems of a bank of water lilies and disappeared from view.

As the nymph moved slowly through the forest of stems, nothing appeared out of place until she swam around a large, dark green forest of Canadian Pondweed. Squidget accelerated and flitted into the weed, causing it to release countless tiny bubbles of pure oxygen. The bubbles clung to her wings and body like a million tiny pearls. The oxygen was absorbed through her skin and she instantly felt fresh and alert and was able to see far better in the gloomy water.

A large, dark cylinder was lying at the deepest part of the pond. The nymph swam cautiously towards the object. It was a huge, black container which was open at one end. As Squidget swam closer to investigate she saw that it was a black plastic dustbin, lying on its side, and that it was full of frightened fish.

"What are you all doing in there?" she asked.

A large goldfish moved slowly towards the edge of the dustbin. "There's something strange beyond the reeds! It was screaming to get out! And it's made a water beetle go mad!" said the fish.

"What do you mean, go mad?" asked the nymph. The goldfish moved slowly back into the darkness of the dustbin.

"Well it keeps grabbing it to eat it, but it can't touch it!" Squidget could not understand what the fish was talking about. She moved away from the sunken dustbin and entered the reeds.

It took Squidget a few minutes to thread her way through the closely packed reed stems. Beyond them was an expanse of clear water framed by the towering black cliffs of a bank of dense pond weed.

In the darkness of the distant weed she saw a tiny reflection. Cautiously Squidget glided across the open space towards the twinkling light. As the nymph approached the mass of weed she gradually saw what was causing the reflection. It was a milk bottle lying almost upside down on the mud. The base of the bottle was floating above the mud due to a pocket of air trapped within it. Something in the bottle moved. Squidget darted into the weed. A swirl of yellow mist trailed up from the mud, raised by Squidget's passing. There was a violent disturbance in the weed above her as a black shape shot out into the clear water above the milk bottle.

It was a huge water beetle which, alerted by the disturbed sediment, had resumed its attack on the bottle. The large, black and yellow insect, its legs paddling frantically, was enveloped by bubbles from the weed. It thrashed madly towards the suspended milk bottle. Bubbles were released in their thousands, spiralling away like silver smoke. The beetle launched a frenzied attack on the bottle. Six powerful, hair- covered, yellow legs grappled and scratched across the slimy glass, the insect maddened by something in the bottle which it could not reach.

Squidget watched the drama from the safety of the weeds. She had never known a Dytiscus act so strangely – and she had never before seen a water beetle as large.

Clouds of yellow sediment billowed around the bottle, dredged up by the swirling water. Eventually the beetle, frustrated in it's attempts, swam rapidly away towards the distant surface and vanished in the gloom.

Squidget emerged from the weeds and cautiously moved into the cloudy water. She reached the bottle and, peering through the yellow haze, saw that there was a small piece of wooden debris floating inside the bottle. The water was clearing and the nymph could see that draped across the wood was a tiny body – it was Elliel. Squidget had found the little lost Fairy. The nymph emitted a high-pitched squeak which vibrated through the thick glass of the bottle. The little figure moved a hand. She was still alive!

Above the surface, Snaps the cat wasn't very happy. His owner had been behaving very oddly recently. There were strange humans coming and going all over the place disturbing the peace, and his food was being served at peculiar times – if at all. That evening Miss Forgetmenot, lost in anxious concentration, had unwittingly scraped the contents of a small tin of spaghetti hoops with tomato sauce into his bowl. Snaps had decided to go hunting.

He crept silently out through the hated cat flap and moved swiftly to the cover of a flower border. Gradually Snaps worked his way along the edge of the garden, hidden by the unkempt foliage and the fading light. The cat stopped and pricked up his ears as he heard the snorting, snuffling of the hungry hedgehog. He sneaked past one of the apple trees that overlooked the adjoining waste ground. Then suddenly, Snaps stopped and lowered himself down into hunting pose mark one. He had heard a voice, a tiny fairy voice! The cat snaked his way hurriedly through the long grass as though on wheels. His legs pumped up and down but his head and body remained arrow- straight.

The voices grew louder. It *was* fairies! Snaps grinned and very carefully pushed slowly forwards. He remembered the night of the storm and his painful experience.

"Okay you little winged swine," scowled Snaps, "it's snack attack time!"

He continued creeping forwards until he was within leaping distance of Wazzark and the others. He frowned when he saw the goblins, but then caught sight of Ghisette and Mirithin. The cat sank down again and remained motionless, awaiting his chance to dash out and grab one of them. The fairies were intently watching the surface of the water, anxiously waiting for Squidget to reappear.

Squidget squeezed in through the neck of the milk bottle and swam up to the floating wood. She surfaced next to the semi-conscious fairy and tugged at her shoulder. There was very little breathable air left in the air pocket. The water nymph stopped pulling at Elliel and looked around her. This was going to be difficult. She was going to have to carry the incapacitated fairy down into the water-filled bottle, struggle to get her out through the neck, and carry her all the way to the surface – avoiding carnivorous beetles on the way.

"Impossible!" thought Squidget – which it was, especially as Elliel could not swim even when she was well and, more to the point, unlike her water-nymph cousin, the fairy could not breathe under water! Squidget leant back against the cold wall of the fairy's glass prison. A bubble of marsh gas wobbled out from the mud, passed over the bottle and climbed away to the surface.

"That's it!" shouted Squidget and she dived back down into the bottle and out through the neck. The nymph plunged into the pond weed, covering herself with the pearly bubbles. She returned very gently to the milk bottle and shook her wings under it's neck. The shaking of her body and wings released the oxygen into the bottle. Squidget repeated the exercise several times, releasing more and more bubbles into the bottle.

After fifteen excursions to and from the bank of weed collecting bubbles, the nymph was just about to fetch some more when she saw Elliel sit up on the little wooden raft. Squidget darted inside the bottle and swam up to the fairy.

"Elliel, Elliel!" spluttered Squidget, "are you all right?"

"Squidget, where are my sisters? What's happened to them. Where am I?" cried Elliel as she reached out to the nymph. Squidget held the fairy by her arms to comfort her.

"Shh! Don't be frightened, they're perfectly all right," and she pointed above her to the pond's surface. "They're waiting for you up there, right this minute!"

The oxygen in the bubbles had not only restored the exhausted fairy, it was also doing exactly what the water nymph had hoped. The milk bottle was gradually rising up through the water. Squidget looked up and saw that it was getting slowly lighter.

"We're going up, Elliel!" said Squidget happily. "As long as this bottle doesn't get stuck on anything, you'll be fine!" she said, straining her eyes through the thick glass.

"What's that, Squidget?" cried the fairy suddenly.

"What's what?" asked Squidget.

"Something moved in those weeds!" said Elliel.

Squidget looked to where Elliel was pointing and saw a disturbance in the distant pond weed. An explosion of bubbles and algae was foaming up through the water.

"I wish she'd hurry up!" said Podfudger. The goblin was chewing his thumb nail and looking nervously around. "I don't like standing in one place for too long, it makes me nervous."

"Oh, stop moaning. She'll be back in a minute," said Wazzark grumpily, although he felt no less nervous himself.

"Oi don't moind standin' in one place for a long toim," added Cousin Moykle. "As long as it's by a bar with a point of ale in me hand!"

Snaps concentrated on the group, waiting for Ghisette to move away from the goblins. His tail twitched and his mouth began to water.

"Get ready, Elliel," said Squidget, "we're getting close to the surface."

"But Squidget, I can't swim. How am I going to get out of here?" cried the fairy in panic.

"Don't worry. I'll carry you out, you'll just have to hold your breath for a second."

Squidget stared hard in to the face of her cousin, seeing the terror in her eyes. "It'll be all right, I promise," smiled Squidget. "Now come on, put your arms around my neck and keep your wings closed tight," said Squidget.

The milk bottle reached the surface of the pond, gently breaking into the evening air. Elliel clung on to Squidget and took in as deep a breath as she could. The water nymph dived down to the neck of the milk bottle. In a second they had wriggled free. Squidget turned and swam towards the evening glow. Safety was only inches away, the mirror surface reflecting them as they swam towards it.

Elliel saw the creature first. A shape appeared behind them in the mirror. The black and yellow of its armour glinted as it hurtled towards them, its great yellow legs writhing in the water. Squidget looked back over her shoulder to see the horrific bulk of the insect looming up beneath them. Elliel screamed and bubbles gushed from her mouth. At the same instant they splashed through the surface of the pond.

"Fly!" screamed Squidget.

Elliel released her hold on the nymph and the two separated in flight. The fairy unfurled her wings and skimmed across the surface of the water, flying for her life. Squidget continued climbing into the still air. She glanced over her shoulder in time to see the monstrous insect erupt from the pond in a plume of spray. The great water beetle, consumed with raging anger, opened its heavy, grooved wing cases to reveal two strong, leathery wings. The nymph stopped and hovered, watching the approaching insect.

"Look!" shouted Podfudger. "It's Elliel! Squidget's found Elliel!" The goblins and Cousin Moykle rushed to the water's edge, shouting and waving.

For a second Ghisette and Mirithin were unprotected. The grass behind the two fairies swished aside as Snaps sprang from his hiding place. In a ginger blur he charged towards the sisters, singling out Ghisette as his victim.

The great beetle, clicking its jaws in malicious hate, flew straight at Squidget. The nymph continued to hover, confronting the approaching terror. The beetle's compound eyes glittered as it buzzed towards her.

Snaps accelerated, silently bearing down on the fairy.

"It hasn't seen me!" gloated the rushing cat. Flecks of spittle flew from his mouth, as he narrowed his eyes for the kill.

The flailing, crazed insect opened its jaw as it surged towards the water nymph but, in a blur of speed, she darted sideways. The great beetle flew past in a flurry of beating wings. Then, realising what had happened, tried to turn. The huge wing cases stretched fully open in a desperate braking manoeuvre. It was too late! The beetle had completely missed its prey. Consumed with rage, the insect decided to bury its jaws into the first living thing it saw...

The first living thing it saw was an approaching ginger cat. Snaps saw the great black insect heading straight for him. He dug his back paws into the ground, and tail erect, skidded across the wet grass.

The fairy sisters, hearing the hissing cat, leapt out of the way as Snaps slithered past them, a look of horror on his face. The beetle flew headlong into the cat, striking it above the eyes, buried its powerful legs into the cat's face and sank its jaws into one of his ears.

A blood-curdling, screaming, hissing, yowl rent the still evening air, terrifying every cat in the neighbourhood. Snaps ran shrieking and squealing for home, with the monstrous alien creature stuck over his face!

"What in de name of all dats holy was dat?" exclaimed Cousin Moykle in fright.

"It was just that daft cat again!" answered Wazzark.

"I think he was sneaking up on us," trembled Ghisette.

There was a flutter and a swish of tiny wings as Squidget and Elliel joined the friends. Elliel flew straight into her sisters' arms. The three fairies rose into the air in a dance of hugs, tears and kisses. Joyously they swayed to and fro, rising and falling.

"Nice one, Squidget!" said Wazzark.

"Where was she? How did you find her?" asked Podfudger. Squidget began to tell the whole story as they all headed back to the Rockery.

Snaps was running for his very life from the thing digging and clawing into his fur, hissing and clicking as it chewed his ear. The cat screamed across the lawn, careering towards the kitchen door. For the second time in his life, he launched himself, at full speed and from some distance, at the cat flap.

He missed. There was a muffled thud and a dull clang as the cat smashed headlong into the adjacent drainpipe. There was also the splattering sound of thick liquid being ejected and a sickening, splintering sound like shattering bone.

Luckily for Snaps it wasn't the sound of his head breaking, it was the sound of the beetle disintegrating. The Dytiscus had taken the full impact of the cat's unintentional head-butt and pieces of cartilaginous material now slid down Snaps' face, lubricated by the dead insect's bodily fluids.

The cat collapsed on to his back with his legs in the air, watching the pretty-coloured stars spin around his head. Then he passed out.

There was a party that night under the Rockery, a party to celebrate Elliel's return. It was a very happy occasion, which was just as well because, very shortly, there would be an end to happiness for the fairy folk at Number One Romany Way.

CHAPTER EIGHT

FALSEHOODS &
FALSE HOODS

· 8 ·

FALSEHOODS & FALSE HOODS

THE HOBBS FAMILY decided to stay on at the Dorchester for a week while they planned their immediate future. They finalised the agenda for the holiday that Harriet had demanded, and began to enjoy the freedom of being obscenely rich.

Harriet also demanded that Henry should go out and buy a new car. Back at the flat, the neighbours had poured so much scorn on Henry's previous wreck that Harriet had made him get rid of it.

"Well, what sort of car do you want?" asked Henry as they sat in their hotel suite on the Monday morning.

"I don't know," said Harriet, "just go out and get something posh... something that people won't think has been dumped every time you park it!"

Henry frowned. He knew that Harriet was referring to the time they had parked their car overnight whilst staying with friends. The next morning it had taken Henry half an hour to remove the 'Police Aware' stickers.

"Okay, I'll go and get something posh," he said, reluctantly.

A week later the Hobbs family left the luxury of the London hotel in their new family car. Thirty years ago, when Henry had been an impressionable youth, he had wanted the type of car that all the nobs and gangsters drove around London, and so, during their stay at the hotel he had gone out and bought his favourite dream car – a Jaguar. However, despite his now being one of the richest men in Britain, Henry had not let wealth change him. He remained a slob and a skinflint and couldn't see the point of buying a brand new car when a perfectly acceptable second-hand one was available.

"But why didn't you buy a new one?" asked Harriet for the fourth time since crossing the River Thames on their way south.

"What d'ya want a new one for? What's the matter with this? You like it don't ya?" yelled Henry.

"Well yeah, it's gorgeous … but it's *fifteen years old*."

"Of course it's fifteen years old! They don't make 'em like this any more!" shouted Henry.

"I wanted a big fast motah like James Bond drives, Dad, wiv rockets an' guns an' that! Why didn't you get one of them, eh Dad? … Dad?"

Henry couldn't be bothered to reply and tried to change the subject by pointing out of the window.

"Oh look, a field with a tree in it!"

"I still don't know why you didn't buy a new one…" repeated Harriet, as Henry approached the motorway that would lead them to the Sussex Coast.

An hour or so later, the shiny blue Jaguar, complete with roof rack and tasteful plastic adhesive fingers stuck to the boot lid, cruised into Bogham. A flood of childhood reminiscences swept over Harriet as she gazed upon long-forgotten landmarks. Henry tried to concentrate on his directions. The decibel level in the car continued to rise as Harriet's childhood holiday adventures were described in minutest detail.

Eventually Henry arrived on the road that ran the length of Bogham Beach. The Jaguar purred past the remaining holiday-makers, past the old pier, the amusement arcades, candy floss and whelk stalls, miniature railway and miles of golden sand.

Harry had never seen the sea before and was as excited as his mother.

"Oh look, Henry! That's where me dad's 'at blew under a bus!" exclaimed Harriet, pointing back through the rear window.

"Shame 'is 'ead wasn't in it," mumbled Henry, who disliked his father-in-law intensely.

"Oh and look, look! The pier … me Mum and Dad used to take me on the pier to look at Mouse Town."

"Mum, Mum! Look … dodgems!" screamed Harry.

"It was a little town all made like dolls 'ouses, 'enry, only it was full of mouses!" shouted Harriet with glee.

"If it's still there we can take the cat to see it," scowled Henry under his breath.

Mercifully for Henry, the entrance sign to the holiday centre came into view. The Hobbs family drove in to Maislins Riviera World and were welcomed by the Managing Director, who had been alerted to their visit and was on standby to give them the VIP treatment. With much ceremony, they were escorted to their luxury, flower-and-champagne bedecked chalet.

Harriet went in search of late summer sun. Harry went in search of virtual reality machines. Henry went in search of a pint and found several. Their holiday had begun.

ON THE FOLLOWING THURSDAY MORNING Harriet decided that she wanted to go exploring. The last few days of lazing in a deckchair without a care in the world had made her more and more maudlin. She had even shed a tear when, dozing in the late summer heat, she remembered the golden, distant days of those holiday excursions with her parents. She realised, with a nostalgic sigh, that she had always wanted to live in Bogham. Seconds later, she remembered that now she was fabulously wealthy, she could … and would! Her childhood dreams could at last come true.

So, after breakfast that Thursday morning, she put her plan into action. Harry was playing with a remote-control racing car in the kitchen when Harriet called him.

"Now 'Arry," said his mother, handing the boy a bundle of twenty pound notes, "me an' yer dad are goin' out for the day. So we want you to 'ave a luvvly time while we're away. We'll be back at tea time luv. You got that money so you can buy a burger if yer hungry. Now give Mummy a kiss." Harry snatched the money and gave his Mother a fleeting kiss as he ran out of the chalet and headed for the amusement hall.

"Right, come on 'Enry 'Obbs, we're goin' 'ouse 'unting!" said Harriet triumphantly as she pulled her husband out of the chalet by his elbow.

"Whoa … whoa … 'ang on 'At! 'Ouse 'unting? What you mean? 'ere in Bogham?"

Henry tried to stop his wife manhandling him as they walked along the path towards the car park. Other holiday-makers had paused to witness the display as Henry jogged about like a defensive boxer.

"Well, where'd you think I meant … Cairo?" said Harriet sarcastically. Henry continued struggling as he whispered as loudly as he could,

"Well, no, but…," suddenly embarrassed at realising his public humiliation. Harriet stopped walking, released Henry's arm and stood facing her husband with her hands on her hips.

"But what?" she demanded, tapping her foot. Henry shuffled about, glancing at the onlookers.

"Well, Hat… Bogham? You can't be serious, love! I mean, look at it," he swept an arm towards the horizon indicating the entire resort. "The pier's collapsing, the sea's so polluted that you can walk on it, the place is full of yobs and dogs, you can't park anywhere, the average age of the population is about two hundred, they drive like zombies … they even have to buy sand in from a builder's merchant to put on the beach! I ask you, Bogham, Hat? It's a music hall joke!" Henry's voice had risen from a whisper to a crescendo. As he finished his tirade, the onlookers broke into spontaneous applause. Harriet was furious.

"Oh yeah? Where'd you suddenly get all this expert knowledge from 'Enry 'Obbs, eh? Where?"

"A bloke at the bar told me," replied Henry with an air of authority.

"A bloke at the bar," repeated Harriet slowly. She nodded her head, fuming with rage. Silent for just a second, she then leaned back, took a great breath and, with a mighty swing, clouted Henry around his ear with her handbag.

"Music hall joke, eh?" she stormed. "Well you'll be all right then. You can get a job there. You're a flaming comedian!" Harriet shoved Henry in the back and he staggered forward, holding his ear and muttering furiously under his breath. Amazed and open-mouthed, the onlookers continued to watch the spectacle as Harriet prodded and poked her husband towards the car park.

In a stony, brooding silence, Mr and Mrs Hobbs left Maislins Riviera World main entrance in search of Harriet's dream. The time was just after ten o'clock.

By four o'clock that afternoon, Henry had driven nearly forty miles in and around the town looking at vacant properties. Harriet had still not seen the elusive property that she knew was 'out there somewhere'.

Henry was becoming increasingly irritated as he fought to negotiate the unfamiliar roads and local traffic. There was, he noted with derision, a great difference between skillful London drivers and the comatose rabble who played at driving in Bogham! After he had been stuck behind three milk floats, cut up by an irate lorry driver, suffered a string of obscenities from an old woman in an electric buggy and finally had realised how much fuel he was using, he rebelled.

"I've 'ad enough of this, 'Arriet! Look for an estate agent!" he demanded.

"I don't want to look for an estate agent. I'm 'appy just driving and exploring," remonstrated Harriet.

The conversation that followed took up the next fifteen minutes, but nothing of any great interest was said on either side. Suffice to say that Harriet gained the upper hand and Henry's Jaguar resumed crawling along the busy main road as Harriet, sitting in the back, continued looking for her dream house.

"Get the ***!!? out of the **!!#!?!! road you stupid *!!??#!!" came an interesting comment from a local taxi driver as he passed the dawdling Jaguar.

"Right, that's it!" shouted the exasperated Henry, who had repressed his rising temper with increasing difficulty. The thought of a brother cabbie confusing him with a civilian driver was the last straw and he accelerated away towards a distant row of shops.

"Where are you going 'enry?" yelled Harriet as she was hurled back in her seat by the force of the acceleration.

"There!" replied Henry defiantly, pointing at a building amongst the row of shops and offices.

Enoch Filch was standing at his window watching an extremely attractive girl with, as he remarked to himself, particularly impressive mammary glands, when he noticed the blue Jaguar pull up and park behind his Range Rover. He watched with growing interest as Mr and Mrs Hobbs stepped out of the car and looked towards his property.

"Now, did they go into the bakery below or did they ...?" thought Filch. Before he could conclude his contemplation, the office doorbell rang. Filch smirked in a self-satisfied way and straightened his tie. "Mmm, it must be them!" thought the estate agent. "Yes, classy car... classy people. Classy people ... classy cheque book!"

Enoch Filch strode to the door, opened it and welcomed the Hobbs's into his office. His first observation – which certainly did not require much intuition to determine – was that the pair did not appear to be very happy. The estate agent switched on his most helpful smile and extended his hand. "Good afternoon, Madam, Sir. How may I help you?"

"Er, yes mate," said Henry Hobbs begrudgingly shaking the proffered hand, "I want you to find a house fer the missus."

Enoch Filch's curiosity was rising fast. Who were these common people who had stepped out of a luxury car? And why had they chosen his business? Something didn't feel right. Filch began his gentle interrogation.

"I'm sure we can find just the property you have in mind," he smarmed. "Have you come far, Sir?"

"Yeh, from London."

"And have you visited many property consultants since you've been here?" probed Filch.

"No mate, you're the first," said Henry.

"The first ... ah ... the first. Well, if I may enquire, Madam, Sir, do you have any particular property in mind?"

Harriet strolled over to the photographs of buildings pinned up in Filch's display area. She looked at a photograph of a large thatched cottage that Filch had cut out of a *Home and Country* magazine.

"One somefink like this would be very nace," said Harriet in an affected voice. Henry wandered over to see the picture that had attracted his wife's attention. He looked closely at the price. The amount reflected the property's true location: nowhere near Bogham, but actually in the very best part of Ascot in Royal Berkshire.

"How much?" screeched Henry in an unnaturally high voice. "That's nearly a million quid!"

"Shuttup 'Enry," hissed his wife out of the corner of her mouth.

Filch strolled around to his desk and sat down. He looked for a note pad that he knew was somewhere on the untidy desktop. His initial suspicions about the couple were deepening by the minute. With a slight hint of irritability, he lifted his newspaper and discovered the note pad laying beneath it. He folded over the cover of the pad and lifted his pen.

"Could I take your names, please, Mr and Mrs...?"

"'Obbs with a haitch," said Harriet, as the couple turned to face the estate agent. "Mr and Mrs 'Obbs... of London!" she added, as though it made a difference.

"Er ... quite," said Filch, looking up from his note pad with an ingratiating smile.

As he began writing their names, he suddenly became aware of a peculiar sensation. His eyes were being manipulated by an extraordinary magnetic force. Instead of seeing the pad he was writing on, his vision began to travel. The notepad dropped out of his field of view to be replaced by the folded newspaper. Now, before his astonished eyes, the front-page photograph came into focus. The photograph showed three people holding up a giant cheque which had a staggering amount written across it in huge numbers.

The blood drained from Enoch Filch's face and he felt the cold sweat of cheap novels on his blotchy forehead. He looked slowly up from his desk, not daring to hope that his suspicions could be confirmed – but they were. For right there in front of him stood the winners of the biggest prize in National Lottery history: Mr and Mrs Hobbs – of London.

Very gently and in what seemed almost like slow motion, Filch turned over the newspaper and slid it under some other documents. He tried to speak, but the words staggered out in a nervous castrato pitch.

"I take it ... humph!" Filch composed himself and began again in a normal register. "I take it that you have a budget prepared for an acquisition?"

"Eh?" queried Henry. "Whotcha mean, ol' son?"

"How much can you afford?" smiled Filch with new-found reverence.

"Well actually..." began Harriet.

"What she means is we aint made o' money, but we aint skint neiver, know what I mean?" interrupted Henry, who glanced slyly at his wife and winked. Harriet was annoyed at her husband but decided to let him carry on. By now Enoch Filch had smelt their rat, but he was sure that they were not going to smell his...

"Well now! As it so happens, you are in luck," said Filch with an oily smile.

"Yeah? Wysat then?" asked Henry.

"There's a property available which is almost identical to the estate shown on the picture your wife was admiring. It does need a little work but that, of course, would be reflected in the price."

"Yeah?" said Henry with interest.

"Can we see it?" asked Harriet.

"Of course you can. We can make an appointment to view and I will contact you later today to confirm the details," said Filch.

"Cor, 'Enry!" said Harriet excitedly, "a thatched cottage in the country, eh?"

"Any pubs nearby?" asked Henry.

"Yes, several," answered Filch with customary exaggeration.

"Well, mate, you sort out an appointment then. All right Hat?" Harriet nodded.

Enoch Filch took their full details. Then he arranged for them to view the property the following Saturday, at a time to be confirmed. The Hobbs, encouraged by the discussion with the estate agent, shook hands, said their goodbyes, and departed. Harriet was in a jubilant mood as Henry drove them back to the holiday centre.

"Shame we couldn't see it today, eh, Henry?" she said.

"Yeah, but you 'eard what the man said, Hat. You can't walk around a 'ouse while they're getting ready for a flamin' funeral!" said Henry.

"Aaah!" said Harriet, with genuine sympathy, "poor old lady."

"Yeah!" sneered Henry, "Lucky for us though, eh Hat?"

Harriet coughed, and looked out at the retirement flats and rest homes that jostled each other for space along the Bogham seafront. "Poor old lady!" she repeated under her breath.

FILCH'S SUBTERFUGE was working! Immediately the Hobbs's had driven away from his office he dashed to his telephone and made a rapid series of telephone calls. He started by cancelling several drinks appointments, then phoned Sonny Patel at the Rest Home.

"Sonny," whispered Filch into the mouthpiece, "we're on old boy ... Saturday, some time in the afternoon. I'll let you know for definite tomorrow ... Yes? ... Good ... This one's a gem ... So I want the old dear treated like absolute royalty ... Good ... Until Saturday then..." Filch put down the phone and immediately redialled; this time he spoke to Charlie Wollock.

"Charles, thank God you're in. Look, dear boy, something very, very nice has happened. I want you to find your charming colleagues Sherbert and whatsisname ... Oh yes, Kneecap! Find them, Charles! I've got a very important task for them ... Yes, that's right, Charles, it is indeed the old seventh cavalry trick ... Yes, the usual black suits and clipboards. Saturday morning at ten o'clock outside the Methodist Church. Oh, and Charles ... don't forget the wreath, the black ribbons and the sign."

Filch replaced the receiver with tender care. Then, filled with expectation, he flipped over another page on his calendar and welcomed the pneumatic Miss September into his office.

Later that evening positive in the knowledge that his devious plan would work as well as it usually did, Filch phoned the Hobbs's and arranged to meet them at his office on the Saturday afternoon at three o'clock.

HENRY, HARRIET AND HARRY thoroughly enjoyed the rest of their week at Maislins. Harriet didn't even mind Henry going off to a new bar he had discovered (and neither did Henry!) – she was so looking forward to seeing her thatched cottage that she ignored Henry's drinking routine that Thursday evening.

Saturday morning dawned. Yet another sunny day had been bestowed on the seaside town. Harriet awoke at seven o'clock, excited at the prospect of the day's events. She woke Henry, who jumped out of bed and dressed shortly after his wife. This was a rare event for Henry, for Saturday morning was usually cursed with a ten-megaton hangover. But Harriet had forbidden him to go out boozing the previous evening and he was thus spared his usual post-alcoholic affliction.

Henry couldn't see for the life of him why they all had to be up so early on that Saturday morning, especially as the appointment with the estate agent wasn't for hours.

"Is that car all right?" asked Harriet as she walked into the chalet lounge from the bathroom. Henry was standing with his back to her, gazing out of the window. He fiddled with his nose as he watched a pair of nubile young girls bouncing voluptuously around with a frisbee.

"Course it is," grumbled Henry.

"It had better be," threatened Harriet. "Don't you dare let me down today, 'Enry 'Obbs."

The door to Harry's bedroom flew open as the boy exploded into the room. He kicked a football, which struck Henry between the shoulder blades at the exact instant that the boy's bedroom door slammed shut.

"Aaarghh!" screamed Henry, as he was sent sprawling across the sofa.

"'Ere, Mum," shouted Harry, completely ignoring his father's plight. "Can I go to the movies? There's a great film on." Excitedly he ran to his mother.

"Of course you can, my petal," smiled Harriet. "What's it about?" she asked in a baby bunny, cutey voice.

"It's a disaster film, Mum! S'about a huge asterix that comes out of space and crashes into the earth, killing everybody and blowing everything to bits!" exclaimed Harry loudly. Harriet smiled and leant forwards. She squeezed her son's cheek.

"It's not an asterix, you silly boy – it's a haemorrhoid!" she giggled.

Henry staggered painfully to his feet. "So that's what hit Bogham!" he grimaced.

Charlie Wollock telephoned for a taxi at 9:45 that same morning and made his way to the Methodist Church. He had not wanted to bring attention to himself that morning, preferring to keep a low profile, and so had left the van at home.

"Wassup? Your van got woodworm?" quipped the driver, but Charlie was not going to rise to the cabbie's cheap taunts.

"Yeah, something like that," he replied, quietly pleased at the cabbie's crestfallen expression.

The taxi dropped Charlie in a street adjacent to the church. After the cab had gone, Charlie donned a pair of dark glasses and turned up his jacket collar. A few seconds later he reached the Church and saw two dark-suited men, also in sunglasses, standing outside the building beside a white transit van. When the men saw Charlie approaching, one opened a rear door whilst the other got into the driving seat.

Charlie reached the van and jumped in the back. The man slammed the door and ran round to join the driver. A few minutes later, Enoch Filch drove up behind the transit in his Range Rover. He flashed his lights at the van and the two vehicles moved off towards their target.

Miss Forgetmenot had received yet another threatening letter that morning from the aggressive Mr Wollock. The leaden feeling of despair had returned to haunt her. Then she remembered the words of the benevolent Mr Filch, which helped to lighten her feeling of hopelessness. "When you come to a decision, please ring me." Miss Forgetmenot stood in the hall holding the letter, her mind numb with doubt. She did not want to consider the terrible consequences of the situation she was in.

The Range Rover pulled into the side of the road. The white van continued on, with Charlie Wollock in the back giving directions. Moments later the van stopped outside Number One Romany Way; its occupants waited for a few minutes while a near neighbour of the old lady drove off in his car. Sherbert and Kneecap opened the van doors and got out, Charlie Wollock crouched behind the driver's seat, out of sight.

"Good luck, lads," whispered Charlie.

The two dark-suited men carrying clipboards walked up the path and knocked on the front door. Sherbert adjusted his thin, black tie.

'Sherbert' was the nickname of this particularly unpleasant individual who was used by Filch on occasions for solving stressful problems. He had acquired the name, not because he was sweet but because, like the effervescent confectionery, he could get up peoples noses and make their eyes water. 'Kneecap', his colleague, had acquired his nickname because he was fond of threatening his enemies with the use of that gruesome form of punishment.

Now they stood waiting on the doorstep of Number One Romany Way. After a few seconds the door slowly began to open.

"Yes ... Can I help you?" asked the old lady nervously.

"Miss Eleanor Forgetmenot?" snapped Sherbert.

"Y ... yes. Good morning," she stammered.

"We are acting for our client, Mr Charles A. Wollock, the plaintiff in this action, in regard to an outstanding debt of thirty-seven thousand pounds owed by you to him," announced Sherbert in his least friendly manner.

"B ... but ... oh ... I, well," stuttered Miss Forgetmenot.

"Do you wish to pay this amount by cheque or by cash?" added Kneecap.

"But I haven't got any money!" cried Miss Forgetmenot.

"Oh well, sorry luv!" said Sherbert and he pushed past the old lady and entered the cottage. Kneecap went back to the van and opened the rear door. He exchanged his clipboard for a large 'for sale' sign.

"Ow's it goin?" whispered Charlie.

"It's a doddle, he's in now," answered Kneecap.

The old lady shuffled after Sherbert in alarm.

"Please … What are you doing?" she cried.

"I'm makin' an inventory," barked Sherbert, "to see how much all this stuff will make at auction."

"Auction?" gasped the old lady in shock.

Kneecap lifted the sign and drove it into the soft grass, then picked up a mallet to knock it further into the ground. Miss Forgetmenot heard the sound of banging and staggered to the door.

"Oh my goodness," she gasped, on seeing the sign. She turned back to confront Sherbert.

"You can't do this. This is my home!" she cried. There was the sound of a car horn from outside as Kneecap entered the cottage.

"How much do you reckon this lot's worth?" he asked Sherbert with a sly wink.

"I'm not sure yet. Is this TV yours luv or is it rented?" Miss Forgetmenot stood shaking her head, tears dropping from her cheek.

Then, suddenly, across the threshold, marched the imposing figure of Enoch Filch, gentleman and knight...

"What is the meaning of this outrageous behaviour?" he bellowed. "Who the devil are you men?"

Sherbert and Kneecap stood beside each other and, in feigned anxiety, nervously backed away from the estate agent.

"Sorry guv, just doin' our job! The old lady owes a stack of money. We are the bailiffs," lied Sherbert theatrically.

"Oh dear! Oh dear! Oh dear! Miss Forgetmenot I did warn you that Mr Wollock was right in his claim," said Filch. He stood close to the old lady and leant over, whispering in her ear. "I think I know what we can do. Who is the property to be sold by? Who is the Estate Agent?" asked Filch.

"There ain't no estate agent. We're handling the sale for the Court."

"Indeed," said Filch. "Do you have your official documents with you?" asked Filch.

"You mean these?" answered Kneecap. He handed Filch an out-of-date court summons he had been sent for a motoring offence. Careful to hide the relevant detail, Enoch Filch passed the form which bore the Royal Coat of Arms with the words 'County Court Summons' under the old lady's nose.

"I'm afraid this is all in order. They do have a legal right to do what they're doing, I'm afraid," said Filch in an almost heart-broken tone.

"That's right, lady. An' I tell you this, all the stuff you've got in this place is not going to get you a quarter of that," announced Sherbert.

"What will happen then, Mr Filch?" cried the old lady.

"You'll get evicted and we'll sell the house!" shouted Kneecap.

"Evicted … Oh my!" Miss Forgetmenot swayed on her feet and was immediately supported by Enoch Filch, protector of the oppressed.

"Desperate times call for desperate measures!" said Filch to the weeping old lady. "How much do you intend to sell the property for? I warn you, I am an estate agent; I know everything there is to know about property values," declared Filch.

"Thirty-seven thousand pounds," said Sherbert.

"But the house is worth far more than that!" proclaimed an indignant Enoch Filch, putting his arm around the old lady.

"We don't care how much it's worth, we only want our client's debt repaid," sneered Kneecap.

"Well how much is it worth?" asked Filch.

"You tell us – you're the estate agent," said Sherbert.

"I jolly well will! This house is worth at least sixty thousand pounds!" blustered Filch in a masterly understatement of the property's value.

"Well you buy it then," replied Kneecap, with a particularly unpleasant curl of his lip.

"B ... but M ... Mr Filch!" stuttered Miss Forgetmenot, who was completely lost amongst the whirling developments. Enoch Filch raised his hand in grandiose authority.

"Do not fear, dear lady!" Filch asserted. "I will not stand here and see you robbed by these people!" The estate agent dramatically pulled out his cheque book. Kneecap turned and looked out of the window, the hand in his pocket pinching the inside of his thigh to stifle a fit of the giggles. Filch flourished a pen above the cheque book and wrote out a cheque for thirty-seven thousand pounds and another for twenty-three thousand pounds. He then held them both in front of Miss Forgetmenot.

"There you are, dear lady. I think the problem is solved!" He turned to Sherbert and presented him with the cheque for thirty-seven thousand pounds. Holding one hand on his lapel and pointing to the door with the other, he ordered Sherbert and Kneecap out of the house.

"Right you are, that's what we came for! Goodbye Missus," said Sherbert as he and Kneecap departed slamming the door. The two men hurried to their van and drove out of Romany Way.

"And?" asked Charlie Wollock over their shoulders. Kneecap waved the cheque in front of him.

"As rubber as a box of condoms!" laughed Kneecap.

"Blinkin' right," frowned Charlie, "these ain't though! 'ere y'are lads!" Charlie leant over and handed each man a bundle of banknotes.

"Very nice!" said Kneecap as he counted the cash.

"Okay, stop here and wait for Filch to go past," said Charlie. The van pulled into the side of the road and parked.

Back inside Number One Romany Way, Enoch Filch stood watching the old lady finish the cup of tea he had made for her. She was sitting in her armchair, totally perplexed by the situation. With a trembling hand, she returned the rattling cup and saucer to Filch.

"Oh my ... Mr Filch, what a to do. What have I done?" she asked despairingly.

"You have done a wonderfully courageous thing," said the estate agent triumphantly.

"You have beaten those men at their own game. Now, dear lady, here is a cheque for twenty-three thousand pounds. This is the balance of the money for the sale of your property, after the repayment of your debt."

Miss Forgetmenot took the cheque and looked at it in total bewilderment. She looked at the figures which, to a lady of her age, represented a colossal sum of money. Gradually the reality of what the payment was for began to sink in.

"Does this mean I can't live here in my home any more?" sobbed Miss Forgetmenot.

"Now, now, dear, dear lady, I want you to put all these unpleasant things from your mind," said Filch as he put the cup and saucer on a table. He then walked to the far side of the room and picked up the old lady's coat.

"I have a surprise for you! Up we get. Some very good friends are waiting for us," said Filch excitedly, as though addressing a four-year-old child. "Now come along – you'll enjoy this."

Deep in a vortex of confusion, the old lady felt herself being helped out of her chair and into her coat. The next thing she knew, she was being escorted to the estate agent's car.

Miss Forgetmenot had not been inside any form of private transport in over twenty years and was immediately overawed by the nice Mr Filch's Range Rover. Filch made sure the old lady was seat belted and comfortable, then drove away from the house and headed in the same direction as Kneecap and Sherbert's van.

Several minutes later the Range Rover passed the white Transit van and, so as not to alert his passenger he did not sound his horn but instead flashed the rear fog lamps.

"There they go," said Charlie. The van spun around in the road and headed back to Romany Way. When they reached the cottage, Kneecap jumped out, carrying a supermarket bag. Filch had made sure to slam the door behind him when they left, for the benefit of Miss Forgetmenot, but he had slipped the catch, allowing it to be opened by his accomplices.

Kneecap furtively entered the house. Once inside he took several lengths of black ribbon and a wreath out of the plastic bag. He draped the black ribbon over the mantelpiece, the windowsill, and the curtain pelmet. The last of the ribbon was used to surround a photograph of Miss Forgetmenot.

Before leaving, Kneecap hung the wreath over a coat hook on the inside of the front door, which he then carefully opened. Making sure he was unobserved, Kneecap quietly shut the door behind him, again making sure it was on the latch. He then walked briskly to the van and got inside. The three men drove away to disappear into the streets of Bogham.

'We welcome Miss Forgetmenot' was written in large letters on a long, white banner. The banner was stretched between the two marble columns that flanked the entrance to the Ingletimber Residential Home for Gentlefolk. A red carpet had been laid down, leading up the steps to the reception hall.

Enoch Filch arrived at the home and turned into its tree-lined driveway The Range Rover slowly approached the large, white building, allowing Miss Forgetmenot time to take in the splendour of its surroundings.

Sonny Patel walked down the steps to greet the arriving visitor whilst Enoch Filch manoeuvred the vehicle to a position where his passenger would step out on to the red carpet. The old lady was warmly welcomed by Patel and a nurse. The owner fussed and fawned on his very special guest, helping her up the steps to the entrance.

As Miss Forgetmenot entered the building with the ebullient Mr Patel, another uniformed assistant presented her with a beautiful bouquet of flowers. She was then shown into a very large guest room where she was introduced to a group of residents who, knowing nothing of the visitor's circumstances, welcomed her as though she was about to take up residence.

The other residents were all approximately the same age as Miss Forgetmenot and, steered by Filch and Patel, she was soon deep in conversation with them. When Filch was certain she was relaxed and happy he stood up and made his apologies to leave.

"Dear lady, ladies and gentlemen, it is nearly two o'clock. I'm afraid I have some urgent business to attend to. Once I have dealt with this tedious matter I will come back to collect Miss Forgetmenot and take her back home. In the meantime," added Filch, smiling and addressing the group, and the old lady in particular, "I have arranged for you to take high tea in these salubrious surroundings." Filch noticed that the old lady did not seem taken aback by his departure.

"Good," he thought, "it's beginning to work." He turned to leave adding, "I will return at seven o'clock this evening. Goodbye Miss Forgetmenot for the moment." Filch left the residential hotel and drove back to his office. Once there, he made a phone call to Charlie's drinking club.

"Oi, Charlie! Phone!" shouted the barman.

"Hello?" said Charlie, furtively. "Yeah ... all done, doors unlocked ... Yeah, right ... See ya!" He put the phone down and returned to drink with his cronies.

Like a teenager anticipating a first date, Enoch Filch waited nervously in his office for the Hobbs to arrive. He was wracked with doubt. Surely with all that money they didn't have to wait for a property, and this one was in serious need of repair. He weighed up Harriet's apparent enthusiasm against the cold, hard logic of the situation. One thing was for certain, he was taking a gamble.

The appointed hour of his meeting with the Hobbs came and went. By 3.15 they had still not arrived. Filch was suffering with a strained neck from looking out of the window, as well as nervous hypertension. Hot and cold flushes swept over him as he contemplated failure.

The doorbell to his office rang, Filch leapt into the air and rushed to the window. There was no sign of a blue Jaguar. He strode to the door with mounting anger; he did not want to see anyone at this particular moment. He flung open the door.

"Yes! What is it, I'm … so pleased you could make it," said Enoch Filch as he came face to face with Henry and Harriet Hobbs. "I … I didn't see your car outside."

"We got a cab," said Henry. Harriet smiled politely, even though she was furious with Henry, for their new car was suffering from a burnt-out coil.

"Do you have a problem with your motor car?" enquired Filch.

"No!" said Harriet sharply.

"Yeah," said Henry. "The blasted coil's knackered! I'd better watch out, eh, in case the car gets pregnant! Ho, ho!" joked Henry, trying to lighten Harriet's dark mood. Harriet however, was definitely not at all amused.

"You're a pillock, 'Enry 'Obbs! Why ever didn't you buy a new one?" hissed Harriet under her breath.

Filch put on his coat and prepared to leave. "Oh well, no harm done. These things happen," he said, understandingly.

Led by the estate agent, the Hobbs climbed into Filch's Range Rover. He apologised for his vehicle's condition, flattering them by referring to the worthiness of their own beautiful, if temporarily incapacitated, Jaguar. The Range Rover sped to Romany Way, with Enoch Filch briefing the Hobbs's on the history of

RomanyWay (not that he knew it) and of why they would reap the benefits of living at such a unique address.

They arrived. Harriet got out of the vehicle and instantly fell in love with the cottage, which she had already made up her mind to own even before seeing it. Filch strode to the front door, which he pretended to unlock, then he stood back and bade the couple enter.

The first thing to strike the Londoner's eyes were the draped black, funereal ribbons. Harriet nudged Henry's elbow and gestured towards the photo of Miss Forgetmenot.

"Was that the old dear who lived 'ere then?" asked Henry. Harriet leant over to her husband and whispered in his ear. She then nudged him again, urging him to speak. "Um, The missus wants to know like ... well ... she didn't ... like ... die here, you know? Like ... in the house?" asked Henry as delicately as he could.

"Oh good gracious no! The unfortunate lady passed peacefully away in the arms of her loved ones at a nursing home near here," lied Filch.

"Well who put all that stuff in 'ere then?" asked Harriet.

"The deceased's housekeeper and friend placed them as a mark of respect before she left the area," added Filch in a sanctimonious tone. "Now, let me show you the rest of the house and the extensively nurtured garden."

Enoch Filch took the couple on a thorough tour of the property. The estate agent masterfully lied his way through several observations the Hobbs had made, such as why all the old lady's possessions were still in the house.

Despite the obvious amount of work needed to restore the property, Harriet was already sold on the idea of living at Number One RomanyWay. As they went from room to room, her imagination was happily shopping for matching curtains, bedspreads, carpets and wallpaper.

"The place is a dump!" observed Henry, whispering in Harriet's ear. Harriet – who had still not forgiven Henry for embarrassing her earlier in the 'Get out, it's not going to start' episode – was infuriated with her husband.

"Excuse me, Mr Filch, I would lake a word in prayvate with may husbond," said Eliza Harriet Doolittle Hobbs.

"Of course, dear lady," said Filch, as he stepped out of the room they were in and quietly closed the door.

Harriet looked at the door and then grabbed Henry.

"Now you look 'ere 'Enry miserable skinflint pisshead 'Obbs. Just you remember who paid for that flippin' lottery ticket. I want this 'ouse! And for once in my life I'm gonna have what I want! If you don't like it you can sod off back to London – me and Little 'Arry is gonna live 'ere. You 'ear me 'Enry 'Obbs? We're gonna live 'ere – right 'ere!"

For a fraction of a second, Henry saw himself sitting in his frayed and battered armchair watching the 2:45 race from Goodwood. In his vision, the room was stocked from floor to ceiling with cans of lager, whilst a blonde girl with huge breasts wearing a French maid's outfit stood nearby with a tray of pork scratchings, assorted rolling tobacco, and green papers. The moment passed and Henry returned to reality. That reality was – even though he would not have readily admitted it – that he was actually very contented with his lot in life. He couldn't and wouldn't contemplate life without Harriet and Harry. Well, not for ever.

"All right, all right, keep yer 'air on woman! If you wannit so much we'll 'ave it, I'll tell the geezer. Flippin' 'eck!" Henry called Enoch Filch, who returned instantly (having been listening outside the door) and resumed the guided tour.

There was only one unfortunate incident during the remaining part of the tour. As they were passing through the kitchen to view the garden, a horrific, mutant ginger cat appeared from behind the cooker. Its face had pieces of a black shell-like substance plastered all over it, and it appeared that its brains were dribbling out of its head.

"YAAEEEEK!" screamed Harriet.

Snaps took one look at the strange people and fled in panic through the hated cat flap. The remnants of the huge dead beetle had congealed on his head and dried into his fur like concrete. A week had passed since his encounter with the horrific insect and he still had not managed to rid himself of all its remains.

"What on earth was it?" trembled Harriet.

"I don't know!" said Filch, genuinely surprised, "but don't you worry, dear lady, I'll have it dealt with … whatever it was!"

The tour of the house was finally complete and they had returned to the front room.

"Well there we are," said Filch tapping a finger on his pursed lips.

"'Ow much?" asked Henry directly.

"Er, um …well … I … The property is a little dilapidated; it could do with a small lick of paint here and there," said Filch.

"Don't take me for a plonker mate. The place is a flamin' dump! It needs thousands spent on it. 'Ow much?" replied Henry smartly.

"W … well …not a dump … certainly not a dump! Besides, I do have some other buyers interested in this…"

"'Ow much?" repeated Henry, interrupting Filch.

"Three hundred thousand," announced Enoch Filch in an instant, swindling reflex action.

"Th … three hundred.." shouted Henry at the top of his voice, but before he could finish repeating the amount he was kicked in the shin by his wife.

"Aaah! Blimey, Hat, that 'urt! All right! Listen moosh, you've got a deal if you fix the place up – proper like, understand? Savvy?"

"Why of course, Mr Hobbs, Mrs Hobbs. Nothing would give me more pleasure! Oh, how wonderful to think that you will soon be living amongst us here in Bogham." Enoch Filch grabbed the man's hand, and shook it vigorously. He, Enoch Filch, would become the stuff of legends throughout the drinking halls of West Sussex after pulling off this deal!"

The estate agent drove the couple back to their chalet at Maislins. He arranged for all the paperwork to be sent to them at their London address, then made his apologies and departed.

Filch drove rapidly back to Number One Romany Way and entered through the unlocked door. He swiftly removed the wreath and the black ribbon. He then opened several windows, pulled the aerial out of the back of the television and set to work replacing several healthy light bulbs with blown ones that he had brought with him. Filch also entered the old lady's toilet and removed nearly all the toilet paper from the roll.

When he was satisfied that life would not be very comfortable in the house, he left, carrying incriminating evidence in a plastic bag.

"Charlie Wollock! Phone ... again!" shouted the barman at the Fort Baxter, the drinking club frequented by the painter and decorator. Charlie picked up the phone.

"Yeah ... Phwor! ...Good one! ...Yeah ... Half past nine? ... Okay ...See ya!" Charlie went back to the bar with a huge grin plastered across his face.

Enoch Filch returned to the rest home to collect their honoured guest.

"Dear lady, I'm so sorry to have kept you. I do hope you have been well looked after," Enoch Filch enquired ultra-politely of Miss Forgetmenot as she sat amongst her new-found friends. The old lady was indeed very content. It was now ten minutes past seven in the evening. Once she had started reminiscing with the others, time had simply flown by. The atmosphere in the residential hotel was warm and friendly; she hadn't known such conversation for years.

Filch apologised again, but informed her that he had to return her to Romany Way. Miss Forgetmenot said goodbye to her new friends and made her way, clutching her bouquet, to Filch's Range Rover.

Half an hour later she was back in her living room. The house felt damp and cold, and the old lady discovered that several light bulbs were not working. The helpful Filch found a spare bulb in the kitchen and replaced one of the blown ones. He then made her a cup of tea and drew up a chair beside her.

Filch then explained the situation she was in. By giving the awful bailiffs a cheque for Charlie Wollock's bill, she was now clear of her debt. He had brought her home and had a cheque for twenty-three thousands pounds made out in her favour.

"Unfortunately, dear lady – much as I regret it – I shall, however, have to sell this house, as I have to recoup the money I have spent on your behalf."

The old lady listened to the kindly Filch and understood the dire situation in which she now found herself. Miss Forgetmenot had one very important question to ask Mr Filch which, considering what he had done for her, seemed almost too selfish to ask!

"M... Mr Filch, I don't like to bother you b ... but where do I go from here?" she asked apologetically.

"Well now," said Filch excitedly, "perhaps this afternoon could give us some ideas on that score. Did you enjoy yourself this afternoon at the residential hotel?"

"Oh yes, Mr Filch, I had a wonderful time, simply wonderful!" replied Miss Forgetmenot, breaking into a smile despite her worries.

"In that case I think I have some good news for you: I happen to know that they have a vacancy," he said.

Enoch Filch put the last stitches into his carefully embroidered subterfuge, explaining that she could never buy a property for twenty-three thousand pounds. He went on to tell her about the available suite at the Ingletimber Residential Hotel and of the facilities available to her.

"Why don't you think about it overnight," said Filch. "It would not be right to rush you, dear lady. However, I would point out that such a room will be in great demand…" And this was his parting shot as he took his leave of the lonely Miss Forgetmenot.

Filch drove home, changed, showered, ate a quick snack and telephoned for a taxi to take him to the Fresh Ferret. By nine thirty, when Charlie Wollock came in to the pub, Filch was already on his third gin and tonic. He welcomed his colleague with much back-slapping and congratulations. After Charlie had received a pint of ale from Filch, the pair sat in their usual darkened corner.

"Two weeks' work, I think it was?" asked Filch. "For you and your young spotty friend, correct?" he continued.

"Yeah … I had a lot of expenses to pay out you know, Enoch: petrol, gear an' that."

The estate agent pulled a fat, brown envelope from his coat pocket and slipped it quickly across the table. He invited Charlie to inspect the contents. Charlie Wollock was preparing himself for the expected underpayment.

"Blimey!" Charlie whispered loudly, his eyes widening.

"Enough is it, dear boy?" enquired Filch in a supercilious tone.

"Cor, yes … yes! Blimey! Cheers Enoch, nice one!" smiled Charlie. He settled back in his chair and tried to remember if he knew any other old ladies who lived on their own in big houses?

"To the next storm," proposed Filch with a sly grin.

"To the next storm!" seconded Charlie, enthusiastically.

CHAPTER NINE

THE APPALLING CRIME
OF 'ARRY 'OBBS

THE APPALLING CRIME
OF 'ARRY 'OBBS

MISS FORGETMENOT GENTLY CLOSED THE DOOR as Enoch Filch walked away from the cottage. She shuffled cautiously back through the dimly-lit rooms of her home. The warmth and happiness she had shared all afternoon with her new-found friends made the silent emptiness of the house almost over-whelming. She went into the front room to turn on her television; at least that would provide the comfort of fellow human voices.

The television crackled and hissed into life as a gradual, grey light brightened into a snow of fizzing white dots and lines. Miss Forgetmenot changed the channel again and again, but the result was always the same unpleasant hiss, with no picture. Despairing of the faulty television, the old lady moved across the room and switched on her ancient radio, only to find out that it was not working either!

After switching off those lights that still functioned, she decided to go to bed. Miss Forgetmenot wearily climbed the stairs to her bedroom. The stairway light was, she thought, thankfully working, but when she switched on the light in her bedroom nothing happened. She groped her way across the cold, damp room until she found her night-clothes at the end of the bed.

Outside, in the night sky above her garden, ragged clouds were moving across the moon. The little statue of the god Pan was slowly covered in deep shadow as the garden was lost to the dark.

Miss Forgetmenot was soon asleep in dreams of warmth and friendship, cucumber sandwiches and cream teas, day trips and beetle drives, bingo nights and conversation.

Sunday morning dawned grey, wet and blustery. The wind swept across Maislins as the Hobbs family prepared to leave for London in their car – now fitted with its new coil.

Charlie Wollock would not wake for a further six hours. He was suffering the after-effects of a severe case of body abuse that had involved drinking nearly two crates of Fresh Ferret Ale. Enoch Filch, professional drinker, had exercised more caution the previous night and was consequently awake and alert early on Sunday. He had much to do, and he was going to enjoy doing it.

The Hobbs's arrived back in London without incident and were relieved to find the contents of their flat in one piece. This was not that surprising as a 24-hour guard had been placed on the humble apartment by the Lottery company, Tintagel. Once home, Harriet set about filling in various forms sent to her by Enoch Filch and the local borough council (who had been informed of the Hobbs's new financial situation and were anxious to recover their council flat).

Miss Forgetmenot walked slowly and stiffly to open her front door. The damp and cold of the house had aggravated her rheumatism and walking had become painful. Enoch Filch greeted the old lady and comiserated with her over the various troubles she was experiencing, both physical and electrical. He then spent the best part of an hour explaining the various options regarding accommodation that were left open to her.

Filch had brought a small file of information on vile bedsits, virtually uninhabitable slums and condemned hovels. He went on to add that if she was to buy one of the described 'accommodations' she would be left with little if any money. Filch described in depressing detail how, because of her age, she would have great difficulty in persuading anyone to rent her a property, and in any case the only rented properties in and around the area were expensive and on third, fourth, and in some cases, fifth and sixth floors. Filch spread the file across a table and then played his masterstroke.

"Of course, dear lady, I know how much you value your peace and quiet, and at least you would be alone in any of these accommodations …" Filch paused to look at the reaction on the old lady's crestfallen face. "Otherwise I would have suggested you take the vacant suite in the luxurious Ingletimber address, which ironically you could afford," he continued.

Miss Forgetmenot stared at the array of photographs. She thought of the decaying house, which was deteriorating rapidly despite all that money spent on repairs. She thought of the damp, the cold, the loneliness, her age and her fading health, then in a momentous decision she said, "Mr Filch, could I really live at the Ingletimber res…?"

"Of course, of course," Filch interrupted her before she could finish the question. "It is the obvious choice for anyone in your predicament. I hesitated to press you before as I didn't think you would be too keen on mixing with all those other ladies and gentlemen." Filch scooped up all the paperwork he had brought with him and stuffed it back in the file.

It was the penultimate piece in his scheming jigsaw puzzle plan. He would now organise the removal of the possessions that were dear to her from the cottage to the nursing home. The remainder he would sell off, the profit from which would go to Sonny Patel and himself.

The old lady found herself totally in his hands. She gave him *carte blanche* with respect to her affairs. The trap had closed.

A week later the world had become a very different place for Enoch Filch, Charlie Wollock, Miss Forgetmenot, the Hobbs family and Snaps the cat.

Miss Forgetmenot had settled into her new room at the Ingletimber Residential Hotel for Gentlefolk. There had been only one setback and that was the sad matter of her beloved cat. The Ingletimber had a strict 'no pets' policy, which came as a bitter blow, but once again it was her saviour, the kind Mr Filch, who sprang to the rescue. He explained that a very good and kind friend of his owned a cattery, and he was quite sure that Snaps would find the very best of homes there.

"I will return to your old house and try to find your cat. Then it's simply a matter of driving him to his new home," announced Filch. Miss Forgetmenot was won over by Filch's plan, but she still had one or two reservations.

"What is the name of your friend's cat hotel?" she asked. "Is it far? Will I be able to visit my poor little Snaps?" she continued.

Filch had to think quickly. It was trivial complications such as cats or dogs that could wreck a well-oiled confidence trick. He blurted out an answer and then winced in embarrassment, closing his eyes tightly.

"Um … er … Moggy … 'Moggy-Coddled'. The name, er … of the cattery is 'Moggy-Coddled' … and it's only two or three miles from here." He opened one eye and looked at her. She was smiling, seemingly content with the answer. Filch continued the deception. "So you see, I can take you to visit him regularly, and you'll never have to worry about him again," he reassured her.

The estate agent found it harder to catch the cat than to swindle the old lady out of her property. Snaps had eventually managed to rid himself of the last remnants of dead water beetle and, apart from his cauterised tail, looked once again like an ordinary cat. However, he never had taken kindly to strangers and the traumas he had suffered recently had made him even more nervous.

Filch eventually caught the half-starved animal by leaving a trail of titbits from the garden into the kitchen. He watched from the side of the house as Snaps moved slowly towards and then in through the cat flap. Filch rushed to the door and jammed the flap with a piece of wood.

After half an hour of swearing, stumbling and incompetent rugby tackles, Filch managed to grab the hissing, spitting, scratching, biting animal and confine it to a cat basket. He slung the wicker basket into the back of the Range Rover and, sucking the blood from the back of his scratched hand, got in and drove away. It was seven o'clock in the evening and it had started to rain.

An hour later he was half way to London and in the depths of a wealdland forest. The Range Rover pulled into a lay-by and stopped. Filch jumped out and waited for a few moments until he was confident that he was unobserved. He lifted the vehicle's tailgate and removed the cat basket, which he opened. Snaps tore out of his prison as though fired from a catapult, running as fast as he could and leaping into the welcoming cover of some thick woodland fern. He watched the distant figure of Filch disappear into the vehicle and turn back towards Bogham. When he was sure it was safe, Snaps emerged from his hiding place and looked around. The forest was dark, wet and silent. He sat down on a patch of soft moss, scratched his ear with his back leg and looked at the surrounding darkness. It was getting late on that Sunday evening, the rain was swirling through the trees. Snaps sighed and his shoulders drooped as he surveyed the surrounding landscape. "Where the hell am I?" he wondered.

He had a wretched day and spent hours walking through wet and tangled undergrowth trying to find his way home until he eventually found a place he recognised. Unfortunately, it was the soft mound of moss that he had started from. Snaps sat down to think. The first thing he thought of was that he was going to die of hunger; he hadn't heard anything, no mice, no birds, there weren't even any tasty fairies in this wood...

But there were elves! Two of them sat high in a tree directly above the cat. The storm had spared this part of Sussex, and although the foliage was beginning to turn to its Autumn hue, there was still plenty of it. The first elf held an acorn, his colleague held a large, ripe Blackberry. The elf with the acorn held his hand out and released it directly over the cat; a second later the other elf released the Blackberry.

The acorn hit the cat on the back of his neck. In a swift reflex action, Snaps looked up to see where the object had come from, and received the Blackberry straight in the face. The blur of the ginger cat streaked through the dark forest just above ground level! Snaps didn't care where he was going just as long as it took him out of the ghastly place.

Eventually he emerged exhausted on to the side of a main road. He sat for a while and decided to follow the road downhill. Luckily for Snaps, it was the right decision, for the road would eventually lead him home.

THE NEXT MORNING, Enoch Filch received a telephone call from Harriet Hobbs. She informed him that a banker's transaction was being arranged so that he could instigate repair work to the cottage. She also informed Filch that she and the rest of the family were off on a world cruise and would be gone for two months.

Filch made a telephone call to a local firm of builders and arranged for them to start immediate renovations on Number One Romany Way. He knew that this firm was not of the Charlie Wollock variety. They would not be cheap, but they would get the job done satisfactorily.

There was an atmosphere of foreboding under the Rockery. The feeling of unease had even permeated the great hall of the gnomes. The fairies, goblins, elves and pixies had been making their usual nightly forays in search of food but with little success. More disturbing was the fact that the old lady had completely ceased to leave out their regular titbits. They noticed too that the house appeared to be empty; even the troublesome cat had vanished.

Life for the fairy folk finally changed on the Tuesday morning when a rumbling sound shook pieces of earth and grit from the ceilings of their Rockery rooms. The rumbling grew louder as a fleet of lorries, vans and builders' vehicles arrived at Number One Romany Way. Soon the whole site was a thoroughfare for builders, plumbers, electricians, roofers and half a hundred other artisans.

When Snaps the cat eventually reached his home at the end of that week, he thought at first that he had made a mistake because the house had been transformed into a building site. When at last he realised that it was indeed his home, he fell into a pit of despair. Where was his mistress, his bed, and most important of all, his food? He hurriedly left the turmoil of the building and headed for the fields beyond the houses, where he lived wild for the next few months.

Wild, for the bewildered cat, meant exactly that, wild! The refugee pussy cat soon discovered that the popular impression of the peaceful English countryside given by calendar photographs and suchlike was a sham. The 'paradise' of rustic Sussex was teeming with zoological maniacs!

The first problem the evicted cat faced was that of shelter, and he soon found that every inviting outhouse or farm building had its own resident psycho-cat who would instantly appear in a hissing, claw-slashing fury. In his search for shelter, Snaps was chased by dogs, assaulted by a badger, mobbed by birds and in one nasty incident, chased by a huge dog fox. Most humiliating of all, he was 'mistaken' by a large buck rabbit who must have had an eyesight problem! It was a lucky escape – Snaps did not stop running for a mile!

After much searching he eventually found a shelter of sorts: an old, hollow tree in which he sat for hours, contemplating his wretched existence. For food, the cat managed on a frugal diet of small birds and the occasional vole or field mouse, but mostly by raiding farmhouse dustbins and by eating disgusting dead things he found lying around in the fields.

While Snaps was living an enforced exile in the adjacent fields, the fairy folk of Number One Romany Way lived in constant fear of the same upheaval that had driven the cat away. Wazzark and the rest of them watched as hoards of humans descended on the old lady's former cottage in a frenzy of activity. Food-gathering became increasingly difficult during this time. It was almost impossible to venture out during the day for fear of being seen. Because the old lady no longer handed out goodies, they had to forage further afield, which meant risking 'close encounters of the worst kind' – with dogs and humans.

The noise of machinery kept them awake during the day and humans would often wander over the Rockery and around the now-unkempt garden. The fairy folk lived in constant fear that they would be discovered at any moment.

The unwanted intrusions to their domain had one or two advantages, however. As long as they were careful not to be spotted, foraging had a number of bonuses, especially as the workmen had created a huge pile of unwanted material – unwanted by them, but very useful for the Rockery inhabitants. The number of half-eaten, abandoned packed lunches came as a pleasant surprise.

Wazzark would arrange for a pair of the inhabitants to set out on the evening forage about an hour after the last workman had gone. During one memorable occasion on a September evening when Effans and Elfie had been dispatched to search for provisions, some workmen returned unexpectedly from a local pub. They had left some gear unsecured in the garden and had returned to lock it up. Just in time, the two elves leapt for cover in some bushes half way between the pond and the house. One of the men walked away from his mates and headed towards the bushes. Elfie was a few feet away from Effans. He watched in horror as the man walked to the exact spot where the Welsh elf was hiding. He could almost hear Effan's teeth chattering in terror as the human stood directly over him.

"What's he doing?" wondered Elfie. Then he saw what the workman was doing! The Scottish elf slapped his hand tightly over his mouth and pinched his thigh painfully with his other hand as he desperately tried not to laugh, for it would have been a disaster if he had been heard. Elfie nearly choked as he watched the human directing a stream of urine onto the red-headed, bespectacled figure hiding in the bush below him. The man turned and walked away, totally unaware of what he had done.

Elfie wouldn't have missed it for the world! With tears streaming from his eyes, he pointed at the aghast Welsh elf and doubled up with laughter. Effans stood stock still, his mouth and eyes tightly closed and a look of unadulterated horror on his wrinkled face. As soon as he realised he was safe, he blundered out of the bushes, ran to the pond and pitched head first into the weed-covered water in a desperate effort to cleanse himself!

It was an incident that encapsulated the whole unfortunate situation for the fairy folk of Romany Way. They appeared to be helpless as insensitive human beings continued to defile their world.

The situation deteriorated for them as the renovation work continued into the autumn. They had thoughts of quitting their Rockery home altogether, but that was fraught with difficulty and besides they all loved the old place so very much. It couldn't go on for ever, they decided, things had to improve – and for a while, they did.

September became October, then November arrived with a crisp, frosty morning over Romany Way. The building work was complete and the Hobbs family, fresh from their world cruise, were finally settled in their new home.

The Hobbs family now included their black and white cat, Jackson ('wittily' named by Henry because, like a certain well-known celebrity, it wasn't clear if the cat was more white than black or vice versa). Jackson soon became accustomed to his new surroundings and very quickly caused havoc amongst the local wildlife. The fairy folk, aware of his presence, made sure to keep well out of his way.

Mrs Harriet Hobbs, having completed the interior design of her new home, decided to turn her attention to the sprawling back garden. She hired some landscape gardeners who set about the beautification of the area with all the delicate finesse of Jack the Ripper.

Harry Hobbs wasn't too interested in the activities of the garden designers. He was only interested in hunting; that is shooting anything that moved with a high-powered air rifle. The boy's safari antics soon landed him in trouble with the gardeners, who took a dim view of air gun pellets zipping past them as they were trying to work.

Exasperated by the mad sniper, they decided to complain to Harriet about the boy's behaviour. Harriet took the criticism personally as an attack on her baby boy and dismissed the gardeners on the spot. The next team of gardeners who were hired suffered the same fate, and by the following spring the grass and weeds were spreading unchecked. Harriet had a problem, for she soon found she had been boycotted by all the local gardeners.

"Who do these people think they are?" shouted Harriet to Henry, who was watching an Australian soap opera on the television.

"What people?" grunted Henry.

"Gardeners! I can't get any gardeners to mow the lawn and do the weeding," she replied indignantly.

"Get 'Arry to do it then," said Henry.

"Wha?" exclaimed Harry, who was oiling his semi-automatic turbo-powered Lee-Enfield air rifle with infra-red telescopic sights. "I'm not going to mow the lawn!" he screamed.

"You'll do as you're bloody told, boy!" barked Henry.

"Don't you swear at my son," retaliated Harriet angrily. "If 'e doesn't want to mow the lawn he don't 'ave to! You get off your lazy backside 'Enry 'Obbs. You get out there and sort out the garden!"

Henry instantly forgot about the television programme. The conversation had suddenly become unpleasant with the introduction of the subject of hard work.

"Me!?" he coughed. "Mow the lawn? You've got to be jokin'! As far as I'm concerned you can tarmac the whole flippin' lot!"

"Now you listen to me," started Harriet, the words which were usually the prelude to a full-blown row.

"Yeah! An' I can have a rollerboot park, and a BMX track? Brilliant, Dad!" interrupted Harry.

"Is that what you want then, darling?" asked his mother, instantly changing her tone.

"Right lad! I'll sort it out in the morning," proclaimed Henry in an unusually warm and affectionate tone.

"Don't you think you've charmed yer way out of that, 'Enry 'Obbs. I know your game. You just make sure you get 'Arry what he wants – you 'ear me?"

"Yes dear!" replied Henry meekly, since he felt – not without good reason – that he could afford to be gracious.

Harry Hobbs rushed out into the back garden to look at where his BMX track and skateboard park were going to be. He ran around the lawn in the twilight, kicking the heads off several chrysanthemums. With arms outstretched he ran down the garden towards the pond. He was a stealth fighter as he flew to the edge of the pond and landed. Harry threw some stones into the water for a while before his attention was caught by the little statue of Pan.

The boy looked at the statue in a puzzled way. He had noticed it there before but had not really paid any attention to it. Now, he began to wonder about the little goat-man. What sort of creature was it supposed to be? It looked weird with its stupid, bent goat legs and curly horns he thought. At that moment, he decided he didn't like it. It never occurred to Harry that he might not always get his own way. If he didn't like it, it would not stay in his garden. He kicked it hard and stamped down on it, knocking the figure off its pedestal.

A tiny, almost indiscernible, tremor spread through every living organism in the garden, a tremor so small that it was hardly felt by anyone. Harry felt a shiver run up his back; it was getting chilly! At the same time he heard his mother calling.

"'Arry... 'Arry, come in, yer suppers ready." Harry Hobbs bent down and picked up the little bronze figure by its left leg, swung it around his head and, in a catastrophic piece of ill-judgement, hurled the little statue over his head and out of the garden. The little god flew over the bramble hedge into the waste ground next to the garden. With a thud and a splash it landed in a muddy puddle.

"Bombs away!" yelled Harry as he took off again and flew his last mission of the day back to base.

Another tremor, this time stronger than the last, shivered through the twilight air, causing a mesh of tiny ripples on the pond.

"Whoa, somethin' just walked over me grave!" exclaimed Cousin Moykle as he came out of the room heading for the great hall of the gnomes. Several adjoining doors opened and he was joined by the others who had been awoken.

"What wassat?" asked Podfudger.

"You felt it too, then?" asked Wazzark.

The three entered the hall and were soon joined by everyone else. They had all experienced the strange tremor. Something, they all agreed, had occurred; something ominous which they couldn't understand.

Elfie and Effans had been chosen to go scavenging that evening. The others wished them luck as the two elves set off, each carrying a haversack. They walked out of the tunnel and down from the Rockery in silence. The two were conscious that something was amiss.

"Keep yer eyes peeled fer that bastard cat, Effans," whispered Elfie.

"Don't you worry, boy. I'll let you know all right if I see it."

Elfie couldn't help thinking that Effans' eyesight was so appalling that by the time the Welsh Elf had seen Jackson, it would probably have eaten him.

"C'mon Effans, we'll try next door's dustbins first – we might get lucky."

"I bloody hope so! I'm starving," complained Effans. They walked along the path beside the pond and were about to head off across the rough grass when Effans stopped dead in his tracks.

"Bloody 'ell!" he exclaimed.

Elfie swiftly and instinctively crouched down. If Effans had seen the dreaded cat, that was just the sort of noise which would bring it straight towards them. What was Effans up to? "Where?… Where is it?" he hissed.

"I dunno boy … That's it, isn't it!" said Effans.

"What da ya mean ya don't know?" growled Elfie.

"Well it's not there!" said Effans in a puzzled voice.

Elfie stood up and snarled at the Welsh elf. "Effans! What the #!!**! are ye gabberin on aboot? I thought ye'd seen that dratted cat. What isn'a there?"

"The statue of his Lordship. It's gone!"

Elfie looked around and back to the place where the little man usually stood. He realised with some embarrassment that he hadn't even noticed the statue's absence.

"*#!!#*#!!?? Yer raight!" exclaimed Elfie. "C'mon, Effans, we've gotta get back to tell the others!" The elves ran hurriedly back to the Rockery and down into the tunnel. They arrived in such breathless haste that the others soon gathered that they had some exciting news to tell.

"Well it can't just have disappeared," said Wazzark. "Are you sure it wasn't blown into the pond?"

"That's an oidea! Maybe de little fellahs gone to foind me poipe?" said Cousin Moykle.

"Wud ye shuttup aboot yer paipe, ya fat bastard!" shouted Elfie, who still hadn't forgiven the Leprechaun for treading on his prize sausage and was apt to find any occasion to argue with him.

"Oi tink you an' oi better step outside!" exclaimed Cousin Moykle as he formed two fists and started to weave about like a boxer.

"All right, all right, pack it up, you two!" insisted Wazzark sternly. "We've got enough problems without you two pratting about! Ghisette, Elliel, Mirithin, you have the best chance of finding it. Go and search the garden ... and keep an eye open for that Jackson."

The fairies had taken up residence beneath the Rockery whilst Elliel recovered fully from her terrible ordeal. They were intending to return to their apple tree, but with the upheavals in and around the house they decided it was safer under the Rockery, which is where they stayed throughout that winter. Now Ghisette led her sisters cautiously out of the tunnel. She looked very carefully before emerging into the open, for whereas Snaps had been just dangerous, the new cat was psychotic.

Ghisette flew up into the dark, followed closely by Mirithin and Elliel, and for half an hour they searched the garden for the little bronze statue. They found nothing. After a while, their wings began to get weary and Ghisette was beginning to think they would have to stop for a rest.

It was Elliel who heard the voices first. Two Hedgehogs were deep in conversation on the other side of the overgrown bramble hedge. Ghisette soared up into the cold evening air and looked down on the adjoining waste ground. She spotted the two hedgehogs standing next to a muddy puddle, discussing an object that was lying in the middle of it. Ghisette descended until she was close enough to the enigmatic object to recognise it as the missing statue. The fairies lost no time in returning to the Rockery with news of their discovery.

"Upside down in a puddle?" gasped Wazzark.

"How did it get there?" asked Podfudger.

"Never mind how it got there. We've got to get it back!" said Wazzark.

Cousin Moykle and Elfie had made up their differences, and were standing at the bar, drinking and listening to the discussion.

"That's sacrilege, that uz," Elfie called across the room. "We gotta get the wee man back."

"You're right," agreed Wazzark. "But it's going to take all of us to lift it – that statue is made of solid bronze."

In the dark, quiet of the cold spring air, the fairy folk moved quietly through the lush new undergrowth until they had reached the puddle. They set about removing the statue with the aid of a large crowbar and bundles of string. After much heaving and straining, the statue was finally pulled free from the gluey mud. Working swiftly, the residents of the Rockery used the same string and some pieces of wood to construct a cradle for the little bronze man to lie in. Apart from Effans stumbling over Elfie's foot and falling face down into the mud, they managed to drag the statue back into the garden without any major incidents.

Once the statue had been safely recovered, Wazzark and Elfie decided to hide it under a cover of some grass and hay. The goblin didn't know how the little man had come to be in the puddle, but it was obvious that it was an act of desecration and that they had to try and prevent it happening again.

With the goat-man hidden close to the roots of a large hawthorn tree, the fairy folk returned to the Rockery. Many glasses of ale and cider were drunk, and many fingers pointed at the mad Welsh mud-man as they celebrated the statue's rescue.

The next morning began quietly, with no hint of the impending disaster that was to strike the garden. The milk float clinked and rattled along Romany Way. The squeak of the postman's bicycle came and went, as did the early chatter of school children trudging their way to school.

The rumble started just after nine o'clock. Once again, the inhabitants below the Rockery were awoken by pieces of rock and plaster falling from the ceilings. The rumbling grew to a thunder that caused real fear amongst the residents.

"What da hell's dat awful noise?" cried the leprechaun, hopping around on one leg as he tried to put on his other shoe. Wazzark, who was already dressed, rushed up the tunnel and carefully looked out. The noise was now deafening but he could see nothing amiss.

"What is it?" asked Podfudger as he joined his friend.

"I dunno ... I can't see. Wait, look! What's that?" Wazzark pointed towards the house. Puffs of blue exhaust smoke were belching out from behind the roadside hedge. The Goblins watched in amazement as the overgrown hedge began to bulge into the garden before splitting and rolling under an advancing wall of shining steel. Having bludgeoned its way through the hedge, the machine turned towards the lawn. Great metal tracks clanked across the new-grown grass as the huge machine continued its advance.

"It's a tank!" cried Podfudger, who had once had a lucky escape whilst walking across a military firing range at Aldershot, where he had nearly been blown to bits!

"Worse than that," said Wazzark in a low voice, "it's a bull-dozer!"

The pair watched the great red and black bulldozer grind to a halt, as another huge machine crashed through the gap in the hedge.

"What's that thing then?" asked Podfudger.

"It's a tractor, an excavator!" said Wazzark with alarm. "I don't like this, Podfudger ol' mate … I don't like this at all!" he muttered between gritted teeth.

The machines stopped on the lawn by the house, whilst the two drivers received their work instructions from a third man. Harriet and Henry Hobbs watched the events from a bedroom window.

In a roar of diesel smoke, the bulldozer began to clank its way across the lawn. Turning towards the pond, it lowered its shovel-like blade and began to push up tons of turf and topsoil as it advanced down the garden. The machine was slowly pushing a wave of earth and debris towards the pond – and the Rockery.

"Oh no!" cried Wazzark. "C'mon we've got to get everyone out of here!" The goblins scampered back down the tunnel towards the great hall, Wazzark slung open the door and yelled at the others.

"Out, now! All of you, quickly!" The others sensed the fear in his voice, and without hesitation they ran or flew up the tunnel towards the daylight.

The machine had pushed a great bank of soil to within a metre of the pond. Every time it moved up and down the lawn, it added more earth to the bank until only the top of its cab could be seen from the tunnel entrance.

"Now," called Wazzark urgently. Effans, Pidwidgin and Cousin Moykle ran over the Rockery and away into the bushes and trees behind it.

"Now," repeated the goblin, as Ghisette, Mirithin, and Elliel half-flew, half-ran as fast as they could after the elf and the leprechaun. The fairies were terrified, and not just of the bulldozer and the mountain of earth. Only in extreme conditions did they ever venture out during daylight, for apart from the ever present danger of cats, there were hawks, rooks and crows to worry about and, most dangerous of all, humans (or human children to be exact).

Wazzark and Podfudger were the last to evacuate the Rockery. They ran quickly to the cover of the trees where they joined the others in watching the scene of destruction.

By noon the bulldozer had apparently finished its task for the day, for after the men had returned from their lunch it was the digger that was being used to fill a lorry with the excavated topsoil. When the workmen finally finished, a large area of the garden had been levelled. Gone were the bramble-bush homes of the birds and hedgehogs, the flower beds and the crazy-paving path; all of it had been sliced away by the bulldozer.

Wazzark was the one who seemed to be in control, to take charge of the situation. He decided that they needed to know more about what was happening to the garden, and he knew that the best person to undertake such a dangerous task was the fairy Ghisette. It would be easy for the tiny creature to slip into the cabs of the vehicles and see if she could discover any plans. Hoping she would agree – and very much afraid that she would refuse – Wazzark spoke to Ghisette, trying to make the job sound as reasonable as he could. Ghisette knew exactly how dangerous a task it was, but she also knew how vital it was that they understood what was happening. And she was a very gutsy fairy, so without hesitation, she agreed.

Elfie looked hard at Wazzark. He realised that they were coming very close to breaking the sacred law of non-intervention by fairy folk in the affairs of humans.

"Och! Wazzark, yerr sailing close ta the wind, ye ken," he warned.

"What's Elfie mean, Wazzark?" asked Podfudger.

"He means we're not supposed to interfere in human activity," replied the goblin with a stony face.

"But surely to God dis is an emergency!" said Cousin Moykle. Pidwidgin looked at the leprechaun and nodded in agreement, even though she wasn't sure why.

"I know, but still we're not supposed..." Wazzark rubbed his chin with his rough, leathery hand and thought hard about their predicament.

While this discussion was happening, Harry Hobbs had been on the beach throwing stones at seagulls when he realised that the sun had gone and that it was past his tea time. He jumped on his brand new Ninja Commando bicycle and pedalled furiously home. When he reached the cottage he saw the great hole in the hedge and the earth-moving machinery in the back garden.

"Wow!" he shouted as he stood in the middle of the large, bare patch of earth.

"'Arry 'Obbs, where on earth have you been? Yer tea was ready an hour ago!" called his mother angrily as she walked across to the boy.

"What's this, Mum! Is it for me skate park?" asked Harry excitedly, ignoring his mother's question.

"Yeah, well..." said Harriet, her mood mellowing as she saw her son's obvious excitement. "They did all this today, and tomorrow they're gonna take all this lot away, fill in that smelly pond and get rid of that pile of rocks over there. Then they'll cover it all over with tarmac and you can have yer skate park, yer DMZ track or anything yer want luv," said Harriet affectionately.

"Cor, magic! Fanks, Mum!" said Harry.

"Right now, inside and 'ave yer tea," chided Harriet.

The tiny figure of Ghisette emerged from under the tank track of the bulldozer. She had not found any clues as to what was being planned from searching the vehicles but instead had heard all she needed to know from Harriet Hobbs.

Ghisette risked flying high above the garden as she sped back to Wazzark and the others. The fairy found her friends gathered around the base of the large hawthorn tree near which they had hidden the statue. They were anxiously awaiting her report and she was quick to tell them everything she had discovered.

It was clear that the great machines had arrived to destroy their homes and surroundings! Elfie was the first to voice what he thought should be done:

"We must call on the Guardian of the Green," he announced, and silence fell on the assembled group as they all looked from one to another with worried expressions. Such an ancient rite of appeal to the supernatural overseer of all that they held dear – the garden, the fields and the forests – had to be taken very seriously. They would have to use the Invocation of Arcadia to call on the Guardian, an ancient, rarely used plea for help, an incantation invoked by fairy folk only in the gravest of circumstances.

They stood in silence for a few moments, considering the situation. They all looked to Wazzark to take the final decision. He had considered the situation carefully, and would be the first to admit that circumstances didn't come much graver than the one they were in.

"Ye've got ta do it mon," insisted Elfie.

"Oh yes indeed, boyo. He's right enough," said Effans.

"Oh God, yes, ye'd be an awful eedjut if ya didn't," agreed Cousin Moykle.

Podfudger looked at Wazzark and nodded his head in agreement with the others.

"Right, we'll do it then!" declared the goblin.

During the night, Wazzark, Podfudger, Elfie, Effans and Cousin Moykle managed to pull the little bronze goat-man into a standing position. He was actually leaning against the hawthorn tree, but that was good enough. Night gave way to the faint blue aurora of the approaching dawn. The friends stood around the statue in respectful silence. Ghisette, her sisters and several other garden Fairies produced the light for the ceremony. They began the strange chant: a low, booming noise mixed with a soft whistling, which continued for exactly three minutes. All was silent for half an hour, then the chant was repeated for another three minutes.

By that time it was daylight and the first rays of the sun were probing the clear, dawn sky – and underneath the hawthorn tree, something strange was beginning to happen...

The statue gradually began to lean forward until, unsupported, it stood completely upright. Wazzark and the others stepped back and watched a point in mid-air between them and the goat-man. The air itself was behaving strangely. It appeared as though it was becoming solid, like water spiralling down a plug hole but in reverse. Tiny pinpoints of material were flowing from the surrounding trees and bushes. Minuscule beads of a glass-like substance were being drawn to a space in front of them. To Wazzark, it looked as if coloured raindrops were 'falling' sideways and even upwards.

As this was happening in front of it, the statue itself began to change. The colour was being drawn from the metal. Wisps of bronze-tinted, mother of pearl vapour swirled into the disturbed air. The mists streaming from the statue began to build into an opaque shape, whilst behind it the once solid metal figurine had become as clear as glass. More and more material was flowing into the hovering form as it became a tangible object with a solid outline. It was the silhouette of the goat-man.

The opaque smoke rapidly solidified, turning to black. The fairy folk stared, mesmerised, into the interminable blackness and watched with amazement as it filled with stars and galaxies. Then the black, star-filled figure stepped forward. The lights inside it faded as the creature became solid with colour. A rush of air rippled and swished through the leaves and tall grass and they heard the sound of a million whispers.

"When you sail from Palodes proclaim that the great god Pan is alive," intoned the voices three times.

Podfudger looked at Wazzark, who shrugged his shoulders. Neither knew what it meant, but both presumed it was important. The rustling of the leaves stopped and the little goat-man spoke.

"Why have I been called?" he asked in a deep and authoritative, but somehow comforting voice.

Pidwidgin moved slowly behind Cousin Moykle and peeked around the leprechaun at the goat-man. She felt uneasy about the little brown figure. It wasn't just the horns and the little beard she found disturbing, or even the creature's woolly thighs and goat-like legs. It was the unusually large dangly bits in the middle that worried Pidwidgin.

Wazzark stepped forward and, removing his cap, bowed respectfully towards the little god.

"Um… er… Sir. We need your permission to dabble in a bit of magic – only we've got a big problem at the moment."

"And what is this big problem?" asked Pan.

"Well, it's like this…" continued the goblin. Wazzark went on to tell Pan of how the Hobbs were destroying the garden and explained that later in the day, the machines were intending to demolish the Rockery and fill in the pond. The little god listened patiently, showing no emotion until the goblin explained how they had found his statue in the mud. Then the little man's blue eyes turned to a red glow.

"What is the creature who has dared to do this?" asked Pan impatiently, rising to his full height and looking down at them through his flashing eyes.

"Its name is Harry Hobbs, your majesty," answered Wazzark. "It lives in the house with it's parents. Please help us. We have to stop it from destroying our homes."

Pan looked towards the great bank of earth and the newly thatched cottage roof beyond. He stroked his beard for a few moments, deep in thought.

"You have my permission," he announced solemnly. "Do whatever is necessary to teach these humans respect for my domain."

"Does that mean we can call the Boggart?" asked Wazzark in a hushed whisper.

"Yes… even the Boggart," Pan agreed solemnly. "Is there anything else?"

The goblin shook his head and bowed in thanks. The others followed Wazzark's example and they too bowed and curtsied in gracious politeness as they said goodbye. Pan stood facing them. He lifted his glittering blue eyes to the sky and began to fade, his body becoming thick smoke. In an instant there was a silent explosion and a billion tiny points of light streamed away into the surrounding trees, bushes, grass and earth. The glassy figure of the goat-man swirled with a bronze-coloured smoke until it was solid metal once more. With a soft clink, the statue fell back against the hawthorn tree.

When the little god had completely evaporated, Wazzark spoke.

"Okay everybody, you heard what he said! We're all in this, every one of us, and we've got to stop them. Queenie, take your lot and fly to the house. Use whatever magic you can, find the targets of opportunity and use them. Get over there and do your worst!"

Ghisette called all the garden and woodland Fairies to her. They huddled around, listening to their instructions. Then she flew into the air and led her sisters away. The fairies flew over the Rockery and scattered in all directions, peeling away towards the machines, the house and the Hobbs's.

CHAPTER TEN

WAR

· 10 ·

WAR

IT WAS BREAKFAST TIME at Number One Romany Way on a beautiful spring Tuesday morning. Harriet, as befitted her new station in life, had now employed some domestic help in the shape of Mrs Rigg, whom Harriet referred to as her 'maid'.

Mrs Rigg was a small, tubby woman with short blonde hair. She was in her late fifties and lived near Bogham Railway Station. She arrived in Romany Way each morning in a small white car that had been made in Mongolia or Bangladesh or somewhere. It was riddled with rust and Harriet had promised to buy her a new one. In the meantime she was asked not to park it in their new drive or directly outside the house.

The woman placed Harriet's sausage, egg and chips breakfast on the pine table in front of her.

"Your breakfast, Mrs Hobbs," she said.

"Thank you, Mrs Rigg, very nace I'm sure," said Harriet.

"You're welcome, madam. By the way, you'd better be careful until twelve o clock this morning." Harriet looked up from her paper and stared at Mrs Rigg.

"Eh? What d'ya mean?" asked Harriet, puzzled.

"Well, look at the date on your paper!" Harriet turned the newspaper around to look at the front page and found the date.

"It's April the first. April Fool's Day! Heh, heh," chuckled Harriet.

Upstairs Harry Hobbs was putting on his school uniform whilst Henry was staggering into the bathroom. By now, four Fairies were already inside the house.

Henry opened the bathroom door and walked to the sink. He turned on the hot tap and dabbed his stubbly face with water. Opening the cabinet door, Henry took out his shaving foam and, pressing a small amount in his hand, proceeded to spread it around his face. It took a second for the foam to react. Henry suddenly felt an intense stinging, burning sensation all over his face. In a panic, he looked into the mirror.

"Aaaaargh!" screamed Henry as he smeared away a little of the mass of foam to reveal his face, which had turned a vivid orange colour. He fumbled for the cold water tap and had only managed to give it half a turn when the top rocketed into the air, sending a jet of cold water into Henry's face and up his nose.

Harry rushed to the bathroom to see what was causing the commotion, but when he saw his father's dilemma, he just burst out laughing. "Mum, Mum, come 'ere! Look what Dad's done!" screamed Harry to his Mother.

Desperately struggling to replace the top of the tap, Henry had managed to blast the foam off his face in the jet of water. The foam had gone, but his face remained a livid orange.

What's more, in his frantic attempts to rid himself of the burning foam he had managed to splash some of it onto his sparse greying hair, which was now dotted with florescent orange spots.

As Harriet entered the bathroom, she saw her husband bent over the bath, violently washing his hair with shampoo. Henry groped for the shower tap to wash away the bubbles that were stinging his eyes. Once he had rinsed his hair, Henry grabbed a towel and vigorously rubbed it dry. Harriet and Harry stood staring at him, their mouths open wide with amazement at what had then happened to him.

"Have you seen what this shaving foam's done to my face," shouted Henry Hobbs. Harriet and the boy nodded, and in unison lifted their arms and pointed to the top of Henry's head. Henry waited for an answer for a second, then became suspicious as neither of them said a word, but just looked at him with astonished faces.

"Wha'? Whatchalookin'at?" he gasped.

He dashed to the bathroom cabinet and looked into the mirror doors. For a split second he failed to recognise his own face. Then he did.

"Aaaaaarghhwhatthe**#!!??" roared Henry.

The shampoo had also been sabotaged. Now that his head and hair were dry, the bright orange of the lower part of his face had been complemented by the almost luminous lime green of his forehead, scalp and hair.

"Ah… Ha! Ha!" screamed Harry in delight. "It's Mr Pumpkin 'ead!" Harriet doubled up with laughter and, still pointing, shouted through tears of giggles.

"April Fool!"

"What!?" screeched Henry.

"Didn't you realise it's April the first today – April Fool's Day!" replied Harriet.

"Yeah… and you're the fool, Dad!" laughed Harry.

"You mean *you* did this!" grimaced Henry as his fists and teeth clenched in mounting anger.

"That's right!" cackled Harriet.

"How'd ya do it, Mum?" asked Harry, turning to his mother.

"Eh? I didn't do it, you did! Didn't you?" asked Harriet, the smile fading from her face.

"No, Mum!" said Harry genuinely.

Henry had heard more than enough. He roared in fury and made a lunge for the boy.

"You bloody little liar! Just you wait till I get me 'ands on you!" he screamed.

Harriet made a grab at her husband's pyjamas as he barged past her in pursuit of the fleeing Harry.

"'Enry 'Obbs, don't you swear at my boy. You leave 'im alone. Where's yer sense of humour?" She had managed to grasp the drawstring of the pyjama bottoms as Henry blundered past, detaching it in one swift movement. The trousers dropped around his ankles and Henry fell, ploughing into the landing carpet, his unpleasant hairy backside wobbling in the air.

Harry dashed down the stairs, through the kitchen and out of the back door. With one hand thrust into the arm of his green school blazer and the other clutching his school bag, he fled the house as fast as his legs could carry him. The boy opened the new garage door, snatched up his beloved mountain bike and pedalled furiously away from the house.

Harriet was just about to lay into Henry for frightening her darling boy when she was silenced by a piercing scream from the kitchen.

Mrs Rigg had filled the food blender with bits and pieces to make some soup. But inexplicably the top had shot off, and an eruption of slimy, wet gloop had exploded over the kitchen floor and ceiling. At the very same moment the door to the built-in larder freezer opened and a wave of thawed foodstuffs splashed out. The six brass electrical wall sockets fused, belching blue smoke which activated the smoke alarm. The washing machine went into hyperdrive seconds before its door broke off, sending a cascade of soapy water and tangled clothes across the floor.

When Harriet reached the kitchen, Mrs Rigg was in virtual hysterics, the floor was awash and a pall of blue electrical smoke hung in the air. The fizzing of electric wiring could just be heard under the ear-splitting 'beep beep' of the smoke alarm and the high-pitched shrieks of Mrs Rigg.

Outside the house on that Tuesday morning, things didn't seem to be going much better. The contractors had arrived to continue the work of levelling the garden. The bulldozer driver got into his cab and started up the engine of the powerful vehicle. He waited until the engine had reached working temperature, then pulled the lever to engage forward drive for the tracks. There were two loud bangs and, simultaneously, both of the bulldozer's tank tracks rolled off the driving wheels and curled up in front of the vehicle like two armoured Swiss rolls.

"!!**?!!?" said the driver, looking on in amazement.

The chaos in the kitchen had finally been brought under control. Mrs Rigg's hysterical crying had been halted by the sight of Henry's green and orange head and she had begun to cry in uncontrollable fits of laughter. As a result of that final humiliation, Henry stormed out of the house wearing a large hat, sunglasses and a scarf pulled up around his mouth and ears. He climbed into his car, looking like the clothed version of The Invisible Man.

Henry was still in pain from the acid shaving foam and had decided to go immediately to the doctor's surgery. As he drove the short distance to the Health Centre he began to notice people in the streets were pointing at the car. Other drivers began to flash their lights at him. At first Henry thought that they must have been able to see his strange-coloured face, then he realised something was wrong with the car.

Since leaving Number One Romany Way, Henry had only looked in his rear view mirror twice. The first time he had switched on the rear window de-icer to clear the screen of frost. He looked again; the frost was still there, only it was now a brownish-white colour.

'Wait a minute? How can it be frost, it's too warm?' thought Henry suspiciously. The Jaguar screeched to a halt by the kerbside and Henry leapt out. Behind the car, stretching back as far as he could see, was a trail of oily soap suds. Henry ran round to the back of the car to see masses of foam being produced from the car's twin exhaust pipes.

"**#!!!??" screamed Henry in front of two old ladies.

Meanwhile, the excavator simply refused to start. There was nothing wrong with the battery, it had fuel and everything seemed in good order – it just would not start. It took nearly two hours to fit the tracks back on to the bulldozer but when it came to starting the vehicle, it too stayed silent. The drivers and the foreman were baffled and spent hours delving into the bulldozer's innards. Finally, after cleaning and checking the entire electrical system, they decided to try again. It was now five o clock in the evening and not an iota of work had been carried out that day.

"Well here goes," said the driver, pressing the starter. The diesel engine roared into life, the men cheered, and the driver shouted that he was putting the vehicle back alongside the excavator. He engaged forward drive, there were another two loud bangs, and another two armoured Swiss rolls appeared in front of the bulldozer.

"**#!!!??#!" said the men.

It was six thirty; Mrs Rigg had gone home; the contractors had gone home. Henry Hobbs had come home (with some skin cream), Harriet Hobbs was at home and Harry Hobbs was outside his home.

The boy put his bike in the garage as quietly as he could. Then he crept round the back of the house and entered through the kitchen door. He had almost made it to the stairs when he was grabbed by Mr Pumpkin Head.

"Aaghh, Dad! Leggo! It wasn't me! I didn't do it!"

Henry pulled the wriggling child into the living room where his mother was waiting for him. His Father pushed him down into an armchair where he was cautioned, and threatened about the havoc he had caused with his practical jokes, not to mention the cost of repairs.

"It wasn't me!" screamed Harry for the umpteenth time, then burst into floods of uncontrollable tears. His mother's heart melted and she ran to Harry and put her arms around the sobbing child.

"Maybe it was the workmen?" asked Harriet.

"Yeah? And maybe it was the fairies from the bottom of the garden!" yelled Henry angrily.

"Stop shouting, you're frightening 'im," scolded Harriet.

"Well, of course it was 'im! Who else could it be, the maid?" scowled Henry.

That evening Harriet sent for a huge pizza, Mrs Rigg had not been in any fit state to do the cooking and had consequently gone home early. The Hobbs family sat in front of the television eating their pizza supper in an atmosphere of subdued tension. An uneasy truce had descended over the house. Harry was sent to bed early. Harriet did her best not to talk to Henry, and the pair eventually went to bed independently. Henry sat on his own watching a video whilst Harriet was having a bath. He drank four or five cans of lager before going to bed an hour or so after his wife.

It was probably due to the amount of lager that he had drunk that Henry Hobbs woke up in the night desperate to use the toilet. He shuffled to the bathroom and sat down to relieve himself. When he had finished he stood up and flushed the toilet. He watched as the evidence swirled around but to his horror, instead of the water falling rapidly away, it began swiftly to rise up and over the bowl. Nasty objects slid over the seat and plopped softly on to the new, beige, thick-pile carpet.

"*!!#!!" said Henry as he desperately tried to hold back the flow in a parody of King Canute.

Suddenly some very large bubbles wobbled up from around the U-bend and Henry heard the unmistakable sound of deep, mocking laughter. He slammed down the toilet seat cover, which squashed some unpleasant objects that had clung to the seat.

"Right, you little git!" shouted Henry and he strode along the landing towards Harry's bedroom. He went to open the door but it was locked. Henry started to pound on it with his fists.

"'Arry! Get out 'ere, 'Arry! I know it was you that done it!"

Harriet came rushing out of their bedroom, awoken by the banging and shouting.

"What on earth is goin' on? What's 'e gone and done now?" she shrieked.

"'E's sabotaged the khazi, the little git!" screamed Henry, banging his fists on Harry's bedroom door. "'An 'e's locked 'imself in 'is room!"

"I'm not surprised with a maniac like you rantin' and ravin' outside 'is door!" was Harriet's brusque response.

"It's true 'At! He laughed at me up the U-bend!" insisted Henry.

"It weren't me Mum, honest," came a muffled voice from behind the door. Harry lay under his bed clothes, only the loaded barrel of his air rifle showing as it pointed up at the doorway.

"It can't have been 'Arry!" said Harriet angrily, "'Ow can he be shouting up the toilet and lying in bed at the same time, you stupid old fool." Henry stood perplexed. He thought about what his wife had said and it appeared to make perfect sense, even though he knew it had been the boy. Desperate for a reason to continue the argument, but failing miserably to come up with anything, Henry reluctantly decided he had no choice but to let the matter drop – for now.

Jackson the cat was fast asleep in his luxury cat bed, dreaming of eating birds and fairies, ravishing the local female cats and doing unpleasant things to the neighbour's herb garden. His dreams became more intense as he slipped into an unusually deep slumber. Meanwhile, tiny lights and flickering shadows moved rapidly over and around the comatose cat as its fur fell gently from its body...

When Henry came down for his breakfast the next morning he felt more tired than he had before he went to bed. For one thing he had spent what felt like hours cleaning up the mess in the bathroom, and for another he had lain awake most of the night trying to comprehend how Harry had managed to talk through the toilet's U-bend.

Harriet was making a cup of coffee and Harry was dipping his toast soldiers into a boiled egg when his father arrived at the table. Henry glared at Harry as he sat down opposite the boy. Harriet walked over from the kitchen work surface and almost threw Henry's coffee down in front of him.

"Get yer own sugar!" she said brusquely.

"Mmmm," grunted Henry as he stared at Harry and picked up a teaspoon which he pointed at the boy. He was preparing to say something but Harriet returned to the table and he relented. She sat down and poured herself a cup of tea as Henry lowered his spoon and shovelled two heaped spoonfuls of sugar into his cup. The cup started to tremble and vibrate in its saucer and then in a series of effervescent convulsions a rapidly expanding mass of brown foam began to well up from inside it.

Henry sat abruptly back in shock, and as he did the pinewood kitchen chair disintegrated beneath him. As the chair collapsed, Henry made a grab for the edge of the table and managed to send his coffee cup flying, emptying dollops of foaming coffee all over himself.

Harry's mouth fell open and he dropped his spoonful of runny egg. The boy glanced swiftly at his mother with not even the hint of a smile on his face. He knew the performance had nothing to do with him! Equally, he knew he was about to get the blame.

As Henry began to struggle to his feet, consumed by a boiling rage Harriet suddenly pointed to something over his shoulder and started to scream. Henry spun around and saw a horrific pinkish-white creature which resembled a mutant, bug-eyed, naked rat standing close behind him.

"Aaargh whatisit – gettaway!" screamed Henry, falling over again on the slippery kitchen floor. The pink monster hissed and ran out of the kitchen.

"That's Jackson!" shouted Harry.

"Jackson!?" screamed Harriet. "What d'ya mean Jackson?" She ran to the cat's little four poster bed and saw a pile of black and white fur lying all around it.

"'Arry you cruel, cruel boy!" yelled Harriet with tears welling in her eyes.

"Flamin' right 'At, I could've been killed!" cried Henry.

"Shutup 'Enry 'Obbs, I didn't mean you," sobbed Harriet.

"It weren't me, I swear it!" shouted Harry as he stood up and backed away from the table.

"Don't you move 'Arry 'Obbs!" screamed Harriet across the kitchen. "I don't mind you trying to kill yer useless father," she choked.

"Eh?" said Henry.

"But to do that to my poor pussy cat!" sobbed Harriet.

"IT WEREN'T ME, MUM, HONEST!" screeched Harry and tears began to flood from his eyes.

His Mother blew her nose on some kitchen towel, then with one hand resting on the table she pointed at the boy, who was backing towards the kitchen door.

"Now, you listen to me, I want the truth 'Arry 'Obbs. Did you do them things or not? Answer me!" demanded Harriet.

"No, Mum, I didn't. It weren't me, I swear," sobbed Harry.

"The little liar! Just wait till..." began Henry.

"Shut up 'Enry, and leave this to me. 'Es sworn to 'is Mummy that it weren't 'im," she said decisively.

"An' you believe 'im? You soppy mare! Can't you see? All this stuff – foaming sugar an' all that – it's straight out of a stupid joke shop! 'An who goes into joke shops in this family? 'IM!" ranted Henry, pointing accusingly at his son.

"'Arry wipe yer face and get off to school right this minute!" commanded Harriet. The boy didn't need telling twice. For the second time in a week he rushed as fast as he could to the garage, grabbed his bike and pedalled off to school.

"'Enry 'Obbs, don't you ever call me a soppy mare again..." were the words that started a colossal row that lasted all morning until Henry stormed out of the house. He preferred to suffer the stares and comments caused by his peculiar facial colour than to be nagged to death at home.

The contractors were still struggling with the bulldozers tracks when Henry came out of the house. He stamped off down Romany Way just as a large tipper truck swung into the back garden. It was the first of several lorry loads of sand and gravel scheduled to unload that day. Because of the unforeseen mechanical anomalies, tempers amongst the men were becoming frayed. The driver of the tipper truck could not get past the obstructing excavator/tractor and in an annoyed voice shouted at the bulldozer driver. He asked where he was expected to put the load of sand and the driver made a less-than-constructive suggestion. This almost led to a punch up which was only avoided by the arrival of Mrs Rigg, who began shouting at the man to move his lorry so she could unload the back of her car. Mrs Rigg eventually managed to get her car into the drive and remove a large floor polishing machine.

After Mrs Rigg had moved her car, the tipper driver had reversed his vehicle into the back garden and dumped the load of sand, while the other men had returned to grappling with the bulldozer tracks. The tipper truck drove away just as the bulldozer driver announced that the machine would have to be returned to the depot to be repaired. It was at that point that he saw the small mountain of sand right in the middle of the entrance. It would need a bulldozer or an excavator to shift the mound in order to retrieve the bulldozer and excavator. They had only one bulldozer and one excavator and both were useless.

"*!#?!" said the drivers and both went home.

Henry arrived back home at six o'clock. He had spent the day playing snooker and answering embarrassing questions at a local social club he had recently joined. He walked into the kitchen and noticed the newly polished, sparkling kitchen floor. Mrs Rigg was talking to Harriet as Henry entered. She was of the Methodist persuasion and thus took a dim view of the demon drink. Henry smiled at her and hiccuped.

"Time for me to go I think, Mrs Hobbs," she said as she squeezed past the half-plastered Henry Hobbs. I'll see you first thing tomorrow."

"Thank you, Mrs Rigg. Goodbye for now," replied Harriet.

Harriet glared at Henry, and as soon as 'the maid' had gone began to scream at Henry to get his dirty shoes off her nice clean kitchen floor. Henry retreated to the living room, kicked off his shoes, sat in front of the television and began to roll himself a cigarette. Henry Hobbs may have been extremely wealthy but he still enjoyed the simple things of life.

Harry arrived home about half an hour after his father had wobbled in. He had been engaged in after-school mischief with some of his delinquent classmates. Harry had become very popular amongst a close-knit group of his school friends – otherwise known as a gang of yobs – which had everything to do with Harry's parents being fabulously wealthy. Harry's friends guarded their new-found comrade jealously, especially as he always had money in his pocket.

That afternoon, young Hobbs and his cronies had cycled down to one of the seaside amusement arcades. They had made a nuisance of themselves in the arcade before moving on to the dodgems. There, they monopolised the cars, driving away the little kids and the girls, before being 'politely' told to leave by the owner.

Harry then pulled off a masterstroke of mischief. He bought all his friends as much food and drink as they wanted, without eating anything himself apart from a small burger. He then paid for them all to have five rides each on the Alien Monster Whiplash ride. Harry declined to join them on the ride himself. After all, as he pointed out, he was still eating his burger. The planned result was inevitable.

Harry's mates – Pellett, Grynyer, Gompertz, Cutler, Elphick and Whitmore-Jones – flew around and around and from side to side, full of hot dogs, candy floss, ice cream and fizzy drinks. Young Hobbs was delighted to see his mates enjoying their first ride on the machine. It also encouraged him that so many bystanders were watching. The first ride became the second. By the third, the gang had fallen strangely silent. By the fourth they were strangely silent and strangely coloured! They all seemed to vomit on cue thirty seconds into that fourth ride. Harry quietly pedalled away from the scene as the screams and shrieks of disgust rose from the packed crowd of onlookers the second they realised what was showering down upon them...

Harry Hobbs was still chuckling loudly to himself as he cycled jauntily into Romany Way. Bouncing into the back garden, his bike leapt over the deep mud ruts that had been carved through the gap in the hedge. Harry ploughed his bike through the edge of the obstructing sand mountain and headed down the garden to the earth bank that had been raised overlooking the pond.

He left his bike at the base of the bank and scrambled up the loose, muddy soil to the top. Harry found a wealth of handy-sized stones on top of the mound and began throwing them into the pond. The boy was soon so engrossed in throwing stones at the distant goldfish that he neither heard or saw his bike stand up and slowly wheel itself back towards the stricken bulldozer. Beside the bulldozer lay a puddle – a cocktail of diesel oil and mud through which the riderless bicycle splashed. The machine then lifted off the ground and hovered to the kitchen door, which opened of its own accord to admit the mountain bike.

Harriet walked into the living room, sat down and scowled at her husband, who was engaged in the ritual rolling of a cigarette.

"Just look at the state of you," she sneered, "there's me stuck in this house, cleaning and tidying, while you swan off to a pub all day."

"Club ... not pub ... Harr ... hic! Harriet dear!" said Henry.

"You're pathetic 'Enry 'Obbs. I don't know why I..." but she never did finish the sentence.

While she was talking, Henry lit his cigarette. There was an immediate spray of sparks at the end of his roll-up and a tongue of flame erupted from the cigarette. Red and green flames sent tiny embers over Henry's shirt and trousers. He screamed in agony and leapt up from the armchair as the sparks burnt into his crotch.

Harriet screamed as she saw tiny flames popping up all over the expensive new carpet. She rushed to the kitchen and slung open the door, intending to fetch some water from the sink, instead of which she took three steps and was launched into mid air.

Harriet's feet had skidded on something incredibly slippery. She fell flat on her back in the centre of a Spiragraph pattern of bicycle tyre tracks printed all over the kitchen floor in diesel oil and mud. Harriet screamed again in pain and fury.

Harry's bike, still covered in incriminating oil, settled back on its side at the base of the earth mound. Harry had at last scored a direct hit on a large goldfish and had now become bored and, more to the point, hungry. The boy slithered down the bank on the seat of his school trousers. He was about to get on his bike when he heard a voice beside him.

"Oi! 'Arry 'Obbs, we want a word with you!"

CHAPTER ELEVEN

FIRST CONTACT

FIRST CONTACT

HARRY SPUN AROUND to see who had called to him, and at first saw nobody. Then he looked down as a small man with a beard and wearing a hat walked out from behind a laurel bush. He was joined by another similar little man, who also had a beard, a hat and pointed ears.

"Yeah... we thought you might like to know who has been playing tricks on your Mum and Dad!" said Podfudger.

Harry was astounded at the appearance of the two goblins. He wanted to run but he couldn't move.

"Queenie!" shouted Wazzark," come out and show yourself to our friend here – in case he doesn't believe us."

Ghisette and her two sisters flew out from the bush and hovered in front of the boy's immobilised face. Wazzark stepped over to Harry and looked up at him.

"So, there you are then! It wasn't your fault; we know you didn't do it because it was us."

With that, Wazzark, Podfudger and the fairies disappeared back into the undergrowth.

The spell was broken and Harry was released. He snatched up his bike and pedalled as fast as he could back to the house. Arriving at the kitchen door he threw the bike down and dashed headlong, sliding across the slippery kitchen floor. He reached the living room and ran in to be confronted with another surrealistic tableau. His father was leaping up and down with smoke coming out of his trousers while his mother was hobbling around throwing cups of water over little smoky patches on the carpet. Harry opened his mouth and uttered some of the most ill-chosen words since the marketing slogan for the *Titanic* ('Not even God could sink her'!)

"Mum! Dad! It was fairies and goblins what dunnit! I've just been talking to 'em in the garden!"

Later on that fateful Wednesday evening, when peace had finally descended on Number One Romany Way, a small hedgehog was walking briskly past the large mound of ivy and briers that had overwhelmed the old Austin Cambridge that stood next door on the piece of waste ground. The creature stopped for a second and listened. It heard voices. 'They' were having a meeting.

Under the mound of foliage, inside the old hulk of a car, the front bench seat had been removed and Wazzark stood in front of the dashboard and addressed the others who were seated on and around the rear seats.

"Right!" said Wazzark loudly as he performed a quick head count. "Elfie, Ghisette, Elliel, Mirithin, Effans, Pidwidgin, Cousin Moykle and Podfudger. Good! Everyone present." The goblin asked each in turn for an update on the day's activities and after they had described the mischief that had been caused, Wazzark smiled, turned to Elfie and said, "Great! Are we ready yet, Elfie?"

The Scottish Elf smiled and said, "Aye, Wazzark, that we are!"

"Then we're agreed, it's time to summon Boggart the Bogey-thing!" called Wazzark.

"Boggart the Bogeything!" they all shouted together, waving, clapping and laughing.

That night the fairy folk gathered far away from the Rockery under the oldest oak tree in the area. They had hung chains of ivy in its lower branches and garlands of spring flowers around its roots. Now they began another strange chant, similar to the incantation they had used to call Pan but shorter and with a higher pitch. The chant was sounded three times at intervals of seven minutes, then Wazzark called for silence.

Nothing happened for exactly thirteen minutes.

Then the great tree trembled, its leaves gently rustling. A soft splintering noise was heard as part of the bark around the tree's ancient trunk peeled away to form the shape of a figure wrapped in a cloak and hood. The strange figure moved forwards and grew in height until it towered above Wazzark and the others.

The Bogeything spoke to them in a voice that sounded as though it was talking whilst gargling with thick mud in its throat. "Oo has summoned Oi?" it asked in an old Sussex accent. "Oi is the Bogeything and Boggart is me name."

"Oi 'as... er, I have!" answered Wazzark as he looked up at the cloaked figure. Two points of light sparkled from under the huge figure's hood as it leant down to talk to the goblin, it's bark cloak crackling in the still night air.

"An' what would you be a-wantin' then, little man?" gurgled the Boggart.

Pidwidgin hid behind Cousin Moykle again and wondered what unpleasant surprises this horrendous creature could possibly have in store.

"In the name of Almighty Pan we summon you, oh great Boggart, and command you to help us in our darkest hour!" said Wazzark in the most serious voice he could find.

"Ooh ar... an' what be the trouble loik?" asked the Boggart.

Wazzark puffed out his chest and, waving his arms a lot, began to explain what had happened to their garden and who the culprits were. He told the Boggart what they had managed to do over the last few days. The Boggart listened intently as Wazzark divulged their plan.

It was decided that they were to stage a spectacular event and that Boggart the Bogeything should be the one to tell the horrible

Harry Hobbs about the forthcoming display. The Boggart agreed and promised that he would confront the odious child the very next day. The meeting with the Boggart ended and the strange bark-cloaked creature dissolved back into the oak tree.

Harry Hobbs' life changed dramatically for the worse after the Wednesday evening disclosure of his meeting with fairies and elves. Firstly, his mother gave him six smacks on the backside with a slipper and he was sent to bed with no tea. On Thursday he was driven to school by his father who gave strict instructions that he was to be detained in class until collected at the end of the day's lessons.

Henry then drove to a charity shop where he donated the boy's mountain bike, air rifle and collection of Tormented Turds CDs.

When Henry arrived back at Romany Way the workmen were busy moving the pile of sand out of the way of the dumper trucks.

In a last desperate attempt, the bulldozer driver and his colleague had managed to reattach the troublesome tracks and by late morning had got the machine functioning properly. The rest of the day went without a hitch. The footings for Harry's racetrack had been laid and the area was ready to be covered over with tarmac, even though Henry had told Harriet that they should scrap the idea to teach the boy a lesson. Harriet's response was that they should let the men finish their work and then decide what to put on the new surface.

Mrs Rigg and Harriet set about cleaning the house and Henry had been despatched to organise a new carpet and replacement electrical items. By the time Henry went to collect the disgraced Harry Hobbs, the events of the dreadful April Fool's day were beginning to fade.

At six o'clock that evening the Hobbs family sat down for their evening meal. It was a sombre affair with Harry's parents refusing to speak to him except when absolutely necessary and treating him as if he were invisible. But by the end of the meal, when Harry had asked about his missing bike for the fifth time, Harriet's hard attitude had begun to soften. Harry may have been extremely naughty but he was still her baby boy!

Eventually Harry asked if he could go out into the garden. His father said gruffly that he could not and was immediately overruled by his mother who said he could, as long as he didn't wander off anywhere. Henry, his pride punctured yet again, stormed off to watch 'Meet the Planks', his favourite family game show on television.

Harry went out into the back garden. He walked across the newly laid footings and eventually reached the earth mound. The boy decided to take out his frustration and anger on the enemy golden submarines, so he climbed the bank and began hurling rocks and stones into the now muddy pond.

He had only been on top of the bank for about ten minutes when he heard his mother calling him to come in. The boy angrily threw one last rock into the pond and stood up, unaware that his every move was being closely watched by the fairy folk in the trees behind the Rockery and by something else much closer to him.

"'Arry 'Obbs get in 'ere now!" yelled Harriet. "I shan't tell you again."

Harry slid sulkily down the slope and, kicking the grass, walked slowly back towards the house. His slow, meandering progress was being observed by Harriet from the kitchen window, and when she was certain that he was actually coming in, albeit slowly, she walked away from the kitchen to join her husband.

Harry had reached some trees that lay along the edge of the garden. He was dawdling past one of them when he once more experienced the horrific feeling of being frozen in time and space. Although he could not move he was aware of what was occurring next to him.

Part of the tree's bark began to unpeel and rise up towards him, forming the monk-like shape of a hooded figure. From under the flowing bark robes, an arm emerged. A hand made of knotted, twisted branches clutched his throat and he heard a chilling voice gurgle into the depths of his brain.

"Beware oh 'Orrible 'Obbs, beware, for it is Oi, Boggart the Bogeything, and Oi is very unappy with 'e! Strange things will be a-happenin' to 'e and thoine, starrtin' tonoight at noin o' the clock! And tomarra noight at noin o' the clock! And mark moi words well. 'Arry 'Orrible 'Obbs, fer oi will appear to 'e in yer livin' room at noin o' the clock on this Saturday noight in person! So beware o' the Boggart, 'Arry 'Obbs... Beware! Beware!"

The sinuous, skeletal, branch arm and the hooded figure was absorbed back into the tree trunk, the liquid voice faded and Harry was released. Able to move again, he fled in panic to the safety of the house.

Henry Hobbs, can of lager in hand, was waiting with baited breath to see if the Spanner family would win the star prize of a foreign four-wheel-drive truck. The large-breasted, leggy host-esses, for whom Henry was really watching the show, draped themselves erotically over the glittering vehicle. The toupee-crowned quizmaster heightened the tension with a low, almost reverential voice. "And for tonight's star prize of the Jeep and five thousand in cash, here is your final question..." The man opened a sequin-studded gold envelope and, with the flourish of a conjuror, produced the question on a gold card.

"For tonight's star prize, Martin Spanner, a history question. Please take your time, Martin, here is the question. What was Hitler's first name?"

Henry waved a pointing figure at the screen contestant and began shouting words of encouragement and acquired wisdom.

"It was Heil!" screamed Henry.

"Adolf," said the contestant.

"You plonker!" shouted Henry.

"Oh shut up!" said Harriet.

"It was Heil! Everyone knows that! Heil Hitler!"

"Adolf is the correct answer!" cried the quizmaster and the television audience erupted in a stage-managed frenzy.

"**#!!#?*!" said Henry.

The door to the living room slammed open with such force that a picture frame fell off the wall.

"AAAAAAAARGHHHMUMMY!" screamed Harry Hobbs as he flew across the room, his arms outstretched towards Harriet. Henry leapt out of his chair in shock and dropped his can of lager down his shirt and trousers.

"*#!!!*!" shouted Henry in fright.

"What on earth's the matter?" asked Harriet, fearing some dreadful accident. "What've you done?"

"Mummy! Mummy! Mummy! A monster! A monster got me in the garden! An' its comin' 'ere tonight at nine o'clock... WAH!" sobbed Harry hysterically.

"Gordon Bennett!" shouted Henry as he watched lager soaking into his clothes. "I'm going to swing for 'im one of these days, so 'elp me!" he scowled.

"Shut up 'Enry!" shouted Harriet. "Now 'Arry, calm down. What monster? What monster's comin' 'ere?"

"A boggy or somefing," blubbed the frightened boy. "A bog ... boggy ... monster is going to make somefin' happen 'ere tonight and tomorrah night at nine o'clock ... and it's comin' 'ere in person on Saturday night at nine o'clock! What we gonna do, Mum? What we gonna do?"

"You can get to blinkin' bed! That's what you can do, you little liar!" shouted Henry as he fumed over the loss of his drink.

"C'mon 'Arry love, upstairs, let's get you ready for bed, you've had a 'ard day!" said Harriet in a soothing, sympathetic voice.

"'Ard day, 'ard day? Comin' in 'ere screamin' about bog monsters. I tell you 'At, 'e's not right in the 'ead that kid of ours, an' look what 'es done to me lager!"

"Oh shuttup 'Enry!" snapped Harriet as she led the boy out of the room to run him a bath. The time was twenty minutes past seven.

At ten minutes past eight, Harriet, having put Harry to bed, walked back into the living room and sat down near her husband.

"'E's gone to bed," she said.

"Good," growled Henry.

"What d'ya think he was on about?" asked Harriet.

"I dunno, but if anyfing else unpleasant 'appens around 'ere, I'll murder im!"

Harriet watched the television in silence for a while. Harry's peculiar story had unnerved her and she began to ponder recent events.

"What's the right time, 'Enry?"

"Eh? Oh comin' up to nine o'clock," answered Henry.

"*Nine* o'clock eh?" repeated Harriet in a hesitant, nervous voice.

"Oh don't you start 'At. One idiot in the family's bad enough," moaned Henry as he cracked open a fresh can of lager and glanced around the room for any sign of weirdness. Nothing was amiss so he took a swig of lager.

"What's the time now?" asked Harriet again.

"Oh for... It's a minute later than it was when you last asked!" said Henry with mounting irritability.

"Nine o'clock then," confirmed Harriet.

"YES! It's Ni..." Henry had swung around to face his questioning wife when a movement to his side caught his eye. He stopped still and slowly turned his head towards the disturbance. What Henry saw next amazed him so much that he could do nothing but sink down into his chair and calmly watch events unfurl before him.

The television rose gently into the air and glided serenely across the living room. Harriet clasped her face in her hands in astonishment as the large-screen TV floated across to where

Henry was sitting. It stopped directly over his head – and dropped like a stone.

"AAAAAAARGHHH!!" screamed Henry.

"AAEEEEEKKK!!" screamed Harriet.

At one thirty the next afternoon Enoch Filch was having a Friday lunchtime gin and tonic at the Fresh Ferret with his colleague Charlie Wollock. They were both leaning up against the bar whilst Filch recounted a strange phone call that he had received earlier in the morning.

"Yes, dear boy, I don't know what is going on. Maybe it's too down market for them or something. Anyway they'll have to go a long way before they can put one over on yours truly, I can tell you," announced Filch defiantly.

"Yeah, but what do they reckon's wrong with the gaff? I thought you had it done up proper?" enquired Charlie Wollock.

A bespectacled figure, dressed in blue jeans and a casual jacket, was standing with his back to Charlie Wollock. The man was half hidden behind a pillar and so neither Enoch or Charlie saw him remove a note pad from his pocket and begin to take rapid notes in perfect shorthand.

"I *have* had it 'done up proper' as you put it Charles; that is not the issue. The problem, as they see it, is that the property is *possessed*!" said Enoch Filch.

"What like, 'ornted?" enquired Charlie raising his eyebrows.

"Quite so, Charles, quite so! Haunted!"

"What by?" asked Charlie.

"Well, apparently a TV set attacked the husband last night!"

"Ah ha," slurred Charlie, "I know what that was Enoch. It was a ghost picture on their telly – a ha ha ha!" chortled Wollock.

"Very droll Charles. Anyway if they think they can pull the wool over my eyes – They more or less suggested I knew it was haunted – by the old lady!" added Filch.

"But she ain't dead yet, is she?" sniggered Charlie.

"Shh, not so loud, Charles," whispered Filch. "I don't want anyone knowing too much about this."

"'ere, Enoch. You could be in a spot of bovver 'ere y'know! The woman who ain't dead could come back as a ghost to tell the 'Obbs that she's still alive… and that… ha ha… that your a… your… a… ha ha flippin' liar!" Charlie Wollock, cheered by drink, guffawed into his pint glass, spraying froth over his cheeks and shirt, the bar and Enoch Filch's hand-crafted brogue shoes.

"Shh!" growled Filch through clenched teeth into Charlie's ear. "Keep your damned voice down you fool. You're in this too remember."

The young man who was standing with his back to Charlie Wollock abruptly finished his orange juice and quietly left the saloon bar of the Fresh Ferret pub. He walked around to the car park and unlocked his drop handlebar racing bicycle and took a last look at his note book before replacing it in his jacket pocket.

The cyclist in blue jeans was Gerry Smythe, Chief Reporter of the *Bogham Advertiser*, the premier local paper. There are certain key words in the English language that immediately start alarm bells ringing for any journalist: words such as 'mistress', 'blackmail', 'kinky', 'love child' or 'haunted'. 'Haunted' was always a good one; much better than UFOs. UFOs fly away; hauntings generally stay in one place.

Gerry Smythe remembered faces and names easily. However Gerry's real gift was remembering the context by which the names and faces were related. When he heard Enoch Filch and the word 'haunted', he soon guessed that the Hobbs family (as in 'Lottery Millionaires move to Bogham', a story which he himself had written only a few weeks before) might be involved.

He had recognised Charlie Wollock's voice, especially on hearing the phrase 'had it done up proper!' That clinched it for the reporter. The new millionaire residents had a ghost; it and they lived at Number One Romany Way. Before leaving the car park he made a quick telephone call to his newsroom on a mobile phone, then made several more calls to media colleagues in both local and national television and radio stations, Smythe made them all aware that there was a 'possible' brewing.

The reporter enjoyed his cycle ride to Romany Way. It was one of the quieter parts of Bogham where he was less likely to get knocked off his bike by inattentive motorists. The area was abundant with lovingly maintained gardens. Regiments of daffodils stood guard along the front gardens of the houses that he cycled past; cherry trees blossomed, polyanthus blazed from trim borders and sweet-smelling hyacinths pushed up through drifts of snowdrops. Smythe cycled into Romany Way and noticed the splendour of the freshly clothed horse chestnut trees, their new leaves almost glowing green in the spring sunshine. It was indeed a beautiful world he thought as he dismounted his bicycle outside Number One and trod in a pile of dog's mess.

The journalist swore and awkwardly hopped to the verge where he wiped the edge of his shoe on the grass. Harriet Hobbs happened to be upstairs in a front bedroom putting away some clean clothes when her attention was drawn to the dancing figure outside her house. She watched as he emerged from behind the front hedge and walked up the path, note book in hand.

Smythe stood under the pediment and columns of the Hobbs's plastic Grecian porch and pressed an illuminated door bell. It played 'The Lambeth Walk' on an irritating electronic music device. Harriet Hobbs opened the door to the fresh-faced young reporter.

"Mrs Hobbs?" he asked. "Good morning, my name's Gerry Smythe, I'm a journalist for the *Bogham Advertiser*. I thought you might like to say a few words about your... er... poltergeist?"

"How'd you find out about that so quick?" asked Harriet.

"Oh, I keep my ears open, you know...", smiled the reporter.

"Well, you'd better come in I s'pose. Wipe yer feet will yer?" said Harriet.

Gerry Smythe was led through the hall and into the large living room, where he was confronted with the eccentric sight of the pyjama-clad Henry Hobbs lounging in an armchair with a white, conical surgical collar around his neck. Henry glowered across the room at the approaching reporter. Smythe stared at Henry's green head in the huge collar. It looked like a cabbage inside an old gramophone trumpet.

"Who's 'e?" snapped Henry rudely.

"Manners, 'Enry!" responded Harriet sarcastically.

"Good afternoon, sir. Sorry about your accide..."

"He's a reporter from the local rag," interrupted Harriet. "He wants to do a story about last night! This is my 'usband 'Enry," she continued. Henry squirmed uncomfortably around in the armchair, the collar was aggravating him intensely.

"Last night? I don't care about last night, it's tonight I'm worried about!" grumbled Henry.

"Oh, so you do believe 'im now then, eh?" said Harriet, pointing an accusing finger at her husband.

The reporter was intrigued. "Tonight? What's happening tonight, Mr Hobbs?" asked Smythe.

"*!!#?! knows!" snarled Henry.

"'Enry 'Obbs, you watch yer language in front of the young man!" shouted Harriet.

Harriet invited Smythe to sit down. She went into the kitchen and organised Mrs Rigg into making some afternoon tea and biscuits before returning to the living room. The tea duly arrived and the reporter made notes as the Hobbs described in detail the previous evening's unnatural events.

On hearing the full story of possessed televisions, fairies, elves and haunted toilets, Smythe made an urgent phone call to one of his close colleagues, Louise Eden, a freelance photographer, and arranged for her to be at Romany Way with a video camera half an hour before the predicted phenomena were due to manifest themselves.

Gerry Smythe left the Hobbs house at four thirty that afternoon and raced back to the Advertiser's offices. He prepared a report for the paper which went to press that very evening. If anything interesting did happen at nine o'clock, there would just be enough time to get it in the paper. Gerry also uploaded his story to the Reuters and Press Association web sites.

He stayed on at the office until seven o'clock, by which time the story was beginning to break. He had already received several e-mails, faxes and phone calls requesting more information, names, addresses, etc before he switched on the answerphone and left the building.

While Gerry Smythe was trying to keep other journalists busy without disclosing the Hobbs's name and address, Harry was being escorted to one of his friend's houses where it had been arranged that he would spend the night. Harry didn't want to miss the sight of flying televisions, but his mother had insisted that he was not to be in the house if anything dangerous threatened.

A new television set arrived at Number One Romany Way just before five o'clock. Henry had demanded that they claim for the new set on the house insurance although Harriet wondered how they would explain the damage to the previous one – 'broken by a kamikaze ghost' didn't sound too plausible.

After young Harry Hobbs had been safely evacuated to his friend's house, Henry and Harriet settled, as best they could, in front of their new TV set. As the dreaded hour approached, Harriet became visibly more agitated. When, just before eight thirty, 'The Lambeth Walk' struck up on their doorbell, she leapt up and uttered a shriek.

Shaking like a leaf, Harriet walked to the front door and admitted Louise Eden, photographer, and Gerry Smythe, journalist. Harriet ushered the pair into the living room where the pretty blonde photographer was confronted with the peculiar sight of Henry Hobbs. Henry was still sprawled in the armchair, still in his pyjamas and still wearing the huge cone neck protector over his head.

Harriet was much happier now that she and her husband were not alone, and she bustled around trying to be helpful. Louise unpacked her equipment, setting up a large digital camcorder on its tripod and connecting its light system. She then loaded a stills camera which she positioned on a nearby table.

When all the equipment was in place, the Hobbs's and their guests sat speculating as to what might have caused the television set to fly across the room. By the time it was one minute to nine, no one had proffered any logical explanations to the mystery. Gerry Smythe stood up.

"Everybody ready?" he asked. "It's nine o'clock," he smiled, not really believing that anything untoward was about to happen.

Louise started the camcorder on the stroke of nine o'clock. Somewhere in the house they heard the sound of a cuckoo clock as it heralded the hour. Like Smythe, Louise did not believe anything would happen either. This didn't stop her experiencing a nervous shiver as she started recording. The girl decided to get some human-reaction footage: close-ups of the potential victims of this silly-season yarn. She was getting some good material, zooming the camera in on Harriet's twitching face and Henry's green, sweating brow when they heard the first bang.

Harriet sucked in a throat full of air and put her knuckles in her mouth. Henry didn't hear anything because of the cone around his head. Gerry Smythe swung around to face the door to the kitchen. Louise panned the camera around the room.

"What's goin' on?" asked Henry nervously.

"Shh!" said Gerry, putting his finger to his lips.

"I tell yer, 'At if that door opens and that little git 'Arry walks in I'll…"

Henry was interrupted by another bang, which he *did* hear.

"'Arry!" shouted Henry. "Is that you, yer little sod?"

The door to the living room clicked and very slowly began to open and Gerry Smythe began to feel the hairs on the back of his neck stand up.

Louise gently swung the camera to face the gradually opening door. Harriet was now extremely frightened and, in a very unladylike way, broke wind.

"Ooh er... beg pardon," she whimpered. Louise and Gerry began to giggle, the fart having released the tension.

"What the **!!??'s 'appening?" shouted Henry, frustrated at his inability to see around his head and neck cone.

The door had now opened, fully revealing the shadowy hallway and the darkened kitchen that lay beyond it. The noise was coming from the kitchen and increasing in volume as it approached the living room. Clinking, banging, rustling, and cracking sounds were getting louder; something was nearing the door. Then Henry heard it again, the sound that had puzzled him for so long, the U-bend laugh, reverberating through the house.

"It IS that little bastard! 'Arry, get in 'ere, NOW!" screamed Henry Hobbs as he tried to turn his face to the doorway.

"Oh no it isn't – look!" shouted the reporter.

Louise, the consummate professional, ignored what she was seeing and carried on recording. Harriet screamed and sank as far into the corner of the sofa as she could.

Into the room came a large, plastic dustbin covered in slime and dripping mud. The bin floated in at head height and slowly spun around on its axis. Orbiting the dustbin were hundreds of pieces of junk. The combined aerial objects floated to where Henry was sitting and came to a halt directly over him. The dustbin very slowly turned over in a rolling motion so that the overawed Henry was staring up into the depths of the black bin. There was a sudden, bloodcurdling cackle of laughter mixed with the deeper U-bend voice of mocking derision. The dustbin fell out of the air and dropped with precision over the startled Henry Hobbs. The orbiting junk was released, showering the room and everyone in it with obnoxious bits and pieces. The door slammed and the laughter faded away into the distance.

"Wow!" breathed Smythe.

"AEEEEEK!" screamed Harriet.

"Got it!" shouted Louise triumphantly.

"**!!??#!" bellowed Henry in a muffled voice.

The reporter tore the mobile phone from his jacket. Sweating with fear and excitement, he dialled the newsroom and waited impatiently for someone to answer. "Duggy?" he asked. "Hold the front page – This is BIG!"

Louise drove Gerry back to the Advertiser's office as fast as she could in her little car. They rushed to the newsroom where she switched on the TV monitor and loaded her tape from the camera. It was all there! The apprehensive Hobbs, the flying dustbin, the ricocheting junk shrapnel, the laughter and the screams. Gerry and Louise hugged each other and jumped up and down in triumph.

The reporter began a series of excited telephone calls to the media associates that he had rung earlier in the day, telling them that events had developed beyond all expectations! The Romany Way anomaly was a flyer! And not only that... they also had irrefutable video footage of the phenomena.

While Gerry was on the telephone, Louise busied herself making several copies from her master tape, then she quickly arranged for a courier to take the master copy to the publisher's headquarters in Southampton.

In the early hours of Saturday morning, the video footage of the astounding events in Bogham was downloaded into the publisher's computer system and was immediately made accessible throughout the entire planet via the Internet.

The fizzing blue touchpaper reached the gunpowder shortly after two o'clock on Saturday morning. Reaction to the story was immediate, but when the video evidence was shown around the world the effect was dramatic, especially when they read Gerry's account of the Boggart's promise to make a personal appearance that very evening.

Gerry Smythe was becoming very optimistic about the way his story was developing. He knew his boss, the regional editor, would also be very pleased. The newspaper would do well out of this one if they were lucky! Not only would the circulation be increased dramatically but, with any justice, so would his Christmas bonus! He also realised that he could include all the weird events in a book. He smiled as he considered potential titles for his international best-seller about the spooks of Romany Way.

The first vehicle arrived outside the Hobbs's house shortly after five o'clock in the morning; it was a large truck loaded with broadcasting equipment. The driver had found Number One Romany Way without difficulty, since Harriet had insisted on leaving every light in the house switched on, plus the television set and CD player! The Hobbs's haunted property blazed like a suburban lighthouse.

Two more technician's vehicles arrived shortly after the first and began to unload their satellite broadcasting dishes. Henry, by this time, was fast asleep in a lager-induced slumber. The shock of being entombed in a flying dustbin had been too much for him. Harriet had helped him up to his bed where he had guzzled his way through half a crate of Fresh Ferret lager before passing out.

Harriet had taken several sleeping tablets, eventually fading into a semi-coma next to her snoring husband. That was why neither she nor Henry heard the many telephone calls or the repeated chimes of 'The Lambeth Walk' at their front door.

The neighbours along the entire length of Romany Way were awoken by the swelling presence of media vehicles. Satellite dishes were sprouting like mushrooms in the road and on the pavements and grass verges. Powerful lighting stands were being erected and the floodlights were being attached to them.

The first Police car arrived at ten minutes past six, just as dawn was breaking. The officers were amazed at the sight that greeted them. They had been summoned by residents complaining about a disturbance in the road and were expecting to find drunks urinating in flower beds. They were quite unprepared for the army of technicians and media people that were pouring into Romany Way.

Gerry Smythe managed to snatch a few hours' sleep at his apartment. He had recorded a special message on the answerphone giving details about the forthcoming manifestation. Half an hour after he had fallen asleep, the tape on the machine was crammed full of enquiries.

Harriet Hobbs awoke at half past eight when she heard a faint banging. As she became fully awake, she realised that someone was hammering at the front door. She then heard the sound of a lorry's air horn blasting outside.

"Good God! It's half past eight!" she cried in surprise, having initially forgotten about the events of the previous evening. She turned to look at Henry who was still fast asleep.

"'Enry! Wake up. There's someone at the door!" Harriet shouted into his ear. There was no response from her husband except for a pig-like snort. "Wake up, 'Enry," she repeated and pinched his bottom hard.

"Aayurkk!" cried the dormant Henry.

"Get up! There's someone at the door!" Harriet said again.

"Tell 'em to sod off!" grunted Henry as he tried to pull the bedclothes back over his aching head.

"Oh, fer 'eavens sake!" snorted Harriet angrily as she realised that he wasn't going to stir from the bed. She hauled herself out and walked over to the window, hoping to see who was there. Harriet grasped the curtain, still nagging the dozing Henry. "Get up, 'Enry it's half past... Oh my GAWD!" she cried.

Harriet had pulled back the curtains and received the shock of her life. She stood in her flimsy night-dress, arms outstretched as she held the curtains, and came face to face with at least a hundred people pointing cameras at the bedroom window. There was an instant broadside of flashlights and a rush of people across the road. Harriet slowly backed away from the window.

"'ENRY!" she screamed. "LOOK!" Henry rolled over to face her and saw her backing away from the opened curtains.

"Whassamatter?" he mumbled, painfully easing himself out of bed. He shuffled over to the window, one hand across his greenish forehead, the other scratching his backside. Henry peered out of the window and was temporarily blinded by another fusillade of flashlights.

"GORDON BENNET!" he cried.

Some aspects of local life did continue as normal, however. A lorry-load of hot, steaming tarmac had arrived on schedule and was trying to get into Number One Romany Way to deliver its load. The driver was leaning out of his cab shouting at several people who were blocking the way. It was the last load of tarmac needed to complete the first stage of the planned playground and BMX track. Behind the dumper truck was a huge low-loader truck to remove the bulldozer and deliver a heavy road roller.

The bulldozer driver and his mate had arrived minutes earlier to be confronted by the growing ranks of the press. At first they had been bemused by the barrage of questions. 'No they hadn't noticed anything weird yesterday!' and 'No they didn't know anything about spooks' and 'Yes they had been having trouble with their machinery!'

But by the time the dumper truck and low-loader had arrived at their destination the two drivers were getting quite used to being treated like celebrities.

CHAPTER TWELVE

NOW IT IS THE TIME OF NIGHT

· 12 ·

NOW IT IS THE TIME OF NIGHT

SNAPS THE CAT AWOKE to another day of exile. He poked his head out of the hole in the fallen, hollow tree trunk that he had made into his home and looked warily around. Snaps had lost a lot of weight since he fled from his real home. He was no longer receiving his meals on a plate from his mistress, and on the one occasion that he had returned to his former home to beg for food, a black and white maniac cat had shot out of the house and ferociously attacked him.

Fairies had blighted his nocturnal forays by following him around and using their phosphorescence to illuminate him so that every mouse in the area could see the floodlit cat and keep a safe distance. On this particular morning he decided to risk the mad usurper cat and grub through the dustbins around Romany Way. He crossed the field and entered the thicket at the bottom of Number One.

"Oi!" shouted a voice. Snaps froze, nervously looking about for the source of the voice. Wazzark dropped out of a tree in front of the cat, who sprang up into the air with a frightened hiss.

"Oh it's you, Ampucat! 'Ow's yer tail?" the Goblin asked sarcastically.

"Leave me alone!" said the miserable cat.

"Now why would I want to leave you alone, Fluffball? So you can creep up on one of me mates, eh?" said Wazzark in a threatening way. Cousin Moykle emerged from a bush and stood next to his goblin colleague.

"Oh God! Would ye look at that. If it isn't himself!" stated the Leprechaun.

"Och! Lookie here, if ut is'nay the ginger bastarrd in pairson!" added Elfie, emerging from some foliage behind the frightened cat. "Wassup? Yon Jackson givin' ye a hard time, eh ginger?" he added.

Ghisette and her sisters, feeling safe with their friends around them, flew over the cat high enough to be out of paw-striking range.

Snaps went into fight-or-flight mode – flight won and he decided to bolt for safety. What was left of his tail shot up into the air and he surged forwards to escape – but nothing happened. He was frozen in mid-dash. Snaps wanted to yowl in panic but he couldn't even open his mouth.

"You're not feeling threatened are you, Snaps?" Ghisette called down angrily. "I do hope you are, then you'll know what real fear is like – when you know someone wants to kill you … like you wanted to kill me!"

The three fairies landed on the ground in front of the cat. Ghisette had something behind her back, which glinted in the sunlight. She stepped up to the cat and stood in front of his face. In her hand she held a long sewing needle, which she levelled and pointed at the cat's nose.

"Aye! Right lassie! Forrget the bastarrds nose! Stuck ut in his ay!" shouted Elfie.

Ghisette held the shining needle in both hands and raised it towards the cat's right eye. She drew it back, ready to lance her victim.

But the whole threatening encounter had been stage-managed. There was never any plan to harm the cat. Even so, Wazzark was slightly nervous about the way Ghisette was acting; she may have been tiny but she had a reputation for being very aggressive. The goblin stepped forwards and gently held her arm, removing the needle from her grasp. Wazzark rolled the needle between his finger and thumb as he put his face close to the petrified cat.

"So, there you are! We've got powers you never dreamt of, pussy cat! Powers to return things to the way they were. Now you can either stop hunting my friends here…," Wazzark gestured towards Ghisette, Mirithin and Elliel, "…and help us protect the garden, or…" he paused to savour the moment, "or I'm going to let this young lady push this needle through your eye and out of the back of your head! Now, are you with us or against us? Stay still for no, or blink your eyes for yes! What's it to be?"

Snaps blinked his eyes so rapidly they almost smoked!

"Let 'im go!" said Wazzark and he snapped his fingers. The terrified cat collapsed in a shivering heap. "Good," he added, hands on hips, sticking the needle in his lapel. "You've given us your solemn oath so there's no going back… or you're dead! Do you understand?"

Snaps nodded furiously until his neck ached.

"Blimey, 'At look! We're on the telly. Quick!" shouted Henry Hobbs. Harriet had closed all the curtains in the house and was peeking through a gap at the people outside. She walked over to the television and saw their house. The picture cut to a close-up of her and then Harry, followed by images of the haunted dustbin visitation and its aftermath. Harriet found she was staring at herself looking out of her window. The picture changed again to feature the TV newsman who was standing outside Number One Romany Way making his report.

"What's goin' on, 'Enry? How've we got into this mess?" cried Harriet.

"'Im! It's 'im, 'At! It's always 'im, the little git! Well 'es really gone and dunnit this time. He's gone and pissed off the devil or something. How does 'e do it eh?" ranted Henry. Harriet started sobbing. She was beginning to wish they'd never won the wretched money.

The story had now spread around Bogham, for not only was it the lead on every national TV and radio station, but Gerry Smythe had managed to get it plastered over the front page of the *Bogham Advertiser* with the lurid headline, 'April Fool Phantom freaks family – Dustbin attacks Lottery millionaire!' Below the headline was a still from the videotape showing the levitating dustbin about to fall on Henry. The report also went on to describe how 'the phantom' had promised to reveal itself to the family on Saturday (today) at nine pm.

Many Boghamites were now heading towards Romany Way out of idle curiosity. Others saw the chance of a quick buck! By half past ten the first burger and hot dog van had arrived.

Harry Hobbs cycled into Romany Way at eleven o'clock. His friend's parents had been trying to get through on the phone for ages but it was always engaged. The child was astounded at the sight. There were now several hundred people in the street and more were arriving by the minute.

"Unit calling on channel three, go ahead please..." said the crackling radio voice.

"Uh yes control, whiskey four six zero. We need crowd-control barriers and a dog van at Romany Way. Situation beginning to turn ugly!" said a police officer from his hemmed-in patrol car. The public were mixing with the newsmen, and children, as usual, were becoming a nuisance as they were attracted to the many outside broadcast cameras.

Harry pushed his way through the crowd and noticed people streaming into his back garden through the gap in the hedge. He followed the mob and saw that camera crews were spread all over the new tarmac. Harry threaded his way through the trespassers and put his bike in the garage.

"Hey kid!" shouted a voice, "d'you live 'ere?" Harry turned as he shut the door and was met by several people with hand-held tape recorders moving towards him.

"Have you seen the ghost?" said a dark-haired woman in a blue leather jacket.

"Yeah! It was 'orrible!" replied Harry.

"It's the kid, the 'Obbs kid!" shouted a loud voice. "He's here! He's seen the ghost!"

Harriet was alarmed by noises coming from the back of the house, so she ran into the kitchen to pull down the blinds. Scores of people were in her back garden but it was the TV lights by the kitchen door that drew her attention. She ran quickly to the door, opened it and with a deft movement grabbed the new celebrity and pulled him inside the kitchen.

"What're you doin' 'ere, 'Arry? You're supposed to be at yer mate's 'ouse," Harriet asked.

"The phone's always engaged an' I wanted to come 'ome Mum. What's all these people doin' 'ere... is it 'cos of the Bog thingy?" asked Harry as he dipped his hand into the biscuit barrel.

Harriet pulled down the remaining blinds and was about to admonish the boy when 'The Lambeth Walk' sounded yet again, only this time it was accompanied by a loud knocking and shouts of "Mr Hobbs... Police! Can you open the door please."

Henry's head and neck ached painfully, but he refused to wear the surgical collar. He had, he thought, looked such a total moron on television that he didn't want to become an even bigger laughing stock. Henry opened the door to a police inspector and two constables, who did not look at all amused.

"Yeah whassup?" asked Henry.

"Mr Hobbs, we'd like to talk to you about this – whatever it is, that's happening here! What *is* happening here?" asked the Inspector as he turned and pointed to the crowds behind him.

"You tell me mate, I haven't a clue. You'd better ask Fred," sighed Henry.

"And who's Fred?" enquired the Inspector.

"He's our poltergeist!" said Henry, flashing an instant smile which vanished just as abruptly. The Inspector gritted his teeth and leant over to whisper in Henry's ear.

"Look here, Sir. Because of all this lot I'm going to have to bring some of my lads in from their weekend break; they're not going to be at all happy! So will you kindly tell me what is going on so that I can put an end to it."

"Be my guest," said Henry and he beckoned the officers to enter. They walked into the living room where Harriet and Harry were standing.

"Oh! So you're back," said Henry as he realised that Harry had returned home. "There you are, mate. You wanna know what's goin' on, ask 'im. The devil's a mate of 'is." Henry pointed towards Harry.

"Oh shuttup, 'Enry," complained Harriet. "It's not the boy's fault."

"Not the boy's fault? Not the boy's fault?" screeched Henry in a rising crescendo as his terrified son slid behind his mother. "Whaddaya mean not the boy's fault! Who else was it conjured up the powers of darkness, eh? The ruddy cat?"

"If I might be allowed to interrupt," said the Inspector, "all I want to know is what exactly is happening and when is it going to be over?" Before the Inspector received an answer 'The Lambeth Walk' started up again.

Gerry Smythe and Louise had managed to push through the crowd and had reached the police officers who now guarded the front path to Number One. Harriet opened the door and was confronted by a policewoman. Behind the officer, a battery of cameras clicked and Harriet's name was constantly repeated.

"Excuse me, Madam, there's a Mr Smythe says he was here yesterday and can he see you?" said the Policewoman.

"Oh yes, yes, let 'im in," replied Harriet. Gerry Smythe and Louise were allowed into the house accompanied by the police-woman. They walked into the living room and joined the Hobbs and the police officers. Harriet introduced the reporter and photographer to the police, then went on to inform the Inspector all about Harry's encounter with the Boggy monster and its chilling promise to appear in the house that evening.

The crowd outside had attracted the police. The activities of the police, especially the arrival of a circling police helicopter, had attracted the crowds. The Inspector repeated the earlier request for crowd-control barriers and a dog handler, and these arrived at just after one o'clock.

During the afternoon, certain television news reports carried items on the possible identity of the promised supernatural visitor. Several 'experts' speculated on what had caused the phenomena. They had picked up on the young Harry Hobbs 'Bog' or 'Boggy Monster' and deduced that he was referring to the old English or Scottish word 'Boggart'. There then followed a gallery of artist's impressions of what a Boggart might look like, with images ranging from a yeti-like creature to things that looked like the Loch Ness Monster and Darth Vader.

By six o'clock that evening, the appearance of 'The Bogham Boggart' had become the subject of international conjecture. The end result of these imaginative speculations was even more people cramming into Romany Way.

At the nursing home, Miss Forgetmenot had not been well for a few days; she had been cursed with a bout of what she called 'a funny tummy', probably caused by the food or the unusually warm central heating in the nursing home. Whatever the cause, she found herself confined to bed. The old lady had slept most of the day, finally awaking at just after three o'clock. She turned on her television using the marvellous new (to her) remote control handset and, not wanting to watch the sport, began to browse through the various channels.

The local news was just starting and she decided to watch it. But at that same moment a nurse knocked on her door and asked how she was feeling. As the two women began talking, Miss Forgetmenot turned off the sound to the television, consequently while she was looking at the day's menu with her visitor she did not see her old cottage appear several times on the TV screen.

"Now look, sonny..." said the policewoman to Harry Hobbs, kneeling down to look the boy straight in the eye, "you're absolutely certain you're not making all this up?"

"No, no I'm not! Tell 'er Mum!"

"All right, I believe you," continued the Policewoman patiently, "and you say that this... whatever it is... is going to be here in this room..."

"At nine o'clock! Yeah!" interrupted Harry.

The policewoman stood up, and she and the Inspector moved away from the Hobbs for a momentary *tête-a-tête* in the corner of the room.

"I don't like this," said the Inspector with a concerned shake of the head. "All these people... and they're going to see bugger all. Some of 'em have been waiting hours and a lot of 'em have been in the boozer. When nothing happens, we could have a riot."

The police eventually decided to do nothing more controversial than put a few crowd-control barriers at both ends of Romany Way and a cordon around the front of the Hobbs' house. They then waited for the anticipated non-event to finally not occur. By their calculations, it would all be over by ten o'clock at the latest. The Police Inspector predicted that the bored and disappointed crowd would then gradually disperse to seek last orders at the pubs, cups of cocoa at home, take-away chicken tikka masalas, or head for the night clubs or the midnight movie.

The same Inspector, anxious to let as many people as possible witness the drama of absolutely nothing happening in the Hobbs's living room, decided to ask a local firm to erect a giant TV screen. The screen was in place by seven-thirty. By eight-thirty there were at least seven or eight thousand people crammed into Romany Way and the adjoining area.

Inside Number One Romany Way, Harriet was sitting beside Henry and Harry nervously watching the activity around the room as police officers tried their best to keep out of the way of the outside broadcast crew. She was glad she had made Henry get the large, oval, patterned rug that now lay in the centre of the room; it covered a multitude of sins, including burn marks and lager stains. Harriet looked up from the rug and made a disturbing observation. There was a camera crew of four people, one reporter, one photographer, four police officers and three members of her family. She felt her heart go into her mouth – there were thirteen people in the room.

Suddenly, a huge cheer erupted outside as a camera crew that had linked access to the giant screen interviewed a well-known local eccentric whose vocation in life was to walk around with a sandwich board proclaiming that 'too much sex', 'the eating of peas and lentils' and 'sitting' were sure to bring about the end of the world. Another cheer followed as an even more certifiable Boghamite began to rave into the camera about the imminent arrival of 'the greys' from a far-off galaxy. Proof that 'Looney Toons' were alive and well and living in Bogham!

The carnival atmosphere and noise of the crowd began to subside as the ETA (estimated time of apparition) ticked down towards zero. At one minute to nine, an ominous silence descended over the crowd.

Different thoughts filled different heads inside the living room at Number One. At ten seconds to nine a mental 'newsflash' crossed their collective minds. All thirteen of them heard an inner voice say:

"This is my world and you are destroying it. This is my life and you are ending it. Beware humanity! This realm was always mine to give and never yours to take!"

Then they felt their thoughts go blank. They could think of nothing but the deep and meaningful message until, suddenly, all of them heard the identical mud-gargling voice say, in a strong Sussex accent:

"Now piss off the lot of yer!"

Thirteen heads turned and glanced around the room looking for the owner of the voice. For the first time, the Inspector was alarmed. Perhaps there was something in this after all. He decided to give the Hobbs's the benefit of the doubt for the moment.

"Er... when this happened last time where did it come from?" he asked nervously.

"From the kitchen!" cried Harriet.

"Constable! Go into the kitchen and report anything suspicious," ordered the Inspector, and a policeman duly left the living room. The Inspector commanded another of his men to get to the top of the hall stairs and keep watch. Harriet felt relieved. The dreaded thirteen was now eleven. Gerry Smythe checked his pocket tape recorder whilst Louise held her stills camera so tight she hardly noticed that her hands were sweating.

"What's 'appening Mum? Dad?" asked a trembling Harry.

"Nuffin' son," barked Henry gruffly, trying not to sound as if he was scared out of his wits, just like his son.

Henry reached under a cushion on the sofa and pulled out a World War II helmet which had belonged to his father and had last seen 'action' behind a NAAFI canteen near Catterick in 1949 in an 'outflanking manoeuvre' that had eventually resulted in the birth of baby Henry Hobbs. Henry no longer cared if he looked ridiculous; he felt safer. He was convinced that, given half a chance, Fred the poltergeist would try and drop something else on his head. But that is not what happened.

The cuckoo-clock tooted out nine o'clock. The policewoman moved slowly behind Harry Hobbs who was sitting next to his mother and father on the sofa.

"Take that ridiculous 'at off!" hissed Harriet to her husband.

"Nothin's 'appening Mum," mumbled Harry.

The Inspector paced slowly around the room, alternately looking at his shoes then at his watch. He walked to the window and moved the curtain to look outside. The crowd began to sing 'Why are we waiting?'

It was five minutes past nine when the Inspector said to his female colleague, "Well, looks like the con's over, eh? Now all we've got to worry about is that lot out there going home without wrecking half the town!"

Harriet was sitting staring at the floor, and at the new rug in particular, when an odd thing happened. The rug's ivy and acanthus pattern began to move! Harriet thought her imagination was getting the better of her so she nudged Henry and nodded towards the floor.

"What is it, Mum?" asked Harry in a loud voice.

Harriet looked again at the rug. It was not her imagination; the swirling tendrils in the rug's design were moving around the edge of its leaf-pattern perimeter.

"Wow!" exclaimed Harry, as his parents immediately lifted their knees up into the air.

The Inspector swung back from the window to see what was happening. Gerry Smythe and Louise alerted the camera crew, who rapidly moved around to capture the developments. The tendrils in the pattern were flickering and twisting towards a central point in the rug. As they reached the embroidered Tudor rose at its centre, a single, thin black line began to rise up vertically through the room.

"Something's happening! Look!" shouted a voice in the crowd.

"It's… SHOWTIME!" shouted another as a great cheer spread through the crowd, halting the departing sceptics in their tracks. Everyone strained their eyes towards the giant TV screen.

The thin black line continued it's smooth, perfect, vertical climb. Without apparently causing the slightest damage, it proceeded into the ceiling and continued its upwards movement through the house, emerging out of the thatched roof.

The policewoman tapped Harriet on the shoulder and beckoned her to move herself and Harry. Henry didn't need any prompting! He was already swinging his legs over the arm of the sofa to make a clumsy retreat.

More and more tendrils, roots and branches were being generated by the rug's design and were collecting at the base of the enigmatic black line. The snake's-tongue flickering of the tendrils increased as the black line was overwhelmed by the foliage. The knot of fibrous growth that climbed its way upwards was rapidly evolving into a peculiar cone-shaped organism. It was like watching time-lapse film of fungi growing. The base of the structure was swelling and within seconds it had spread beyond the confines of the disintegrating rug. The living room floor began to splinter as floorboards were smashed and split by two vast, wax-like roots that burrowed their way down into the building's foundations.

"Out!" ordered the Inspector, his voice a mixture of fear, disbelief and urgency. "All of you, out now!" he repeated. "Come on, come on!"

The remaining officers ushered everyone in the room towards the front door. The camera crew reluctantly retreated backwards, intent on recording the unbelievable scene as they were pushed and pulled out of the room.

The black line had reached a height of twenty metres above the cottage when it stopped. Because it was black and only centimetres thick, no one below had even noticed it. The crowds were cheering as they observed the panic inside the house.

"It's a triffid on Viagra!" shouted a wag, accompanied by yet more raucous cheers. Suddenly, without the slightest warning, the black line silently exploded into what could only be described as a colossal wiring diagram. The invisible blackness of the filaments instantly changing to a luminous green. At the same moment, tendrils and suckers burst writhing and flailing through the thatched roof as twigs, leaves and shoots began to permeate the filigreed framework. A shape was emerging.

Abandoning any form of police radio etiquette, the Inspector yelled into his lapel transmitter, "Evacuate! Pull 'em away, starting from the back… DO IT NOW!"

The floodlights blazing onto the house illuminated the untidy panic as the occupants fled Number One Romany Way. The door was pulled open as Henry barged past Harry in his haste to get out of the house.

"You little git!" screeched Henry at his son. "Your mate's arrived, flamin' Beelzebub!"

Then the screaming started.

The crowd fled as best they could to either end of the road. A surge of hysterical people flooded down Romany Way, desperate to escape. The mob clambered over cars and hedges, fell through fences and over low garden walls. In a blind panic to get away, the crowd rolled, scrambled and jumped over any obstacle in their path. Others moved slowly backwards, straining their necks up to see the spectacle unfolding before and above them.

The shape of a hideous giant head was now swaying and writhing up through the floor. It began ascending the thick, central spinal column of the expanding structure. The head was a mass of capillary-like filaments and suckers that were made of the same milky wax-like substance as the roots. The form of a headless humanoid creature had now evolved over the building and was clearly identifiable to the mesmerised onlookers.

Two huge mutant root and branch-filled arms groped down into the thatch. Skeletal twig and tendril fingers snaked around the appalling head and grasped it firmly, drawing it up through the building until, half-covered with the straw from the roof, it was dragged above the figure's torso and positioned on its shoulders. At a fantastic rate, the veins and arteries of shoots, twigs, roots and tendrils were covered by a thin skin of leaves and a translucent cloak of bark.

The giant, straw-hatted Boggart had arrived as promised. It towered above all who observed or fled from it. Those that did watch the monstrosity were transfixed. The abandoned TV cameras were in most cases still operating, those that had not been knocked aside in the panic were still trained on the house and the Boggart, but for some strange reason no pictures were received anywhere, just white noise and snow-filled screens.

The pulsating chest of the creature expanded as, agonisingly slowly, it leant backwards. Loud creaking and splintering noises sounded as the figure strained over. The Boggart's hands went to the sides of it's mouth; it was getting ready to deliver its important message to the human race. Like a tree being hit by the full force of a hurricane, the Boggart swung forwards and down as it shouted; its lungs emptied in a deafening roar as it screamed.

"!?!!** ORF!"

The Anglo-Saxon expletive in a rich Sussex drawl echoed and reverberated like a thunderclap across the whole country.

"*!!??# orf and leave us alone!" it added for good measure.

Then it exploded...

The road, the buildings, everything in a wide area was showered with organic shrapnel. The remaining crowd screamed to get clear as the dirt-filled mushroom cloud boiled and rolled up into the floodlit sky, scattering debris all around as it went.

Out of the pall of dust shot a terrified, hairless pink cat as Jackson fled Bogham, never to be seen again.

CHAPTER THIRTEEN

FALLOUT

· 13 ·

FALLOUT

ON THE MARGINS OF SPACE, high above the earth's atmosphere an unmanned surveillance aircraft called Aurora was busy gathering thermal and magnetic imaging over a target on the south coast of England. The black Y-shaped 'skunkworks' aircraft began to process incoming data before slipping behind the curvature of the earth on its unnoticed homeward descent to Nevada.

The Pentagon received the analysis of the data obtained by the Stealth aircraft. It showed 'The Bogham Anomaly' to be just that… a mystery! The only clue that emerged was of a geophysical disturbance, a web-like magnetic field pattern that had centred on the town. Twenty-four hours after the first images had been received, a second batch showed the original magnetic field trace to have completely disappeared.

On the Sunday following the 'Romany Way Event', the British Government were not aware of the results of the second spy-plane mission. They advised their friends in the press to run with a plausible cover story.

The story was so plausible that many inquisitive scientists actually believed it; certainly the mass of the general public were content with the explanation. The general consensus was that it was not the first time such a thing had happened. The story that appeared in subsequent papers put an end to all exotic theories with the lurid headline:

'BOGHAM BLOWS UP! STREET FARTY GOES DOWN TOILET!'

A build-up of methane gas over an old landfill site has caught locals short! After a spate of methane-induced hallucinations, a chain reaction caused the gas – which is the same as that expelled from human and animal bottoms – to explode. No one was seriously hurt in the incident at Bogham in West Sussex, but the home of Lottery millionaires Henry and Harriet Hobbs was extensively damaged. A spokesman said despite all the rumours of aliens, goblins, fairies and the Loch Ness monster, this was just one of those normal things that occur from time to time, leaving a nasty smell in the air!

Miss Forgetmenot was awoken the next morning by the nurse, who quickly informed her of the previous evening's events. The woman turned on the television for the old lady. The local special news report was full of images of the chaos in Romany Way. Suddenly Miss Forgetmenot's house appeared; the awful damage was evident. It was clear that the roof had completely disintegrated and collapsed in on the building, leaving only a shell. The old lady put her head in her hands and wept – she could not understand what on earth had happened to her old home.

The events of that dreadful Saturday night were on everyone's lips, especially the media people who had been present. Not one image transmitted or collected that night had been recorded successfully – everyone's tapes had been wiped, and photographs had all been disastrously over-exposed. The explanation to these mysteries would be revealed later in the week with the Government's disclosure of a bewildering magnetic energy emission under Bogham. Magnetic fields, like X-rays, were bad news for tape and video recorders, and presumably photographs as well.

The witnesses of the Boggart's visitation, the people who had been there in person, were unwilling to accept that they had been gassed into seeing things by a rogue fart. They had seen the Boggart... and they had heard its vulgar warning.

The Hobbs's intended to heed that warning!

The following Monday morning, Enoch Filch received a phone call in his newly decorated offices from a firm of solicitors representing Henry and Harriet Hobbs. He was instructed to put the property up for sale. His clients, the solicitor added, had no desire to ever see the house again.

"What sort of price have they in mind?" enquired Filch. The estate agent was instructed to sell it for the highest price he could get, the family being far too distraught to be involved in haggling over money.

By family, the solicitor meant Harriet. Henry Hobbs was all for getting their money back. Harriet, however, wanted to rid herself of all memory of Number One Romany Way. If they used the money from that property to buy something else, 'who knows what curse could come with it,' she reasoned.

Harry had not escaped without recrimination for, on their return to a luxury hotel in Neasden, North London, Harriet had contacted the local church to arrange to have the boy exorcised. From then on he was referred to as 'Damien' by his friends, and as 'The Big Fairy' by his enemies.

Harriet demanded that they put the horrific events behind them by going on a world cruise in a luxury liner. As the Hobbs sailed off into the sunset, the family's possessions (those few that survived) were collected up by the solicitor's representatives and placed in storage. The contractor's vehicles were removed, the tarmac, much of which had been damaged by the crowd, remained – as did the huge mound of earth and rubble by the pond. Number One Romany Way was a ruin.

Two days after the strange goings-on and explosion, the bomb squad finally gave the police the all clear to allow the residents back to their damaged homes. It would be mid way through June before the road got back to some semblance of normality. The boarded up eyesore of Number One, however, remained as a reminder of the weird events in April!

The 'Site for Sale' sign gradually became weathered as the property remained on the market. No one had contacted Enoch Filch because no one wanted to buy a haunted house or property that was 'doomed by the devil's curse'. Despite what Government scientists, politicians or newspapers had claimed, the Bogham townsfolk knew that unnatural forces were involved! They knew that there had never been a landfill site in that area.

Miss Forgetmenot had caught a bus from the Ingletimber Residential Hotel to go and see her old house. The bus stopped fairly close to Romany Way and the old lady walked for a few minutes before rounding the corner into her old road. She could scarcely believe her eyes. She looked up at a huge, high boarded fence which encircled the building. Large signs warned intruders to keep out. Her house was hidden; she could see nothing! It had been a wasted, depressing journey.

With a feeling of bereavement Miss Forgetmenot returned to her little room at the nursing home where she received another shock. A notice had been put on her bed. It was addressed to the staff and residents. The owners of the nursing home had decided to sell the property to another larger concern. It meant the existing residents would face a severe increase in accommodation fees.

The old lady would not be able to live in her new home for much longer. Where would she go? She would soon have no money left! It seemed to Miss Forgetmenot that the future was a black bottomless pit into which she was helplessly slipping.

The ivy and brier covered car that lay abandoned near the garden of Number One Romany Way had escaped the devastation of the Boggart. On a cool, clear evening in late June, a meeting took place inside the old vehicle. Present were the fairy folk from the Rockery and their new ally, Snaps the ginger cat.

The Rockery residents had been satisfied with the Boggart's handiwork. His intervention had certainly rid them of the vandalistic Hobbs family.

The Hobbs's departure had greatly improved conditions for all of them. Indeed, life had returned to something like normal. They could once again venture out of their Rockery home. Foraging for food and provisions had become much easier now that the area was not infested with humans. The problem was that the whole nightmare could be repeated if the next residents were anything like the last. The first part of the exercise had been successfully completed; the second part would be far more difficult. They had all agreed that Miss Forgetmenot should be returned to her home and everything put back the way it used to be. The problem was how was it to be done?

Wazzark stood under the dashboard of the old Austin Cambridge and addressed the meeting.

"Okay, we've heard several suggestions that won't work, including a lot of talk about using magic!" said Wazzark. "Well, using magic to rebuild her cottage is out of the question – we can't have bricks and cement floating around without being noticed – so are there any other suggestions? Yes, Effans?"

Effans stood up, his red hair shining in the gloom. The Welsh elf lifted a finger and proudly suggested, "We could shrink her down and then she could live with us like, under the Rockery. Yes indeed!" Effans closed his eyes and smiled; his suggestion was very clever, he thought, and he awaited the inevitable applause.

"Och aye, thats a brulliant suggestion!" said Elfie sarcastically. "Thun after herr, we could shrink ye doon an' shove ye up yon cat's arse!" Snaps squirmed uncomfortably and wrapped his tail tightly around his body. "Nay offence, ye ken," added Elfie to Snaps.

"All right, all right!" said Wazzark impatiently. "Anyone else got any *sensible* ideas?"

Effans sat down and hunched his shoulders, folding his arms in a sulk as the leprechaun got to his feet to make his suggestion. "Whoiy don't we see dat builder fellah... de one wid de spotty kid. Oi'll tell him I'm goin' ta cut his head off – then he'll help us so he will."

Pidwidgin, who had grown fond of the visiting Cousin Moykle, looked up at him, a puzzled smile on her face. Cousin Moykle noticed the look on the Pixie's face. "Oh God, here we go, wait for it... Yes, Pidwidgin?" he said to her.

"Well... how could he help us if you've cut his head off?" giggled the pixie. "Tee hee, you are silly."

There followed several more ludicrous, idiotic and surrealistic suggestions from the assembly before Elfie finally lost patience. He slapped his face with his hand and slid it down over his chin in frustration! Then he stood up and shouted "Och! Fer !!**?# sake! We've been sittin' heere for hoors nou! I'm fed up with lustnin' ta this mince! Why do we not just rob a bank and give her the money?" he shouted throwing his hands up into the air. There was an instant blast of laughter at the Scottish elf's suggestion. Undeterred by the laughter he continued, "Alrayt thun! If we cannay rob a bank, lets find her a winning scratchcard!"

A sudden silence fell and everyone looked at Elfie with their mouths wide open. Wazzark punched his fist into his hand and smiled.

"Wha?" said Elfie. "Wha'ave ah doon?" he asked nervously.

"Nothing, Elfie, except come up with a sensational idea! You've cracked it, ol' mate! We'll win her the money to buy back and repair her house!" announced Wazzark excitedly.

"Aye... right!" agreed Elfie, the penny finally dropping as he realised that his offhand suggestion could actually work. The audience burst into applause at his original solution to their problem.

"I was just about to suggest that, boyo," muttered the sulking Effans, but no one was listening. They were all far too involved thinking up a plan to put Elfie's idea into practice.

There was one problem however. Unfortunately, no magic could reveal the winning ticket; it could only be used to cover up the evidence of the search. The only way they were going to uncover a National Lottery scratchcard worth one hundred thousand pounds – all of which would certainly be needed to put the house back in order and set up Miss Forgetmenot – was to do an immense amount of scratching!

Wazzark discussed with Ghisette how the task could be accomplished. Ghisette said the fairy sisterhood network could be organised to help. That would mean using a rarely implemented cry for help.

The search would have to be a concerted effort by more or less every fairy in the country. It would have to be a massive raid, and fairies were the only creatures small enough to infiltrate the thousands of shops that sold scratchcards.

"But how will you know if a fairy finds a ticket. It's only the big one that'll help the old dear rebuild all that mess?" asked Wazzark. "It could be anywhere in the country!"

"Star code!" answered Ghisette decisively.

"Eh! What's that then, Queenie?" asked Wazzark.

"It's a secret only the sisterhood knows, but you'll find out later, if you swear to secrecy," said Ghisette suggestively.

Immediately their meeting had finished, Ghisette, Mirithin and Elliel scampered out of the old car and separated. They flew off into the crystal clear night to spread the message to every fairy they could find. Hundreds of woodland, garden, town and city fairies were soon flying off in all directions, passing on the news of the great jackpot scratchcard hunt.

CHAPTER FOURTEEN

MERRIN & CLEROMANCE
(SCRATCHING AROUND)

· 14 ·

MERRIN & CLEROMANCE (SCRATCHING AROUND)

BY TWELVE O'CLOCK THAT NIGHT, using secret whispers and star codes, almost all the fairy population of Britain knew what was happening. Many little eyes were eagerly watching the skies.

Midnight unveiled a summer sky diamond-studded with stars (although it was difficult to see them from the towns and cities). The fairies' star code involved a series of colour-coded messages being flashed from one fairy to another in a network that covered the land. In each town and village, a group of fairies would be positioned on every church, mosque, synagogue and cathedral roof or spire. Just within sight high above them, in mid air, a fairy hovered at a fixed point, and even higher another would be positioned. If anyone did find a one hundred thousand pound scratch card, they would use the colour purple to flash a message to the angel fairy high in the night sky. She would then flash red to all the other fairies so that the search could be called off. Any human observer looking up into the heavens would only see the expected twinkling stars, unaware that one or two were not actually stars at all.

The fairy lights were soon in place. The hunt was on.

In the starlight chill of the dark night, millions of dew-encrusted fairies flitted through the air on their strange quest for a winning scratchcard. So many of them flew that night that they formed a thin smoke, a gossamer mist that drifted across fields, lakes, and streams. It swirled under hedges, along country roads and lanes, searching out remote post offices and little village shops. In the cities and towns of Britain, the same silver vapour cascaded over roof tops and streamed along gutters and pavements.

Tiny fluttering figures entered shops and post offices, malls and supermarkets in their search. They squeezed into buildings through cracks in walls, up drainpipes and down drains, under doors and through air vents. If there was a way in, they would find it – and there was always a way in!

Hugh rolls of scratchcards began to unwind on to floors the length and breadth of the country. Half a dozen little sisters would pull on the roll while others scratched away at the surface. When a roll had been completely investigated it was patched up by another group who would rewind it and place it back into position.

The patching up process did involve magic, but not much of it. The material that had been removed was simply spread back over the card and fixed back in place with the 'fairy dust' of folklore and children's books (It actually *does* exist!).

Wazzark decided that as the goblins, elves and pixies couldn't do anything to help, they may as well go and await news of any developments back at the Great Hall – by the bar to be precise. The bar had suffered greatly during 'the big upheaval'. Vibrations created by the huge machinery, especially the bulldozer, had caused much of it to collapse. After the Hobbs's departure, Wazzark had organised the others and they had managed to repair it.

Debris from the aftermath of the Boggart's manifestation and the workmen's rubbish tip had been pillaged for useful articles.

The bar was now almost fully restored, in fact with its new plaster and additional wooden beams it looked better than before. The only unfortunate reminder of their troubles was that the bar stock was dangerously low – and that was a worrying problem. The goblins and elves stood guzzling ale and cider while they discussed their plans.

Pidwidgin sat next to Snaps at the entrance to the Rockery. Far from feeling strained or compromised by his pact with the Rockery inhabitants, Snaps was actually enjoying their company. For one thing they were sharing their food with him, and for another, they were a link with the way things were. The cat desperately wanted things back the way they were (with the exception of him persecuting fairies, of course!) The fairy folk had promised to help him return his mistress, which would mean regular meals and that was more than okay by him, so he sat quietly next to Pidwidgin, watching and waiting for something to happen.

The tranquillity of Romany Way was not shared by all those involved in the search. The further north the hunt progressed, the worse the weather conditions became. There was no star-filled night over the Cheshire plain that night. A steady drizzle had been falling for hours and a small fairy, sitting on the central pylon of the Jodrell Bank Radio Telescope, was soaking wet and miserable, desperately hoping to see a purple light. She was not alone in her discomfort, for many more star-code angels were unable to fly because of the weather and had instead perched themselves on the highest objects in the area.

That night also saw a spate of alarm calls to local police stations. Infra red alarms were being activated in hundreds of commercial properties as tiny creatures flew through the sensors. Nothing amiss was found at any of these incidents, which caused a lot of raised eyebrows and puzzled expressions among security guards and police alike.

At three o'clock in the morning, the clouds had thinned over the east of England and were drifting away over the North Sea. By three thirty the sky over the Suffolk village of Lavenham was a diamante-sprinkled, black velvet canopy. On top of the massive tower of the parish church, a lone fairy watched intently over the old village that slumbered in the shadows beneath her.

Dishevelled, timber-striped houses jutted and warped over deserted roads as a million stars reflected from ancient windows. Nothing stirred. The brick and flint walls, honeysuckle, iron gates and roses, antique shops and old brass lamps all lay cold and quiet in the soundless night.

A faint rustling and scampering noise could be heard from within one little shop that stood near the ancient cross in the market square. A flickering purple glow reflected from its windows. Inside the shop, on the very last scratchcard available, a tiny fairy called Anisse had scraped away the coating to reveal three matching amounts each of one hundred thousand pounds. It was the card everyone was looking for.

Five little fairies, including Anisse, whispered, rustled and twittered to a window vent in the corner of the shop window. A sixth remained inside the shop and pushed the precious card through a gap under the front door. The card was pulled out into the cool air and hoisted upwards by the excited fairies. They rustled and swirled up into the night sky and as the little band flitted towards the church tower, a soft purple glow was cast across the white plastered walls and moss-covered roof tiles of shops and houses. The tiny purple mist of light flickered towards the church tower. It swept over the market square and away from the Swan Hotel, rising and falling on its journey.

The fairy on the church tower leapt to her feet as she spotted the approaching light. She rubbed her eyes and looked again. It was definitely a purple light and it was moving towards her! Even as she watched the light, it split into several little pinpoints and formed the shape of the letter V – V for Victory!

It was three fifty-seven and the search was over. Back inside the little shop where the winning card had been found, the remaining fairy tidied up the roll of cards and deposited a one pound coin (which they had in case of emergencies) into the till reserved for scratchcard payments. She had a last look around, then fled through the air vent, glowing purple as she rose into the air behind the other fairies. The sisters were reunited on top of the tower. They embraced, holding the prize above them as they danced and hugged in celebration.

Realising the urgency of their mission, the fairy lookout took hold of the card and fluttered up into the sky. Far above her, floating on the weakest of thermals, the angel fairy watched like a tiny hawk. She too became excited and rubbed her eyes. From her position she could see other little angel lights scattered across the sky towards the horizon. They were all still fairy pink – none of them had found anything!

The angel fairy's name was Merrin. She descended towards her rising sister.

"Is it the right one?" shouted Merrin in a tiny, shrill voice.

"Yes, yes! We've found it!" replied her sister as she handed over the card. "Don't lose it and don't forget the star code!"

"Oh, well done!" shouted Merrin, taking hold of the card and flying away in a south-westerly direction. "Goodbye… goodbye."

Merrin changed her colour to a vivid red, as did her sisters. Across the night sky, pinpoints of red light appeared and, at almost the speed of light, the knowledge that the hunt was over spread across the whole country in a twinkling of tiny lights. Their task complete, the ruby snowflakes of light began to tumble out of the air as news of the lucky find spread. Fairy angels and the rest of the sisterhood involved in the huge search were returning to their normal routines.

Everyone that is, except for a special, chosen group. The eyes on the little bronze statue of Pan flashed red: a message had been sent! A message to every sister that was on a direct, imaginary line that ran from Bogham to Lavenham. A ripple of instinct passed along the unseen line connecting the chosen fairies. They all knew they had been called and began to take up their positions in the night sky. As each fairy moved into place, a line of lights began to emerge. A minute red line suspended in the scented air of a midsummer night. A line of vermilion fire pointing Merrin to her journey's end!

Merrin clutched the card tightly as she beat her wings into the misty air. She was soon back at her previous altitude. Many misty, dew-soaked miles away, the goat-man's eyes flashed once again. The fairy swung her head to the south-west. She had felt something call her; not heard, but felt! She looked into the distance and could see a faint line of twinkling scarlet stars. Merrin set off towards the path of red light.

A large tawny owl sat in a tree overlooking the Rockery of Number One Romany Way. It had spent nearly a quarter of an hour preening its beautiful, silent wings. With a final puff of its feathers, it settled down to the serious business of watching for food.

"What d'you think the time is?" asked Snaps.

"It must be nearly dawn," answered Pidwidgin. They both looked up as a meteor cut through the veil of stars, leaving a momentary silver scar across the face of the sky.

Merrin saw the same silver flash as she flew over the Suffolk border into Essex. It was difficult to pick out the fairy pathfinders amongst the backdrop of so many human lights. On she flew, over the lights of Braintree, towards the outskirts of London and the widening River Thames. She clutched her precious cargo tightly as she continued her lonely mission.

The amount of light below her was increasing as she approached the great glowing mass of London – the distant horizon had become a glow of copper fire, smoking up to a deep bronze halo.

Lights were now flashing and zigzagging in all directions, and not all of them were below her. With a whoosh and a thunderous roar, a great jet airliner swept above her on its long descent towards a distant airport. Little Merrin held on to the card as tightly as she could as it was engulfed by the turbulent wash of air that rolled and swirled behind the giant aircraft. The card spun crazily, dipped and barrelled end over end in a vortex of twisted air. She closed her eyes and gripped the edge of the card with all her strength as it corkscrewed violently out of control.

Eventually the air began to settle and the uncontrollable spin became a lazy downward spiral. The fairy opened her eyes and found herself lying on top of the card as it floated towards the approaching Thames. She beat her wings furiously and hauled the prize back up into the sky.

"You're too low!" came a shrill voice.

"C'mon we'll help you!" cried another.

She was joined by two other fairies who had been following her progress and had watched in horror as she was nearly hit by the airbus. They flew to her side, grasped the card and helped Merrin regain attitude. The three of them had been rising into the cold air for about six minutes when one of her new companions cheered and pointed to something that lay ahead of them.

Merrin saw that they were approaching a tiny red light. She was back on course! Her little sisters had aligned her with the next angel fairy on her route and, as she looked beyond the bright ruby light, she saw a line of red flashing lights, a broken laser beam of fairy beacons pointing the way to her destination.

Merrin said goodbye to her little saviours and continued on her long journey. She flew across the Thames to the north of Erith and was soon heading over south London towards Bromley, the galaxies of streetlamps twinkling orange beneath her.

As she passed the fairy beacons, the little creatures would wish Merrin good luck before extinguishing their lights and spinning slowly away into the landscape below.

Black spaces were growing between the sea of lights as she flew on towards the south- west. Soon she was passing over Redhill towards the welcome darkness of the distant Downs. Far below, red caterpillars of light moved away from her as vehicles bunched together on the unlit country roads.

Merrin was watching the progress of the distant traffic when she became aware of a little voice calling to her. It was the next fairy in the chain of beacons.

"Have you got it?" called the voice. Merrin fluttered towards the brightening red light.

"Yes," cried Merrin.

The fairy who was beckoning to Merrin was her replacement for the remainder of the flight. While Merrin returned to her home, Cleromance, the newcomer, would be flying the card to its eventual destination.

"How did you find it?" asked Cleromance as Merrin flew up to her and hovered wearily as she handed over the card, telling the fairy where and when it had been found.

The handover had not come a moment too soon for the exhausted Merrin. She longed to return to Lavenham and her bed.

"Do you know how to get home all right?" asked Cleromance with concern, recognising at once her companion's exhaustion.

"Oh yes, thank you," said Merrin as brightly as she could. "I know where I am, I just didn't know where I was going!"

"Neither do I," laughed Cleromance, and with that she turned, waved goodbye and sped off along the ruby runway. Merrin watched as Cleromance and the precious card was swallowed up by the darkness.

The beckoning fairy-light trail was much easier to identify as it flashed away into the gloomy distance. Cleromance continued to pass the little red markers on her way to the coast. She had no idea where she was going, or who it was that she was supposed to meet. All she knew was that she was being guided in the right direction, and that was all that mattered!

Behind her, to the north-east, the first light of dawn was spreading into the sky. It was becoming light enough for her to see features on the land. Cleromance looked down to see strips of woodland and chequered fields rolling beneath her. She crossed the Surrey border into Sussex and was soon over the black meandering ribbon of the River Arun. Away to the north-west she could see the turrets of Arundel Castle, crenellated islands in a sea of morning mist. The tiny runway of lights dipped down as she crossed the silent splendour of the South Downs. They pointed away across the fertile Sussex plain to a little town that stood beside the iron-black sea.

Cold water flowed sluggishly over the little weir on the Alderbourne Rife. Above it, sitting on her favourite iron pole perch, Squidget the water nymph sat watching the dawn. The line of little red stars that she had been observing for some time were beginning to fade into the morning light. She noticed the tiny rectangular silhouette as it approached from the north-east and wondered whether it was anything to do with all the activity that had been occurring during the night.

Cleromance could just make out three more fading red beacons when they suddenly stopped flashing and began to move towards her. The last three pathfinders were Elliel, Mirithin and Ghisette. They flew towards the approaching Cleromance in anticipation and welcome.

"Is that it?" called Ghisette as she closed in on the exhausted visitor.

"Yes… It's the hundred thousand pound card! Do I have far to go?" asked Cleromance.

"Scarcely half a mile," replied Ghisette with a smile. "Here… let us help you to land."

Ghisette and her sisters fussed and fluttered around the weary Cleromance, helping her with the card. They then battered the visitor with questions about how the card had been found and where she had come from as they guided her down to her destination.

The first rays of the new-born day were fingering the sky; it promised to be another beautiful summer's day. However, it was not a beautiful day for everyone.

The owl in the tree overlooking the Rockery was starving. He had not caught a thing that night. For whatever reason, the little people were causing such a commotion that his staple diet of small rodents were keeping well out of harm's way. He was about to wander into his nearby hole in the tree trunk to sleep, when the sound of fluttering and squeaking caught his attention. The owl was alert and prepared to attack. His feathers flattened and his head nodded as he tried to focus on the approaching possible meal.

Four fairies were nearing the Rockery and about to land. Three of them were holding a piece of card whilst the fourth straggled slightly behind the others. Owls were partial to fairies, but would normally only attack individuals – gangs of fairies could be dangerous. But the owl was famished. Throwing caution aside, he decided to attack the group, choosing as his target Cleromance, the straggler.

"I hope you're not thinking of having a go at my friends?" The rasping voice entered the owl's supersensitive hearing at point blank range. Snaps had been watching the bird for some time and had become suspicious of its motives. To avoid a potential disaster, the cat had crept unobserved to the tree and had crept up behind the owl.

As Snaps spoke, the horrified owl, in an instantaneous reflex action, appeared to explode in a blast of feathers and excreta. It rocketed off its perch only to smack its head painfully on an overhanging branch as it made a hasty exit from the tree. An evil grin spread across Snaps' face as the enemy bird flapped, crashed and squawked off into the distance.

Unaware of just how close they had come to tragedy, the fairies landed beside the waiting pixie at the entrance to the Rockery. Pidwidgin welcomed the visitor and ushered her down the passageway to the Great Hall.

Effans was playing darts with Elfie (who was losing) when Pidwidgin entered the room. The Scottish elf was glad of the interruption, for the half-blind Welshman had an uncanny knack of beating him by hitting impossibly flukey doubles and trebles.

"Look everybody!" cried Pidwidgin excitely, "it's the card! They've brought the card – and it's for a hundred thousand!" The pixie waved the scratchcard in the air. Everyone gathered around to inspect the fabulous object and at once began to celebrate.

"Drinks on de house!" shouted Cousin Moykle. Everyone cheered again as a wave of fairy folk washed up against the bar. Corks popped as the last of the ale, cider and elderberry champagne splashed merrily.

"Listen, everybody," shouted Wazzark over the din. "Now that we've got the card we've got to get it to the old lady – any suggestions?"

"Why not just put it in the post?" said Podfudger.

"Ye cannay do that! Summun'll pinch it," said Elfie, shaking his head.

"Right," agreed Wazzark. "We can't let it fall into the wrong hands!"

"I know – I'll deliver it to her, personal like!" said Effans, folding his arms and beaming from ear to ear. "I always wanted to be a postie, yes indeed!"

Elfie turned to the Welsh elf and looked him up and down.

"Brulliant," scowled Elfie, "just brulliant! An old lady opens her door an' sees all twenty centimetres of your ugly body standin' on her doorstep wavin' a hundred thousand poonds at herr! Och! She'd die on the spot of shock! Ye stupid Welsh bastarrd that ye are!"

"Look 'ere boyo, I'm going to thump your nose for that," shouted Effans.

"Aye you do that an see wha' 'appens!" growled Elfie.

Wazzark stepped forward and pushed the pugnacious elves apart at arm's length. "All right, pack it in!" he said sternly. "This is serious. We've got to get the card to her as soon as possible so things can get back the way they were."

"I'll take it – I don't mind the risk," said Ghisette boldly. "And I can put it through the letterbox without anyone seeing me," she added.

"Sorry, Ghisette, but you won't be able to fly carrying the envelope the card has got to be in! For one thing it'll be too big for you, and for another, if you're seen, well, goodbye old lady."

"I've got an idea!" said Pidwidgin's little voice.

"Oh, saints preserve us! Dis should be worth a laugh! Go on little darlin', let's be hearin' ye!" laughed Cousin Moykle.

"Why don't we let Snaps deliver it to his mistress?" said the pixie.

"Oh dat's a goodun. Give it to de cat! T'be sure, dat must have been a sort of 'snap' decision, so it must!" guffawed the leprechaun as he slapped his thighs.

"That's a great idea!" replied Wazzark earnestly.

"It is, it certainly is! A good idea! Oh yes, well done lass!" coughed an instantly serious-faced Cousin Moykle.

The goblin pointed at Ghisette. "You can carry it on Snap's back," he went on. "Humans won't take any notice of a cat, especially if it creeps through the back gardens. When you get to her room, bang on the door and hide. She'll be so happy to see him, an' she'll read the letter!"

"What letter?" asked Podfudger.

"The one from Snap's friend," smiled Wazzark.

"Fancy dat! A cat dat can write" said the leprechaun.

"It's not from a cat! We'll write the letter and make out it's from someone who's been lookin' after Snaps. And we'll tell the 'ol dear that Snaps wants to live back in her old home!"

"How's she going to get the money, Wazzark?" asked Podfudger.

"Ah well – that's the tricky bit, but I think I've thought of a good way to do it, so she can have witnesses." Wazzark went on to explain his idea. Elfie and Podfudger went out to search for some envelopes, whilst Pidwidgin found Snaps and told him of their plan. The cat listened intently – he did not want to make any mistakes, his future happiness depended on it!

Ghisette went to the guest room behind the Rockery with her sisters and Cleromance. She was tired and needed all her sleep to be fresh for the forthcoming mission. Cleromance, exhausted by her long flight, fell into a little bed that had been prepared for her and was fast asleep within seconds.

Podfudger and Elfie returned carrying two envelopes that they had found in a rubbish skip behind a local factory. The envelopes were the 'window' variety and thus had no writing on them.

Wazzark placed the prize scratchcard inside the smaller envelope and wrote a message on it:

> 'Do not show this to anyone except Mr Rogers at the Aldwhyke Post Office. Ask him to help.
>
> You can trust him.
>
> From a friend of Snaps!'

He then folded the envelope and placed it inside the other in which he had already placed a letter from the mythical friend of her cat, pleading for her to return to Number One Romany Way.

CHAPTER FIFTEEN

SNAPS DELIVERS!

SNAPS DELIVERS!

SNAPS SPENT THE REST OF THAT MORNING dozing in the summer warmth. He had been curled up fast asleep by the statue of the little god when he was awoken by Ghisette and Wazzark calling to him. The cat stood up, arched his back, yawned, and stretched his legs out in front of him. He shook his fur and began to lick his back paw.

"What's the time?" he asked, without looking at Wazzark or the fairy.

"Time to go," said Wazzark. The goblin was holding a small, leather strap with a paper clip fixed to one end. He had fashioned the strap for Ghisette to wear around her waist. The other end, with the paper clip, was to be fixed to the back of the cat's collar.

When Wazzark had attached the device, he lifted Ghisette into place on the cat's back. Then the goblin handed her the precious envelope.

"There you go Queenie, all set! You hold on tight! And keep yer 'ead down. Now, off you go. Good luck!" said Wazzark and waved as Snaps and Ghisette disappeared into the undergrowth.

They crossed the waste ground next to their garden and emerged into a nearby roadside. Snaps looked cautiously around, No one was in sight so he began to walk along the pavement, close to the wall. Ghisette, who knew the way to the Ingletimber Residential Hotel, leant forward and whispered directions into the cat's ear.

They had been travelling for twenty minutes or so when the fairy realised that they had to cross a main road to take a short cut through the garden of an adjacent house. Snaps stopped at the kerbside and turned his head to Ghisette.

"Do we *have* to take short cuts?" he asked.

"Yes!" replied Ghisette firmly.

"B...but!" stammered the cat.

"But what?" asked the fairy.

"Well, there's bound to be other cats in back gardens! I'll be trespassing! They'll get me!" said Snaps.

"Well, you'll just have to run faster than them won't you!" hissed Ghisette.

"Okay," said the cat, with a deep breath, "hold on tight then."

Snaps shot across the road without bothering to look to see if anything was coming. Ghisette turned to her right and stared straight into the offside front headlight, indicator, bumper and tyre of an approaching bus. She opened her mouth to scream but nothing came out as the bus missed them by a few thousandths of a second.

"Don't you ever look before you run off anywhere?" gasped Ghisette as soon as she could control her shaking voice.

"No" replied Snaps. Ghisette gritted her teeth, strengthened her grip, and nervously peered over Snap's head at the approaching scenery.

Snaps' pink nose and then his white and ginger face peeked over the top of the house's back fence. The cat looked cautiously up and down, straining his eyes for unwelcome residents.

"See anything?" he whispered to Ghisette.

"Not this time," replied the fairy, frowning, "not even a bus!"

"Right, here we go then," said Snaps. He hauled himself over the panelled fence and dropped down the other side on to a flower bed full of candy tuft and sweet williams. Snaps sniffed the air then, with his fairy passenger, he set off across the garden lawn. They were half way across the grass, just beside a stone birdbath, when an uncouth voice yelled,

"Oi! WOSYOURGAME THEN?"

Snaps stopped dead and nervously glanced around. A huge, bristling, black cat with three white paws and one and a quarter ears stomped towards them like a limbering Sumo wrestler.

"Oops!" said Ghisette. "I don't think he likes you very much!"

At that precise moment the black and white cat flew into action, charging towards them with a growl and a hiss.

Snaps yowled in fright and ran in panic towards the far side of the garden. He reached a high wood and brick fence which he scaled in three great leaps. Standing on top he looked down and was surprised to see his pursuer sitting below at the base of the fence, making no attempt to follow. Snaps took this to be a sign of victory.

"Huh, wassup, Fatty! Out of condition eh? Fence too high for you is it?" Snaps blew a raspberry at the other cat and slowly descended into the adjoining garden. The black, bristling cat stood up and walked away from the fence with nose and tail held high. He turned his head back and chuckled under his breath.

"Oh! It's high enough all right! It keeps that mad killer dog out of my garden! Heh, heh, heh!"

Snaps trotted down a concrete path that stretched away to the end of the property that they had entered.

"Go down to the wall," said Ghisette. "The road to the nursing home's on the other side."

"Good," said Snaps, "we've got away with it! Only one cat on the whole journey."

"Er... only one cat ... and one dog!" added Ghisette.

"DOG?" shouted Snaps in horror. "What dog?"

"That one there!" cried the Fairy, pointing.

The dog's name was Bubonic. He was a black and chocolate coloured Staffordshire Bull Terrier – a totally insane canine nightmare with a spiked collar, feared by every other dog in the neighbourhood. Bubonic was famous for attacking anything that moved: other dogs, bicycles, motor bikes, postmen, old ladies, bailiffs, policemen (and women), cars, buses and – cats! Especially cats. But cats ridden by fairies? That was a new one!

Bubonic was homing in on the pair like a mad canine locomotive, his legs pumping up and down in a cartoon blur as he blasted towards them along the straight concrete path. The creature's face was an insane mask of fury, Bubonic's boss eyes using his nose like a gunsight as he powered towards his furry target!

"AAARGHHHH!" screamed Snaps and Ghisette together as the cat shot off in another panic towards the bush-topped wall in front of them.

The canine missile was approaching, its legs still a blur, gobs of froth billowing from the side of its mouth like coagulated steam. Ghisette held the envelope and the strap for dear life. She turned to look back over her shoulder. The dog was almost on them. Ghisette realised with horror that they weren't going to make it.

"Snaps!" she screamed. "Close your eyes and run as fast as you can!"

"Whaddayathinkimdoing?" cried the terrified cat.

"No, I mean keep them closed!"

"'Howmygonnaseethewall?" screamed Snaps.

"JUST DO IT!" shouted the Fairy.

Bubonic was a hair's breadth from the stumpy end of Snap's tail. The dog began to open his jaws as he stretched his muscle-bound neck forwards towards the cat. He was going to get them! There was no way the cat was going to jump that wall! He was definitely going to get them!

They were all travelling towards the looming brick wall at just under thirty miles an hour when a totally unexpected event occurred. The cat vanished into thin air! The boss-eyed dog saw its prey disappear right in front of its nose only to be replaced by a brick wall. The animal had less than a nanosecond to react and it failed – spectacularly. There was an extremely loud thud, followed by the clinking sound of cascading bricks and mortar.

"You can stop and look now," shouted Ghisette, tugging on Snap's collar.

The cat opened his eyes and was amazed at the sight that greeted him. He slowed to a gallop and looked in front of him. Where there had been a solid brick wall there was now a wide, grassy bank that rolled down to a road. Snaps panted to a halt and turned around to look back. He was astounded to see that the same brick wall was now behind them. There was a large, dog-shaped hole in the wall just above ground level, and under the hole lay the crumpled, unconscious shape of the mad dog.

"Wha? Whattapened?" asked the confused cat.

"Um… a bit of an emergency." replied Ghisette. "I had to help you – just a tiny bit. Don't go telling anyone!" she added.

"But we've just gone through a brick wall!" Snaps gasped, inspecting himself to see if any other bits of his body were missing.

"Well, let's just say you faded away momentarily," said the fairy.

"How?" asked the puzzled cat.

"Oh, just the old Cheshire cat trick! Have you still got a smile left?" asked the fairy.

"Eh! Why?" asked Snaps, who was finding the whole conversation quite beyond him.

"Oh nothing. C'mon, we're almost there…"

Snaps ran across the road at the far end of which was the Ingletimber Residential Hotel for Gentlefolk where he would find his mistress, Miss Eleanor Forgetmenot.

Snaps scampered along the daisy-speckled grass verges that fringed the ornamental shrubs and walls. These exotic palms and hedges thrived in Bogham's warm climate and were used to border many of the grand estates that straddled the road.

Ghisette pointed towards an entrance beside a large Victorian lamppost, and tugged at Snap's collar.

"That's it! That one there!" she cried excitedly.

"How do we get in?" asked the cat as they arrived at the gateway to a gravel drive. Defending the gateway, on top of two large brick pillars, a pair of white stone lions looked menacingly down from behind their shields. Beside one of the lions a huge white sign had been erected which proclaimed: 'Site Sold'.

Snaps looked up cautiously at the aggressive beasts.

"Over there, run behind those trees and go around the back," whispered the fairy. Snaps lowered himself and, in panther mode (to impress Ghisette), skulked across the gravel and scurried along behind the line of tall, swishing poplar trees. They reached the end of the tree-lined driveway and, without being noticed, slipped behind the main building.

Two cars and a caterer's van were parked behind the rear entrance. Snaps dodged between the vehicles and stopped to look up at the building.

"See anything?" asked Ghisette.

"Mm, yeah! Look there, half way up! There's an open window," hissed Snaps. "Hold on!" The cat ran to a wall and leapt on to it then, with three agile jumps, he had reached the flat roof of an outbuilding. They looked nervously around but no one had seen them. Snaps crossed over and leapt on to the gabled roof of an annexe. They were now only a leap from the enticing open window.

"Anyone about?" whispered Snaps.

"No! In you go," hissed Ghisette.

The cat crouched down, wiggled his rear end, focused on the aperture and leapt through the gap. He settled on the window ledge then, when he was satisfied that no one was about, dropped silently on to the thick carpeted floor.

Snaps and Ghisette found themselves on the landing of a staircase. Somewhere below them they could hear the murmur of voices and sounds of people moving about.

"Where do we go now?" asked Snaps.

"You stay here behind these curtains," said Ghisette. She unfastened Wazzark's little leather strap and jumped down from the cat. The fairy pointed to a space next to a fire extinguisher and handed Snaps the precious envelope.

"Hold on to this! If anyone discovers you, run like hell – and don't drop it whatever you do," said Ghisette, frowning and waving her finger at the cat. She flitted off down the staircase in search of a clue to Miss Forgetmenot's whereabouts.

Snaps sat hidden behind the curtain with the envelope between his teeth. He thought about Ghisette. He had grown to like her. His heart sank and he was filled with guilt at the thought that he had once tried to harm such a beautiful creature.

Ghisette fluttered down through the building, flying from one vase of flowers to another. The stairs eventually led her down to the reception foyer. The receptionist was sitting at her desk. Ghisette saw just what she was looking for: the named and numbered post boxes for the resident's mail. The receptionist, a hugely overweight woman in her mid fifties, had pinkish-blue hair and peculiar yellow, horn-rimmed glasses. She sat holding a cup of tea as she read a magazine which lay open on the desk in front of her.

Unobserved, Ghisette flew low across the carpet and nestled into a bowl of flowers which had been placed opposite the receptionist. Try as hard as she might, she could not read the names on the post boxes. Either she would have to wait for the woman to leave her post, which could be hours away, or she would somehow have to make her leave.

The fairy flitted back up the stairs and flew around, exploring the corridors, until at last she found an open, unattended room. Ghisette flew into the room and landed next to a small bowl of fruit on a bedside table. Besides the bowl of fruit there was a writing pad, a paper knife, an ornamental china dog and a small elastic band that had been used to bind the stems of some pink and white carnations.

She sat thinking for a while, tapping her fingers on the edge of the bowl – then suddenly she had an ingenious idea.

The receptionist had reached the letters page of her woman's magazine and was avidly reading about the politician's embarrassing personal problem of the tram ticket and the Spanish onion, when she saw the horrific black and yellow creature fly under her nose. The long-winged creature had a horrible bloated body which was covered in unpleasant black blotches. It was an enormous hornet, or some freak visitor blown in across the English Channel!

Whatever it was, it achieved the desired effect. The woman erupted from her chair in a spray of tea, which splashed across the desk. In a blind panic, the terrified receptionist fled through the foyer and, arms flailing above her head, screamed out of the building like a demented hippo! The screaming and crunching sound of gravel faded as the stampeding woman careered away down the drive.

The coast was clear. Ghisette landed on the tea-splattered desk under the mail drops. With a grunt she heaved herself out of the hollow tube she had made from the skin of half a banana. The tube had been bound together by the elastic band. It was heavy but the result warranted the effort. Ghisette looked up at the row of names and numbers until she found what she was looking for: 'Room 37. Miss E. Forgetmenot'.

"Yess!" hissed the fairy, taking off and heading back to the staircase.

Snaps was anxiously waiting for Ghisette. As he poked his head around the curtain for the umpteenth time, he saw her returning. She flew behind the curtains, landed on the red fire extinguisher and looked down at the cat.

"It's room thirty-seven," she whispered. They looked up at the wall to a sign with an arrow on it that pointed to 'Rooms 30-40'.

"C'mon," said Ghisette, "it's down this corridor."

The cat crept out from behind the curtains and followed Ghisette as she hovered along the passageway. She flew up to each door number before stopping and beckoning furiously to Snaps.

"It's here," she hissed. "Come on, get ready."

MRS BERYL CRIMP was a middle-aged shrew of a woman. Small and thin, she had dyed black hair and she chain smoked. She was employed as a cleaner at the Ingletimber residential home. This occupation had made her surprisingly wealthier than her meagre wages would have suggested. Her husband, a professional benefit embezzler, had a severe drink problem that was expensive to maintain. Old folk were notoriously forgetful and in a lot of cases over-trusting. The scavenging Mrs Crimp had finely tuned eyes constantly on the lookout for wayward valuables.

Snaps sat at the door to number thirty-seven as Mrs Crimp began to climb the stairs towards the corridor. Her job that time of day was to remove any tea or coffee cups that had been served to the resident's guests (if they ever had any).

"Press the bell! There's someone coming… quick, press it!" cried Snaps in a frightened, muffled voice as he held the envelope tight between his teeth.

"Good luck," whispered Ghisette as she flew to the bell and pressed the white plastic button. The fairy fled swiftly to a flower-filled vase at the end of the hall just as Mrs Crimp's head appeared over the top steps. She had her eyes firmly on the ground; a stray coin here or there was a common event and very useful.

"Hurry up, hurry up!" whispered Snaps, his teeth chattering. He could hear muffled noises of someone approaching from behind the door.

"Oh God, what if it's the wrong room?" thought Snaps, his eyes widening as he thought of the horrific possibilities. "What if it's the wrong room and they've got a bastard great cat-shagging dog in there!" Snaps gulped and started shaking violently.

Mrs Crimp had reached the top of the stairs and was walking along the corridor to where the ginger and white cat was waiting. She glanced through a gap in a half-open door. She was about to enter the unoccupied number thirty-one when something made her look along the corridor. Snaps sat beneath the door to room thirty seven, dreading what might be behind it and desperately hoping it was his long-lost mistress!

He heard the soft click of the latch as the door began to open. He glanced to his right. There was a short, black-haired woman looking directly at him. He looked back to the doorway and saw, standing right in front of him, the marvellous sight of his beloved mistress. The cat was so overcome with emotion that he opened his mouth and cried, "Miaow!"

"Miaow," he said again and dropped the envelope as his eyes flooded with tears. Miss Forgetmenot took a step backwards, her hands went to her mouth in a mixture of disbelief and delight. The old lady wept at the sight of her devoted cat.

"Snaps!" she sobbed. "Oh Snaps! My little Snaps! It really is you." Miss Forgetmenot leant down and with both hands lifted the cat into her room.

Mrs Crimp saw the two hands emerge from room thirty-seven and saw a cat being lifted into the air. The door closed, leaving an envelope on the carpet.

Snaps found himself engulfed in the arms of his best friend, smothered in the remembered warmth of woollen cardigans, and the poignant scent of lavender. He was lost in pussy cat heaven as the old lady spun around with him in her arms.

Mrs Crimp spotted the abandoned envelope. Her scavenging instincts were aroused as she strode towards it. Ghisette watched in horror. She had seen the cat drop the prize out of his mouth but was helpless to prevent the cleaner from reaching the letter.

"Oh no! The envelope!" thought Snaps at that same moment. He struggled frantically to free himself from Miss Forgetmenot's embrace. The old lady dropped him in surprise, Snaps ran to the door and began to scratch furiously at it, yowling piteously as he did so. Miss Forgetmenot was so astonished by his behaviour that she crossed to the door and opened it. She was met by the sight of the cleaner who was bending over, her hand outstretched to the envelope...

Snaps leapt into the corridor and, hissing and growling, sank his teeth into the back of Mrs Crimp's hand. The woman screamed in terror, stood upright and tried to shake the cat off.

"Aaeeeek! Get away! Help!" she shrieked in pain.

Snaps opened his mouth and dropped to the floor, landing by the discarded envelope. Mrs Crimp stood sucking the back of her hand as Snaps advanced menacingly towards her. Ears flattened, fur fluffed up and tail bristling, the cat growled and bared his teeth, stalking slowly forwards as he performed his finest tiger impression.

"Ooh... you horrid creature. I'll have you strangled! You nasty little...." At that moment Mrs Crimp spotted the old lady and began to direct her anger towards her.

"You're not allowed cats in here, you stupid old woman. Just you wait! I'll get you both thrown out, you penniless old bag!" shouted the cleaner.

"*!!#!? off, and don't **!!?# come back, you *!!?#!!" hissed Snaps, translating what he'd learnt from the Scottish elf into catspeak.

As Mrs Crimp hurried off to report the crime, Snaps picked up the envelope, turned to his mistress and walked up to her. He stood on his hind legs and thrust the envelope up in the air with his mouth.

"Oh goodness, what have you got there? Is that for me?" she enquired.

Miss Forgetmenot took the envelope and walked over to her little table. She picked up her reading glasses, put them on and opened the letter. She slowly read the note from the 'friend of Snaps', then looked into the enclosed envelope. She read the instructions and held up the unspoilt scratchcard.

"Well, whatever is this, Snaps? How very strange. There's a note here," she said, looking over her glasses at the cat. "It says it's from a friend of yours! And that you want to go back to our old home. Look, Snaps, I've been given..." she looked closely at the mysterious object and read it. "...a Lottery scratch card! Well? Your friend says I've got to take it to that nice Mr Rogers at the Post Office. Goodness me, how very strange."

Mrs Crimp, by this time, had reached Sonny Patel's office and was waving her bleeding hand under his nose.

"She's got a cat up there! A flea-ridden, dirty, cat! Look, it's taken a chunk out of me hand! I could sue her for that, y'know," shouted the cleaner.

"All right, Mrs Crimp, please stop waving your hand about, you are getting blood all over my desk! Please... I will go and see what the trouble is," said Patel in an exasperated voice. Patel and the cleaner left the office and began to climb the stairs towards room thirty-seven.

Miss Forgetmenot had put on her overcoat and was in the bathroom adjusting a fruit and flower bedecked hat, when Patel and Mrs Crimp walked into her apartment. Snaps had heard them approaching and was hidden under the old lady's bed.

"Miss Forgetmenot," called Patel, "are you there?"

"Just a moment," came the old lady's voice from the bathroom.

Mrs Crimp was looking around the room trying to spot the obnoxious cat, when she caught sight of the unused scratch card lying on the little table. As Sonny Patel moved towards the bathroom and knocked on the door, Mrs Crimp swiftly reached across and snatched the card. The bathroom door opened and Miss Forgetmenot appeared wearing her street clothes.

"Ah, Miss Forgetmenot. I am told that you have a cat here. You know that is not allowed, I'm afraid. You'll have to get rid…" The owner was interrupted in mid admonishment by a loud noise. It was the fire bell, the sound that every under-insured property owner dreaded.

"Oh, my God!" exclaimed Sonny Patel. "Fire… oh God!" he slapped his hand to his forehead and then turned to run out of the door. The owner ran down the corridor shouting at the top of his voice, "Fire! My God! call the Fire Brigade!"

Mrs Crimp turned and rushed to the door. She was half way across the threshold when her feet tangled with the orange blur of a cat.

"Ayeeek!" she screamed as she pitched headlong into the corridor. She had landed flat on her face but had managed to hold onto the scratch card. Opening her eyes after her fall, she stared straight into the face of an extremely unfriendly cat. Snaps hissed and swiped the tip of Mrs Crimp's nose with his best stiletto claw. The woman screamed and clutched her slit nose, dropping the card as she did so. In an instant, the cat snatched up the card and ran to present it to his mistress.

The old lady had seen none of this as she was desperately searching for her handbag, which she eventually found in her bedside cabinet. She turned to leave the room and saw Snaps sitting in front of her holding the card.

"Oh dear, oh dear, a fire. We must leave immediately. Oh thank you, Snaps. I'd forgotten about our present. Now come along dear, we must hurry," she said. The old lady put the card in her bag and hurried out of the door where Mrs Crimp was staggering to her feet, one blood-covered hand spread over her blood-covered nose. Snaps jumped in front of Miss Forgetmenot and took a swipe at the cleaner.

"Mmmmffingurrrkk!" she screamed in a muffled, bubbling curse before turning and fleeing down the corridor. The old lady gave her an astonished glance as she left her room and hurried to the stairs.

As Snaps began to follow her down the staircase, the shrill, ultrasonic sound seemed to grow louder. His ears twitched and swivelled as he tried to locate the source of the noise. Above him on the wall was a little red box with a broken glass panel. Ghisette was sitting on top of the little box smiling.

"There isn't a fire," she whispered. "I did it! I just had to get them out of there!" The fairy stood up and looked up and down the corridor. "You go with the old dear, I'll get back to the garden, and meet you there later."

Snaps nodded and ran off to catch up with his mistress, whilst Ghisette flew to the landing and disappeared out of the window.

Miss Forgetmenot reached the foyer and was swept along in a swirl of people evacuating the building. Snaps ran almost unnoticed through the forest of shuffling legs and out into the drive where more people had gathered and were looking up at the roof. No one noticed the old lady and her ginger cat as she wandered off along the white gravel driveway. They were far too occupied in looking for enormous flames and thick billowing smoke. The gleaming red and silver fire engine swept into the gateway just as Miss Forgetmenot and Snaps were walking out into the street. Not even the fire crew gave the old lady a second glance as they prepared to do battle with the non-existent fire.

The Aldwhyke Post Office was sited on the outskirts of Bogham in a road full of little shops and offices. It stood on the corner of a one-way street which consisted of private houses, a double glazing firm, an off license and a pub. A shiny red pillar box stood sentry outside the building, which doubled up as a chemist's dispensary.

Mr Rogers was in his mid fifties, a tall cheery man with a fine head of swept-back white hair. He had spent most of the afternoon helping his female assistant to hand out pension cheques and was now looking forward to a well-earned cup of tea. The man looked over his steel-rimmed glasses at the dwindling queue of elderly people standing in front of his counter. Miss Forgetmenot entered the shop and quietly took her place in the line. A few minutes later she was standing in front of Mr Rogers.

"Hello there, Miss Forgetmenot. Your pension's already been collected by the matron. you know," he said in a friendly voice.

"Oh yes, I know," said the old lady in a satisfied voice. "I'm not here for that, oh no! I'm here because I've been given a present. But I'm afraid I don't know what you're supposed to do with it," she said smiling up at the postmaster.

"A present?" he asked.

"Yes, look, here it is." Miss Forgetmenot took the envelope out of her bag and withdrew the scratchcard. She learnt forwards and handed it to him over the counter.

"It's a scratchcard!" he exclaimed.

"Yes, it is! But I'm afraid I don't know how they work. The person told me to bring it to you and that you would help me." She looked up at Mr Rogers with a bewildered expression.

"Of course I'll help you, Miss Forgetmenot," said Mr Rogers holding the card up to the light as though it was something more than just a humble scratch card. "And, er… who is this person who gave it to you?" he asked.

"I don't know. It's someone who is a friend of my dear cat."

"Your cat?" smiled Mr Rogers, and he went on to explain to the old lady how she should play the scratchcard game. She was none the wiser when he had finished, especially as some more elderly folk had entered the shop and were swamping her with alleged advice.

"Waste of time!" declared one old boy at the back of the queue. "That money should go on our flaming pensions." There was a lot of tut-tutting from the ladies in front of him who were not impressed by the octogenarian hooligan's disgusting language.

"Would you do it for me please? I would be so grateful. My eyesight is just not what it used to be!" said Miss Forgetmenot.

"Of course I will. Here, let's scratch off your first panel."

Mr Rogers picked up a small coin and began to rub off the panel's silver coating, smiling broadly as he revealed the first amount. "Two pounds!" he said.

"Ooh! Have I won two pounds?" asked the old lady.

"I'm afraid not. There's five more panels to go, and you have to match three numbers," he explained. Miss Forgetmenot stood looking at the card as it lay on the counter. The whole thing was still a mystery to her. The postmaster scraped away a second panel to reveal the figure of one hundred thousand pounds. "Ah, that's more like it!" he said. He continued scraping and uncovered another two pounds.

"You might be in luck here after all," said Mr Rogers, "just one more of those and you will have won two pounds."

"Ooh isn't it exciting!" exclaimed Miss Forgetmenot.

"Yeah, and isn't it taking a long time!" moaned the old man at the back of the queue. The old ladies turned and looked at the grey-haired yob and frowned. "What are you lookin' at?" he growled. Mr Rogers looked over the top of his glasses at the troublemaker.

"I'll be with you in a minute, Sir," he said, then scratched away another panel.

"Oh dear, it's a five," he sighed. "That's no good, it's another two we want, two!" He scraped the coin rapidly and another amount began to appear. It was not the anticipated two – it was another one hundred thousand. "I think they're playing tricks on you. Let's keep our fingers crossed for the last one. We want that two, don't we!"

It hadn't occurred to the postmaster to get excited about having already revealed two huge amounts, for despite protestations from the organisers that they hardly ever put two jackpot numbers on one card, everyone suspected that they did. Mr Rogers' adrenaline rate remained passive as he looked at the last panel. He saw the number ten appearing as he scraped away the covering. "Oh dear, no good I'm afraid – it's a ten!" he sighed and continued rubbing.

"Oh, never mind!" said the old lady. "Well thank you anyway, Mr Rogers. It was very kind of you to take the trouble. Goodbye!" She began to move away from the counter. Mr Rogers said nothing as he very slowly opened his fingers. The penny had finally dropped.

"Goodbye Mr Rogers," repeated Miss Forgetmenot, as Mr Rogers continued to ignore her and stare down at the counter. The old lady began to walk away. She had become embarrassed over the postmaster's silence. He must have heard her and yet had chosen to ignore her, which was not at all like the polite Mr Rogers.

He looked down at the three matching amounts, his eyes flickering from one set of five noughts to another. The fact that the three one hundred thousand panels were staring him in the face had not at first registered. The postmaster slowly turned the card around towards the customers and began pointing at it. There was a collective gasp as the onlookers saw the three identical amounts.

Mr Rogers grabbed the card and rushed around the counter, unlocked the door and sped past the queue of people. Miss Forgetmenot was standing outside, her cat rubbing himself against her leg.

"Oh Snaps," she sighed. "My dear little friend, whatever shall I do with you? Whatever will become of us?"

The Postmaster dashed out into the street and stood holding the card up in the air. He saw the old lady standing by the shop window.

"MISS FORGETMENOT!" he screamed. "WAIT! I'VE GOT SOMETHING TO TELL YOU." Mr Rogers ran over to the old lady, who was quite taken aback by the man's peculiar behaviour. "Who did you say gave you this scratch card?" he asked breathlessly.

"Um… 'a friend of Snaps' is what was written on the envelope. Why? Is something the matter?" asked the old lady in a nervous voice.

"A friend of your cat, eh? Well it must have been Dick Whittington! Because whoever it was – they've given you a fortune!" he hissed.

The Postmaster took the old lady by the arm and gently led her back into the shop. The other customers stepped back from the door to let the couple enter, breaking into spontaneous applause, which added still further to Miss Forgetmenot's bewilderment. Snaps followed his mistress into the shop, his tail held high.

Miss Forgetmenot had drunk three cups of tea and eaten two custard cream biscuits before she was finally able to comprehend the magnitude of her good fortune. The old lady had sat quietly drinking her tea in the post office staff room, while Mr Rogers made some very important telephone calls to the scratchcard company organisers.

It was agreed that Mr Rogers would drive the old lady to the London headquarters of the firm, where she would have her card verified and, if all was in order, be presented with a cheque. The postmaster had finished explaining the following day's itinerary, but Miss Forgetmenot was far more concerned about where she and Snaps were going to spend the night.

"I can't go back you know. They won't let him in. I missed him so much when he was taken away before, I'm not going to let him go away, I just won't," she said tearfully.

Noticing her mounting concern, Mr Rogers explained in a calm, friendly and understandable way that because of the money she was about to receive, she and her cat could stay practically anywhere until she had decided where she was eventually going to live.

"Oh, I know where I'm going to live, Mr Rogers! We are going home! Snaps and I are going home to Romany Way!"

The postmaster arranged for her to stay at the Royal Sussex Hotel that night. He booked her a large, spacious room overlooking the sea, with an en suite bathroom – and a little bed for her cat!

The following morning Mr Rogers and his wife arrived to take the old lady on her adventure to London. They were warmly received at the scratchcard company's headquarters, and after a slap-up meal in the organisation's classy restaurant were ushered into a luxurious conference room where Miss Forgetmenot was presented with her cheque for one hundred thousand pounds.

After a marvellous day in London, the three friends returned to Bogham where Mr Rogers made sure that the old lady reached her hotel safely. Miss Forgetmenot climbed into her bed. She was extremely tired, extremely happy – and now extremely rich.

CHAPTER SIXTEEN

GOLD AND SUNSETS!

GOLD AND SUNSETS!

THURSDAY DAWNED clear and breezy. Creamy-white clouds threw deep shadows across the blue-green sea, as a force four south-westerly wind whipped up the tops of the waves into snowy foam.

At ten o'clock Miss Forgetmenot was sitting quietly on her sheltered balcony enjoying the morning sunshine when there was a knock on the door.

The hotel manager entered and told her that she had some visitors, a Mr Gerry Smythe and a Miss Louise Eden. The old lady put her hand to her chin; she was trying to place the names.

"They're from the press," added the manager. Miss Forget-menot agreed to see them and asked for some more coffee. Snaps yawned and made himself comfortable on the large sofa.

Gerry and Louise were shown into the apartment and were warmly welcomed by the old lady. She had assumed that they wanted to ask her about the peculiar destruction of her old home. It came as a surprise to her when Gerry Smythe asked her if it was true about her Lottery win.

The newspaper man relied heavily on the Bogham 'grapevine' and rumours of an old lady winning a fortune in a post office queue had spread rapidly. Stories about the Lottery had been very rewarding for the reporter and the photographer – apart from the small matter of almost being killed in the Romany Way incident!

Their coverage of the debacle had made them, and their employers, a handsome profit. Smythe took out his notebook and asked the usual how? when? why? and wheres? It rapidly became evident that this was far more interesting than 'just a scratchcard win', especially when the old lady revealed that the scratchcard had been a gift from an unknown third person, who was apparently, a friend of her exiled cat. The story became even more weird with the revelation that it was the cat that had delivered the card to her door, carrying the envelope in it's mouth.

The old lady mused about that afternoon's strange events.

"By the way," she asked "there was a fire at the Ingletimber on Tuesday. Was it very bad? I didn't see any smoke. I should have stayed, but I had to get Snaps away and..."

"Oh that! No, it was a false alarm," interrupted the reporter, who wanted to know more about the real story. The old lady sighed with relief. She had been worried about the effects of a fire on her few remaining friends, not to mention the possible damage to her own meagre possessions.

"Where did you live before you went to the nursing home?" asked Gerry, bringing the old lady back to the original story.

"I had a house in Romany Way," she replied. "But it was so badly damaged in the big storm that I couldn't afford to keep living there..." she said unhappily.

Gerry Smythe looked up at Louise. They both experienced a feeling of trepidation mixed with excitement. The reporter, who was sitting on the edge of a chair, leant forward slowly with a pen poised over his shorthand pad. "Romany Way? It wasn't Number One Romany Way by any chance, was it?" he asked carefully.

"Why yes!" she exclaimed, "that was my home."

Smythe looked up at his colleague again and raised his eyebrows. He sucked in a lung full of air, held it for a few seconds, then exhaled violently. This, he thought, was shaping up nicely into a definite front pager – two jackpot winners from the same haunted house. "Wow!" he said under his breath.

Louise felt another shiver run down her spine. She was looking through the viewfinder at the woman who had once owned the infamous Number One Romany Way.

When all the photographs had been taken and the questions completed, Gerry Smythe and Louise left the Hotel and returned to their office to prepare the story for the next edition.

Enoch Filch stood looking out of the large plate glass window of his new offices in the town's high street. With one hand in his pocket and the other holding a large Cuban cigar, he watched intently as the pretty young things bustled to and fro on their lunch breaks. The tapping sound of the word processor stopped.

"Mr Filch, what's a *peed at er*?"

"Eh?" answered Filch, turning to face a twenty-two-year-old blonde bombshell who was almost dressed in a red and white striped blouse and a white mini skirt. Gloria Spanker was Enoch Filch's newly acquired secretary. She had trouble reading and writing but boy, did she look good! Filch realised that she looked very good in clubs and pubs when she accompanied him on his 'business meetings'.

"A *peed at 'er*... it says it 'ere. Is it some sort of toilet?" she asked again.

Filch sauntered over, happy to stand behind her and look down at her big problems.

"Not *peed at 'er* my dear girl, thats a *'pied a terre'* – a temporary or part-time lodging or dwelling place. It means 'foot on the ground' – it's a French phrase." Filch drooled as he gazed down Gloria's ample cleavage.

"Well why don't it say so... Why's it written in foreign, eh?" she asked.

"Time for a spot of lunch I think, Gloria," said Filch as he extricated himself from an obviously doomed conversation. He looked up and stared at the photograph of the Romany Way site.

Number One had become a bitter-sweet experience for the estate agent. Selling the property to the appalling Hobbs brood had made him comfortably well off, but trying to resell it was proving to be a nightmare. Nobody wanted to buy a haunted, cursed, useless, unsaleable piece of real estate that was apparently directly over a flatulent volcano. Filch couldn't really blame them. He had read both the ghost stories and the scientific explanations – whatever the real truth, he certainly would not want to live there either!

The door to the agency opened slowly as an elderly woman entered the room. Enoch Filch, professional gentleman, stood up straight in acknowledgement of the woman's presence and walked around from his secretary's desk. He adjusted his tie and walked towards the visitor, waving aside the cigar smoke as he crossed the room.

"Good morning, madam, how can I hel..." Filch suddenly recognised the old lady. His heart began thumping, he visibly swayed slightly as a deep booming voice echoed through his guilt-encrusted conscience.

"Litigation," thundered the voice, "revenge... ruin!"

"How nice to see you again," said Miss Forgetmenot sincerely, as she smiled sweetly at the estate agent.

"G...ah...hee!" said Filch as he made an incoherent response, not wanting to commit himself to a sentence until he was certain about the old lady's intentions.

"I wonder if you could help me, I understand that you are still trying to sell my old house," she continued.

"Uh... yes... well... in a manner of speaking," Filch lifted his chin and needlessly adjusted his tie. His nerves were beginning to crumble.

"I would like to buy it back," said Miss Forgetmenot firmly.

"B-buy it back? You want to buy it back?"

It was beginning to dawn on Filch that the old lady had no hidden agenda. She really had no idea that he had conned her out of her old home! "My dear lady please sit down won't you? Gloria, a cup of tea for the lady please," he said in a deeply patronising voice.

"Eh? I fort we was goin' out fer lunch, Mr Filch?" frowned Gloria.

"Not now, Miss Spanker," Filch frowned, hissing through gritted teeth. "Let me see if I have understood you correctly," smiled Filch, turning his attention back to Miss Forgetmenot, "you wish to buy your old house back."

"Yes," she answered, just as firmly as before.

"But I'm afraid it is in rather a poor state of repair. It could do with a lick of paint," said the estate agent in another masterpiece of understatement.

"Yes, I know. I've seen it," replied Miss Forgetmenot.

"You have? And you still want to buy it?" asked Filch nervously.

"Oh yes!" she replied confidently.

"Do you have a price in mind?" Filch asked.

"A thousand pounds?" said the hopelessly out-of-touch old lady. She sat patiently looking up at the estate agent, who clasped his hands together over his chest. Tapping his thumbs together he looked up at the ceiling and made a soft, whistling sound.

"I don't believe this! The old bat wants to buy back the biggest disaster area in the south of England... Oh, thank you, God!" he thought.

"Call it fifteen hundred, cash, and I think we can say you have a deal," said the benevolent Enoch Filch.

The old lady smiled and stood up from the chair.

"If you would like to come with me I can give you the money now," said Miss Forgetmenot. "Oh and by the by, will you tell your friend who owns the cat hotel that my Snaps has returned to me. He must have escaped. I expect your friend is still looking for him, so please tell him not to worry"

"Er… quite… er…humph! Of course, dear lady, so good of you to be concerned!"

The secretary arrived with the drinks. "'Ere's yer tea," she announced.

"Not now, girl, not now!" hissed her employer.

Filch helped Miss Forgetmenot to the door and together they walked the short distance to the high street bank. Filch was slightly puzzled as to where the old dear had got the money from, but he was quite content to relieve her of it. With his wallet bulging, Enoch Filch returned to his agency and put his head around the door. Gloria was sitting at her desk filing her nails.

"Come on Gloria, now we'll have that lunch. I'm celebrating, dear girl!" Gloria looked up from her filing. "Some bloke phoned. 'E said 'e was the 'Obbsies solicita. 'E said it was important, like, an' can you phone 'im back."

Filch thought for a moment. He didn't see the need to hurry the sale of their property. "They can wait!" he thought. "Thank you, dear girl, now hurry along, your wine will be getting warm!"

Enoch Filch did not phone Messrs Burwitz, Leach and Sangfroid, the firm of lawyers that represented the Hobbs. Instead he spent the next day, as he often did on a Friday, propping up the bar at a local golf club.

That Friday morning, Gerry Smythe was in the offices of the *Bogham Advertiser* preparing his article for Saturday's paper, when he had an unexpected phone call from one of his colleagues in London.

"Hey Gerry," said the caller, "have you seen last night's *London Evening Gazette*?"

"No."

"Well go to your fax, I'm sending you something you're going to love. You owe me a pint… Cheers mate," and he rang off.

Smythe read the fax copy as it curled out of the machine. Ripping the paper out, he hurried back to his desk to read it again. "Good grief!" he said aloud, "This gets better and better!"

He began to rewrite his article on the strange case of Miss Eleanor Forgetmenot, then he picked up the telephone and rang Enoch Filch esquire, to get his reaction at the startling news from London. Enoch Filch's tinny recorded voice informed the newsman that he was not available. He was not available because by now he was well established at the '19th hole' of the Whykham Grange Golf Club.

Filch's Friday afternoon slid into Friday evening but the estate agent did not notice; he was far too busy drinking, indulging in mutual backslapping, drinking, enjoying some manly boasting and ... drinking.

At nine o'clock Enoch Filch, inebriate, took a taxi to The Bishop's Winkle public house. At ten o'clock he was in the Frog and Cowpat. At eleven o'clock he didn't know where he was, and cared even less!

Early the next morning, Gloria was in the estate agent's office trying Filch's home number. Saturday was usually the busiest day of the week. It was unusual for him not to be there when she arrived. She was about to record a message on his answerphone when he spoke to her.

"Filch," he croaked.

"Mr Filch? It's me Gloria, are you comin' in today?"

"Oh God, Gloria! What time is it?" spluttered Filch.

"Nine-firty, Mr Filch."

"Oh God!" he sighed again.

"I shan't be in today, my dear, I have a migraine. You'll just have to handle things yourself! I'm sure you're good at that. There's a good girl, goodbye," he groaned.

"But Mr Filch!" shouted Gloria, "the 'Obbsies solicitas! They've sent you a letta! It says they're gonna sue you... 'ello?... Mr Filch?... You there?"

But Filch had hung up before hearing his secretary's ominous news. The estate agent groped his way into the kitchen, found a bottle of aspirins, filled a glass with water and swallowed three of the pills. He slammed the glass down and made a face of pure disgust, Filch was of the same aliterative opinion regarding neat water as the great American comedian, film star and drinker, W.C. Fields. "Never touch water! Fish *#*!! in it."

Filch tottered away to his bedroom and sank gently down onto the bed, clutching his throbbing temple.

He awoke later that afternoon feeling considerably better. He remembered that it was Saturday and that he had something to celebrate. He dressed and made himself a strong cup of coffee. Lighting a cigar, he sat down on his black leather sofa and picked up the phone.

"Charles, dear boy, how the devil are you? I've got something to tell you... ah, you'll have to wait! Why don't we meet at the usual place? Seven thirty?... Jolly good! See you there!" Enoch Filch replaced the phone and sank back into the soft, creaking leather. He took a deep puff of the cigar and produced a broad, self-satisfied smile.

That same Saturday afternoon, Miss Eleanor Forgetmenot was taking tea with her friends Mr Rogers and his wife. They were discussing her future plans, especially the repairs to her newly recovered home. This time she would be given good advice on who should carry out the repairs. At last she was amongst true friends!

"Charles, dear boy... What's your poison?" Enoch Filch strode across to the bar of the Fresh Ferret. It was just past seven-thirty and Charlie Wollock was on his second pint of ale. Charlie looked up from his newspaper. It was a copy of the latest edition of the *Bogham Advertiser* and he was looking at the property guide section.

"'Ello Enoch... I'll 'ave one in the bin... Cheers!"

Enoch Filch waited for his gin and tonic, then pulled Charlie Wollock away from the bar towards their usual secluded table. They sat down and leant forwards in furtive discussion. Filch told the builder and decorator how the old lady had appeared out of the blue and paid to have her old house back.

"Not only that," hissed the gloating Filch, "the daft old bat actually gave me one hundred pounds for all the help I'd given her. I don't mind telling you, old boy, I damned near wet myself." He guffawed loudly.

Charlie Wollock lent back in his chair and threw his head back as he joined in the infectious laughter. As he did so, he knocked his paper on to the floor and almost sent his pint of ale flying.

"Ooh! Careful, old boy, that was a close call! We can't have you involved in drinking tragedies!" Filch picked up the newspaper and unfolded it. He closed it again in the right order and placed it front-page upwards onto the table. He then looked at Charlie Wollock, took a mouthful of his drink and… went rigid!

"Whatsamatter, Enoch? Too much tonic in yer gin?" chortled Charlie.

Enoch Filch slowly opened his mouth and the unswallowed drink dribbled from the corners of his mouth and over his lips, dripped down his tie and across his jacket. His eyes opened to the size of dinner plates and he began to shake violently.

"Enoch! You okay?" asked Wollock jumping up from his chair in alarm.

"GGGAGGLEEGGUGUG!" gurgled Filch and, without looking down, he picked up the newspaper and slowly raised it in front of his face. Several seconds later he stood up and let the paper fall from his hands as he turned away from the table, arms still out-stretched, and walked robotically towards the pub toilets.

Charlie looked down at the newspaper that had fallen on to the table. He hadn't bothered to read at the front page. He had only bought the paper to find out who was selling what and for how much in the world of real estate. He gasped as he realised what he was looking at.

"Bloody hell!" he exclaimed as he read the huge black letters that were spread across the front page proclaiming:

'LOCAL WOMAN WINS £100,000 SCRATCHCARD JACKPOT'.

Below the headlines, Charlie Wollock gazed on the photograph of a remarkably familiar face! He read the strange account of a local woman's lucky scratchcard win, then he widened his eyes in amazement as he saw the equally large headlines that appeared below the top story:

'LOTTERY MILLIONAIRES TO SUE LOCAL ESTATE AGENT'.

Charlie read with growing anxiety of how the *London Evening Gazette* had learned that the 'Record-breaking Lottery Winners, Mr and Mrs Henry Hobbs, formerly of North London and Bogham, were instigating proceedings, via their legal representatives, against the estate agent who had sold them a haunted property in Bogham.

'It was alleged,' Charlie read on, 'that Mr Enoch Filch had assured them that the previous owner had not died in the property, but had continued with the sale knowing the house to be haunted'.

Charlie Wollock continued reading. The article went on to describe how in a 'sensational new development' to the *London Evening Gazette's* story, the *Bogham Advertiser* had discovered that the previous occupant of the Hobbs' Bogham house, the now notorious Number One Romany Way, was actually still alive! The mysterious woman was none other than the lucky winner of the scratchcard jackpot, Miss Eleanor Forgetmenot!

The article concluded that both the *Bogham Advertiser* and the Hobbs family lawyers had tried in vain to contact Mr Enoch Filch over the past twenty-four hours but that the estate agent was 'unavailable for comment'.

Charlie Wollock ran into the gents toilet.

"Enoch," he shouted. "You're been rumbled!"

As the estate agent sat quivering on the toilet seat, the image of the old lady holding up the giant cheque began to fill his brain. He could hear her laughing. She was looking out of the newspaper at HIM, she was laughing at HIM. All along he had thought that she was the simple one! A simple, naïve, clueless, old dear! Now it was clear to him! No one could be THAT stupid! She had known all the time that the place was cursed. He hadn't conned her – SHE had conned HIM!

The bottom had fallen out of Enoch Filch's world, and with those few doom-laden words from Charlie Wollock echoing through his head... the world fell out of Enoch Filch's bottom!

The estate agent was arrested later that evening. He was staggering out into the road on his way home from the pub when he was nearly hit by the very police car that had been sent to pick him up.

"You've saved us some petrol, Mr Filch," said the officer in the passenger seat as he lowered his window to look at the collapsed form of Enoch Filch lying in the gutter. "I'm sure the taxpayers will be very grateful! Now if you would like to accompany us to the station?"

Enoch Filch was remanded in custody for a week to face charges of theft, deception, fraud, VAT and tax evasion, offences under the Trades Descriptions Act, bribery, improper accounting, breaking and entering, criminal damage, being drunk in a public place, having no vehicle road fund licence ... and having an out of date TV licence!

Early on the Monday morning, whilst Enoch Filch was languishing in a police cell, Gloria Spanker was at her desk in Filch's office. She was fending off a barrage of complaints that had flooded her telephones from the moment she had arrived. By Monday lunchtime, Gloria had had enough! Her ears were ringing with the sound of dissatisfied customers. The person they were all complaining about had disappeared from the face of the earth ... and worse, she had lost an earring *and* broken a nail.

At ten past eleven, Gloria unplugged the phones, sat down at her desk and waited for the absent Enoch Filch. Shortly after she had disconnected the phones, people – very angry people – began to arrive at the office demanding to see Filch and threatening to sue the agency. It soon emerged that every single customer who had dealt with the hapless Filch now claimed to be experiencing some sort of supernatural activity. Every property he had ever transacted, or so it seemed, was now supposedly haunted!

Gloria put her make-up in her bag along with her magazine and a photograph of her dog, got up, and walked out, never to return. By the following Thursday she had a part-time job working hard at The Bishops Winkle.

Whilst Gloria was dealing with irate phone calls in Enoch Filch's office, Charlie Wollock awoke to the incessant ringing noise of his doorbell, accompanied by a ferocious thumping and knocking.

"All right, all right! Hang on a minute!" growled Charlie. He had half-expected to see the police standing on his doorstep. It came as a short-lived relief to see, not the expected blue uniforms, but a man and a woman dressed in business suits.

"Mr Wollock, Mr Charles A. Wollock?" asked the woman.

"Yeah... Wassup?" asked the bleary builder.

"It's about your income tax," she continued.

"What about it?" snapped Charlie.

"We'd like to talk to you about some discrepancies. May we come in?" said the man with the piece of paper and the briefcase as he slipped past Charlie and entered the apartment.

"Eh? Whaddayamean discrepancies?" said Charlie as he bounced up and down behind the man, trying to look over his shoulder at the piece of paper.

It appeared that some previously overlooked information concerning figures for the previous ten years' income had come to the attention of the regional tax authorities in Bichester. The figures confirmed that Charles A, Wollock's income placed him firmly in the supertax bracket and that he had failed to declare his vast income or pay tax on it.

"I must say you don't look like a multi-millionaire," said the smartly dressed woman.

"Supertax?" laughed the builder out loud. "This is a wind up! Who sent you... Jimmy Hunter?" he asked angrily.

Charlie Wollock was arrested the following Wednesday and remanded in custody for two weeks. He faced several charges relating to the non-payment of taxes, non-disclosure of income, and having a vehicle on the public highway with insufficient tread on three out of the four tyres!

Enoch Filch appeared in court and was sentenced to two years. He was forbidden to hold a company directorship for ten years and all his assets were seized to pay his back tax and outstanding fines.

Charlie Wollock appeared in court and was also sentenced to two years' imprisonment. His assets were also seized (which in Charlie's case did not take long) The authorities were puzzled as to where his 'considerable fortune' might be hidden, but the pixie and the elf who had managed to get inside the tax office and 'embellish' Charlie's tax records, were not. On hearing the news of Charlie's arrest they took off from where they were sitting beside a little river that flowed between the tax offices and a milti-storey car park and flew towards the nearby cathedral, laughing like drains.

The Hobbs family, satisfied that the estate agent had been in league with the devil and had got his just rewards, settled down in their new home close to Staples Corner in North London.

Harriet bought herself a little poodle to replace the absconded Jackson, and within a year owned a string of poodle parlours that specialised in trimming, clipping and shampooing. The shops were soon commonplace all over North London, with their large red signs proclaiming, in all innocence: 'Hobbs for Blow Jobs' with a picture of a happy French poodle holding a hair dryer.

Henry bought an ailing taxi business and the fish and chip shop next to it. He spent most of his time as happy as Larry, miles away from his wife and child, sitting in front of the taxi firm's television watching the racing.

Little 'Arry 'Obbs played in the ten-acre back garden of their new home. Ten acres of tarmac and concrete with not a bush or a blade of grass in sight; no flowers, no birds, no bees and most of all, no elves, goblins or fairies!

Six months after she had won the scratchcard jackpot, Miss Eleanor Forgetmenot moved back into her refurbished cottage. The building was as good as new with its golden thatched roof and sparkling conservatory. The garden had been restored, trees replaced and the vandalised pond cleared of debris. The repairs had been very expensive and threatened to deplete her of her 'nest egg'.

But fortune again intervened. The gardeners had found the concealed statue of the little goat-man as they were clearing away the undergrowth from below the old hawthorn tree. They had presented it to the old lady, who was thrilled to see the little figure again. She had the workman dig a hole so that this time the little statue could be replaced on a permanent stone plinth set in concrete.

It was as the men were digging the hole for the concrete that they discovered the large, lead box. With the old lady watching excitedly, the box was carefully opened. Miss Forgetmenot and the men stepped back in amazement. The foreman grabbed his mobile phone and immediately called the police.

The box was taken to the police station, where it was kept under guard until it could be collected by the appropriate authorities. The find was deemed to have been accidentally lost, and therefore as no owners would ever be traced, the full commercial value could go to the person on whose land it had been found.

The hoard of Roman jewellery, including the finest gold artefacts found anywhere in Britain was later auctioned in London. Miss Forgetmenot received a staggering three-quarters of a million pounds for the contents of the battered lead box. It had taken many fairy folk many hours to find enough gold to fill that box!

It was now almost the autumn end of Summer. The great cherry-red sun had finally, defiantly sunk into the mist-swamped fields beyond the little seaside town. The warm air held a scent of damp hay mixed with the sound of clicking bats and the last swallows of summer.

Beside the garden pond of Number One Romany Way, an old lady sat holding a small bunch of flowers. Her ginger cat sat beside her. She looked down and bent to retrieve something half-hidden in the water.

"Well, well! Look at this, Snaps, a tiny little pipe. It must be a child's toy! I'll just put it here by the little man! Now come along, Snaps!" said the old lady softly, "it's time for your supper."

Miss Forgetmenot turned and walked slowly back to her cottage. Snaps looked up and saw his friends Wazzark, Podfudger, Elfie, Effans, Cousin Moykle, Pidwidgin, Ghisette, Elliel, Mirithin and Squidget all smiling and waving at him from the rockery. Just for a second, he thought he saw the little goat-man wink and flash a smile. He scampered after his mistress towards the warmth of his old, new home.

"Magic!" whispered the cat.

To be continued in... 'REDEMPTION' (Retribution Part II).